NATHAN M. HURST

Xenogene

Also by Nathan M. Hurst

Tusk
Clarion

To Fiona. For sharing the journey.

ACKNOWLEDGMENTS

Special thanks as always to Fiona Viney for making sense of the noise, for her copyediting and wise nudges toward the right path. For the constant support of my wife, Jo and her 'pew-pew-pew per page' action ratio, applying true science and rigour to my work. To the excellent Nicolas Bouvier (Sparth) for his awesome cover art. And to Brian Herring for his energetic and inspirational pub-chat on everything sci-fi.

Finally, a heartfelt thank you to all my readers, for picking up my books during this period of pandemic. I wish all of you and your families well.

Xenogene

PROLOGUE

He was not the same. He was reborn.

Mud caked his hands as the driving rain lashed his face. He frantically scrambled over the dark, cratered landscape in a desperate effort to escape the exploding violence around him.

His body had been changed. He had little memory of anything but the last few minutes and a distant past—he remembered that. But nothing was as he expected. He should be on the *UTS Endeavour*. He should be under interrogation for crimes against the fleet. He should be, but he wasn't.

Born into terror, his body and hands were thinner, nails like razors in chrome, muscles stretched and wound tight with power, face gaunt and predatory behind a mirrored visor. He wore an armour he did not recognise: silver, skin-tight interlocking hexagonal platelets shimmering with a translucent liquidity. A pack on his back crackled and howled as it wound down a spray of hinged rods, folding flat like the skeletal wings of a bird, the purpose of which being seemingly to pull him into existence in the centre of a battle.

Plasma beams lanced across the sky above him and sonic booms followed missile strikes and artillery shells, which took tonnes of rock and earth and threw it indiscriminately into the air along with shredded metal and evaporated alien forms. Life struggled for meaning. Every breath hard and ragged was another second of minor success, while his eyes scanned the horizon for an escape route from the carnage.

From his peripheral vision, another figure matched his stride and pointed past him, gesticulating that he should change direction and follow a gully to his right. It took them both off the horizon and would give them a chance to orient themselves.

An intense florescent light struck the ground behind him and the energy lifted his surroundings and launched him through the air. The visual information through his visor was blurred and useless, the horizon was spinning, and his mind unthinking, reacting. The ground came up to meet him hard, and with the momentum of the blast he slid the last four metres into the gully, coming to rest with an abrupt crunch.

Alerts flashed in icons across the inside of his visor, red and orange indicators to the failings of his suit and his body. There was a dense spider web crack across his vision which obscured his view, and his display flickered with static as it too began to die.

Moving himself back he slumped against the gully wall, his left leg dragging as he went; it was completely unresponsive, mangled. Oddly, he felt no pain. A frustration grew inside him built from the unknown in the situation, from the violence without explanation. What was he even doing here? He took hold of his visor and ripped it from his helmet; throwing it in a roaring rage at the wall opposite, it embedded itself in the mud.

Without his visor the gully became more real, with death and decay invading his nostrils and the strobing of laser fire lighting shapes and forms like so much garbage and debris discarded on the ground. The body of the soldier who had indicated the gully to him lay broken, hanging inverted down the opposite trench wall, face open to the night with shards of a destroyed visor spiking wickedly from its features. His features.

He had been in this situation before, on the *Endeavour*. His team had been of differing ages, but all him. His DNA, his mind and seed consciousness. But now, this wasn't any part of that place—he was planetside and, from what he could make of the stars above, the constellations were all wrong, the moon too large in the sky. This was not Earth, or Hayford b, the Earth analogue they had planned to colonise. Where was he?

Another violent explosion shook his soul. Clods of earth fell like rain, then his other self slid from the trench wall, coming to rest awkwardly across him, gore spilling out of a gaping wound in its abdomen and covering him up to his waist in snakes of gruesome intestines. He felt bile rise in his mouth and slid to the floor trying to fight his way out from under the lifeless body sprawled across him.

As he struggled, a pattern of laser fire streaked across the trench casting an unnatural shadow, and something base and animal in him made him freeze. His breath stopped, the only movement a slow sideways glance down the gully and towards a huge form, slowly making its way in practiced fashion amongst the corpses, checking for life and snuffing out any it found. It was tall and humanoid with a muscular build. He could see no features, only its outline in the flickering light. The torso supported four arms, which it utilised to dispatch the dying with swift powerful manipulations—no need for weapons when you had that kind of grappling strength.

His eyes began to widen as the Xannix got closer, his heart beginning to pound in his ears as panic set in. Looking down at his free arm, he realised his pulse sidearm was free, set into a gauntlet in his armour; he pointed it at the threat and fired. The silhouette was momentarily illuminated; bolts of light sprayed across the short distance between them. Falling into obliterated parts, the Xannix died instantly.

Letting out a sigh of anxious relief, his breath turned to mist in the chill air. His eyes followed the wisps rising up the trench as he slumped back to the ground, his body complaining, his mind overloaded with tension. The world around him stopped in the next instant, his eyes finding those of another, poised aggressively at the lip of the trench wall. Black opal eyes squinted back with malice. He had lost the initiative—there was no way he could respond to the new threat in time. His mind seemed to explode with scenarios, running each in milliseconds but each reaching the same hopeless conclusion. There was no fight to win. He looked up at the stars; they were wrong. Everything was wrong.

He let out a final relenting breath as the Xannix fired. The stars flashed to black.

ROUX

He came around and his body went into a short fit of spasms. Restraints prevented his legs from kicking out, but his arms struck the enclosed hull of his escape pod. In that odd state of awakening where the body and mind were not yet fully connected but the mind conscious and limbs responsive, there was a certain level of helplessness. There was noise all around him of blaring alerts and flashing lights, with the underlying tone of perpetual thunder.

As his body connected and he opened his eyes wide to the tiny world of the escape pod, he looked for information to help him make sense of the crazy psychedelic colours and sounds bombarding him.

Red and amber alerts were everywhere and the alarms were backed up by an over-calm voice stating simply, "Terrain. Terrain." He looked quickly for some key information—height, speed, attitude. He wished he hadn't. The artificial horizon was spiralling and out of control, the speed was way too fast and his altitude way too low. Part of him wished in that moment that he had never woken up.

A pain began to make itself known to the side of his head. His hand went to it almost involuntarily as he concentrated on the screen of digitised instruments before him. The sensation came back warm and sticky; looking to his fingers, they were now red with blood. Memories of the re-entry started to return. The impact had been harsh and sudden. That was the last memory until this moment.

He experienced the tumble of the escape pod like a fever. His head throbbed, his coordination was impaired by the rotating forces fighting every move of his body, and it was hot like the humid heat of a sauna. Life support had failed and CO_2 build up would kill him soon enough, but probably not before the ground did, as he smashed into it at over 800 kmph. The alerts wouldn't shut up. Whatever he had hit or had hit him as he had made it through into the upper atmosphere may as well have finished the job then. It seemed particularly cruel that fate had allowed him to survive only to awake moments before snuffing him out for good.

Struggling frantically with the controls, some part of him wouldn't give up. The base biological function of self-preservation. The pod span wildly against his control inputs, like a bronco bucking to unseat its rider; some inputs failed, others over-corrected, but he couldn't tell whether it was his poor judgement or a physical failure of the pod. He had trained for this—the tumble could be corrected. He should be able to orient the pod and point its retro at the ground, as he had hundreds of times before. Even the aerodynamics of the pod should self-correct its flight without his intervention, but in the simulator the pod had never been this damaged.

Running out of options, he began to try things that he knew would fail, but there was little else to try. He deployed the emergency drogue-chute, but at the speed he was travelling he heard it rip itself clear with a thump. He tried to redeploy the primary air brakes, but the damage to two of them simply increased the buffeting and wild vibrations. The auto-stabiliser was clearly damaged and there was no way he could fire the thrusters manually in a sequence that corrected his descent. His final action was that of a doomed, desperate man. As he passed through 1000 metres with seconds until impact and the jagged mountains below, he fired the main retro.

The pod display was already showing all kinds of chaos as the view spiralled and twisted to the ground. He could barely make out the terrain, but colours flickered dark grey, white and green in rapid succession. The roar of the retro rattled him to the bone and applied more unbearable forces on his body, more than it could contend with. His vision began to tunnel and fade as the g forces escalated.

He didn't really know if he was in pain, but his body was

informing him of intense stress. Everything was too heavy, too dark, too tired. He couldn't even breathe.

There was noise, sudden thrashing sounds as the pod breached the top of the forest canopy, then there was a lurch and jolt which inverted the pod and threw him against his harness. An impressed dent appeared instantly across the mid-section of the hatch in front of him, the cylindrical space within the pod becoming compressed to the point of pinning him in place.

Darkness came with the next impact.

*

"Commander," said a voice. "Sir, what are your orders?"

He looked up from his confusion and saw Commander Holt at his station, the navigation officer asking for direction; he needed to make a decision. Scanning his console and the primary tactical screen on the bridge, the situation seemed hopeless. The *Intrepid* and the *Indianapolis* were in free formation, but they were all trapped by the Xannix satellite defence network. A network they had mistakenly assumed to be some high-level communications jammer, but which had turned out to have a more sinister purpose. The rain of energy weapon fire they were now receiving made their mistake all too evident.

Looking for answers, he consulted the ship's Volatile Encounter Resolution Simulator, a tactical system which ran millions of iterations of varying permutations using the current real-world variables of the ship's sensors and active operation as seed inputs. The VERS gave him few options. The destruction of the *Endeavour* and the fleet was the answer returned with a confidence interval of 99.999%, which was the system saying there was no way out. But something in him resisted. This answer was flawed; it was a machine answer to a human problem. He knew what he had to do.

"Commander, take us through the satellite grid. Make a hole." There was a pause while Holt considered the implications of his words. "Now, Commander." Every moment was vital.

He turned to Dawn, the ship's AI, standing diligently by his side observing the scene with a look of concerned concentration.

"Dawn, what is the status of the non-essential crew? Are they ready?" he asked.

She turned to him without hesitation. "Yes, Captain. All non-essential crew are in their escape craft and awaiting your order."

Nodding in confirmation, his hand went to the control console and opened the link to a ship-wide broadcast.

"This is Commander Roux. Launch escape pods for non-essential crew. And Godspeed." At his sign-off, Dawn raised an eyebrow. Religion was rare, but not forgotten. The odd phrase stuck around in moments of stress.

With his command given, a spray of escape pods suddenly littered the display, each with its own telemetry identification marker chasing its icon. There were hundreds; some single pods, others lifeboats built for ten to twenty. As he watched, the first of the pods was struck by fire from the satellite defence grid, becoming a momentary blip of light against the void, the valuable and vulnerable human lives inside lost in an instant. Another and another suffered the same end. Within a few seconds it became apparent that the escape pods were being deliberately destroyed in sequence. The fire was becoming more intense everywhere, the main external screen showing almost completely red, as if the energy falling on the *Endeavour* was blurring his vision with the blood of those he had just committed to their death.

"No!" shouted a voice. Was it his? "No! No! No!"

The bridge around him began to deconstruct. The bright red of the screen becoming brighter and brighter, to an almost pink-orange.

"No! No! This can't happen!" The voice screamed. "What have you done?"

Those around him started to disintegrate and blow away like dust on the wind, black and red faceless screams pulled into the void as the ship around him barrelled through the defence grid and suffered huge amounts of explosive and decompression damage. A swathe of destruction cut through the Xannix defences at the expense of his crew. It was their sacrifice at his hand. What had he done?

The sounds of the ship breaking apart around him clawed at his ears and the light became bright and intense. He felt his face cold like an intense white pain.

*

7

Gasping a lungful of air like it was his first, he cracked his head hard on a contorted structural spar of the pod. He instantly recoiled, coughing and spluttering whilst trying to gain his bearings. There was bright white light and sparking electrics only centimetres away from his face, the display screen was shattered, and power cables shorted against exposed metal.

The watery haze began to clear from his vision. He could see daylight streaming into the tiny space through ragged holes and gashes, punched and gouged in the hull. The whole escape pod was twisted, contorted and battered out of shape; it had taken a severe amount of damage but miraculously it had done its job. It had kept him alive. With a sudden, desperate need to be free of the crushed craft, he fumbled for the harness release, the bar clicked but hardly moved. He was wedged in—the escape pod seemingly reluctant to let go of the life it had saved.

Wriggling an arm free, he reached across to the hatch and triggered the emergency release. Four tiny explosives fired, but the door didn't release as expected. It should have been pushed clear of the pod, but instead something had pinned it in place, possibly wedged between rocks or tree trunks. The hatch ricocheted and rattled as he tried to eject it from the pod, coming to rest diagonally across the door jamb. The noise clattered and clanged, ringing the pod like a bell.

"Stars and blood!" he shouted in alarm at the buckled hatch, as his ears complained at the noise. Losing his composure, with the small amount of additional wriggle room he pushed and kicked at the door, in the end pulling his legs up to a squatting position and forcing the hatch with his feet diagonally away from the opening. He kept at it, working away some of the pent-up adrenaline and frustration of the last few hours. Finally, the hatch had been inched away from the opening with just enough room to wriggle out.

He flopped back onto the pod couch panting away the effort of forcing the door and looked out to the world beyond.

White clouds of powdered snow swirled in spirals outside the pod, bitingly cold air rushed in to attack his body and turned his breath to smoky wisps. It was a cold that chilled him to the core. He didn't know exactly how far off course he was, the targeted landing zone for the escape pods had been a ten-kilometre square area in a temperate region of the planet. He estimated the temperature here to be far below zero Celsius, maybe ten or twelve degrees below, which meant he didn't have long to get covered up and warm. Even with the survival kit the pod was packed with, surviving for any duration in this environment would be tough.

With the dented hatch no longer pinning him, there was nothing to prevent his harness from releasing and he sat forward to climb out of the pod. He tentatively put his hand to the metal rim of the hatch to test the temperature of the metal. It was hot to the touch but cooling with the meltwater flowing over it from displaced and thawing snow. With the gloves and thermal kit, he would be fine for the few moments it would take him to clamber out of the pod, skin protected for the short contact. He began to rummage around the pod for the survival kit packed into a neat compact ruck sack to the base of the couch.

As he pulled the bright orange thermals from their vacuum-packed wrapping, he used his bio-comm implant to interrogate his physical status. Considering the trauma the pod had received, he was a picture of health. A few minor lacerations which he began to attend to with the on-board medical kit, several nasty looking purple and black bruises, and a wicked headache, possibly concussion, but nothing broken. He was mobile and would be on the move soon.

Keeping himself busy, he tried to avoid introspection, but it was impossible. His last actions had destroyed the *Endeavour* and, although he had probably saved the *Indianapolis* and the *Intrepid* in the process, the loss of life and the loss of the ship was a heavy burden. He knew there would be nightmares; he was already hallucinating and reliving the event as he sat there. Nervous adrenaline-fuelled anxiety began to set in. Initial signs of post-traumatic stress. It would have to be dealt with later; there was no time for that now. Now it was about survival. Taking stock of events—that could come later.

Newly stapled skin was raw and hurt like hell. The gash on his scalp had been bleeding badly, so he had decided to tend that wound first. He had foregone any painkiller or sedative; some level of guilt had convinced him that he didn't deserve the sedative. Beginning to lose the feeling in his fingers, he decided that he couldn't wait any longer and bundled himself into the thermal suit. Clicking a control at the neckline, the expansive sack-sized suit moulded itself to a close, snug fit, and a second neckline slide control regulated the suits temperature, power drawn from a skinline battery weaved into the lining of the thermal layer. Battery and thermal layer in one, the suit surface a solar capture mechanism for battery recharge. The gentle warming would keep his body at a comfortable working temperature, as long as it didn't drop below minus 40 Celsius.

Next on his long list of things to do was to find shelter. He had rations for a few days and water to get him started, but he needed to recon the place and see if he could find any shelter better than the bucket-of-holes he had landed in. Slinging the survival kit over his shoulder, he began to squeeze himself through the broken hatch space.

It was beginning to get dark as he popped his head through the hatch; night would be only a matter of an hour away and he could only guess at the drop in temperature when that happened.

Dropping to the ground, he looked back at the pod, giving the skin of the hull a gentle pat of appreciation.

"Thanks," he said. "Maybe I'll name my first kid after you." He caught the ident tag on the side of the pod: ELP-27. "Catchy."

Balancing himself against a tree for support, he realised just how lucky he had been. Looking about the pod to appraise his situation, he found it had come to rest wedged between a rocky outcrop and a tree trunk, a trail of destruction led in a straight line up the mountainside. Trees cut down and shattered to splinters, meltwater and mud all about where once deep snow had lain. He didn't like to think about the probability of him surviving such a crash; it would be low, very low. And yet, here he was. He would make it mean something. A frown of determination worked across his features at the thought.

The trench the pod had carved out of the mountainside was deep, the snow and ice packed hard, which meant that to get out he would have to track back up the mountain until the trench wall became low enough to climb out. Alternatively, he could work himself an ice-hole in the snow. He would be able to work his way in from the trench wall, which would be easier work than digging in from above. For a moment he considered his ice-hole collapsing as he slept. Maybe he would climb out after all and make his ice-hole the more conventional way.

A tone had been steadily building. Initially, this had not been so loud that he had even noticed—it was like the whine of a mosquito from afar. But, as he began his climb, the noise became more pronounced; solid, closer. For a moment, he stopped his ascent to scout the horizon. The view across the mountains at dusk was breath-taking: the deepest orange flared across the peaks as light curved its way through the atmosphere and took its last moments in the day.

The thunder arrived and shattered his perfect moment of awe. Intense white light drenched him and reflected off every surface, and snow whipped around him and stung his face. He raised a hand to the source of the torrent of light, partly to protect his eyes and partly to shield himself from the biting ice and snow. Winds rushed around him and he found himself moving closer to the ground. The last thing he wanted on a mountain slope was to lose his footing, so he hooked his arm around a shattered tree stump.

There were shadows all about him now: tall, muscular shapes in black. One came in close and loomed over him, goggles and mask covering its features, but the physical form—the upper torso with those powerful limbs—betrayed it as Xannix. The Xannix scout overcame his struggles with ease and clamped him diagonally across its chest in a carry with two of its arms. A moment later they were off the ground and moving ever closer to the light. He closed his eyes against the pain and brightness, but he could do nothing to shut out the thunderous noise.

Something bit his neck. A sharp, sparkling pain turned quickly to darkness. The thunder rumbled into the background of his mind.

PATTEN

As the plane descended through ten thousand feet, the seat belt sign lit up with a familiar ping and a rapid succession of clicks filled the cabin as other passengers complied with the instruction. He lazily searched for the buckle ends of his own harness and pushed them together, joining the chorus of scratching, clicking locusts, locking himself into the seat. Looking across to his left, Ellie remained asleep, unaware of the flight crew's request. He leant over and softly shook her knee.

"Wake up, sleepyhead." She shifted a little in her seat, but only enough to move away from the annoyance that was trying to wake her from her comfortable slumber. He decided to continue to arrange his harness and tighten it to a more firm and fitting position.

"Ellie," he said a little more forcefully. "Time to wake up. We're landing soon."

She gave out a moan of recognition and stretched out a little.

"Can't you tell them to circle for another ten minutes?" she asked, rubbing her face to try to invigorate and motivate herself awake.

"You look like you could do with some sleep," he said.

"Funny man."

"I try."

"I think you need to try harder."

He smiled at her response while checking down the aisle, looking out for a steward.

"Where do all the stewards go when you need them?" he asked aloud as the thought passed through his mind. He really wanted a glass of water.

In truth, they could both do with some sleep. They had been working flat out this last month. The Accelerated Quantum Alignment or AQuA project had advanced at pace since his research findings, and Ellie had been brought in to assist him with the additional workload. He couldn't fault her, she was brilliant, but he could do with three more just like her; the work was just too much and there was so little time.

The resulting drive engine pulled from the theory had been coined the Magnetar or Mag drive, simply due to the size of the containment field needed to manipulate the forces involved and the thrust produced. The theory was not new—truly new ideas were the work of genius and he was far from one of those—but innovation? He could do that. This was a new implementation of quantum field theory which improved on the power output of current star drive technology by almost 200 per cent. The improvement was vast, the implication of which was to extend the reach of human star travel, to bring the time to travel the billions of kilometres to the nearest star systems within reach. Alpha Centauri was now one short single generation distant from Earth but there was nothing of interest there, nothing that could sustain life, Proxima b having been found to be much more like Mars than Earth—too cold and atmosphere too thin. The problem with this leap in technology was that it didn't matter. As the world died about him, he may as well have just mastered alchemy; he might turn lead to gold but, in the end, they would be just as dead. The nearest group of habitable planets were still 135 years away. It would take three generations of people to live harmoniously in a giant tin can for any mission to successfully colonise one of these newly discovered habitable worlds.

It was a fiction if anyone believed it could be done; people were just too damn territorial. The greater the population density aboard ship, the more explosive the mathematical models predicted the outcome. People just didn't like living in a sardine can. And it wouldn't matter whether you selected your initial crew based on traits that could cope with claustrophobic conditions, as their offspring could not be selected. Passive personality traits could not be guaranteed in further generations and, at any rate, you would need hardy, forceful people once they arrived at their destination. Building a colony was an extremely gritty and overwhelming process which required a high level of determination. Whichever way you looked at the issue, if the mission had to run across generations, the voyage appeared doomed from the outset.

He rubbed his temples, the lancing pain back again, rushing pressure behind his eyes, as if his brain was trying to escape the confines of his skull. It was all connected, the pressure to resolve the power issues to the star drive, the rationing of food and water, the attacks against research facilities by the French terrorist organisation La Guerre à l'Intelligence Artificielle (known more simply as GAIA) and the stress of the deadlines. How was anyone meant to work under these conditions? He had to find a way. Sliding another painkiller from its pouch and popping it into his mouth, he crunched the pill between his molars until the acute pain turned to a dull ache.

"More headaches?" asked Ellie. He nodded. "We'll be back at the lab soon. You can catch some proper sleep."

A short laugh escaped his lips. "Thank you, but you know there's no time for that."

"Look, you need to be clear headed." She paused to consider her options. "Here's the deal. You get some sleep while I prep the next experiment. You've done more than enough prep. I can handle the final set up. You get some sleep and I'll come wake you when we're ready to start running the tests."

He was still rubbing his temples. It sounded like a wonderful idea, but it was his responsibility, so he should be there.

"I don't know."

"Okay, final offer... I'll let you take me out to dinner once we're done."

That derailed his thought process. He stopped rubbing his head and stared at her. Had he been that obvious? Obviously. He sighed, then smiled at her.

"Are you sure? I'm a terrible cook."

"Oh, I know. So, you're not. You're taking me out. I think Neo Azure; I hear they do great old Italian."

"You appear to have it all planned. Sounds wonderful."

"Yes, it does. Deal?"

He had no excuses. "Deal."

*

The transfer to the Formillun Institute helijet had been smooth, as usual. It had been waiting for them on the pad when they landed, and the security team ushered them aboard. They were off the plane, aboard the helijet and wheels-up in less than three minutes. Back in the air for the short final hop to the Stelling facility, a purpose-built underground lab with its main test bed on a fixed sea platform twenty miles off the coast. For now, they were headed for the Stelling lab control room; the final oversight of the engine test could be done from there, then he would do a post engine firing on-site inspection later tomorrow, after the test.

From the window of the helijet his mind wandered over the test detail again. This was the final test and there would be a raft of dignitaries in the viewing gallery to witness the outcome. They were a serious distraction, but he knew they were necessary—the funding and political support for his work had to come from somewhere. He only wished the observation room could have been on the end of a vid-link. At least then he wouldn't have the constant prickle at the back of his neck as a wall of eyes scrutinised his every move, his every decision.

They passed over the London New Wall perimeter. A defensive wall to keep out the millions of unfortunates and marauders that roamed the lawless zone beyond its boundary. Since the decline, the Great Decline as the media were beginning to call it, billions of people globally were dying or displaced. Ever since the asteroid strike which destroyed the eastern European country of Ukraine and its local ecosystem, the delicate balance of geopolitical power had shifted as millions of migrant peoples looking for sanctuary and food became a torrent. The governments of the region could not contain the flux in such an acute timeframe. Global overspill of the problem caused economies to collapse and governments to fall. Scientists warned of the worldwide devastation that was coming: the strain on the supply chains and the altered, violent weather which would do further damage to the civilization man had created. It was a depressing cycle of events which many predicted would be the end of humanity. He had initially thought it was the media exaggerating for effect, as they did to hook people into the feeds, but then he was approached by the Formillun Institute to work on a then-secret project. They were building colony ships; the plan was vast. They would need star drives to reach the nearest identified habitable planets, and they would need to be completed and launched within ten years. That was all the time humanity had left on this rock. Ten years.

Water sparkled and twinkled in streaks as they flew low following a river. Grass and trees were turning as autumn approached, blurring his peripheral vision into a green-brown.

His Mag drive had been born of this desperation. Suddenly, there was a need to get off the planet and he was invited, his ticket was the drive system that he had invented. He told people it was an altruistic act, that he only had others in mind, that the survival of humanity was everything. But in the quiet moments he would reflect on his selfishness. He had a golden ticket, billions of others were not so fortunate, including a large number of his team. What was moral about any of this?

Regardless of this soul searching, he took the ticket and the responsibility. Did that make him bad? He pushed the thought aside before he went crazy. Going mad would do no one any good.

And now Ellie had been introduced into his world. They had hit it off the moment they met. She had been dazzling. His feelings for her were new, but very real. As real as the end of the world. What about life was fair? He had decided then that he would need to squeeze a lifetime into the next few years, and, so far, he was giving it a damn good try. But he was finding speaking to her on a personal level… problematic.

He forced himself to think about work. That was safer, more comforting. Equations and certainty, the power and grace of mathematics applied to an infinite universe. It was where he thrived. The Mag drive would be ready as planned, but more was needed. His innovation was to move away from carbon fuel and into quantum tech and build on research which he had spent a lifetime studying. His drive manipulated the quantum field and sequenced particles into chains which could be used to generate thrust. For some reason, he had also been reading about a piece of dead-end research on electro-magnetic drives. The research had been side-lined for two reasons: firstly, the force generated was very weak, on its own too little to generate thrust for anything of substance, and, secondly, no one at the time could formulate any sensible theory behind why the effect worked—it just did—and that was never an explanation that sat well with scientists. But he had theorised that he could use the principle as an amplifier to his quantum drive. A quantum drive afterburner. It worked. As with the scientists before him, he had no idea why the effect worked, but there was an identifiable difference between the scientists of that time and him. Humanity was desperate and he didn't care. He didn't have time to care; he just needed results. The fact that it worked, and he could control it, was all he needed. All humanity needed.

There was a jolt which gently bumped his head against the window; he hadn't realised he was so close. His focus returned from his daydreaming and musings; they had just touched down at Stelling. Clamps took hold of the helijet and the engines wound down with the discordant howl of dying beasts. With a deep clunk, the landing platform began to move, descending slowly below the surface. Situated outside the London New Wall, the Stelling research facility was afforded no protection from the city authorities and therefore had to defend itself from the lawless. Consequently, the complex was heavily fortified with the majority of its structure underground. As the helijet platform edged its way down below the surface, a protective roof cover began to slide across the opening, the clear cyan blue of the sky slowly becoming a thin line before being shut out, replaced by the sodium yellow of the hangar lights. A hollow boom indicated their arrival as the hangar cover closed and the platform came to rest at the first subterranean level of the complex.

There was a short ping across the helijet's internal comm which he hardly noticed. He'd been on this flight so many times the mundane nature of the commute had started to turn the volume down or drop out the repeated noise. "Welcome to Stelling. The brightest minds for the brightest future." The announcement always made him cringe. What future?

Doing the commuter shuffle down the aisle of the helijet, Ellie took his hand as they made their exit from the rear ramp of the aircraft and out into the hangar. He found himself grinning like a teenager, his heart pounding with the excitement of a new unknown. It was a short walk to the lobby area and the first security checkpoint, beyond which were the elevators to their quarters. He suddenly felt exhausted, as if Ellie had given him permission to relax and for the natural state of his body to catch up with reality. Until now he had been operating on a regime of caffeine and micro-naps, just enough to keep him going and able to function.

Passing through security, the world began to appear as if viewed through a mist or a frosted window. He felt as if on complete autopilot and in a trance-like state.

"I think I need some sleep," he mumbled, as he missed a step and stumbled forward. She managed to keep him upright. In what seemed like a couple of seconds later, there was a door in front of him, on which he could just about make out the number – room 18, level D. He fumbled for the key card in his pocket and dropped it.

"Easy, Scott. I've got it," said a beautiful female voice. Light, bright and seductive. "There you go."

The door opened to a dark room; the lights remained off. He felt a comfortable cotton pillow against his cheek, his body relaxed into the softness of his bed's embrace. Sleep came easily.

ELLIE

Walking into the canteen area, she took a tray from the rack and headed for the serving hatch. There was an array of healthy options on display, but she needed the energy hit. The next few hours were going to be long and tough. She needed to be awake. A coffee and two energy bars; one for now, one for later. The guy behind the serving hatch passed her the coffee with indifference. It was coming up to shift change, and he was likely bored and counting the minutes until he could escape to the recreation level. It was where she would prefer to be. She tapped her ration card to log her purchase and picked up the tray, noticing a momentary tremble as her hands betrayed her anxiety. She fired the guy a quick smile to distract his attention then turned her back to him, eyes searching the dining hall for a quiet seat.

Finding an empty table, she sat and took a large gulp of the coffee. It tasted great and had an odd counter-intuitive calming effect. It normalised the moment: she was just a regular physicist taking a coffee break. Releasing a deep breath, she relaxed into the chair and watched the room. There were techs, engineers and research scientists everywhere, all engrossed in work or lunchtime conversations, all ignoring her. That was good.

She slumped a little in her chair and put her hands in her lap to disguise her next action. Picking briefly at her palm, she raised the edge of a circular translucent patch and carefully folded it in half, then, using the palm adhesive of the patch, she stuck it to the underside of the table while pulling herself and her chair closer.

The tranq-patch might be discovered in the trash—it's where people are supposed to dispose of evidence. Hiding it in the canteen would give anyone on her trail a much bigger haystack to search. It would give her time.

Flicking on her cell, she checked her messages: there were two from her mother, one from her brother, a slew from various work colleagues on the AQuA project, then the one she was looking for. The subject was marked as junk, identified by the system as spam or other superfluous incoming nonsense which the net generated on a daily basis, but to her it had more significance. She took a sip of coffee and scrolled through the message. Today's message was particularly creative, an advert for the new trend in unlicensed augs, a company willing to fit her up with a bio-comm implant or neural enhancers, or to improve her immune system with the latest nano tech. All for only a month's salary. Bargain. In truth, a top of the range bio-comm alone would set her back five year's salary; there was no way people would ordinarily be able to afford this stuff. Black market sales and the lure of high-grade kit for a cut-down price was too much for some. People were warned about it all the time, but some still took the risk in the back-street chop houses and tech slums of the city. The cost was very often too high, faulty parts or infection all playing a part to degrade their life rather than enhance it. Death was also a regular side effect.

She scanned the message and clicked on the third link. Neural enhancement, nano tech and go juice to open up the pathways in the brain responsible for recall. A less invasive option and one which could be taken as a pill. Nano tech would do the rest over several days. Highly illegal.

Clicking around the linked page a little, checking out the blurb and testimonials, she closed the page down. Her message sent. Mission running to plan.

Patten would have a hell of a headache when he woke up, but it was a compromise she had made. She had grown to like the guy – a lot. So much so, that she had argued with her handlers that the operation didn't require his death. She had won out. Was it love? No. She was sure of that. But he had won her over. He was a good guy, caught as a cog in the AI machinery. He could be spared.

Slugging back the remainder of her drink, she rose and began to make her way out of the canteen.

"Excuse me."

She turned sharply, quickly masking her surprise as she felt her heart rate spike. Be casual; it's just another workday at the office.

"Hi," she returned, looking at a security guard holding out a hand. A card with her face stared back at her.

"I believe this is yours. You left it on the table."

"Oh, thank you," she said, taking her security pass from him. "You just saved my afternoon. Last thing I need is to lose this little thing just before a corporate presentation."

"No trouble. I hope it goes well."

"Yes, thank you. That makes two of us." She gave him a broad smile and waved the pass thankfully, then headed out.

*

The lab was a hive of activity, everyone busy with final preparations and checks for the drive test. Quickly scanning the team, she noted that no visitors had been brought in yet, although an area of the lab had been set up with a temporary bank of chairs, a small theatre to the events that would unfold in a few hours.

Making her way directly across the lab to a row of offices at the far side, she weaved her way around workstations and people using VR ocular interfaces. It was reasonably easy to navigate the room without being intercepted or noticed by any of her work colleagues. She closed her office door behind her and quickly logged into her workstation. The front of each office was a floor to ceiling glass window with a desk behind it; it afforded her little privacy, but it was enough. With others all too busy with their own tasks to notice her arrival, she started to check via remote link on the progress of the system set up and any last-minute issues, of which there always were a few to iron out. This time she was pleased to see they were ahead of schedule. They would be ready to test half an hour earlier than forecast. That was a comfortable margin and would mean people were nice and relaxed for the test.

It would mean they would be confident. Fallible.

She reviewed the status of the checklist and saw that the accelerator module had been checked and signed off—that was her mark. Casually, she noted that the office next to hers was empty, as Hubbard, the senior liaison to the press office on this project, was due to be greeting the guests and VIPs and briefing them on the test before he brought them through to the laboratory. A few moments later she was in his office at his terminal. His password had been easy to obtain, as he was overly relaxed about security, believing his work to be non-critical to the security of the facility, but misunderstanding how access to his terminal could be misused. She had watched him several times entering a simple password: his son's name and date of birth combined. He had even let her use it to log in once to obtain files that she had needed when he had been out of the office. He would have failed a security audit in a heartbeat. It was the easiest social hack she had ever performed, but likely the most important.

Opening a browser to the net, she clicked through to a local news feed. Nothing unusual. Searching for news on the institute, a raft of stories became available. She didn't bother clicking through to any of them and instead scanned down the page for an advert, and there it was. BIOMETRIC AUGS *Enhance Your Life*. Rather than clicking on it, she dragged the image to the terminal desktop where the file that should have appeared then disappeared. The complex hack had begun; it should take moments. A screen popped up.

"Enter new value for lambda:_" She punched in the first number that occurred to her.

"Enter a corrective margin (0 – 1.0):_" She typed, "0.275". Hitting the return on the terminal killed the popup window and she shut down the browser. She logged out. Hallard would be none the wiser.

It was done.

The Mag-X accelerator module reconfiguration she had just performed would not be detected at this late stage, the checks having already been performed on that module. Punching a bunch of random numbers into the drive config would throw the optimised thrust output off, diminish the effectiveness of the Mag drive and ultimately show the assembled dignitaries that the project was going nowhere. GAIA will have pulled off a bloodless victory and destroyed any chance of the colonisation effort leaving the confines of orbit.

To members of the GAIA faction, this colonisation fleet was the ultimate betrayal to humanity. A bunch of elitist AI setting off on a mission to spread themselves throughout the stars, while those who had conceived them and raised them up as saviours would be left to perish on a toxic world. Machines could no better save a doomed planet than those who created them, but for some reason the AI and a chosen few were being given a life beyond the bounds of this dying planet. Why should such a small elite number survive? She could not reconcile the morality; the price was too great. People in this AI equation were expendable, that was clear to her. She, and others like her, would stop this entitled group from escaping the fate of the masses at all costs. What made *them* so superior? Now, after missing all the opportunities to help the populous, the greed and selfishness of the elite hung like a cloud of darkness over them all.

She hadn't started off as part of GAIA—she had met them later—but you didn't need to be part of a group like that to be disgusted by events. You just needed to watch the newscasts; it was all in the feeds. Her decision to do something about it, rather than feel impotent and unable to affect the wider outcome, was taken when she found herself among a group of like-minded people. These were people driven by the same motivations and able to further inform her of the dreadful outcomes associated with AI development and overreliance. They took her down the rabbit hole and revealed not just the stories but evidence of AI atrocities, mass murder and genocide. Arrongate station and a few other incidents had hit the news casts and media outlets, but it was one of many, the tip of a much larger iceberg, others covered up and hidden from the wider populous. Technology development had been unfettered and unchecked, moving faster than regulations and oversight could be applied. As she learned more, and had her eyes opened to the terrible danger AI really posed to society, she became increasingly enraged and driven to act, to put a stop to their corrosive effect on the world.

She found herself back at her desk, her mind wandering again. It was not so much a daydream as a waking reminder of the nightmare she was battling to avoid, her subconscious reinforcing the purpose for which they all fought. Whatever course humanity found itself taking, whether destined to find a way though the devastation fate had wrought on their planet or not, *people* would find a way, not AI. Being led by a machine was like giving up or trading gods—one human constructed hoax for another—each designed to control the masses and ensure dominance of a ruling minority.

A knock on the door shook her from her thoughts. Abel Okoro

looked back at her through the glass door, a broad smile across his face. It was infectious, and she found her face instantly react to his good nature by returning the smile. The lead engineer on the project opened the door and popped his head into the room.

"Are you ready for some good news? You look like you could use some."

"Sure. Come in," she said. "How's the final test set up coming on?"

"Oh, all good. We're ahead of schedule, at the moment, by 30 minutes. But don't let anyone out there know—they'll be sneaking off for a coffee break."

"Not today. If I have to face the brass from Formillun, so do they." She smiled to make light of it, but there was truth there.

"Talking of top brass, where's ours? I thought Patten was with you?"

"He was, but the flight back from New York must have taken its toll. He crashed out as soon as we got back. I'm sure he'll be joining us for the main event later."

Okoro shrugged his shoulders, a look of concern across his face. "It was only a matter of time. He works too hard, and I know he doesn't get enough sleep. I call him on any shift I work and he picks up like he's expecting my call, wide awake. You should have a word with him."

She shook her head. "Wouldn't help. We've had those arguments before. It's his baby we're building, and he won't be swayed."

"We all know he's committed to the project, but he's going to give himself a heart attack," replied Okoro. "If you can't persuade him, what hope have the rest of us?"

It was her turn to shrug. "He'll be here."

"You know I'll have to run the show without him if he doesn't turn up before Jessop and his friends?" Okoro asked. "It would be a real shame. I know he'd want to run this one."

"I know," she nodded in agreement. "But, like I said, he'll be here." She waved him out of the office. "Now, let me finish up here and I'll be out. You can run me though any last-minute issues."

"Sure. I'll be with Greene." The door closed with a click and she watched him make his way back out across the control room.

Alone again, her smile dropped from her face, unable to keep the mask any longer. Infiltration of this team had been tough, with the rigorous background checks and personal interrogation being intrusive and the hardest to overcome. But she had been briefed well; GAIA had been infiltrating the critical structure of key technical and political positions ever since their inception. They had become very good at it. But when it came down to it, there were only so many specialists at the cutting edge of astrophysics and spacecraft propulsion. Even if Formillun security had suspected anything, they may have just tagged her and put her under 24-7 surveillance. They still needed her knowledge.

To secure her position, she had marked Scott Patten as a target and had lured him into a honeytrap. She was intelligent and beautiful, but she had still found getting his attention somewhat of a task, drawing his focus away from his work had been frustrating and confounding. In the end, her seductions had to become blatant, as he just wasn't receptive to subtle charms. On one particular critical test of the Mag-X, she had made sure she was standing next to him. As everyone had cheered the success of the engine test, becoming extremely excited by the prospect of project advancement and the renewed funding that would bring, she had grabbed him and planted a kiss squarely on his lips. His frozen face had been exactly the reaction she had wanted, the breakthrough she had needed. She was suddenly the sole focus of all his attention. In that moment, the trap had sprung and her prey ensnared. "Sorry," she had said coyly. "I seem to have become a little carried away."

From that moment on, she had worked her way fully into his confidence—and his bed. It was an espionage tactic as old as time. GAIA had placed her as a middle-ranking scientist at the facility, but now all Mag-X project information was within her grasp, and some other projects too. It had worked out better than they had planned.

The main control room door opened and Hallard entered leading a gaggle of suits, all grim-faced and demanding to be impressed. Next to him was Sir David Jessop, president of the Formillun Institute and their esteemed leader. They were conversing easily and casually to the others, giving the suits the grand tour before the presentation.

It was about ten minutes before the start of the test firing. She got up and made her way to the door of her office, opened it and stood just outside, casually observing the room and watching the primary screen, which pictured a live view of the Mag drive test bed. Various readings populated the primary display and mission monitors on the front wall—the temperature of key components, test time countdown, power output, drive efficiency, fuel consumption rates, quantum field stability and particle ladder generation rates—the list of data all currently nominal and green.

Okoro caught her eye and tapped his watch. *Where's Patten?* She shrugged a response. *Don't know.* He shook his head and walked over to the control desk where six engineers were all busy performing their final checks. An elevated chair with an integrated terminal and comms panel was situated a meter or so behind them and he climbed into it with a reluctant sigh. Checking his watch again and the mission clock on the primary room display, he waited.

Voices gently burbled across the room as the visitors discussed their observations, pointing occasionally to indicate an item of interest. The scientists and engineers checked and reported that they were set and ready for the test. The drive was ready for ignition, conditions optimal and data capture was good across all sensors. She looked back to Okoro as he stood to address the room.

"Ladies and gentlemen, for the record this is Mag-X drive test 212. We are now ready to commence. In the absence of Project Director Patten, I will be taking charge of this test firing. All stations confirm your Go-No Go status." There was a moment's pause as the news was digested, and a few of the engineers looked back to him in surprise. The visiting group with Jessop and Hallard began to exchange concerned comments.

All the stations began to report in. She checked them all off in her head and watched the primary display as the station acknowledgments lit up with a green Go status.

A sudden cry interrupted the test, derailing everyone's concentration. Expectation and tension evaporated as all eyes turned to the main door. The two posted security detail seemed to be wrestling a person to the floor. No, not wrestling, she thought, helping. There was care in their actions and worry on their faces. Curled waves of dark hair on a head, which flopped and tried to control itself while being failed by muscles and motor actions, obscured her identification of the person. Then she found herself in shock, a physical thrust to her heart as it was hit by a shot of adrenaline. How had Patten made it to the control room?

Reacting rather than thinking, she ran across the room, the concerned and worried girlfriend. She looked down at Patten as he lay in a sweat on the floor, his eyes seemed to be having problems focusing, bulging and bloodshot. She knelt down taking up his head in her hands, a tranq-patch shouldn't have had this affect. She held his hand tight.

"Ellie," he said, a grin on his face, though it could equally have been a grimace. "Help me up. I need to run the test."

"Are you kidding?" she replied. "We need to get you to medical. Get you checked out."

"After. Right now, let's get this test done. I've been waiting years to see this run. It's my bloody life's work. I'm not missing it for a fever. Who catches a fever on the most important day of their life?" He was insistent. "Now, please. Help me up."

He was already struggling to stand himself. Okoro had joined her and, between the two of them and the security detail, they helped him over to a chair.

There were concerned faces about the room, all startled at how ill Patten looked. And he looked bad. His skin had taken a grey pallor and his eyes looked black and sunken. It had only been a couple of hours since she left him in his room, but now he looked like a different man.

Jessop appeared like a ghost at their side, without warning and in silence. To her, Jessop was dangerous. He was tall with an easy charismatic charm and a startling scalpel-sharp intelligence. But for those who knew him, worked with him, there was a side of him you didn't want to see. Cross that line and he turned into a dark daemon, sucking the air and life from the room in moments. She had seen him intellectually dismantle a guy once, a researcher from another team that had tried to manipulate and massage his research findings to save his research grant. She could even remember what he had been researching: nano-machine motion and propulsion in non-Newtonian fluids, to move and control nano-bots within the human bloodstream. He had claimed success but Jessop had torn him apart at a conference in front of his peers. The day after, she had seen the researcher leaving the facility, being escorted off the premises. Gone.

You didn't want to be 'gone'. While you were working and your research was of value, you and your family were taken care of by the institute and the government. You and your family were given citizenship, you and your family were given a suburban house and full provisions, a life of protection within the city boundary and a lifestyle which many millions could only dream of in these days of global decline. Lose the favour of the institute, or government for that matter, and you and your family were out, thrown back on the pile.

"Patten, what is going on here?" asked Jessop. "You look terrible!" He paused, waiting for an answer. "I presume you have a good explanation for all the theatrics?" His manner was breezy, but everyone in the group knew what the wrong answer might elicit.

"No, sir. No, I don't. It may be flu, but I couldn't miss this test. I'll see the doc after the run." His skin was a sheen of sweat. "Okoro, could you continue with the test for our guests? I know we are all excited to see the outcome."

All eyes fell on Okoro, who was momentarily surprised by the attention. "Of course," he said, and made his way back to his command.

She continued to hold Patten's hand, a gentle but firm squeeze to confirm her part, give him the physical comfort a girlfriend would. Then without letting go, she grabbed a nearby chair and scooted it to a close position next to him, then sat so she could speak closely with him. Jessop was still standing over them, imposing and threatening but in a calm and quiet way. He was clearly trying to calculate whether he was being made fool of, or if Patten's situation was genuine.

"Please express my apologies to our guests, Sir Jessop," Patten said evenly. "Enjoy the test."

Jessop nodded, but before he turned back to his companions, he looked at them both with piercing blue eyes. "This better work, Patten." He stared at them a moment longer then returned to his own tormentors, to put a spin on events and rebuild confidence in the coming engine test.

"You should be in medical," she said, shaking and squeezing his hand and setting her face to a frown to convey the mix of concern and insistence she felt.

"Soon. This will all be over in ten minutes," he replied, holding her hand in both of his but not taking his eyes from the main display screen. "You can pack me off to medical the moment we're done here."

"Hmmm," she said in a nurse's tone.

*

"Commence ignition process," called Okoro across the room.

"Ignition start," responded the duty engineer. "In three… two… one."

The control room main screen showed a white-hot glow from the rear of the machine, the engine exhaust directing the generated particles away in a high velocity stream, which at the beginnings of the test meandered as any stream finding its way. Energy sputtered and flashed, but the fluctuations settled quickly into the recognisable constant flow anticipated by all the simulated data. The system stabilised.

She had to purposefully relax her grip on Patten's hand, which she realised she had been gripping tighter and tighter as the engine test went on. She hadn't taken a breath since Okoro's command to ignite the drive.

"Vacuum holding," came an anonymous voice from the bank of controllers.

"Throttle at ten percent and holding."

"Okay, good," said Okoro. "Attenuation in the stream is minimal. Increase the throttle to fifty percent on my mark… Mark."

The room was silent. With the test being carried out in a giant submerged vacuum chamber under the offshore platform and built into the seabed, there was no sound to hear. But the visual capture was hypnotic, and she found herself staring, unable to look away. A magnesium line of blinding energy born from a small man-made star.

"Fifty percent," said a voice. Brunner; she recognised it this time.

"Bring in the EM accelerator," said Patten, transfixed by scrolling data, as it moved continuously across a nearby workstation monitor. Okoro heard the instruction and nodded his confirmation. They all knew the test sequence and what step was coming next.

"Throttle at fifty percent," stated Brunner.

"Engage the EMA," commanded Okoro.

"EMA engaged," replied Brunner.

Her heart skipped a beat. It was sabotage pure and simple, and it was down to her. Her mind leapt ahead: catastrophic failure of the test site, the energies involved evaporating the metal and concrete of the vacuum chamber, turning sea water in the immediate area to vapour in an instant. She found herself wide-eyed and as captivated by the main screen as Patten, but for an opposed outcome.

Light intensity increased as the afterburner engaged, power output readings began to climb as expected but, as she watched, a sudden rush of anomalous spikes began to appear in the output stream and things started to go wrong. A spectral stutter in the pure white of the stream—colours flickered and lanced out from the exhaust in all directions.

"Massive power fluctuations!" said Brunner, seemingly stating the obvious. "Experiencing unstable EM resonance in the chamber."

"Severe vibration throughout the drive frame," announced another engineer.

There was a disbelief in the room. The test was beginning to run counter to hundreds of simulations, thousands of man-hours in preparation and checks. But then, that's why you performed physical tests, she thought. Nature always had a surprise in store— the thing you hadn't thought of, the unknown-unknown. She rehearsed her arguments even then, as the drive began to fail.

"Begin emergency shutdown." Okoro was resigned in his order, disappointment thick in his voice.

Patten squeezed her hand and levered against her, mustering all his strength to stand. He was full of adrenaline, fired up and disbelieving. "No!" he shouted across the room. It was a bellow of command and took everyone by surprise. All eyes turned to him in expectation. "Throttle to full! Power through it."

"Think of the energies involved! You'll blow the facility!" pleaded Okoro.

"I know the risks! But this is wrong. There's no time—just do it," Patten countered, sternly, looking with blazing eyes at Brunner.

Brunner, looked back to Okoro then Patten, weighing up the relative consequences of acting against either man, then turned back to his workstation and pushed the throttle to full.

Initially, there was no response, the drive emitting spears of light erratically as it appeared to struggle to function.

"Thrust degrading, down ten percent."

Glancing at Patten, she saw that he was frozen in expectation and still grabbing her hand. The angle at which she was seated meant that her wrist was twisted in an unnatural way and there was pain which she hadn't noticed a moment before. She pulled her hand from his grasp; she didn't think he even noticed.

"Hold it," Patten said. "Be patient."

Then, as if Patten knew it would happen, the power output began to pick up. The star bright white of the screen began to become more intense and the visual flux of energies became smooth and linear. A sudden pulse of thrust exploded from the drive exhaust and the power output readings began to climb rapidly. A stable engine burn had been pulled from the brink of disaster, the power output now exceeding expectation. As the thrust elevated past 33 million Newtons and continued to climb, the mood in the room changed to one of elation. People started to clap and, as the stability of the drive improved, there were whoops of joy, urging the performance levels on to greater heights.

Patten slumped back into his seat.

"You did it!" she said, in real astonishment.

He shook his head and looked up at her. "*We* did it. We all did it."

The room was jubilant. Okoro was trying to keep control of proceedings the best he could but it was difficult when you were caught up in the moment. She noted even Jessop had a smile on his face.

"Time to get you to medical," she said over the noise.

"Yeah," said Patten, who seemed to deflate like a punctured tyre. "I think that's a good idea."

BOYD

"It's like a coyote pissin' in the wind," he mumbled in frustration under his breath. No one but Ellie heard him.

'Is that a saying in Texas?' she asked via his bio-comm.

'It is now,' he responded dryly, staring back at the three Zantanath troops suddenly standing dotted about his workshop. 'Where the hell did they come from?'

In the closest workshop to main engineering, he and his team had been working to fabricate parts to bring main engineering up to operational effectiveness as quickly as possible, and to repurpose the available Rem-Teks aboard with the new 'soldier' mod of his own design. The order had been for all this to be done 'yesterday', and he understood the urgency. Main engineering was pretty chewed up from the chaos of the last few days, with everything patched together, rerouted, reworked or just plain broken. The place had energy weapon holes in panelling about the corridors, and monitors and consoles were shattered and in splinters. Considering that he and his team had only had a few hours to patch things up before people started shooting again, he had thought this progress pretty good.

The workshop had been locked down under heavy manoeuvring, and his team ordered to their crash couches for the battle. However, as the ship settled into a level course for a moment, strange figures had turned up out of nowhere. Shimmering, mirrored balls appearing across the room, their surface undulating like the reflective surface of a lake on a bright and sunny day. They had grown from the size of a pinhead to that of a tall human in the space of a few seconds. Everyone in the room had become confused and transfixed. He on the other hand, had feared the worst and, based on the events of the last few days, he now felt more than vindicated. He was rarely wrong, and his instincts had served him well to this point; why would they fail him now?

"Move!" he shouted.

He watched, almost as a spectator. People scattered, releasing harnesses and jumping from crash couches to take cover where they could, but they were too slow. The intruders had immediately taken down two of his work detail, and the three guards assigned to them. Within moments, the others were standing, frozen, hands up, rounded up and herded over to the wall furthest from the workshop entrance. But not him. In that instant he had gone to ground, hidden behind a workstation and out of sight. Whatever was going on seemed to him to be a capture-and-hold exercise, these new mirror-suited murderers now sealing off the room and defending their little corner of the ship. The good news was that they weren't here to exterminate the crew; the bad news was that they, as a ship, were now occupied.

'Anyone else get a terrible sense of déjà vu?' he asked Ellie, as he kept low and moved around the corner of another workbench, grabbing a Rem-Tek control interface as he did.

One of the techs in the team had managed to modify a Rem-Tek receiver unit and enable it to pair with a bio-comm interface. However, she had been finalising this work at her station before the latest fleet skirmish and had pulled the receiver unit directly from a working Rem-Tek. If he had any chance of saving this team, he would need to reactivate this Rem-Tek with an untested receiver unit, then arm it and repel boarders.

'It's not going to work,' said Ellie.

'Bullshit. It'll work.'

'I've run the VERS. The outcome is not good… for you.'

'Are you going to help me or criticise me?'

There was a pause as Ellie considered his question.

'Both.' As she said this, the workshop doors closed. All exits were now blocked.

'By closing the only way out of here? Good move, genius.' He positioned himself to lay on the floor at the foot of the target Rem-

Tek and quietly began to refit the communication interface.

'Wait,' said Ellie in a flat tone, showing as much frustration with his manner as she ever really showed. He froze in place, holding his breath, eyes wide and looking about without moving his head.

'What?'

As he worked, she fed him a streamed vid-link of the workshop security cameras. This showed that the larger of the three intruders, the one with a pack on its back with what appeared to be skeletal wings folded behind it, had moved away from the opposite side of the workbench that he was hidden behind. The Zantanath were now more interested in the unexpected closure of the main door, which allowed him the precious seconds he needed to get the job done.

'I guess that's a 'Thank you' moment,' he said.

'You're all charm. Just work faster.'

He picked up the pace. Within ten seconds he had the modified comm unit in place and the Rem-Tek systems booting up. He was thankful that the boot sequence was silent, with only a couple of flashing lights on the front of the chest panel giving away the start-up. The Rem-Tek was now being completely ignored by the Zantanath, who were focused on the door and looking the wrong way. A little subtle misdirection by Ellie was giving him—giving them—a lifeline.

Once the boot sequence was complete, he kept low and snuck away to the stairs leading to the elevated control room. He wasn't interested in the control room this time, instead his focus was on the storage area to its right as a place to take cover before he started causing trouble. Squeezing between a couple of containers, he noted the markings on the side indicating titanium pellets for the 3d-fab unit. *Perfect*, he thought, with a full dose of sarcasm. He imagined one of the containers being hit by weapons fire, and in his mind the effect would be like that of a claymore mine, with pellets of super-accelerated metal punching holes in everything from where he sat to the back of the storeroom. He shook his head and sat down. He didn't have time to find a better spot. Hopefully, being out of sight was more important than being behind useful cover.

Settling into the dark shadows of the storage area and closing his eyes, he opened the control connection to the Rem-Tek. It had been based on a lite version of the more fully integrated haptic link, which could be initiated from the haptic suites dotted about the ship, or aboard the fleet shuttles. He received a visual binocular view from the Rem-Tek sensor array located in the head of the unit. The height of the Rem-Tek was that of an average human, which was by design. Most of the maintenance work a Rem-Tek performed during normal duties was within the working environment of the ship, on corridors and maintenance conduits which were built to human proportions. In addition, when Rem-Teks were piloted via the haptic link, a human found it far less disorienting if their visual position was where it was expected to be. All sorts of problems began to manifest themselves if the human pilot was too tall and perceived the world as a giant—

mainly issues of apparent clumsiness. Scaling people up, even via remote technology, just messed with their motor functions and coordination.

His bio-comm link with the Rem-Tek on the workbench reported active and all systems were green. Immediately, he dropped the Rem-Tek to the floor and positioned it prone and out of sight while he manoeuvred it to the weapons rack at the wall under the elevated control station. With head forward and the caterpillar tracks folded under it, he made it to the weapons rack in another couple of seconds.

Removing two Longman-Cooper carbines and a couple of magazines of .22 soft-nosed ammunition, he utilised the four forward limbs of the Rem-Tek to rapidly load the magazines into the carbines, then grabbed a couple more replacement magazines to go.

'That got their attention,' said Ellie.

'Busy,' he stated, flicking off the safeties to both carbines.

Spinning the Rem-Tek on the spot using the caterpillar unit, he stood the machine tall, above the line of workbenches and in clear sight of the Zantanath, who were now prowling their way forward across the workshop. He took aim at the two nearest and, to his surprise, the Rem-Tek took control and provided him firing solutions, angles, velocities and trajectories, all instantly available and displayed as orange dotted lines from his carbines to the red circled target icons about the Zantanath troopers heads. All he had to do was provide the fire command.

From his position behind the container units, he heard the loud explosive rattle of the carbines as they fired their rounds across the short space between the Rem-Tek unit and the Zantanath. The sound seemed to amplify in the bare-walled metallic environment of the engineering workshop, a tinny shrill pain stabbing at his ears with every round.

Sparks lit the space in front of the Zantanath, their hexagonal, plated armour shimmering as energy dissipated across it and bullets were redirected and ricocheted about the room. But, as panic began to rise within him at their continued unrelenting advance, one jerked its head in an unnatural fashion and fell to the ground. The Rem-Tek recalculated its firing solution and both carbines came to bare on the second Zantanath, as a bolt of energy lanced across the space. He tried to evade the strike but the Rem-Tek's reactions were not fast enough and the energy sliced through its upper shoulder, an arm—with carbine chattering in anger—fell to the floor.

In that moment, he looked for a place to retreat and give space enough to reload and press the attack, but he was hard against the back of the workshop, the weapons rack giving him no further room to move. But the instruction to the Rem-Tek was acted on. To his surprise, the Rem-Tek began to back up and climb, its available limbs gripping exposed pipework and structural beams, hauling itself on powerful chimpanzee-like legs up into the roof space, its caterpillar drive folding to its midsection. Climbing up past the control room and into the ceiling space, the Rem-Tek reloaded its carbine and unleashed another barrage against the nearest Zantanath trooper.

The trooper's head seemed to explode under the weight of fire, a third of the faceplate and frontal skull hung weakly from the body as it slumped to the floor, the rest of the brain matter sprayed a bright red across the floor and nearest workstation.

Reorienting quickly, he tried to find the third trooper, as the work team, no longer under the scrutiny of their captors, had started to find cover. A flash of light drew his attention, but there was nothing to see other than the main door and bulkhead. Sweeping left and right, the final Zantanath had gone. A confusion set in, the main door still locked and untouched, the workshop floor clear.

A second later a growing light from the storage area flashed out, then the Rem-Tek feed simply stopped, plunging him into darkness. Opening his eyes in confusion, he crept slowly to the end of the gap in the containers and his hiding place. He looked up at the place he knew the Rem-Tek to have been, high in the ceiling space. The Rem-Tek hung there, hands locked and anchoring it in place, the head fixed looking out into the room, carbine pointing toward the main door. A large, blackened hole had been punched in its chest, severing its control pathways and taking out its vital circuits.

Without really thinking about it, his mind traced the trajectory of the hole he was looking straight through to a scorched carbon splash in the wall behind the Rem-Tek. He slowly turned his head—

in the confined space he found looking behind him difficult—but from his peripheral vision a shadow cast across him. His heart spiked with adrenaline and his eyes grew wide.

The third trooper—wings spread and crackling with energy like a daemon emerging from a dark dimension, the jump pack spinning down and spines folding in behind it—stood on top of the containers, pointing its gauntlet-mounted weapon straight at him. He fell to his back and tried to scramble himself out of the way, but he was fooling himself. There was no way he was going to escape. The wall slammed him in the back as he back-peddled. Looking down the barrel slowed time.

Noise erupted all about him, sparks and fire. He closed his eyes and thrust his hands to his ears, pulling his legs up to protect his body. It was the only shield he had available to put between him and the chaos about him. The silver trooper altered his aim and unleashed a stuttering barrage of energy from his gauntlet weapon, and in response there were screams and shouts from behind him in the workshop. He could not make out the commands over the returning gunfire, just deep bellows which directed and concentrated the fire, pounding the Zantanath trooper into submission.

A heavy blast lanced past him and accompanied more screaming, but the team were not deterred and the carbine rounds continued to rain onto their target. The relentless nature of the attack was clearly becoming too much for the complex platelets of armour the trooper wore. The suit failed, overcome by the weight of fire and unable to dissipate all the energy of the rounds falling upon it. The shimmer of energy, looking like ripples on a pond from a thrown stone, had protected the soldier from the incoming anger, but in a moment the armour flashed out and bullets found their mark.

The trooper fell to one knee and tried to return fire but, however advanced his systems were, it knew it was doomed. In a last effort for life, it started up its local transport system. The spines unfolding from the backpack and the low whine building over the gunfire, Boyd watched in fascination and fear, his engineer's mind suddenly captivated by the alien technology. The shimmering field began to build around it and solidify, but in that last second one of the team's rounds struck something critical. The field hadn't completely formed, and it lost power, shrinking the diameter of the sphere in the moment it solidified and completed its matter transfer. The sphere disappeared and for a moment floating in space was the dismembered head and shoulder section of the Zantanath trooper, a left hand and the right arm and gauntlet weapon severed above the elbow. The gravity plates through the flooring of the workshop eventually took affect and the extremities of the trooper fell, bouncing off the top of the container units, coming to rest on the floor.

"Shit!"

He looked to the entrance of the storage bay and Craig Li was staring at the accumulated, random body parts scattered about the floor, still holding his carbine pointed at the head section of the dead trooper, as if being cautious at this point was a good idea. The lead mechanical engineer in the team, Li's main responsibility was building and modifying the Rem-Tek chassis to accommodate the additional shielding to the power core of the machine. He had found out the hard way that an unshielded Rem-Tek core breach by weapons fire in a confined space was more than a little devastating and could make a real mess of the ship, let alone organics in the area.

"Couldn't have put it better myself," he said, getting up and taking a few steps closer to the remains of the trooper and the space in which he had been hiding a few moments before.

"Where did you learn to shoot like that?"

"10-8 Rifles."

"Army?"

"Before this life, we all had another," Li said.

"True," he replied, his mind momentarily wandering to the many resuscitation suites he had woken up in over the years. He was definitely an old soul in a young body. It was one of the tricks of the splicing process. Once you were spliced to your new clone host, no one had a clue how old you were. When you all look 25, the only differential that he had found as an indicator to a person's real age was how much bullshit you put up with. The older souls tended to be less accepting of the bullshit.

"What a way to go," said Li. Others began to crowd into the storage area, to try and take a look at the perpetrator of the chaos and death of the last few minutes.

"Better him than us," said a voice from the back.

He moved closer and knelt in front of the body parts, assessing and examining. Accessing his bio-comm, he began to record what he was seeing. The fact that the weapon had been left behind was particularly intriguing to him. Possibilities of reverse engineering the Zantanath weapon were tantalising—too much of a prize to pass up.

"Man, pull yourself together," he said, trying to lighten the mood. He wasn't sure it was working, and there were a lot of very tightly wound people standing around with weapons. He didn't like it.

"Li, help me out here. The rest of you, go and see if we can help any of our guys in the workshop. Tyrell, Cooke, I need another couple of Rem-Teks online as soon as we can manage it. That's your priority. Now, go!" The group moved away with an urgency, a couple loitering for a moment, not quite able to take their eyes away from the remains of the trooper in front of them, each of them still processing the situation. A moment later, he and Li were on their own.

Pinning the lower arm of the trooper to the ground with his boot, he pulled hard but carefully against the gauntlet and the weapon it housed. After a short struggle and a little manoeuvring, the weapon came free. He rolled it over in his hands examining every detail.

"This is some piece of kit," he said.

"We need to get more of those," said Li. "Even the playing field."

"Risky, getting them. But we might be able to build one ourselves." He looked over to Li who was equally fascinated by the exotic technology he held. He extended his arms and offered it over to Li, whose face became one of surprise. "You up for the challenge?"

"You sure?"

"Over to you. Strip it down, learn its secrets, duplicate."

"It's going to take time. Probably time we don't have."

"Need to make a start sometime. May as well be now."

"Right. I'm on it." But Li didn't move, just stood there looking back at him expectantly. He understood the delay in action. Li looked past him at the masked helmet on the floor, then back to him.

"Curious?"

"You bet. I think we need to know what we're dealing with here."

Nodding his reply, he moved over to the disembodied head. Trying to keep out of the pool of red, slick blood which had leached out onto the floor, he found the visor release on each side of the helmet. Taking a careful moment to get his hands in place, he pressed the release. There was a click and hiss as the seal was removed then, gripping the face plate tightly, he slowly lifted the visor away to reveal the trooper's face.

"Stars and blood!" he said. "I know this guy." The face was calm and pale and appeared somewhat malnourished, but there was no mistaking the features. "It's Lieutenant Larsen."

Li moved for a better look. "Can't be. Must just be coincidence."

"No. This is something else. The likeness is exact... well, apart from being a few pounds leaner."

"You mean, having just been sliced up by a huge silver ball?"

"No, you idiot. Like he's been at the gym for months but not eaten, that sort of leaner," he snapped.

Standing, he continued to look down on the decapitated remains of Larsen. This made no sense.

"You get to work on that weapon. I'm going to report to the bridge, find out what's going on and who these guys are," he said. "And keep those doors locked. There will be more of these things lurking around the ship."

"Not sure how much use that will be, given how these guys turned up in the first place."

That had slipped his mind.

"Shit."

ROUX

He lay awkwardly and his neck stung with a bright pain. Trying to touch his neck to assess the damage he realised his hands were cuffed, legs too. Wriggling himself to a seated position he took in his surroundings, his groggy head blurring his vision, his hearing dull. Light and noise were now tolerable, no longer the whirlwind and blinding whiteout of his capture, but there was still an underlying droning noise to the space and the scene was low and subdued, maybe indicating utility, a military space. Whatever the transport, he was still in it, and they were on the move.

A face loomed out of the shadows as he woke, grabbing an overhead handrail to steady itself over the motion of the transport. The Xannix was still wearing its combat mask and a chameleon poncho around its shoulders shifted with the light and blurred his sight, his brain momentarily telling him that parts of the Xannix were disappearing sporadically, messing with his perception. It made him want to look away. It leaned in and with a powerful single armed lift, picked him clean off the floor and placed him roughly into a couch a couple of metres across the cabin. It spoke into the darkness further down the cabin and another figure stepped forward, smaller, of a lean, slight frame and with features which were very human. Powder white skin almost glowed in the dim cabin and large, manipulative ears stretched like the wings of a bat, guided by a twitching upper ridge which moved much like the tail of a cat. Highly attuned directional hearing with forward facing opal black eyes; this humanoid was a predator, keen and perceptive.

Zantanath.

Stepping closer, the male Zantanath examined him like some laboratory specimen, special attention paid to the sore area at his neck. A chill passed through him, a reaction to being so close to something so dangerous; the Zantanath exuded malevolence. He tried not to let the fear show but he felt like his body was letting him down, sweat pricking his skin and eyes wide. The words it spoke were meaningless, but the soft intonation and sneering smile conveyed an intention to him; nothing good was coming.

The Zantanath took something from within his camouflage chameleonware robes, a small flat handheld device which he placed against Roux's chest and collarbone. Looking down his nose and just about able to see what was happening, he saw the black shiny surface become transparent, as the Zantanath tapped the screen in sweeping and button-like motions, the transparency dropped into his chest, a red rectangular cavity through muscle and bone revealing his upper left lung. He made an involuntary yelp, the Zantanath just smiled and carried on tapping at the controls. The view changed and refocused until he was looking at a cutaway of his collar bone, all the meat and skin visually stripped away by the device.

Part of him was repulsed by the hole in his chest, part of him was now fascinated by the device. It didn't last long. When the pain struck, he forgot almost everything, his neck felt like it was being eaten away, bored through from the inside. Something within him was moving and slicing its way through him to do it. His mind was shutting down again with the incandescent pain, vision fading to grey then tunnelling to black. A sharp slap struck him across the face and he felt his lip split then an iron red taste on his tongue.

Into the window in his chest moved a murmuration of tiny spiderlike dots, moving slowly to wrap about his collar bone. Once in place, the Zantanath medic muddled with the controls some more, further instructions to the burrowing nanotech. Each of the dots began to dissolve the surface of his left clavicle and moments later had disappeared, morphing into the bone material.

A white light pinged on the panel, the medic smiled and removed the device. The pain as acute as it had been, stopped instantly. More words he had no understanding of were uttered between the Zantanath and the crew. He could hear them getting ready in the shadows of the cabin, preparing: the rustle of clothing, the test operation of equipment, possibly weapons, the stowing of kit. Then he realised the Zantanath was centimetres from his face again, those deep opal eyes staring into his soul. A grin on its features, he could only guess at the meaning; the creature was evil and made his skin crawl.

"Free," it said, using a word which made his heart skip. He was being set free? The single word without context was confusing, and his face reflected this miscommunication. The Zantanath started speaking at him again in yet more indecipherable words, then it backed off and shouted to the crew. The instruction caused an instant hurricane in the cabin as a loading door began to open, lowering to become a ramp out into the slipstream of the craft as they threaded their way down a craggy walled valley. His eyes fixed on the opening, he could now make out snow and a grey snaking line of water meandering its way to a point. As they descended closer, the water began to froth and swirl.

A couple of metres from the ground, the craft came to a hover, and he was unceremoniously picked from the couch and dumped out of the rear of the flyer. Striking the lip of the ramp with his trailing leg as he fell, the world about him began to tumble. The ground struck hard, his left side complaining and his head slapping into wet, mudded soil. Opening his eyes and squinting up at the downdraft from the flyer, his rucksack splashed into the shallows of the river. The whine of the engines increased and the blast chilled him, grit and ice biting at his exposed skin. Seconds later the flyer was heading across the river, the Xannix who had ejected him from the craft holding his gaze as the ramp closed. A moment later, the flyer banked hard and followed the contour of the cliff face, then dipped and disappeared over the ridge.

Rolling to his back, he ached. He held his side, exhaled and stared straight up. The sky was overcast, the shades of grey and white subtle and stratified, sliding over each other in wispy irregular platelets. He tried in some way to understand what had just happened. He had no idea what they had done to him. Perhaps he had been tagged with some kind of tracker to survey the new invading species? Data collection and study. Regardless, he knew three things: firstly, they didn't care that he knew; secondly, it hurt like the rage; and, thirdly, he had no idea where he was.

Deciding to move, he worked his way to his knees and took another moment before standing. Checking for the sun, he tried to orient himself with the big white ball in the grey of the clouds. Plugging the detail into his bio-comm, which took a couple of seconds to respond, a compass rose swung into his view and augmented his horizon; the valley headed off to the north-east. Knowing his escape pod had crashed wildly off course, he had had no time since the crash to really pinpoint where he was; he only knew where he needed to be. The main group of survivors would be his best hope—out here on his own would be a challenge, and with the cold he didn't like his chances. The best thing he could do to extend those odds would be to make his way down the valley to a warmer altitude and try to make contact with the main group. He double-checked his bio-comm for a signal from above—perhaps the *Intrepid* or *Indianapolis* could assist—but after the chaos he had left behind he thought it unlikely; they would have their own problems.

He would first head for higher ground and see if the survivors of the *Endeavour* were broadcasting a beacon, or look for any others in the wind like him. He needed to know which way to head before he started putting any serious effort into breaking out in any particular direction. At least he knew he wasn't short of water, his shelter was in his kit, and he had food—he mentally ticked off the checklist. Surveying the surrounding valley, he found a likely crest to the ridge line, steep but not too tricky.

Hauling himself up and dragging his kit bag from the river, he set off for the ridge.

SPENCER

White. His existence could be described in a single word. From the blinding brightness of the isolation cell—a bubble small enough to tuck him into a foetal position, cramped and unyielding—to the white intensity of the pain that crashed over him in waves. He would feel an electrical charge building all about him over agonising minutes of anticipation. The hairs over his body, the nape of his neck, across his scalp were then all energised and standing from the surface of his skin, as if he was at the centre of a human-sized capacitor. Then the charge would flow through him, discharging across his body, causing every muscle to contract violently.

His voice felt hoarse from the screaming. Confusion was almost complete, thus focus on anything was just an unachievable state of mind. He tried to remember how he had got there, but he couldn't; nothing offered itself from the depths of his memory to answer even that most simple of questions.

He tried to be strong, to resist the pain, but after a while he found yielding to it took the edge off the worst. To bear the unbearable.

The searing light suddenly and without warning went out, plunging him into a darkness where only his mind provided the input, conjuring up further tortures yet to be experienced. Visions of what might come next raced through his thoughts, a journey with a single destination—a fractured mind. He willed his end to come soon.

A dead mechanical clunk; a short punch of vibration all about him. His world moved a little. Something began to whir and the sensation of motion became more pronounced. Trying to reason with the limited sensory input he had, he felt like he was being taken somewhere, but he had no idea where he was *now* to understand where *somewhere* might be. The motion of his cramped cell slowed gently, then stopped. His chest pounded, his heart fuelled by the adrenaline flooding his system, but to no purpose, as he could not fight and there was nowhere to run. Panic was beginning to take hold.

The cramped confines of his cell disappeared. As gravity instantly took hold, he plunged downward, splashing into a warm liquid which enveloped him and seemed to hug and hold him as if he was returning to mother. It was an unexpected sensation for his body and he felt himself slowly unfurl from his curled position, a swelling of relief in his chest. Long arms and legs stretched out and eyes opened to the blur of his new environment. He tried again to make some sense of what was happening to him, but he found no answers, just strange shadows, lights and movement which provided him with more questions.

As his motion in the fluid stabilised and the swirl of shadows became a steady image he moved forward, propelling himself with a languid motion of his long legs. Reaching out to the shadow with his hands he felt a barrier press against his fingertips, there was a limit to his world yet again. But the image began to clear as he moved his face closer to the edge of his new enclosure. Three faces; but one felt familiar, a white face framed by short dark hair, eyes round and full of fear… or shock. He wanted to ask where he was, he wanted to know who he was, but he found only frustration, no way to communicate or reach out to the floating faces on the other side. A ball of emotion within him forced a sound from his chest, to him it was coherent. *Where am I?* No one answered him, but the familiar man the other side of his world became almost frantic, the two others looked on emotionless, calm.

Another dark shadow moved in his peripheral vision, another figure but this time much closer to him, pressing at a panel the other side of the barrier, lights flashing at its fingertips. A whir of motion and a snakelike umbilical swam through the liquid towards him and locked to a socket in his abdomen. It happened faster than he could respond and for a panicked moment he struggled and rolled about frantically to pull the umbilical free. But within a moment a lethargy began to flow through him, a peace which took all the fight from him, made him forget what he was struggling against. Turning back to the familiar face, it was now closer, hands pressed hard up against the barrier trying to get to him, to help and comfort him. As the darkness of sleep came, he reached out.

Father.

*

Spencer watched helplessly as the figure in the gestation tank before him drifted off into what he hoped was a peaceful sleep, features relaxed and calm, a hand reaching to touch his through the membrane of its enclosure.

When Yannix had stated that he needed his help, this was not what he had had in mind. Help to overcome the Zantanath aggressors he could understand, and he was almost willing to agree, given the evidence with which he had been presented—the grotesque clone of Larsen bio-engineered into some advanced killing machine, augmented with modifications and armour which could transport matter or manipulate spacetime to create a localised personal gateway. He was unsure of the specifics, as Yannix had not wanted him to assist in any technical way that he was aware but as a donor. A compliant donor of bio-material. His DNA. In order to beat the Zantanath Larsen clones, Yannix intended to build his own army. The facility he had at his command had been infiltrated and slowly subverted away from its Zantanath technical crew and into his control.

Political games. All the Zantanath on the fabricator station were now under Yannix's command. Converts to his cause of taking back control of his people after all these years of Zantanath rule. Generations of time that had seen the erosion of the Xannix civilisation and the decimation of their number. The Zantanath had systematically reduced the planet's population to manageable levels, levels which could be easily controlled… and farmed.

The disgusting irony of subverting the control of Fabricator Two, was that Yannix had to keep the façade going. In order for his under-cover operation to go unnoticed, the station had to continue its operation as normal. The supply of ships and cloned technology to the Zantanath homeworld had to be uninterrupted.

For the greater prize, Yannix was ensuring this status quo, he and his small army of loyal Overseers. But, in this, Yannix had at his command all that he needed to raise his rebellion. As far as he could tell, the Xannix Overseer leader was playing the Zantanath at their own game.

"Can he feel anything?" he asked Yannix as he touched the gestation tank, as if by doing so he was in some way in physical contact with the clone inside.

"Not now," replied the Zantanath tech who stood at the controls administering a cocktail of nutrients and growth hormone into the newly hatched body. The Zantanath's porcelain white skin furrowed in concentration as he spoke, ears pushed back against his head, and the tips of the upper ear— a smooth snakelike structure with skin to the lower ear—flicking and twitching as he worked. It reminded him of a cat twitching its tail, unthinking and reflexive, but at the same time orienting to direct the quietest, slightest sound. "He will sleep during the next growth phase. It is necessary only to wake them during the birth process, to check the accelerated construction of the clone was successful and that it is fully functional. It is a diagnostic check, if you like, to test all neural pathways and motor function works as anticipated."

Yannix stepped forward to scrutinise the new clone more closely. "In the next phase intellect and purpose will be programmed. This particular model will be part of the infiltration units."

"Is that what was identified as my primary attribute? I'm a doctor! I save people. You understand? I'm not a killer!" His hands balled into fists against the tank, his frustrations building at the unjustified assessment.

"You cannot deny your true purpose, Doctor," said Yannix. "And, to correct you, an infiltration unit is designed to scout ahead, identify the path, find a way through. You have a keen insight in finding a way through, Dr Spencer. That is what the Zantanath have found in you. The killing part, that is your species as a whole. You are predisposed to it. You cannot deny it."

Spencer could not respond, his mind whirling through human history to find examples to counter the argument, but he could find none. Earth was a place of endless conflict, war was an ever present part of human nature. During a global catastrophe like the Great Decline you might expect a grab for resources, people making claim to food and water to keep their countrymen alive, to keep their clansmen alive, to keep their families alive. It was a struggle on every level. But prior to that, even when the world was stable and governments had resource enough for populations of millions, they squabbled and bickered over lines on maps, minerals and water which were not even in their own territories, food and energy resources, each civilization believing that because they had the bigger weapons they were somehow entitled to claim whatever they wanted from wherever it could be found.

Belief and entitlement, an eternal cocktail of disaster.

His face contorted into a furrowed ball of anger, his fists clenched tight. He could not escape the truth of who he was: humanity could not avoid its propensity for violence.

"You are a species of hunters, Dr Spencer. It is simply that element of your nature that is being exaggerated by the Zantanath."

"That, and the tools to execute your purpose," said the Zantanath tech while continuing to work. "You have been given greater strength, your skin toughened, your skeleton hardened, lengthened slightly and made lighter to increase your speed. Reaction times are faster due to increased neural connections and your sight is enhanced to cope with low light and a wider spectrum."

"You have weaponised our species."

"Yes," said Yannix. "But then, as I stated, that is what the Zantanath do to all of us. Those ships out there, with what you call chameleon hulls   that is just one of the outcomes of their many years harvesting and torturing our species. It has to end, Doctor, and this is the first step."

He tried to calm himself. He was becoming too emotionally invested and identifying too much with this specific clone. He worked with clones all the time, preparing them for hosting their spliced memory, ensuring that the gestation and growth of the new body was normal and that the brain structure was an exact copy of the original. What the Zantanath were doing was the same but there was a difference, a moral difference, one which early on in the cloning program the Formillun Institute had defined and carved in stone. A clone was an exact copy; there would be no alteration or manipulation of the DNA to augment, enhance or modify the bio-structure. Duplication was required to ensure the safe and lasting splicing of the sentience and memories back into the host in any case. This wave needed a very specific and sustaining matrix to operate within, namely the very structure from which it originated. Hosting a mind in a foreign brain was possible; however, it was highly unstable and illegal, as the consequences could be dire. The moral path to cloning was fraught, but with the necessities forced upon humanity, choices had had to be made.

Through no design of his own, he now faced the consequence of actions the Formillun Institute had implemented moral codes to avoid. The weapon in the tank before him was a tool, a resource to be used. Consideration of the person inside was not even secondary. The clone was expendable, disposable. He wondered at this moment whether, to Yannix, he was any different. Was he just an expendable resource to achieve a goal? The answer was easy. Yannix was an exceptionally driven individual, that much was obvious to him, but a driven individual without a moral compass, which made him dangerous. Combined with the amount of power Yannix wielded over the people of Xannix, it could be catastrophic. Yannix was already colluding with the Zantanath to reach his perceived goals, but to what extent was he being played? The thought occurred to him that however much Yannix thought he was in control of the situation, the Zantanath had always been a step ahead.

"A first step to peace," he replied, like he had heard the line before, a level of resignation breaking through in his tone.

"Yes, Doctor. For the first time in countless cycles, endless Setak'da, the Xannix will enjoy peace."

"I just hope the cost is not too high."

"After all that we have endured, Doctor, there will be nothing they could do to us that we have not already overcome. To survive this long against such an enemy gives us strength."

"Excuse me, Cardinal. Your next appointment." Commander Elstron's skin tone lowered to a submissive blue hue as he interrupted the conversation. Yannix nodded, a human affectation he had picked up from their earlier encounter, when he had been forced to tutor Yannix in human language and history. The Xannix returned a brighter blue as confirmation to Elstron's information.

"We will talk more, Dr Spencer. Until then, feel free to become accustomed with this facility. It will educate you on the importance of our alliance." Yannix and Elstron turned back to the administration rooms and left him with the Zantanath tech, but on turning to examine what the tech was doing he realised he was alone, the tech having also moved off.

A creeping chill slowly spread across the back of his neck. The clone in the tank before him moved lazily in its sleep, a twitch here and there to show that it was alive.

With Yannix taking advantage of his own people, manipulating the genetics of his own species towards the goal of saving them at some imaginary point in the future, he considered what the final stage might be? How could he use his own people in that way? Was it justifiable to say that, as they had been at war for so long, their self-worth had decayed to such a low point that even the life of another of their own species had little meaning? Was each of them simply a resource in the struggle, a number on a page?

And how many had there been so far? There seemed to be a single Xannix in each of the gestation pods he could see, but there were hundreds on this level, and on the elevator down he had seen hundreds of levels. There were thousands in this facility alone, all to be engineered and resequenced into various machines of war.

He put his hand to the pod and touched the warm surface. He realised he was considering this from his human point of view. The two species had only just met, and there was much yet to learn. Both sides needed to be open minded to each other and their differences, and embrace the similarities. This ability to sacrifice their own in these numbers was shocking to him, but Yannix was a leader of a species farmed by the Zantanath as a simple commodity. Perhaps after years of such oppression, humanity would have the same extreme thoughts in trying to reason a solution, plans becoming wilder and far more risky, more perverse as time went on.

Building a secret army of advanced soldiers to counter the Zantanath threat on the face of it seemed a normal response, but it was the sacrifice of his own people to achieve that goal and in vast numbers which, even after all his days of wrangling with the complex issue, he found he still couldn't come to terms with. There had to be a better way. A way to shortcut the madness and stop the savage behaviour of a species, and perhaps the fall of his own kind to the same fate.

The clone in the tank moved again, languidly shifting in the warm embrace of the amniotic fluid, lost in a deep world of its own, a world of reprogramming, of learning.

His eyes widened and his jaw slackened as an idea dropped into his head like a stone into a pool, the ripple across his mind seeming to consume his every thought. A moment later he was sprinting for his workstation.

PATTEN

He didn't get it. All the simulations he had run, the calculations all indicated a perfect test run with an estimated 20 percent uplift in performance. What they had seen was an uncontrolled, almost catastrophic runaway drive which had very nearly destroyed the test facility. The performance gain, however, had been recorded in excess of their wildest expectations. He had made some brief mental calculations as he lay in the medical bay being fussed over by various medical staff and Ellie, and his conclusions were that with six or seven of these drives, a sustained 0.1 lightspeed could be achieved by the current design of colony ship.

Jessop had been elated with the result and had ordered the project renewal before the results had been formally reported, research work secured for the foreseeable future. It made him pleased for the people working for him, but it unsettled him that he didn't know why the results had been so far away from his forecasts.

In his office, he sat in his chair, feet up on the desk, staring intently at the wall screen rerunning the feed data and video stream of Mag-X drive test 212. It must have been the fifteenth time he had been over it but nothing leapt out at him as anomalous; he would need to go deeper. He rubbed his face and, realising the time, dropped his feet from his desk and started prepping to leave, securing files, backing up files, sending files to others who might need to know.

Turning to leave, he looked up just in time to see Ellie

approaching his office door. She entered with a smile on her face and a paper carry-out from the canteen. Noodles. He loved noodles.

"You hungry?" she asked. "You've not left your office all day."

"I love you," he replied, clearing some space on his desk.

"Beer?"

"I suddenly love you more."

"I know it's just the hunger talking, but I appreciate the thought." She smiled.

Within moments the desk was a clutter of noodle boxes and beer pods. He took the chopsticks and started to eat. After the first mouthful, he was wolfing the food in large, knotted balls of starch, the chicken adding the protein his body needed.

"The doc asked me to tell you to go see him. Make some time tomorrow; he wants to check you over again, make sure there are no lingering side effects."

"I've been ignoring his calls. Too much work to do. I received a message from Jessop too. The last time I received any praise from him was the day of my recruitment. Now, suddenly, five years later, I have two glowing comms from him in one day."

Ellie was shaking her head while listening to him, and at the same time stalking around her noodle box for the last piece of chicken.

"He's just taking care of his new golden egg." Her face turned to a frown. "How does that happen?"

"What happen?"

"I thought I had another piece of chicken. Now I feel chicken deficient, and still hungry."

He laughed and looked down at the three pieces in his noodle box.

"Here. I'm done." He pushed his mostly finished dinner to the edge of the desk and picked up his beer. Twisting the seal, gas fizzed excitedly in its escape. He took a long drink and sighed. It was good.

"Three pieces? You spoil me." She finished the last of his meal too.

They both sat for a few moments, in a post-noodle haze. Doctors called the digestive process after a meal 'dumping'—he called it bliss. Suddenly very relaxed, the stress of the day began to ease away. Ellie knew him. She knew how to press his buttons at times but also knew when he needed to relax. His smile was that of contentment.

"So, what's next?" she asked.

"I don't know. What did you have planned?"

"Easy there, flyboy. Your doctor has you under a strict regime of relaxation. And *that* is not relaxing."

He made a face. He was beginning to hate doctors.

"I meant," she continued, "what was your next step in the investigation?"

He shifted in his chair, looked back at the wall screen and pursed his lips while collecting his thoughts. The wall was now running a screen saver, a green meadow and lush wildflowers slowly undulating in an invisible breeze. A memory of the world before its decline.

"Well, there's nothing obvious in the test results, no smoking gun. There was nothing activating, engaging or changing other than the gentle increase in throttle, before the observed erratic behaviour." He shrugged. "It means tomorrow the guys out there start the grunt work of going through the logs and correlating with config and code, while we take a trip out to the test site and supervise an on-site inspection."

"I love a field trip. When do we leave?"

"Right after my doctor's appointment."

"I don't believe it," she said with a smile.

※

The helijet seemed to be the only place he got any time to think. And since his morning trip to the doctor, he had more than his usual number of issues to work through. The doctor had dropped a new little piece of information in his queue, and it had gone straight to the top of his critical list.

How much did he know about toxins? 'Nothing,' was the answer. Why would he? He was an engineer, not an assassin. So, there were two scenarios the doctor had suggested as possible— that he had accidentally come into contact with a small dose of a toxic substance which he had reacted to badly or that the toxin had been administered intentionally without his knowledge.

After he had recovered from the initial alarm of the situation— realising that someone may be targeting him for reasons which completely eluded him—he had been escorted to a room where a couple of the facility security had taken another hour of his time to ask him about the period of time between his flight back from NY-Met and the lead up to the Mag-X drive test. He could think of nothing. Everything had been normal, mundane even.

Ellie sat by his side, working through log files from test 212. She was also speaking to and collecting the initial results back from the other lead engineers and scientists on the project. He was being shielded from the large body of low-level work so that he could conduct the investigation more efficiently. Ellie was reporting any significant information as it arose. Finer detail was available if he requested it but, on the whole, the detail was leading to dead ends.

He turned again to the helijet window, water speeding past as they followed the Thames estuary to the open waters of the English Channel and where it met the colder waters of the North Sea. Huge white windmills glinted in the sun, standing like pillars of chalk sticks rising from a mirror of glass. The sea was calm, breeze minimal, but there was just enough to turn the blades of the turbines in lazy arcs. From the power farm, there was another ten minutes before they would be at the test site. He closed his eyes and exhaled as he relaxed into the seat, trying to focus his mind on the questions he wanted answers to when they arrived.

There would be Techs on the platform already. A ship was always on station nearby in case of emergency with a ready-team able to lock down the site or give fast initial comms and data collection if there was a catastrophic problem. He had sent them in ahead of their arrival to start retrieving on-site logs from any isolated terminals and check for obvious damage to the outer workings of the drive unit. Strict instructions had been given to be non-invasive and if they found anything suspicious to inform him immediately. He estimated they had been there for a couple of hours already and, as he had heard nothing, he surmised there was no superficial, easily obtained evidence.

Where had the power fluctuations come from? Where had the toxin come from? The more he thought on the matter the more his mind wandered and merged ideas, the more his thoughts became conflated, the problems of the day becoming one. You can't poison a drive test, it was ridiculous to think so, but you could sabotage a drive test. And if someone was eager enough to sabotage the project mechanically, they would certainly by capable and probably motivated enough to sabotage the project physically, personally, at a human level. After all, killing him would have fundamentally the same affect.

The project was under attack. Was he just being paranoid? Could it be coincidence that both these events occurred within the time window they did?

He closed his eyes and brought up his bio-comm to scan through some of the logs himself. Maybe getting into the minutia would be a good break from the bigger problems, giving him a distraction and space to let his mind consider other thoughts.

Icons flashed and lines of code began to scroll through his vision, floating in the blackness of his closed eyelids. His bio-comm aug had been fitted free a month after his recruitment to the Formillun Institute; all the technical and research staff had them fitted as part of their induction. It had been meant to speed up their ability to interface with terminals and equipment in the facility, increase their productivity by giving easy access to incredible quantities of historic test and technical data, and instant communication to anyone via voice or text, but it never worked quite that way for him. As a child he could remember being fascinated with the workings of *things*, the cogs and movement in his grandfather's old automatic skeleton watch, the beauty in the smooth aerodynamic design of his model flyers, each intricate link in his first fractal neural construct. He would spend hours in deep thought and intense concentration, the resolution of his own eyes never seemingly good enough to give him the detail he wanted from the object he was fascinated with in that moment. The bio-comm seemed to encourage the opposite, a superficial transient thought process which skimmed information and disregarded understanding in favour of quick iterative methods, a try and forget approach. He found it unsettling that superficial understanding was all that was expected and accepted these days. There were certainly some things that couldn't be treated that way, things you only had one chance to get right. Now was one of those times.

All of this meant he found himself scarcely using his bio-comm. But, at times like these, it was convenient.

Words flashed up before him, navigating through the code structure to the core config files. Randomly, he clicked through a couple, reading then quitting the view. He selected the Mag-X accelerator module config and started working his way down the lines and parameter settings. Scrolling down the page as he read, his eyes skimming the detail and ticking off a checklist of items from memory, he suddenly stopped and frowned to himself. It was as if his brain was catching up with the information it had just seen, processing slowly, triggering uncertainty. He scrolled back, up and up again.

There, among the thousands of parameters was an error. The corrective margin was set too high, almost five times higher than it should have been. He tagged it for further investigation and moved on. If this was wrong, what else might have been set incorrectly? He didn't expect to find the next one so quickly, the lambda parameter was also wrong. Wildly wrong, there was no way that was human error. Both values were intentionally far from where they should be, and he had no explanation why.

While he worked a surge of anger rose within him which drove him on. Who? It took him moments to find out, but the answer made no sense. Hallard? He was basically press liaison, how did he have access to apply config and code changes? A further moment of system interrogation and the answer was equally baffling: he didn't have access to the code base. He was being led on a wild goose chase. Regardless, these initial findings told him a lot. They told him that his team had been infiltrated, and that there was an active plot against his project—certainly to sabotage it, possibly to remove him by force.

Everyone around him would be in danger. He sent a bio-comm link to Ellie; he needed to warn her. Her response was immediate but questioning.

'What's so secret? You never use your bio-comm.' He could see the smile in her eyes. 'And I'm sat right next to you. All very cryptic.'

'I've found something.'

Her eyes went wide, a stunned reaction. 'Really?'

'There's a discrepancy in the core config to the accelerator module. Numbers are way off. It's definitely not a typo. The numbers have been tampered with.'

'Shit. Have you been able to trace it back?'

'Hallard.'

'Are you serious? He's not written a line of code in his life. He wouldn't know the first thing about updating the config.'

'Config isn't code. But, agreed. I'll need to dig deeper. However, it shows we have a problem.'

They looked at each other in silence for a moment. Eyes locked together, thoughts racing.

'I know one thing,' she said across the sub-vocal bio-comm.

'What's that?' he asked, lost in his own thoughts.

'Jessop's going to be pissed.'

A chime sounded as if to emphasise her words, and the pilot's voice began to announce the commencement of the landing sequence. They would be at the test facility within moments. He huffed a response. Jessop would be pissed—and that was an understatement. It would mean that the Formillun Institute's screening programme was full of holes. If a single person could get through and circumvent the process, it meant there could be more. There would be more. The institute would be wide open to attack and vulnerable to espionage. He didn't want to be the bearer of that bad news but at the moment he didn't see any way around it. His team was compromised; he may as well wrap up the project now.

'Let's hold off on telling him anything yet. I want to be absolutely certain of what we're dealing with before we go telling Jessop.'

Ellie nodded back while continuing to read reports via her bio-comm and multitask, her eyes unfocused and scanning side to side.

The helijet pulled into a tight turn and the engines wound up to counter the increased g. He looked out of the window and saw the test facility platform below, a huge 'H' their target.

'Ellie, you're not on Dr Clayton's CORE programme, are you?' It was more a confirmation than a question. The CORE programme was a new experimental research programme which had found some initial success in advancing the capability of AI technology using human mind splicing. The technology was complex but promising, so promising that all the senior research leads were now required to undergo the splicing procedure daily. It was reasonably quick, non-invasive and completely painless. The test case had been Clayton's own daughter, Dawn, who was reportedly now helping him with his research.

'No. Why? I've not heard of such a programme.'

'It's pretty new, but I'll make sure you're on it. I'll put in the application when we get back.' He forwarded her the programme induction documentation he had received from Clayton. 'Read these when you get some time. You've become pretty key to this research project, and... think of it as security. I wouldn't want anything to happen to you.'

'You say the most romantic things.'

CLAYTON

Stepping from the life pod, he turned to assist his wife and the other medic down the steps. It was the first time his feet had been on solid ground for over 135 years and, even though the circumstances of the event were marred by the desperation of the situation, he savoured the sensation, stretching his toes in his shoes and rising up and down on his calves, as if to experience the small sensation of natural, planet-born gravity again. The air hung heavy with spent retro fuel, and the sound of sonic bursts as escape pods streaked overhead like shooting stars. Roaring retros gently placed more human life on the alien world, which had been planned as their new home. The wider implications of that would have to wait. Right now, his focus was on minute-to-minute survival.

Having lost one of her team in the descent, Jemma was in sombre mood. They were all covered in the gore of the man, whose death had come with the rain of fast-moving shrapnel from the disintegrating *Endeavour*. The man had not escaped his fate, and the rest of them could do nothing to save him, a fist-sized hole punched in his chest. From his injuries, he had been surprised that Jemma and the other medic in the pod had been able to keep him alive for as long as they had.

"I'm really beginning to dislike this place," she said to him as they looked out across the field and the hundreds of arriving life pods. "And we've only just arrived."

He nodded. It was the only way he could think of replying which wouldn't add to her moment of sorrow. He took her hand

61

and gave it a gentle squeeze. They stood watching the scene in silence.

People were stepping from their escape pods and watching their crewmates do the same. For the moment, while there was so much activity with pods landing in any available space across the stated landing zone, people were staying close to their own pods. It was foolhardy to wander at this time and find yourself in the path of another pod as it touched down.

There was a sudden high-pitched whistling, increasing in volume as it neared. He scanned the sky for the source but saw nothing. Without an instant visual, the sound gave him a sense of danger and foreboding which chilled his spine. He found himself instinctively throwing Jemma to the ground, jumping down to cover her head with his arms and yelling for the other medic to do get down and take cover. Jemma shrieked in surprise. The whistle became a roar as a pod led a trail of smoke and flame from the sky. It was travelling with all the vertical kinetic energy of an uncontrolled re-entry; no aerobraking, no retros. The pod struck the ground half a kilometre away like a missile. The people already on the ground and within close proximity to the strike were vaporised in an instant, and those 50 metres further away were simply thrown like rags into the air, some flayed and torn apart. Debris and dirt cascaded and rattled down about them. Feeling a sharp stinging sensation on his lower left leg, he gave it a shake to kick away whatever had landed there, but the pain stayed. Looking down through the dust and grit, he saw a blade of jagged metal protruding from his lower leg. Visual confirmation seemed to intensify the pain, and he gritted his teeth against it.

"You okay?" he asked Jemma.

"Yes. What the stars was that?"

"Uncontrolled pod, I think. Maybe a chunk of *Endeavour*, difficult to tell."

"We need to help them. Check for survivors."

He worked through a chain of bio-comm options and selected a report of his crew's health status, then overlaid that against a raw local map of a two kilometre square of the impact site. There were survivors, shown as orange and yellow dots in a 200-metre radius of the site. Green dots were already congregating around those in need.

"I'll grab the first aid kit from the pod."

He rolled over and crawled to the pod, taking care not to move his wounded leg too much. The heavier debris had stopped falling and the dust was thinning, but the air was grey and smoky, making it difficult to breathe.

Climbing back into the pod, the small pocket of air less clouded than outside, he glanced at the lifeless and bloodied body of the medic still strapped into his couch. His skin was as white as chalk with black sunken eyes, which were closed and at peace. His struggle was over—with the loss of the *Endeavour*, there was no way to bring him back, as all his clone tissue was gone and his mind's storage stack destroyed. He was one of the first of his crew to be lost this way that he knew of, but he wouldn't be the last. They were all at risk now. Life was fragile again, at least for his crew, until they could reach the *Intrepid* or *Indianapolis* and rescan.

Life was fragile.

Slumping into a couch, he reached under and pulled out its first aid kit, placing it on his lap. Opening it, he worked his way through looking for local sedative and skin sealant. He put the first aid kit to one side then looked at his calf. He was lucky: the metal was a twisted triangle about 10 centimetres long and hadn't penetrated far. Applying a spray of the local sedative, he then pulled the metal, but it still made him wince. Before the blood started to seep from the wound, he applied a spray of skin sealant. Less than a minute later he was back with Jemma, two first aid kits in hand.

"Ready?" he asked them both. They nodded. He looked at the medic from Jemma's team; he didn't recognise him, but then the *Endeavour* was a big ship. He put on a confident and reassuring smile. "How you holding up...?" He let the question hang, acting as an introduction but also an invitation to give a little detail, some personal context.

"Okay, considering, sir. Thanks."

He nodded in agreement. He passed over one of the first aid kits and the other took it, extending the shoulder strap and slinging it over his shoulder as they started off for the crash site.

"What's your name son?"

"Gregson, sir."

He nodded again. "We'll get through this," he said, trying to give some comfort in the moment, maybe to convince himself. He needed to get people organised and working on the basics, as there were a lot of people suddenly turning up on the surface of the planet without the support kit which they had planned to land with. Staying alive was going to be their first and last objective for the foreseeable future.

"First things first," he continued. "Let's go help some people."

"Yessir."

He upped the pace.

*

Losing people; leadership in the face of personal loss. It had been an academic lecture he had received back at fleet training— how to deal with the trauma, how to deal with the remorse, how to deal with the guilt. Words in a book, psychologists preaching in front of a presentation of bullet points and nameless case studies.

Just words.

The reality of it was far worse than the words had led him to believe. Empty words by people who had never experienced the subject they studied.

Dust was settling, and the devastation leached out of the landscape. An horrific crater of black charred rock described a spiked circle of death in all directions. Body parts were dotted across the ground and the wailing and moaning of those in pain carried on the wind. There were people urgently trying to save the wounded and others who sat in a stupefied silence, staring at their daemons on some unfocused personal horizon.

Jemma and Gregson had gone to work as soon as they arrived at the crash site, helping where they could, trying to save those who could be saved. He, however, had collected some able-bodied survivors and organised work parties to build shelters and dispense what rations could be collected from the landed life pods. Giving people focus at this time would give them less time to think on the larger issues, or the trauma of losing colleagues and friends. They did their part.

Night came in the blink of an eye. Time seemed to have its own agenda and darkness fell before they were ready. A sea of orange two-man tents, and the occasional four-man tent, spread out within a circle of life pods. Although they had done a good job of providing shelter for all those who had started to arrive at their location, there were still some who decided to sleep in their life pods. With the door up, a pod made a good shelter, but they were heavy and could not be moved. Most people preferred to group together, as it was the instinctive thing to do, so people walked from all across the landing zone to congregate with them near the crash site.

A strange positive had grown from the disaster, the crash site and smoke plume had acted as a beacon for those who survived the descent. People slowly drifted in over several hours, bringing what resource they could carry, helping where they could, to provide comfort and kindness to a tragic situation.

Standing at the edge of this small town that had suddenly grown from the dust and rocks of the plane, he cast an eye over the sea of orange bubbles, now masked by darkness but for the comforting glow of lights and portable heaters. To him, it indicated the continuation of life, and he looked on with admiration for those inside. These people were more than survivors, they were pioneers, the last of humanity, each and every one precious, each and every one a fighter. It hardened his resolve. Whatever hardships were to come, he knew he had the best people to see them all through. Even in the darkness, he was encouraged.

They were all exhausted, and some hadn't slept in days. The orbital battle they had been fighting had been a test of endurance for them all, in many different ways. His duel with Asher had ended in a way which left him angered. He was now clear of his tormentor, Asher likely destroyed along with the *Endeavour*, but now within a newly spliced backup clone and waking into the chaos of a descending escape pod, he felt mentally violated and in shock. Asher had crashed into his mind, into his most private thoughts, where there was nowhere to hide, no way to escape. He was not as physically tired as the rest of those on the surface, but adrenaline, fatigue and the memory of that mental intrusion had sapped his energy. The exhaustion was just as real.

Endurance; he felt himself falling into an almost meditative state as he scanned the camp. His breathing rising and falling in a calm rhythm, heart rate an almost hypnotic wave of sound that only he could hear. In his mind he could see the roadside trees slowly sliding past. The run; miles passing underfoot, the clarity of thought. In those moments he found most of his best ideas, his truest decisions. He needed to go for a run, but for now he would have to be content with the memory.

"You okay?" Jemma had appeared at his side, as stealthy as a panther, just suddenly there.

He shook his head, shaking off the question. How he felt was not important right now. Ensuring that his people were safe, that was the focus. He nodded at the camp, lights glowing like an indicator to the life within. "More importantly, how are they?" he asked.

"Considering the current situation, they are doing pretty well. I'm told we have everyone under shelter, all with rations and water for a couple of weeks if we are careful. That's the good news. The bad news is that my makeshift hospital is busy. We have 28 with severe injuries, five of which I'm not expecting to see the night through. And we are working with first aid kits. We need a proper med-bay. Any word?"

She was never one to take the long road when there was a perfectly direct alternative. His answer was not one he could honestly stomach. He had never lied to Jemma, and he wasn't going to start now, no matter how he wanted to delay the answer. He had sent a call out to the *Intrepid* and *Indianapolis* almost as soon as they had landed. There would be life pod beacons firing off all over the plains, and both ships would be acutely aware of their situation and location, but he had received no comms. He was certain others had tried but there was no answer to the call.

However bleak things appeared, there was some small corner of his stubborn mind which wouldn't give in to the idea that all was lost. *Endeavour* might be gone, but he saw no evidence of the others being involved in the destruction. He could not be certain—the pod's instruments were basic—

but he could not bring himself to think that all ships were lost. Not now. Not yet. He needed hope, not just for himself, but as a political tool. He would need to utilise that hope as a guiding light to the rest of the survivors.

"No. Nothing yet. Likely they are orbiting the night side of the planet. A couple of hours and they'll be back in comms range. Or they have issues of their own."

"Surely, someone would have responded."

"They may not be able to. My top working theory at the moment is that if they're not on the night side then they're being jammed."

"The network of satellites?" It had been his first thought, as the vast defence network about the planet had obfuscated the planet from all electromagnetic transmission and comms. It had been the reason for so much that had transpired to this point. The fact that they were here in the first place was due to the result of the initial scientific survey, and scientists stating that the planet was uninhabited. The analysis had been at least inaccurate, at worst incompetent. This was just hindsight and he shrugged it away.

"Possibly. But more likely a ground-based jammer." He scrunched up his nose, a decision made. "I'm going to ask for volunteers to head for the high ground to the west. It's about 20 kilometres distant, so a good day trek, but they might be able to break the jamming and get open comms up to orbit."

"Are you sure that the signal jamming is local?"

"No. But it's worth a try, and right now we need every break we can get."

Both of them had been avoiding the bigger question, but while they were being candid he forged ahead.

"No word from Dawn either." He was looking at the stars now, as if one of them might be his daughter. His eyes searched the heavens, a surge of emotion threatening tears. He hoped Jemma had not noticed. Dawn's escape pod was a modified version of the one they had descended in, the life support system was not necessary, so it had been swapped out in favour of more powerful comms and extended power duration. She could land on the surface and be active for years, solar receptive panels could be deployed to extend her life. As a rover she could roam over reasonably rugged terrain for physical exploration, and she also had sufficient short-range flight capability. But all this only worked if she managed to get to the surface. The fact that he had heard nothing so far had him extremely worried.

"She is okay," Jemma said. "I know it."

He continued to look up, not trusting his ability to contain his emotions.

"Yeah. She'll be in touch."

They embraced warmly, both staring to the stars.

ELLIE

Descending in the elevator to the test facility was the longest five-minute journey of her life. Since the flight and the trust Patten had shown her—the love he had for her—she had felt herself conflicted. She had begun to question her commitment to him, how it was becoming more than the mission, more than the need she felt towards the destruction of the programme, more than the hate she had for the Formillun Institute and its development of AI as a governing instrument. People came first, that was the argument. AI could not be allowed to grow to a position of influence that led to an elevated position of governance—that would be the end of human civilisation. But what demonstrated this people-first principle more than the love one person had for another? The love Patten had for her? She could not let that emotion sway her from her purpose.

But if they had a true connection, would he not understand? She should open up. Let him know how she felt and who she really was. If he truly loved her, he would accept her, and they could find a way through. She would open her heart to him, show him the truth of who she was, and open his eyes to a world governed by AI and the death of humanity under its control. It was servitude under a machine construct, an intelligence more powerful than the human mind by design, self-serving by virtue of its own machine learning. GAIA knew that however humanity safeguarded their future in the design of fail-safes, all humans were fallible, so their design would be fallible, thus AI would be fallible. What's the best way to make sure you don't shoot yourself in the foot with a gun? You make sure you don't have a gun. No AI, no rule by AI. Humanity would control their own destiny.

Now staring at the Mag-X drive unit, they had been greeted by the smiling face of Warren Gill, Chief Engineer of the facility ready-team. Gill's team had been on site for a couple of hours now, collecting logs and local data. He had even begun a laser survey of the test bay, useful for virtual reality walkthroughs by off-site teams. Gill shook their hands enthusiastically, Patten responded with a warm smile of his own.

"How are you, Gill?" said Patten.

"Just great. You've given us guys round here the most excitement we've had in months. Who knew that things going wrong was more fun than things going right?"

"I think that's a matter of opinion," she said.

"Perhaps, but it's not often we get to wind the boat up to full throttle. Getting back here from station was a real ride. Those waves may look calm from the air, but when you're on the surface..? Man, it was a real ride!"

"Yeah, you know, I think I left my sea legs at home," she said, pulling a face of absent-mindedness.

"I lost my breakfast on the boat," he said, patting his stomach as he remembered. "Yeah, that part you can keep, but the rest— fun." They laughed the visual away. When they recovered, Gill turned to the drive.

"So, I expect you'd like to know what we have found so far?" asked Gill.

"Please," Patten replied with a nod.

"Well, the test rig's drive mounting appears fine; however, we have found micro-fractures throughout the mounting—stress fractures due to the sudden extreme load. The thrust force experienced was way off the charts and far more than the rig had been designed to handle. Personally, I'm surprised the drive didn't break loose and destroy the facility." She and Patten shared a worried glance. She understood his thought process; he would be presuming that the altered configuration he had discovered to the drive had been intentional and designed to rip the drive from its mounting. The energies involved would have been uncontrolled and devastating. He was overthinking it, but she went along.

"Sounds like we were close to it breaking free. We'll need a new reinforced mounting for the next round of tests."

"Yes, I think so," said Gill.

As they spoke her eyes wandered around the room, taking in the scale. The room was cylindrical, about fifty metres in diameter and sizable for the tiny three metre drive unit at its centre. There were two entrances to the room both with thick solid pressure doors, which led to engineering workshops, storage bays, staff quarters and elevators to the surface. There was a control room with a reinforced window which overlooked the main test bay and a huge frame structure of rails and runners allowing two crane systems to operate within the confines of yellow markings across the floor.

A key feature to the room was the exhaust pipe which ran from the back of the drive unit, across the bay and out through the wall, it connected to a vacuum chamber which simulated the void of space. The pressure to the test bay itself could also be dropped to that of near vacuum when required, but not all testing required it.

Various units and canister clusters dotted the near vicinity of the drive, with feeder pipes and cords connecting each. Coolant systems, control boxes, monitoring equipment—all had people busy taking readings, pulling logs, acquiring data; each a small piece to build a big picture. And somewhere in the detail: her lie.

Recognition; she looked again.

One of the techs had started walking towards the southern pressure door; a big 'S' stencilled in white identified the door, the letter almost as tall as the door itself. He now had his back to her, but a moment before their eyes had met and the recognition had been instant. Her thoughts sparked about her head with urgency, trying to place the face. There was danger there, but she couldn't place it.

A gasp escaped her as the information arrived to her conscious mind. A picture of him hung like a ghost in her thoughts, framed by a protest rally she had attended. He had been dressed in GAIA uniform; a dedicated advocate.

Almost without thinking, she moved away from Patten and Gill's conversation, drifting towards the canisters the tech had been working on. Curiosity furrowed her face into a frown, eyes searching for things out of place, things added. In this moment, she didn't know what she might find, or what she was looking for, she only knew her instinct was setting off alarms.

Pride cut across her action, why would this tech be here, a GAIA operative on site and she didn't know about it? What was he up to? Why hadn't she been informed?

A small insignificant looking block stuck to the side of one of the canisters, the size of a memcell. It didn't flash, there was no indication that is was active in any capacity, and it didn't look as if it could do any damage. However, the canister cluster it was attached to was highly pressurised...

Her world stopped in a heartbeat. "Scott! Get down!"

There was no pain, only silence and motion. A blur of things: the bright yellow of the crane frame, the orange flash of fire, a spray of deep crimson and the green of the test bay floor, the order of it was confused, the timeline distorted. But it all stopped in a moment as she struck the floor, air forced from her lungs, the internal sensation of splintering bone. She slid uncontrolled to a stop. Her body was unresponsive; eyes stung, lungs rasping and gurgling for every breath. She couldn't understand why she could still see. The floor around her seemed to be changing colour, green was becoming red.

Boots and legs began to run past in all directions, some running away, some running towards her, she was rolled onto her back, a concerned face filled her vision, his lips moving, possibly shouting, but she heard nothing. *Okay*, she read from the motion of his lips, *you're going to be okay.*

Another arrived, a woman in white, red echelons on her upper arm, she threw open a medic kit and got to work.

Patten's face was suddenly there, signalling deep concern, his hair and face smeared with blood from a nasty looking cut in the hairline. But his eyes were intense and locked on hers.

"I'm sorry," she felt herself saying. "I didn't mean for this to happen. This wasn't meant to happen."

She focused on his face as the world around them began to darken. He looked away urgently to the medic, as if a panicked conversation was taking place, and she followed none of it. He looked down at her again and she felt his hands cupping her head and face firmly but gently, like she was the most delicate and fragile thing he had ever held. Darkness started to close in and shade the picture.

"I love you," she whispered.

Don't worry, I've got you. I've got you.

There was a flash of brilliant pain in her chest, it was greater than any pain she had felt before and she screamed as the world returned in brilliant colour.

Lifted into the air, she was placed as gently as they could onto a gurney and they began to travel almost at a run through the rooms and corridors of the labs. Lights strobed and Patten was still with her, touching her shoulder, pushing the gurney, shouting at people to clear the way, directing the plan. She had seen that drive before; a man with a solution and no time to implement it.

The whole gurney jolted as they crashed through doors, and she was jostled to a stop. She was lifted again, this time to a bed in the test facility med-bay. The medics fussed around her like worried bees, and the only constant was Patten—he was still with her. He was saying something, she focused through tear-soaked eyes. *Trust me*, he was saying. *Trust me.*

The bed was pushed into a tube, which looked like an MRI scanner. There was a clunk that she felt through the bed frame as the machine began to work.

She felt tired. As she watched, the barrel she had been placed in slowly began to revolve around her. Pain was now everywhere, and she wanted it to stop. She was just so damn tired. She remembered her childhood, and her mother and father's faces looked down on her, making her smile. They must have dimmed the lights in the MRI because it was getting darker again. She tried to breath slowly, but the effort seemed too much and she didn't seem to care anymore. Maybe she would just sleep for a while.

*

She shifted languidly in bed. A warm summer's morning filtered through shuttered windows. Slowly she stretched out, her muscles responding with a pleasant waking ache as they moved slightly beyond their limit, then relaxed. Opening her eyes, she lifted herself up onto her elbows, and looked around the unfamiliar room. The morning light cast a warm orange glow, a colour which instantly put her at ease, it was the colour of warmth and safety. A dresser; a fire place with logs neatly stacked to the side; a picture of a bluebell infused glade hung above the logs, the other side of the fire place towards the window was an upholstered chair, she thought they called it a nursing chair, low and comfortable. In the chair sat a figure she didn't recognise, smiling kindly, leaning forward, eyes bright and attentive.

"Good morning. How are you feeling?"

Surprisingly, she felt great. The confusion and pain of memories which felt so far away tried to intrude on her perfect moment, but she pushed them aside.

"Hi," she found herself saying, still looking around the room and trying to figure out how she got there. "I feel fine." She paused and reconsidered. "I feel great."

"My name is Dawn," said the girl in the chair. She couldn't have been more than about twenty years old. "Would you like something to eat? I've prepared some breakfast. Would you prefer eggs or pancakes?"

"Coffee, and pancakes. Always pancakes," she said with a smile.

"Okay, no trouble." Dawn rose from the chair and made her way across the room to the door. "There are clothes in the dresser. Kitchen is down the hall. When you're ready, just follow the smell of coffee and pancakes."

She had woken into some kind of fairy tale.

Pushing the covers to the side she stood and moved to the dresser. She was naked. She skipped the question of how that had occurred and opened the top drawer of the dresser. There were loose fitting sweaters and trousers, and she dressed in seconds then stepped into a pair of easy shoes which sat to the side of the dresser. The smell of coffee was intoxicating; she let it lead her to the kitchen where Dawn sat at a pine table with a perfect breakfast spread laid out in front of her.

"Do you take your coffee black?" asked Dawn.

"Yes, thank you." She sat and taking up the coffee she took a sip. It was hot and bitter. Perfect.

They sat in silence for a while. Dawn seemed to watch her casually as she sipped her coffee and began to demolish a pancake. She didn't hold back on the maple syrup.

"How do you like the place?" Dawn asked.

"It's lovely. Where are we?" She looked out of the window, across a green, lush valley with a backdrop of snowy peaked mountains.

"Well, out there are the Austrian Alps. I loved the clean air and pure mountain streams. My parents took me there a couple of times when I was a kid. It made a lasting impression." Dawn smiled as she seemed to drift momentarily through memories of those times. The spell broke and she returned to the now.

Waving a hand around, as if to encompass everything they saw, she said, "In actuality, we are in Formillun labs just outside the London Met."

Things were not really making sense. How could they be in two places at the same time?

"Sorry, you said we're in Austria and London Met? How can that be?"

Dawn drew herself up, raising her coffee cup up and resting her elbows on the table. She was pretty sure her father had told her never to do that. Bad table manners or something. She continued to eat the pancakes. They were good.

"How much of *before* do you remember?"

She didn't want to. There was pain there, anger, confusion. Patten.

"I don't know. Not much. Scott, the last thing I remember was Scott Patten. Not much before that."

Dawn nodded as if she understood. But she didn't, not really.

"Is he here?"

"Not at the moment. But he visits you regularly. He is back at the test site, working on the next phase of his programme."

She shook her head and smiled to herself while taking the last mouthful of pancake. *You couldn't keep Patten from his work, not even from your sickbed.*

"You should be happy you saved so many people, Ellie." Pushing the empty plate aside, she moved the coffee front and centre while listening to Dawn continue. "Thanks to your warning, people were able to take what cover they could. A second or two was the difference between life and death for many."

"I'm sorry, Scott visits me? When?" The smile on her face had transformed into a confused frown as clarity began to emerge from the fog of her mind.

"Most weeks. His work schedule has been stepped up, so it can be difficult, but he is here most Sundays. You are very lucky he is such a quick thinker. He confused the hell out of us when you first arrived." Dawn shifted back in her seat and took a more comfortable posture in the pine chair, legs crossed away from the table legs.

"We initially thought you were Patten. He used his backup

account to store your wave. When we did our regular scheduled wave integrity checks of our principle team, we thought something had gone terribly wrong with Patten's wave storage. Turns out, he had more important things on his mind."

"So here I am?"

"Here you are."

The penny had dropped. She felt sick, and it had nothing to do with the breakfast she had just eaten. Thoughts raced through her mind like a rat trying to escape a ship which was slowly filling with water: it didn't matter which way she looked for freedom, the inevitable outcome overwhelmed her.

She tried to calm herself, to not give any outward appearance of panic, or stress. But Dawn was a step ahead.

"Your feelings are normal. It takes some time to adjust to the concept, but you will find that by just acting normally, thinking normally, as you have always done, it will assist in the transfer. You are you, whether in here, out there, or in your own old biological body. The sentience is you, the host is not. Try and relax into who you are, not what you are."

She was screaming inside, her eyes fixed Dawn with a stare that would have turned others to stone. Hatred burned from her heart; Patten had betrayed her without even knowing it. He had cast her into an oblivion of her worst nightmares. She had become what she loathed most in the world.

Staring at her balled fists, not trusting to look anywhere else, she felt tears, hot and real, line her cheeks.

"This has to be a dream."

"It is the only solution."

"No, no it's not. Put me back. Return me to my body. You took me out, you can damn well put me back." She was shouting now, emotions running high. Dawn was sympathetic and remained calm; there was only understanding and a need to reach out. The rejection was normal; they would get her through.

"Your body…" Dawn said. "It was too damaged. There is no going back."

No going back. She was destined to spend the rest of whatever this existence was locked in a box; a cage of circuits and servers, her new self a collection of fluctuating binary numbers. How could she live like this? It was contrary to everything she had believed in. By her own morality, she should demand they switch her off.

Terminate her. Let her die the death she was meant to die. But she found the more she considered the situation, the more she raged against the situation, the more she wanted things to stop, she found an overwhelming force of nature in her way. Morality aside, a base function of her existence remained within.

Self-preservation. The will to survive at almost any cost was strong; a life force that burned like a fire and grew brighter each time she tried to extinguish it.

"You are strong, Ellie. That you are here right now is testament to that. But like any trauma, you need time to heal. In the same way you would give your body time to heal, give your mind time to heal. We will be with you every step of the way."

Time. How long.

"How long has it been?"

"Since the attack? Almost eight months."

The fight seemed to have gone out of her. She was just exhausted and scared.

"Have we found out who did it? Who was responsible for the attack?"

"GAIA has taken responsibility for the attack, they even seemed quite pleased about it. Hateful people."

"But has anyone been caught? Did we get the guy that did this?" Her focus had shifted, emotions forcing their way up and flaring in sequence, vengeance was now in her heart. The man that put her in this place would reap a whirlwind of pain for the damage he had caused her.

"No, not at this time."

"You're telling me that with all the cameras and surveillance, all the teams of security and people on site, no one else saw anything?" Her voice rose again, Dawn again stayed passive in tone.

"The Formillun Institute is cooperating fully with the security investigation, but nothing has been uncovered at this time. All camera footage of the facility over a 48-hour period in the lead up to the attack, and during the attack has been examined. No evidence has been found to implicate any individual."

Ellie slapped the table. "Then someone is not looking hard enough! Gas tanks don't just blow up on their own."

"They do, 0.0002% of the time," replied Dawn. Ellie just glared at her with expression of dark thunder. "Sorry, that wasn't helpful."

"No."

There was a silence. Dawn seemed to be reflecting on how she could have handled the conversation better.

Shifting in her chair, she leaned towards Dawn. She had made a decision.

"Give me access to the surveillance footage."

Dawn pursed her lips, her look stern. "I don't know if we can. It's not our decision."

"You could ask though? Right?"

"Yes."

"Thank you."

Anger had taken over. Not the anger of thoughtless outbursts and tantrums. She was well past that. Her anger was the most dangerous. A cool fury, calm and concentrated. A clarity of purpose had descended, something she had never felt before. Somewhere at her core, somewhere deep within, that dark place where all forbidden desires and actions roil and churn in a black mass, something slipped free and flowed like ice water through her veins. Surprisingly, it was soothing.

BOYD

There were days when he wished he had more to work with. From the moment they had arrived aboard the United Terran Ship *Intrepid* he had spent more time working in an information black hole than he thought possible. The bio-comm each of them was implanted with streamed information from anyone and anything on the ship, so he could essentially have a conversation with whoever he chose whenever he wanted and access most devices to interrogate their status or affect their operation. Permission level permitting. And there lay the problem.

In the last few minutes, as his work crew and he were about to head out, they had been locked out of all systems. Even the simple operation of opening the workshop door received the irritating 'Access Denied' message.

"Who has the power to do this?" asked Harper, who was already at the door controls and looking for the manual override.

"Not many. The Captain, the XO and perhaps the Chief. Others could lock you out of areas, but not a ship-wide lockdown." He had his arms crossed, scratching his chin in thought. Why would you lock down the entire ship? "I think the bridge has been taken," he said.

"What was that?" asked Harper, pulling away panel sections at the side of the door, his head poked into the dark of the conduit.

"I said, the bridge has been taken. The Captain is likely trying to lock out these guys," he said, thumbing at the Zantanath body parts now on the workbench nearby, then realising Harper couldn't see his action. "Anyway, what's with the door?"

"Easy," said Harper, the exertion in his voice almost masking the words. "Almost..." A low mechanical thud signalled the release of the lock. As there was still power to the system, the door slid easily to an open position. "…There," finished Harper with a huff, and sat back with his back against the wall to catch his breath. "That's harder work than you think."

"Time to move out," he said to himself.

Turning to speak to the team, he noticed the room had gone quiet, and rather than busying themselves in preparation to leave, they had congregated around the workbench where the Zantanath trooper parts lay. Striding over, he found himself being hushed by a hand waved at him. Li finally turned to him and opened the circle of people, giving him room to see.

"What's going on, Li, we have to go."

Li shook his head, "Not yet. Tyrell's onto something."

The electronics specialist Landon Tyrell was leaning over the helmet of the decapitated Larsen clone. Head extracted from the helmet and pushed to one side, Tyrell was working at a small panel of microelectronic circuitry with his utiliplex tool.

"What have you found?"

"Shh. Quiet," said someone, as Tyrell leaned in closer and tweaked the circuit again. In the quiet, there was a static crackle, then voices. Small, tinny voices in a language he did not understand, a language he did not recognise.

They all listened intently, looking at the source of the sound as if the gateway to an underworld they wished to avoid, a world of daemons and darkness, concern etched across their faces. The sound was emanating from a helmet earpiece, but Tyrell had tweaked the output to a level beyond the scope of its normal operation, the volume so high the voices were distorted and garbled. Regardless of that, the voices did not seem overly excited; they were calm, professional, all business.

"This is all very exciting people, but we need to be going."

"Where are we going, boss?" asked Dooley, as he pulled his attention away from the helmet and the alien voices. It was like listening to ghosts while suffering tinnitus.

"Because of Puzzle-boy here, we're likely to have a swarm of his friends descending on us any minute. It's a big ship, and they won't have enough people to control it all. We need to melt away.

Become part of the background. But we're going to need help."

They were all listening now. The squeaky voices from the helmet had been shut off and people were beginning to muster and pay attention.

'Ellie, you there?' he asked. He shook his head and sucked his teeth. Staying out of trouble was going to be difficult enough, but without Ellie's help it was going to be almost impossible.

"Anyone getting any comms from Ellie?" A few heads shook as their eyes momentarily focused on a distant point, then returned to him.

"Okay boys and girls, for the moment we're on our own. We're moving out into the ship, so stay tight and don't shoot any of the good guys. You know what the bad guys look like." He pointed at the remains of the trooper on the workbench. There were nods of confirmation. "We're going to head for the nearest AI core. Hopefully, we'll be able to gain direct access to Ellie and have a little chat."

The faces in front of him reflected a mix of concern, worry and determination. It was the right reaction. If you felt any different, you were likely to be a liability.

He flicked a look at Dooley and the carbine in his hand. "I'll take one of those." He was handed one. Checking it over with a professionalism of long distant memories, he flicked the safety.

"Okay, Dooley. You're on point." Dooley looked at him blankly. "That means you go first. Let's move."

They turned and headed out into the corridor.

*

When Dooley got nervous, he became a talker. The subject didn't matter, and for the last ten minutes it had been like verbal diarrhoea, a seemingly endless random walk through the mind of a worried man. At least the guy had the decency to whisper, though he was pretty sure if there were any of those Zantanath Larsen clones in their shiny suits hanging around, Dooley would be the first they heard.

'Dooley, confine that shit to the bio-comm. We don't need to hear it, and the Steelers certainly don't.'

"Steelers?" said Dooley aloud. The single file group looked up and down the line at each other wondering what Dooley was muttering about now. The out of context word making him sound more and more like a madman.

'The tin men that shoot at you if you breathe,' he stressed. 'Or talk too much.'

'Sorry.'

'Better.'

They walked on in silence.

He had taken them out into the corridors of the ship, but without Ellie's guidance and all-seeing eye across the ship, they were blind, every step a risk. He didn't like to admit to himself, but without the AIs reassuring presence, and the connection to the information that afforded him, he felt somewhat on edge. He made a conscious effort to push his doubts aside; they were no use to him here. He needed solutions, a way through. Getting in touch with Ellie was the first step.

The chain of command had been disrupted, taken off at the head. Workers throughout the ship had also been isolated, he couldn't connect with anyone other than his local team, which meant line of sight bio-comms only. The more he thought about it, the more he considered that whoever was doing this knew what they were doing.

These troops that had suddenly appeared in his workshop, they were not Xannix. He had had the opportunity to study the Xannix up close on their first encounter, down in main engineering. It had been intriguing and revealing looking over their kit, but with the time available to him and the limited preparation, there had been little he could really discover. Weapons were more advanced, strength greater, and they appeared to augment their communication with fluctuations in skin tone. They were a remarkable species, but ultimately aggressive and didn't appreciate the colonisation plan. He could understand that and had a level of sympathy for the position—Earth's scientists had made an error in designating this planet as viable, so the mission here had been a mistake.

Refugees from a dying world, that is what they were now. He corrected himself, with the number of years they had been travelling, all expectation was that civilisation on the planet they had left behind was now dead. Refugees from a dead world. It made something in his chest feel hollow as the reality of his thoughts sank in. There was no going home. There was no home.

The line jostled to a halt. Dooley had stopped suddenly, without warning and was looking down the line at him gesticulating that he join him.

'What's up?' he asked, making his way to Dooley's side. Without responding on bio-comm, Dooley just pointed from his crouched position, with a wiry finger towards the corridor ahead, then to his ear, then back to the corridor.

Listening intently, initially he heard nothing. Then there it was, a muffled thump. It repeated several times then stopped again. He tried to isolate the position of the sound, his head cocked to one side, giving his ears greater vertical separation by which to differentiate the height of the sound; a hawk pinpointing its prey.

'It's in the wall.' He followed the track of the sound with his eyes. A maintenance hatch a few metres up the corridor. A locked maintenance hatch. If a work detail had been in the maintenance crawl spaces when the access lock took effect, that is where they would still be. Trapped in the maze.

Stepping across the corridor, he started to inspect the hatch. As he did so the thumping started again, this time very obvious and pronounced. He sent out a ping with his bio-comm, his personal identifier. The thumping stopped. The local bio-comm signal had some minimal penetration, enough to get through the hatch plate.

'Hold tight,' he sent. 'We'll try and open the hatch this side.'

Turning to look back at his team, Dooley was already at his side and looking for the manual release to the hatch. Everything was going to be done the hard way for the time being.

'Got it,' said Dooley.

The hatch popped open about 5 centimetres around the rim, just enough to clear the wall and hung on its extenders until a force from inside pushed the hatch up and around into a locked position. From inside the hatch appeared a smiling face, hair ruffled, eyes cheerful which, under the circumstance, was not something he had expected to see.

'Glad to see a familiar face,' she said.

Extending a hand, he helped her out of the maintenance crawl space.

'And you are?' he asked.

'Pleased to see you,' she said, grinning. 'I've been trying to pop that hatch from the inside for the last twenty minutes.' She brushed herself down and straightened her kit, then extended a hand to him in greeting. 'Riz Elderson. Lieutenant, *Endeavour* security.'

'Adam Boyd, Electrical Engineer' he replied, a little unsettled. He didn't quite know how to take the attitude coming from Elderson. She seemed a little too happy for the situation.

'You do realise we're in lockdown?' he asked her.

'You know I'm on the wrong ship?' she said in return. A comment which threw him momentarily. He hadn't registered this initially, as he too was originally from *Endeavour* and was reassigned to oversee the construction of the Rem-Tek refit. Elderson, however, had not been part of the Tusk One crew.

'Okay, I'll bite. How are you here?'

'Escape pod. When my pod launched, *Intrepid* was closer than the turn around to the planet surface. I got scooped up and set down in the main bay on deck 60.'

'You're a little off course,' he replied.

'Can't disagree with that.'

He turned to the others in the team and found them looking at the two of them, quizzically. His bio-comm conversation with Elderson was direct link, and he opened it up to broadcast to the team.

'So, how did you get be locked in a maintenance hatch on deck 27?' he asked.

'Probably the same reason you're creeping around this corridor. We were attacked. We were in the galley on deck 60, it has been set up as a temporary reception centre for those escaping *Endeavour*. There were a few of us in there, around a hundred or so.' She looked up around the group. 'I was close enough to the door when the attack happened. Six troopers suddenly appeared in the middle of the galley hall out of nowhere. Silver kit, pretty F-tech. Anyway, they started just lancing people. It was instant chaos. I just dived for the door and disappeared.'

A solid metallic clunk sounded down the corridor. They all jumped and instantly looked in the direction of the sound source. He and a couple of others in his group had their carbine to their shoulder, training and drills overriding instinct. There were a couple of ex-military in his team, and he was glad of that. The others just crouched and stared nervously, whether they had a weapon or not.

They stared down the corridor for a moment, but nothing moved and nothing appeared. He relaxed and lowered his weapon, turning back to Elderson.

'And you were in the maintenance network, how?'

'Ellie. She has been guiding me for the last hour or so. Contacted me the moment I left the galley. Not sure how many others made it out. I'm hoping she managed to help the others. But we got cut off, and here we are.'

'Here we are,' he said. 'Security, huh? Extra gun. Ellie is always thinking.' He turned to Dooley, who was just beginning to stand, but his eyes were still fixed in fear to the end of the corridor. 'Dooley, give Elderson your carbine.'

'Give her my gun?'

'Better in her hands than yours. No offence, but you with a carbine makes me nervous.'

Dooley just nodded and passed the carbine over. Elderson took the weapon and checked it over and attached it to a sling on her uniform.

'You pick up any extra ammo?' Elderson asked Dooley. He checked his pockets and passed over two additional clips. 'Good. Thanks.'

Another metallic sound. 'What are they doing?' asked Li. As if on cue, the lights down the corridor began to go out in sequence. 'You're kidding me.'

'Like I said, they know what they're doing.'

In moments they were in darkness.

*

'Stay here.'

As he watched, the tracker in his bio-comm display moved away from his own marker, and the torchlight silhouetted Elderson momentarily as she moved down the corridor towards the penultimate junction before the local AI core room. They had been lucky so far that there had been no more contact with the alien troopers but that had to change. It would only be a matter of time.

The short walk to the AI core room had stretched time, and every step they took seemed to take forever in the darkness, ears straining for the slightest sound, eyes drawn to the small pool of light Elderson used to guide the way. They were moths to the flame, and any second he expected a giant reflective suit of armour to step into the light and carve them down with a single beam of high energy particles. He had seen it done. He didn't want it to happen to him.

'Three targets,' said Elderson. 'One at the AI core doorway, the other two in the corridor, this side.'

'Guarantee there are two more the far side exit, probably in the corridor there.'

'Negative. It's a patrol. The two in the corridor are moving off.'

A thought crossed his mind.

'I can't see shit. How can you see to the AI core room?'

'Military augs. Enhanced visual optics as part of the new skin.'

'Didn't know they could do that.'

'Select few. Guinea pigs. Left eye works, right eye doesn't. I think I'll take it back when we're done here.' She was quiet for a moment. 'I can probably take one at this range, not all three.'

'Can we get closer?'

'How's your aim?'

'Out of practice.'

'Best odds we're going to get. Won't be a problem if the other two don't come back too soon.'

'How am I going to see them?'

'You'll see them. Close on me and aim at the target. I'll tag them in the bio-comm.'

'Li, the rest of you stay here. Wait for my all-clear then come and join us.'

'Copy that,' replied Li. A couple of others also confirmed.

He looked into the blackness of the corridor ahead of him and started to pad quietly towards Elderson's position. His eyes flared and swam with false light, as his brain tried to create images from a void of information. He kept his focus on the green icon in his bio-comm and used the back of his hand against the wall to his left, keeping the sensory mental image of the corridor mapped in his mind.

His fingertips touched clothing as he approached Elderson's icon, tagged in his display.

'There you are,' she said. 'I thought you'd gone on vacation.'

'I was thinking about it. But you throw the best parties; I couldn't leave.' He imagined Elderson with a wry smile, shaking her head. All he saw was black.

'Okay. I'm going to take out the target at the door. Loud. Then I'll light up the room. When the other two come running, I'll put down the first one. You deal with the second.'

'Copy.' He paused while his mind worked through the scenario. 'Question. How are you going to light up the room?'

'Details,' Elderson said, and the green icon in his bio-comm display moved away.

Shit. He thought it silently, although with the adrenaline beginning to build in his body, he wanted to shout it at the top of his voice. Creeping forward, he touched his way to the corner of the junction and settled into a practiced kneeling fire position, carbine aiming to the left of the icon moving down the corridor at pace. He clicked the safety off.

Blistering noise suddenly assaulted his ears as Elderson fired, staccato and thunderous to his now oversensitive senses. Elderson became silhouetted by her own attack, rounds discharging spat light like a strobe about the AI Core room. A beam of deadly blue light cut momentarily through the air, a particle beam fired wildly as response from a surprised trooper, the arc crackling and fizzing as it ripped the room apart. He felt his finger twitch on the trigger as he tried to find the source, but it was blocked by the evading Elderson. She disappeared into the room and out of sight as the light and sound returned to a pitch black.

'Elderson, report!' he almost screamed across the sub-vocal bio-comm channel. Nothing. 'Elderson. Do you copy?'

A faint blue-white glow started to emanate from within the AI core room, followed a moment later by a blob of light that rolled through the doorway into the corridor. Bouncing off the opposite wall, it came to rest about 10 metres from him. He realised that he had lost line of sight with Elderson, the wall possibly blocking his comms signal.

'Busy,' came a reply. At least she was still alive. He exhaled and began to breathe again. He decided to stop interrupting and stick to the plan. Aiming down the corridor, he readied himself.

More blobs of light made their way across the floor, this time heading out of the far door and into the adjacent corridor. A final two skittered to rest in the corners of the AI core room, adding to the light and illuminating the bait. Elderson was slumped in the centre of the room, carbine on the floor and out of reach.

'You have to be kidding me,' he said. He didn't expect a response. He didn't get one.

Shadows crept like ghosts out of the darkness, pale and

menacing. Their armour reflected the light of the glow sticks, which shimmered across the walls and ceiling, the air languid and liquid. He viewed the scene as if submerged and at the bottom of a moonlit lagoon, dark and otherworldly.

I'll put down the first one. Her words echoed around his mind as his world became intensely focused into the circular sight of his carbine, the head of the second trooper fixed and tracked. His breathing became slow, the physical rise and fall of his diaphragm lifting and lowering the barrel. He concentrated on relaxing and his breathing became shallow, his aim more concise, motion minimal. He waited for his moment.

The first trooper had approached Elderson cautiously, giving her a nudge with his boot. Keeping her nerve, she played her part: the corpse, the enemy defeated. The trooper came in closer, confident of his examination. He waved the second over to check on their fallen comrade. The strike was swift. A glint of polished metal like a lightning bolt from the ground, struck and punctured its target with precision. There was not even a sound from the first trooper as its weight and surprise dropped it further onto the blade.

Focusing down the scope of his carbine, he steadied himself. His breathing ebbed and paused, and his carbine settled to rest smoothly on its target. His training had not left him. He squeezed the trigger. The bark of the weapon punctuated his intent, and the second trooper dropped instantly, without taking another step, as if the puppet's strings had been cut.

Keeping his position, he checked for further targets. He saw nothing, heard nothing, except Elderson struggling out from under the heavy corpse of the now-dead trooper.

'Clear,' he stated.

Elderson stood and started punching and kicking the air towards the trooper at her feet. "Yeah, that's you," she shouted. "How'd ya like that, asshole? See you now? That's you!"

Walking into the room from the corridor, he stopped to look down at the dead trooper.

"I guess that's us done with creeping around," he said to Elderson, as the adrenaline began to recede from her system, allowing her to calm a little.

"Guess so."

He knelt down to the dead trooper lying face down and rolled the body over. Checking the helmet, he released the visor, which hissed its reluctance to open. Gripping the visor with his outstretched fingers, he slowly lifted it to reveal the trooper's face. He shook his head in recognition.

"You know this guy?" Elderson was perceptive.

"We met him already, in the workshop," said Li.

Both he and Elderson spun in reaction, raising their weapons and levelling them on the engineer, Elderson seemingly pulling a pistol out of thin air. The rest of the team had moved up behind them and now stood in the entrance to the room, eyes wide and taking in the detail. Three armoured warriors lay contorted and slumped on the floor, with horrific wounds, flesh smashed or sliced, beginning to pool blood across the floor. Dooley stared transfixed, becoming pale in his disgust, then ducked out into the corridor. He heard the smattering and retching of a man in shock.

"Someone check on Dooley," he said.

"I'm alright," came a strained voice from the corridor. Li rolled his eyes then went to assist where he could.

"Okay, Harper, front and centre. You're up. Need you to bring Ellie back on line. Be nice, hold her hand, whatever you need to do. But we need her running this ship again."

"You bet."

Harper took a moment to open the entrance hatch to the AI Core. "Here, throw me one of those," he asked, pointing at one of the glow sticks in the corner of the room.

"Here, have a fresh one," replied Elderson, cracking and shaking a new glow stick, then throwing it the short distance. Harper caught it with an easy swift motion, then turned and stepped through into the AI Core.

Elderson turned to the two with carbines staring across the room. "I need two volunteers. You and you," she said. She pinged their bio-comms and they returned their names. "Tyrell, Cooke. Perimeter. One on each entrance. Throw a glow stick into the corridor, as far as you can get it. You see movement, you holler." She handed out two more sticks to nods of understanding.

She returned to him as he worked to examine the Larsen clone with the least damage to the armour and kit.

"Their mistakes cost them," she said.

"Yeah. Larsen, the human one, the one I know, he is an engineer. Damn good one. He was never a soldier as far as I know. Everyone has their history, but I don't think he had any military training. These guys would be green. Zero combat training."

"Numbers."

"Yeah. But an army with the biggest number and all the tech in the universe can still throw it away if their opponent is better trained and more committed. I'd say that puts us at an advantage right now."

Elderson didn't say anything but pointed surreptitiously at a couple of his team—Dooley specifically, as he walked back in with Li. Point made. They needed Ellie back online.

"Boyd!" came a shout from inside the AI core. He stepped across the room and through into the confined space of the AI core. Harper was busy working at two terminals simultaneously. He was looking intently at one of the screens, but, knowing techs as he did, he knew Harper would be seriously multitasking at speed. He never quite knew how the techs did it, though he was glad he'd not taken that career path, the number of burn-outs being unacceptably high as far as he was concerned.

"What have you found, Harper?"

"She's not here, Boyd."

"What do you mean, she's not here?"

"Exactly that. Her container is empty at this node, and all other nodes across the ship. Her wave is not here, her core code is missing."

"Deleted? How can that be? Aren't there safeguards?"

"Yes. There is no way to manually drop an AI from all nodes. They are classed as human-sentient. There are laws, there are safeguards. It's murder to kill an AI, same as killing anyone else. I've scanned through the logs, and all was normal up until the attack. Then she stops. Just ceases to exist."

His face was scrunched into furrows that didn't suit the age of his face, his fifty-year-old mind working through permutations and possibilities. None of them good.

"That can't be right. She has to be here."

"Incoming!" came a scream from the corridor outside the AI core. An eruption of automatic fire began to crackle and punch at his senses. Another sound began to build in the background, a sound rising in intensity and volume. It grated at his mind and slowed his reactions, restricted his thinking. It felt like a terrible thunderstorm was building, compressing and closing in. He shook his head and grabbed at Harper.

"Find her."

"We haven't got time. We have to go."

"Find her, dammit." He pushed at Harper, pointing at his terminals to focus him. Harper looked back with a fierce opposition of will, then, relenting, turned back to continue his work. With the search to find Ellie again underway, he turned with urgency to do what he could to help those in the corridor.

Reaching the door, Elderson hit him in the chest like a truck, the impact forcing them both at the wall opposite and to a shuddering stop. The room behind her erupted into light and cold blue fire. Screams of incinerating pain called out then fell silent in a moment, as the AI core door slammed closed. This did not happen quite quickly enough, however, to stop the sudden explosive overpressure from pushing them into unconsciousness.

LARSEN

Things had escalated. Staring unfocused at the floor, he sat on the side of a lounger, rubbing the back of his neck where a headache was beginning to build, slowly but surely. He was being swamped with information, requests to provide answers, technical detail on how he had been able to subvert the Arch'sa machines about the planet and disable them. The Xannix people wanted to know who this new Setak'da was and everything about the species that now rained from the stars to save them from the Zantanath. It was all getting too much, and as far as he could tell this was a side show to the more pressing problems of a Zantanath retaliation.

Sure enough, it had happened, just as Ovitala had stated. He had been able to escape Celestia, the Zantanath regional prime, and take down her immediate attack against him. Doing so had won him the support of the Xannix council and, by proxy, the people of Xannix in some ancient competition to their presidential seat of power. He had become the Setak'da, and immediately inherited all the political strife that entailed.

But his reasoning had been flawed. He had presumed in his naivety that once he had beaten Celestia and become Setak'da to the Xannix people, he would ensure the safety of the human fleet trapped in orbit and now, in part, spread across the northern tundra of the Xannix world.

In the subterranean complex of the Xannix Seekers, he hid from the new world, while he tried to piece it all together. His mind wading through the treacle of half-formed ideas and tenuous answers. He had won the battle, but he was far from winning the war. Celestia had made her move the moment he had climbed, burned and scarred, from the bed of his damaged Arch'sa. The ancient machines were no longer able to function across the world's network, no longer able to command the VR constructs, to instigate their pointless battles, to slaughter thousands of Xannix. The situation had been contrived by the Zantanath centuries before, a period of time which was vague at best, based on some premonition and search of the next Setak'da. He had been that being, the Setak'osso, the pretender to the throne. A challenger who only the Cardinal of the Seeker clan of Xannix could identify, and who the Overseer clan were sworn to test while defending the incumbent.

Traditions had been built up over these centuries to enforce a leader on the Xannix populous who, in reality, was nothing but a puppet to the true power, the shadow rulers of the world—the Zantanath.

It was a regime of exploitation and destruction. The Zantanath had eroded Xannix society, installed corrupt bureaucrats which they could more easily control, trawled and stripped the continents of their resources, and ravaged the world with wars to decimate the population. Uprisings would be crushed, the people controlled harshly with laws, strict and unyielding.

The more he learned from Cardinal Ovitala and her Seeker faction, the more he became convinced that the Zantanath needed to be stopped. His concerns for the human fleet were a priority, but the Xannix had been oppressed for generations. If the Zantanath could do this to the Xannix, there was absolutely nothing stopping them from doing the same to the newly arrived human colonists.

His head throbbed as if all the problems and moral implications of his decisions were pulsing and pushing against his skull, straining to escape. The pain he felt was far more likely to be the side effect of the feedback shock which he had sent to all the Arch'sa during his confrontation with Celestia, to destroy the control crown within the devices and disable the global network. It had taken him days to recover, and even longer to begin to think with any coherence. He had not confessed to anyone, not even Rivers, that he had not expected to survive the move. Overloading the power to the control crown of the device would have delivered a deadly arc of current across the nodes, all users would have been dead in an instant. He had released himself from the crown the moment he had sent the instruction and it had saved him from the worst of the power surge but not all.

He touched the back of his neck again and ran his hand to the top of his head, the sensitivity of the new skin still acute, but soft and smooth. The hair had not yet grown back and he knew he looked like death, but the Seeker doctors had been professional and technically brilliant—their medical technology far in advance of anything he had seen on any human ship—and his burns had all but vanished.

The door to their quarters opened and Rivers walked in with anger in every step; close behind her followed Clarion, a petulant teenager, dangerous eyes glaring at her back. There was a storm raging. He braced himself.

Things had turned bad between them quickly. He understood and expected Clarion to have trouble adjusting to them, the fact that they looked so much like his parents as he remembered them would almost certainly confuse and confound him. For him to differentiate the visual appearance might be one problem, the other was clearly trying to come to terms with the emotional disconnect. Rivers had shown an instant empathy for the child but he had not. That may have been a mistake, but, then, he was a terrible actor and pretending to feel something he clearly did not would have been to set a false expectation and an emotional lie. Better, he felt, to stay truthful and find a course through than to lie and be found out. If everyone knew where they stood, there would be firm foundation for tough decisions later on, and he knew there would be tough decisions. He had encountered plenty of those already.

"What do you mean, we can't go to the fleet? It's exactly what we should do," blasted Clarion.

"You are not listening," replied Rivers, still with her back to him and trying to control her anger. "It is too dangerous. You are not going on any rescue mission. I don't even know why they are calling it a rescue? It'll be a slaughter. You did see what the Zantanath did to the Seeker fleet?"

"But these are my friends, Mum. I can't just let them go without me."

The room went silent. *Mum.* It had derailed her anger, he watched as a look of sadness swept over her features. She turned back to face Clarion.

"I am not your mother, Clarion. No matter how much you may wish it," she said with a sigh. "But I am looking out for her son."

He watched as Clarion flushed with an embarrassed glow, his argument falling flat with the realisation of his understandable mental and verbal slip. He sat heavily next to him on the couch and let out a resigned but angry huff. Clarion fired him a momentary look, possibly hoping to swing the argument.

"If you're looking for an ally in this argument, you've come to the wrong place," he said. Clarion simply scowled back then, shaking his head, got up as swiftly as he had arrived and retired to his room. Rivers flopped onto the couch, taking Clarion's place. Another sigh, this one tired, forearm across her eyes to shut out the torment.

"Still think it's a good idea?"

"What?" she asked.

"Having kids."

She scrunched up her face, still hiding behind her forearm. Jury was out.

"I can understand he has questions," she said, "but it's relentless. And this rescue mission of Ovitala's. What was she thinking?"

"She was hoping to help."

"Who? She has to wonder how her fleet fell apart when the Zantanath attacked. What does she think can be achieved by sending more to the same slaughter? Madness."

"That it may be, but she is trying to help us. I think we need to temper her enthusiasm, but we need her and the Seekers, and the Overseers. We need this planet unified. We just need to think of an alternative."

Rivers sat up to face him, her expression serious. "Your loyalties cannot be split. This nonsense they have you chained to, this Setak'da presidency, you cannot let it override your responsibility to the fleet. I feel huge sympathy for the Xannix, but we have our people to think about."

"I think you're missing the bigger picture. Why did we have to come here in the first place?" He waited for a response. None came. "A meteor strike, a second extinction level event. And who was affected?"

She looked at him darkly. "Everyone," she replied.

"The Great Decline affected everyone. Century long enemies, your next-door neighbour. Didn't matter. My point is, this is a different place, a different time, but the extinction level event is right there in orbit. Waiting for us to make the wrong move."

Rivers sat back, legs crossed, body language defensive; she was worried. He could see her thinking through the events of the last few weeks: the Zantanath attack on the fleet and the destruction of the *Endeavour*. The survivors who had escaped the break-up of the ship and made it to the surface, although they probably didn't know it themselves, were in a safer place than those in orbit. He was equally worried. He just didn't know how long it might be before Celestia would make a strike for the planet. They were against the clock and he no longer had the initiative.

"For the time being, I think we have to trust the fleet captains to work with the situation they have. We need more information on the Zantanath and to profile Celestia—I need to know how her mind works and what is motivating her. I need to speak to Ovitala."

Getting up from the couch, he moved across to the door and it opened. On the other side of the door, a Xannix guard stood attentively. "I need to speak to Cardinal Ovitala," he said to the Xannix.

"Of course, Setak'da. I will take you to her."

"Bodyguards," he said, looking back at Rivers and rolling his eyes. A smile slipped out of Rivers to disrupt her dark mood; she shook her head.

"Get going, you fool."

Job done. He headed out.

*

Ovitala had been allocated quarters close to their own when they had arrived at the subterranean Arch'sa facility of Dessek, which was situated in a remote rocky region to the north east of the city of Alloss, where they had first been introduced. She sat staring into a large aquarium, watching the slow, easy motion of several fish and fish-like creatures lazily moving through the water. He realised that this was the first time he had ever seen a fish, other than in an educational vid or archive. Stepping up to the glass, his face close enough to condense his breath, he watched the colours sparkle and fluoresce. He found himself captivated by the tiny creatures.

Without words, Ovitala raised a hand to the glass and with a slight motion back and forward altered the colour of the skin across her palm in a repeated sequence. The fish responded with a similar colour display and moved as one back and forward in time with her hand. Lowering her hand again, her features became tight and contorted, a look that he had come to understand as a smile, but which looked nothing like the human equivalent. This was another of those nuances of liaising with the Xannix that could cause misinterpretation if unaccustomed, as their smile to any human was pretty frightening.

"We came from the oceans a long time ago," she said. "There are certain forms of communication which are still a common bond between the species." They continued to look at the aquarium where the creatures were still doing a repeated dance and light show. "It is always wise to keep in touch with your past."

With no conductor, the fish began to disperse and go about their business. He continued to watch them, fascinated at their movement.

"Humanity too. Millions of years ago. But we have no connection like this. Communication is incredibly basic between different species, if at all."

"Maybe you have simply forgotten how."

"No. I think it's more fundamental."

"It is not just what you say, Setak'da. Communication is made in many ways, of which the sound you make is just one." Her face flushed and fluctuated between blue and a soft magenta. Ovitala turned and began to walk further into the room to a large rug scattered with cushions and the pedestal type seats the Xannix were fond of using. He followed. He presumed that was what the colours had meant. He was guessing.

Once they were seated, Ovitala handed him a small, clear globe. He inclined his head as he accepted, then popped it into his mouth. Applying a firm pressure to the jelly-like substance with his tongue, the globe burst and drenched his mouth with a citrus-like freshness. He drank the liquid and savoured the flavour. It was one of the small Xannix traditions he had come to enjoy.

"Unity and friendship," said Ovitala, bringing her four hands momentarily to the centre of her chest and then towards him. The motion was easy and casual, repeated routinely.

"Unity and friendship," he repeated, feeling that he should make some reciprocal gesture. It made Ovitala smile again.

"It is not necessary to respond," she said, "but thank you."

They sat for a moment while he composed himself.

"Now, how can I be of service, Setak'da?" Ovitala asked.

"I'd like to discuss the rescue you are planning to attempt. At this stage, I think it is too soon to be sending a team. We do not know enough about the situation, and the number of ships we have currently lost in the defence of the fleet has been high. We need to understand why." As he spoke, he realised he was using the inclusive, *we*. Rivers' words resonated in his mind, but he pushed them to one side.

"I agree. To a point. But the team is decided. And we must find out more, as you say."

"So, am I to understand this is a reconnaissance mission, not a rescue mission?"

"Yes. Reconnaissance."

He was quiet for a moment while he thought things through.

"I presume we have attempted communication?" he asked.

"Yes, and we have had responses from our own ships but not yours. The fact that they have been boarded and are now unable to respond leads me to believe they are under the complete command of the Zantanath at this time."

"You mentioned that you," he checked himself and restarted the sentence, "that *we*, have ships able to respond in the area?"

"Just one, to be precise. The *Essalit*. She is close and was hidden at the time the attack happened."

"The *Hopeful Light*?" he said.

"*Eternal Light*," Ovitala corrected. "Her mission is as a shadow ship. Most of our formations will operate with a designated ship that will run dark at all times. It can be of strategic benefit in many situations."

"And where is she at the moment?"

"Close to your remaining ships. Monitoring, and standing ready to assist on your word."

"Are they able to communicate with us without giving away their location?"

"For the time being, yes. We are using tight beam communications and they are hidden well, in the shadow of the

Endeavour."

The wreck of the *Endeavour* had split into large hulks and now orbited the planet as several unstable, uncontrolled artificial asteroids. It had become another planet-threatening issue. When the orbit decayed, there would be consequences. There were Xannix, currently hard at work trying to determine the impact site.

"Then, for now, we wait. Allow the *Indy* and *Intrepid* crews time to make contact and give us a more detailed report. But please keep me informed of any detail you receive from the *Essalit.*"

Ovitala's skin flushed a light sky blue, then returned to the speckled light grey of her natural skin tone.

He rose from his seated position and turned to leave, but one last thing caught him.

"One last concern, and I'm not quite sure how to raise this without it sounding like a criticism, which it is not. I apologise in advance if I am less than tactful.

"On Earth, we care for and protect our young for as long as we can. I'm sure the Xannix are no different. But I do wonder, at what age you consider your children adults, and allow them independent decisions?"

Ovitala appeared confused, which she probably was. He was being less than clear.

"Clarion has become very insistent today that he be allowed to join the reconnaissance mission. Rivers and I are against this. He is too young to be taking an active part in military operations."

The smile returned to Ovitala, the skin about her face fluctuating between blue and yellow.

"He is very keen and headstrong, but he is yet a child, as you say. I have given him no such indication. I told him, no."

It was the old parental one-two, if one parent said no, try the other. He smiled back in return as he realised they were being played by a teenager. Being raised on Xannix had not altered Clarion's ability to be devious and plain sneaky. Children were children throughout the universe, so it seemed.

"Thank you, Cardinal Ovitala."

Ovitala flushed light blue again and inclined her head. He turned and walked past the aquarium tanks again, the fish swimming lazily about but mimicking the same light blue. Mirrored communication, he thought, as his bodyguard opened the door for him.

PATTEN

It had been a long month since the accident at the test facility, and what followed had been a trial of torments, starting and ending with Ellie. Somehow, Ellie had identified the impending danger and managed to let out a warning to those close enough to hear, before she was swept away like a leaf on the wind. The guilt had been almost instant, the deepest pit of darkness and despair opening in the centre of his chest, threatening to turn him inside out. He had forced himself to stay as calm as he could, but adrenaline flowed and fuelled his actions; the world had slowed to a crawl.

There were people screaming and running in all directions. He had reacted instinctively to Ellie's warning, their eyes locking across the room for a fleeting moment before the explosion. There had been a helpless realisation there, a submission to fate and an inevitable outcome.

As he picked himself up from the floor, his limbs had complained and fumbled to catch up with his brain's impulse to move. Sprinting to her side, he had crashed to the floor and rolled her over to look at him. He had known in that moment that their world had been torn apart. Any future they had dreamt of together had been taken from them, violently and without care. Death was not selective; it made no concession for age, wealth or station—it came and took without mercy.

But he had seen a way through, a path to cheat death at its own game.

He now stared at a box in the labs of Dr Peter Clayton. Every weekend, every moment he could take away from work, he would come here to be with her. It didn't matter that she was physically altered, it mattered that she was still alive. Still part of the world. The future would take care of itself somehow, but he knew that he needed her in it.

He sat at the side of a carbon fibre and alloy cube, one metre in length along each axis and covered in interspersed lines of red light, each undulating with an organic glow and the regularity of her relaxed breathing. Every now and then a faster trace of bright red would work its way around the cube, like an electrical impulse sparking across neurons, or a nerve pathway. He would stare for hours, watching the life exist within and wondering when it might interact with the outside world.

Dr Clayton had introduced him to his daughter, Dawn. She was situated in the lab across the corridor, and was fully integrated with her AI container, having come to terms with her new existence. She had admitted that the transition had been the hardest part of the process. It would take time.

So he waited, patiently sitting at her side, as if sitting next to her hospital bed. He streamed vids and listened to music through his bio-comm, he caught up on some reading. But mostly, he sat close with his hand touching the cool and smooth surface of the machine that now sustained her.

A monitor on the workbench across from him flicked on, and with a swirl of pixels the face of Ellie appeared, sullen and full of sorrow. Tears appeared to be streaming down her cheeks and she wiped them away the best she could, flicked and straightened her hair and sniffed hard to clear her nose. He realised she was trying to make herself presentable for him, to compose herself for their first face-to-face meeting in months. She looked as beautiful as he remembered.

"Hey," she managed eventually.

"Hey." He stood in front of the screen and touched her face. It was cold and flat, but somehow his memory altered his senses and he remembered a warm and smooth skin, a sunny smiling face, and his heart leapt. They sat for several more minutes, both full of emotion and unable to express it, tears welled in their eyes from the simple joy of being together after the months of separation.

Ellie finally broke the silence.

"I guess I should say, thank you."

He didn't know how to react. He had saved her life, but what was she now? What existence did she have to look forward too? He tried to smile, but even that just felt like an apology.

"How do you feel?"

There was more silence as Ellie appeared to struggle with the question. Under simpler circumstances the question was polite and innocuous, but now he felt he had overstepped a line.

"Weirdly, I feel just like normal. Probably better in some ways."

Again, his reaction was wanting. He noticed her scrunch up her nose and look around the room while she thought further.

"I feel no pain from the trauma. My outward appearance is taken and projected from my memories, and I exist in simulated environments of my choosing. Utopias of my own design. But I am not in the world anymore, there is a separation. And however perfect the simulations, there is loneliness. I'm glad you're here."

Whether on purpose or by accident, her words grated and gnawed at his sense of guilt. However much he thought he had cheated death for her, he now had his doubts. His thoughts transferred the experience and switched their places, looking out at a world of which he was no longer a physical part. After all, he was part of Clayton's CORE programme; this could very well be him one day. He had never truly considered the consequences until now. Was this a future he would want for himself?

"So," Ellie broke into his thoughts and changed the subject. "What did I miss?"

"Straight for the small talk," he said.

She sniffed again and cleared her throat. The AI environment had fully mimicked the physical human form inside a simulated world. Dawn had explained to him that it helped in transition, being able to identify with your surroundings was less important than being able to identify with your own physical form, so every effort had been made to ensure the human wave inside the machine could stay connected within an avatar of themselves, which was their *body* within the virtual environments of the cube.

"You know me. Always business."

He let Ellie take the lead. She was obviously still working things through, so it would be detrimental to push her on subjects or issues that triggered memories of trauma. Until she raised a subject, he would keep things light.

Scooping the chair over to a more suitable position in front of the monitor, he sat and got close to the screen. Ellie seemed to move closer too, her image coming nearer so that her head and shoulders filled the frame of the screen.

"So, what have they found?" she asked.

"There was a rouge configuration of the Mag-X drive alignment, within the accelerator module. The numbers selected were not default to the prescribed test. But-," —he paused to check the reaction on Ellie's face; nothing yet— "-whoever, changed those numbers… We would really like to know why they chose those numbers specifically."

"I'm not sure, that's the question I asked," she said. He must have looked puzzled because she rolled her eyes and shook her head. "The guy who took out the test facility."

"Now you're confusing me."

"There was a guy; there was a bomb."

He stared at her. There had been no mention of it in any of the reports. In fact, the idea of a bomb had been discounted early on due to there being a faulty valve found within the remains of the hydrogen tanks which had initiated the explosion.

"It was reported as an accident."

"It was not an accident."

"You are sure of this?" he asked. "I know you gave a warning before the explosion, but it was presumed you identified the faulty valve before it fully failed."

"No, I saw a detonator. It was small and innocuous, but it was a detonator."

"How do you know it was a detonator?"

"I saw the person who set it." She stopped herself. He saw there was more, but she had cut herself short, her eyes wandering about the room as she reached for memories. She exhaled sharply in frustration.

"Saw someone? But the report stated there had been no one near those canisters that day. They had been checked the previous day, all found to be signed off for the test. I reviewed the security footage of the ten minutes before the explosion. You were the only one near those canisters before the accident."

She looked back at him dumbfounded, eyes searching his for answers he did not have.

"So, on top of everything else, I'm now going crazy?"

"That's not what I said." Working through ideas, he came to a quick conclusion. "We need to get the investigation reopened," he said. "I'll inform Jessop."

"No," Ellie said sharply, an anger seeping through the word. She calmed, realising she was becoming harsh with him. "No. Perhaps I was mistaken."

"You have been through a lot. Memories may be a little confused. Disorientation should be expected. Give yourself time."

"Yes. I think maybe you're right."

She went quiet for a while, mixed up in her own thoughts. He didn't want to push matters, but what if she was right? If it truly was an attack on the test facility, it changed everything. The station would still be in danger and at risk to further attacks. And why had the investigation omitted Ellie as a witness? The answer came swiftly to him. Legally, she had died that day.

The fact that she had returned now meant little. They had wanted the investigation closed down quickly, Jessop pushing to get the tests of the Mag-X drive back on track and the newly found technology moved up the production schedule. In his mind, this was premature. There were too many unknowns, the technology was too unstable, and it currently only had around a 20 percent success rate. Most of the time the drive unit deconstructed itself at a molecular level, the last test having randomly disrupted particles within all kinds of material throughout the structure of the test bay, pitting the room full of fist size holes. But he was building a drive unit, not a weapon. The current line of research was a dead end.

Ellie, however, deserved more than a rushed investigation. She deserved the truth.

"I don't know what happened that day, but if you say you saw something, I believe you," he said.

Ellie let out a physical sigh of relief. "I'm on your side. No matter what. We're a team, Ellie. We'll find out who did this to you. I'll start making some discrete enquiries of my own, pull any data I can, review the video again."

"Could you get me the detail? I have nothing but time here; it would help to have something to work on," she said.

"You need something to work on? I've got a mountain of test data and new design simulations to run. If you are happy to pick up some of it, the team would be more than grateful."

"Send it over. Anything is better than sitting here reliving that day."

An impulse took him and he kissed the screen. "Love you," he said. The moment surprising even himself.

Ellie became coy, almost embarrassed. "I've missed you too, Scott Patten."

*

"What are we even looking for?" asked Okoro. "I've been staring at this screen for hours: the footage of the test bay shows the same from every angle."

"And that doesn't bother you?"

"I think you're trying to read something into this that the evidence just doesn't support. There's nothing there."

"If Ellie says there was someone there, then there was someone there. I just need to prove it."

"You said it yourself—she could have been confused. She could be misremembering the order of events, perhaps merging memories from different timeframes, or just ..."

"Okay," he interrupted. He knew the argument, "but let us, just for a minute consider that she was right. How could she be right and the cameras wrong? Theoretically. How could you make someone invisible to everyone, and everything else?"

Okoro stared at him like he had gone mad. Mixed in with the fact that it was late and the end of a very long day, he felt that they could both probably do with some rest. He rose from his chair to pace the room a little and reinvigorate his limbs, and in the process get some more oxygen to his flagging brain cells.

"Humour me," he said.

Okoro shook his head and rubbed his hands across his face to wake himself, focus on the problem.

"Background. You need to be background. Tech staff, engineering staff. People that would be low level but fundamental and commonplace," Okoro began. "The grey man."

"Grey man?"

"Just that. Someone that would not stand out in any way. Average height, average build... you get the picture. These people get mentally filtered out, everyone does it. Who swapped out the faulty light in your office when it failed last week?"

"I don't know, he came in, fixed the light, went away. I was busy."

"She. She came in, fixed the light and went away," said Okoro with a smile.

"People are perceptive to a point. Is that what you're saying?"

"Just so."

While Okoro let the idea sink in, he found himself staring at the wall monitor, a two-minute timeframe before the explosion, playing on a loop. A grey man. But he saw no man. He watched Ellie move across the room to the canisters. She looked puzzled, like she was trying to work something out, or remember something that stayed just out of reach.

"More outside the box," he said. "How do you become physically invisible? How about small, if the thing she saw was too small for the camera system to see?"

"You said she saw a man."

"But it might not have been a man, it could have been something she is just remembering as a person. If you are confused, your mind will rationalise."

"So she is not understanding what she is seeing and rationalising a human form?"

"Exactly."

"Possible. A drone perhaps? But wouldn't it need to be big enough to see? If she is seeing it, wouldn't we see it? How small could something be to be visible to her, yet invisible to the security system?" asked Okoro.

He scrunched up his nose, while his mind discounted his own theory.

"This is getting us nowhere," he said. The video loop clicked back to the start of the sequence and began again. He saw himself and Okoro speaking as Ellie seemed distracted and eased herself from the group. Step by slow pensive step she moved towards the set of canisters. He touched the screen and the image paused. "What is she looking at?"

He traced a line with his finger from Ellie, along her line of sight, towards the far wall of the room. She had initially been looking at the canisters, but as she got closer she had been concentrating on a point leading to the door on the south side of the test bay. The door had opened and a group of people had walked in: three techs and a security officer. Only at the last moment had Ellie looked back to the canisters and then to him. He traced the line again, this time circling the south entrance.

"What was she looking at?"

"The canisters. A bomb?"

"No. Here," he said, pointing at the test bay entrance in the frozen image of the wall screen.

"The door?"

"Why, if you were so concerned about a bomb, would you be staring in the wrong direction?"

Okoro simply shrugged his shoulders. "It makes no sense."

"It does if you're watching someone walking out of the room."

"I only saw people walking into the room," stated Okoro. "The camera doesn't lie."

"Doesn't it?" he said.

BOYD

It had been surprisingly difficult to extricate himself from the tangle of arms and legs he had found himself in. Within the confined space of the AI core entranceway, Elderson and he had struggled for a few moments before finally finding themselves sitting on the floor with their backs against the wall, facing the door which had just slammed closed.

"Are you guys okay?" The voice came from the wrong direction. For some reason he thought Elderson had spoken, but it was Harper, away from the terminal and helping him up.

"The others?" he said. Elderson just shook her head solemnly. It was all she needed to do to convey the tragedy that had befallen the rest of the team.

"Shit," his frustration and anger surfacing. He pushed his head into his hands for a moment, as if to wipe the daemons away. To turn his rageful face into that of calm. He was not sure it had worked. For now, he needed to compartmentalise the rage and anger. Acting impulsively would only gain them the same fate as the others. That needed to be avoided, as did the troopers outside.

"I thought you said those troops were inexperienced?" he asked Elderson.

"I did," she conceded. "But they have bigger flamethrowers than we do."

"They have flamethrowers?" said Harper.

Elderson and he just looked at Harper blankly.

"Did you find Ellie?" he snapped unfairly at Harper, exposing the tension he felt. Harper realised the intention, raising only an eyebrow to the outburst. He was deflecting, changing the subject. It was understandable.

"No," Harper said. "She is definitely missing from all nodes, which simply doesn't make sense."

There was a bang at the door, which made them all look round in panicked reaction. Elderson, with her sidearm raised toward the danger, moved them back further into the already cramped compartment.

"We've got to get out of here. Is that the only door out?" said Elderson.

"On this floor, yes. But not the only exit. This way," said Harper.

They moved around the AI core stack in the centre of the room to a secondary bay. In the corner of the floor, a hatch slid open to reveal a ladder down to a lower level.

"It gets cramped down there—only really meant for a single tech—so it will be single file all the way to the hatch on the lower level. You go first; I'll close up after us."

Elderson stepped forward and lowered herself down through the opening without hesitation. As he stepped from the ladder after her, he found her a couple of metres up the crawlspace at the next corner, attention concentrated along a visual line he could not see.

"Why are the lights on in here? Are they not off across the whole ship?" she asked over her shoulder.

"Don't know," said Harper, who was now closing the hatch behind himself. "I guess they don't want to close down the AI. It's only us they are trying to suppress."

Another deeper thump could be heard above them, as the Zantanath troopers tried to break through into the AI core. It made Harper flinch again.

"They've got the scent," Elderson said. "Less talking, more moving." She headed off down the cramped crawlspace to the next corner; they followed.

The next thump shook the deck and corridor framework around them.

'I don't think they can breech the AI core', he broadcast to the others via bio-comm.

'Whatever they're doing, at least we know where they are,' said Harper. 'Another floor hatch in five metres.'

It opened as they approached, and they dropped through into a mirror of the AI core room they had just come from.

'Harper, we haven't got long before they work out what's going on. You need to track down Ellie. We need her back online and working for us,' ordered Elderson.

'I don't know that I can.'

'Think your way through the maze,' she said as she paced to the door and out into the darkness of the tech room beyond. Light leaked from the AI core, illuminating workstations and throwing cityscape shadows across the walls. His eyes followed her as she disappeared into the inky shadows.

'No sign of movement; no sign of our armoured friends,' Elderson said.

He walked up to Harper. 'You've got this, Harper. What do you need?'

'I need ten minutes with Dawn, or Obi.'

'Right now, that's going to be tricky.'

'But not impossible,' Harper said. 'If I can get to the comms array, we should be able to find a way.'

'You want to go for an EVA now?'

'Look, I've considered our options, and they're limited. I can't find any trace of Ellie here. We could look at using a shuttle for comms, but they'll have all landing bays locked down. Getting to comms internally will be equally impossible. The only place we could possibly work with some probability of success is outside— go to the array directly.'

'Once they find out where we are though, we're wide open,' said Elderson across the sub-vocal system.

'Yes, probably true. But that's where you come in. You did ask what you could do to help.'

'I did,' he conceded. Harper had him there.

Elderson was suddenly closer again, within the pool of light from the AI core, and motioning that they should get behind her.

'What's up?' he asked.

'They have been quiet for a few minutes. I don't trust the silence. We should get moving.'

It was as if she had incanted a daemon. Within the confines of the AI core, a transport sphere began to materialise; rippled silver and light.

'Go! Go!' Elderson shouted. He and Harper both backed out of the AI core into the darkness of the ship's corridors. The bark of Elderson's carbine broke the silence; a terrifying howling and visceral scream filled the air. Looking back, he saw Elderson slide across the floor on her back, firing back into the AI core as she went. An electrical crackle and bright white light flashed suddenly, then the noise stopped.

He and Harper had frozen, looking back into the AI core, their eyes wide in horror. The remains of a trooper, part-melded with the AI core walls and circuits, fizzed and popped with the electricity that shorted and arced across it. A ruined face with contorted features snarled at them through a shattered visor, tormented pain and death written across it.

"Why are you still here?" called Elderson. She ran at them and pushed them into the corridor. "Go, I said. Go, really means go!"

*

The corridors seemed darker somehow.

'How many of those things are there out there?' he asked himself.

'Your guess is as good as mine,' Elderson replied.

'Too many,' said Harper.

They had been walking the pitch black corridors for what seemed hours, his ears strained to hear any sound that could be a threat, but he was so jumpy that even the regular vibrations and background of the ship's infrastructure was playing on his mind. He considered it luck that they hadn't encountered any more of the boarders; the troops with their power suits seemed unstoppable and relentless, so he couldn't believe they were in the clear. Perhaps they were just not dead *yet*. He shook the thought off; they all needed to stay positive. Think your way out. 'It's your big advantage', he heard his training officer shouting at him from a vague memory of his military past. 'You're on home ground and you have a brain—it's your best weapon in any battle.'

Think your way out.

'We need to go back.'

'What?' said both Elderson and Harper in unison.

'Not a chance. We're only another couple of corridors from the airlock,' said Elderson.

'Shit. Okay, but I need one of their helmets. That comm

receiver—I can use it. I've figured out a way of tracking them. Or at least giving us an early warning to their proximity. I can build a proximity tracker.'

'Noted. Next bad guy that comes along, I'll relieve him of his helmet. But for now, we head for that comms array. I'm not seeking out trouble.'

'But if the opportunity arises…'

'It's a dumb idea.'

'Shit.' Keep thinking, he thought.

*

The airlock was still operational and the lights within functional. The horizontal slot that was its window cast a pure white beam of light into the approaching corridor. It transfixed him, as they paced tentatively closer, one small step at a time, Elderson ever cautious to hidden danger, especially at a choke point such as this. It was a prime location for an ambush, they all knew that, military training or not.

'Looks clear,' said Harper.

'I'll take a look,' said Elderson. 'Boyd, same routine as before. Cover me. You see anything moving that's not me, you ask questions later.'

'Understood.' He checked his carbine. 'Ready when you are.'

Elderson headed off down the corridor on a track the opposite side of the corridor to him, keeping the firing angle open. Last thing he wanted was to tag her in the back with a round. He decided then that the three of them would survive this. No one else was going to die today. It was a false hope, but he would hold to it, even if fate had other plans.

Her silhouette became smaller and smaller the closer to the airlock hatch she got. He felt a bead of sweat from his eyebrow leak into his eye and he tried to blink it away, the salty sting only just registering past his intense focus and fear.

Stepping into the light around the entrance, Elderson activated the door and it slid aside with an amplified hiss. Taking a rapid look inside, she motioned to them both to move up. The moment they were all inside, she closed the door behind them.

'Suit up,' she said. 'I'll suit up after you, Boyd. Then we'll head out.'

'They'll have the external hatch monitored,' he said.

'We'll have to hope they are not watching when we open it.'

'That's not very reassuring,' said Harper.

'No. But where's your sense of excitement?'

'I've had quite enough of that for one day.' He clipped his helmet closed and sealed it. 'You hear me?'

'Yes.'

'Comms are good.'

Switching places with Elderson while she got into an EVA suit, he looked out the window slot into the ship.

'You know, I liked it better when we were the only ones in this universe,' he broadcast across his bio-comm. 'Suddenly it feels a little too crowded.' There was a huff of a laugh across the sub-vocal channel, Harper agreeing to his sentiment.

'Time to leave,' said Elderson.

Moving to the airlock's outer door, he started the door release sequence and the air began to vacate the small chamber. It was like an unseen wind, the rush of air past his visor, the noise fading to a disquieting silence. Considering the vastness of space, an EVA was incredibly claustrophobic—your entire world suddenly a thin atmospheric bubble enclosed within a flimsy suit. Fragile. It was the word that always popped into his head when he stepped from an airlock. He pressed the door release and it slid aside to reveal a wide star field.

'One of those is Sol,' said Harper from over his shoulder. 'Looks beautiful.'

'There's nothing there for us now, you know that? Just death and destruction,' reminded Elderson.

'I don't know. Frying pan—fire. We've just traded one for the other, as far as I can see.'

'Hope is what we have here,' he said. 'Sol is lost. Remember that.'

'Okay. Saddle up, cowboys,' said Elderson. 'We've got a job to do here. Let's move out.'

Taking the hand grip across the top of the door, he swung himself outside the ship and round on the horizontal axis with a practiced motion, bringing his feet forward and up into a crouch. His boots landed square to the outer hull and the magnetic clamps fixed him to the surface. He stepped away from the door to allow Harper and Elderson to do the same.

The ship had reoriented to become his world. He found it odd how easy the human mind deluded itself to find the ordinary in the extraordinary. He was currently walking across the side of the *Intrepid*; however, his brain had given him the security of a stroll across a metal landscape, the comms array like a towering tree on the horizon, various dishes on limbs as leaves all pointing in slightly different directions.

'Twenty minutes there; I recommend an alternate airlock on our return,' he said.

'One closer to the bridge,' said Harper.

'No. I have a better idea.' Elderson paused in her march for the comms array and turned to him, her question clear to him in her facial expression. 'But we need Ellie back online.'

STRAUD

The pain across her temples, leaching like acid across the front of her brain, was one born of stress, anxiety and a hard feeling of failure. Her bridge crew had been herded up and removed from their stations, all now corralled into the briefing room to the rear of the bridge, sitting in enforced silence on the floor about the main dais, a single armoured guard overseeing their compliance.

Ejected from her couch, she looked on as a male Zantanath sat in her chair and conducted operations across the ship. He had an easy confidence about him and practiced understanding of the ship's systems. Her eyes bore into this Zantanath with hate and confusion. It was impossible to be that well acquainted with the *Indianapolis*. Above all that, the Zantanath would need her clearance codes to take command of the vessel, and she would not be doing that. She would die to protect the ship and her crew.

Next to the Zantanath male, sat the Zantanath female that had led the boarding party and had removed her from her chair. She had introduced herself as Celestia and was now watching the Zantanath male work through the system with intense concentration.

"I've done all I can to lock down the ship to this point. Now we need her," he said, pointing with a nod of his head towards her. She knew exactly what he meant, and she knew exactly what she would need to do. In that moment, it was as if mercury had replaced her blood and the chill of space had worked its way into her heart. She had never faced death at such close quarters before;

it had always been removed, on a monitor, or a screen. Death was far more terrifying when it was touching you on the shoulder, in person, face-to-face.

Celestia nodded silently to him, at which point his attention turned to her.

"Captain Straud, would you mind providing me with your Alpha code to the *Indianapolis* systems please?"

Two things struck her about the question, apart from the fact that it was expected. Firstly, that this Zantanath knew her by name, and, secondly, that he knew exactly the name of the required executive code required. Even the best intelligence extraction methods could not have worked as quickly; how had this Zantanath been able to obtain this information so fast? It could only come from a place of knowledge—prior understanding.

She hardened her resolve and looked the Zantanath in the eye. "No."

He was not surprised. An understanding smile spread across his face, "I can't say that was unexpected, Captain. But it was worth a try."

Unclasping a section of his belt, it drooped in linked sections across his palm. He inspected it momentarily then got out of the couch with a spring in his step and made his way across to her. As he approached, she found herself taking a step back, her movement blocked by a tall silver armoured wall of a trooper.

"Oh, don't worry, Liz. I'm not going to hurt you, just pick up a little information I need." His accent was perfect Terran English, indistinguishable from one of the crew. Up close his eyes were bright and intelligent, and she found herself focused on them, delving deep, as she looked for the man behind the mask. He noticed.

"In case you're wondering," he said, as he placed the linked device across her forehead, "I used to have a different skin. There was a slight misunderstanding on our first meeting, and to make amends for their mistake, they gave me another." He pressed a button on the device, and it tightened across her forehead, gripping at her temples, sealing evenly over the skin. Tight, but not uncomfortable.

"Now, Elizabeth, a little pop-quiz to check things are working."

"What are you doing?"

"What is your full name?" he said, ignoring her question.

"Captain Elizabeth Sky Straud."

"Sky?" he said. "Now, that's a lovely name." He pressed a couple of buttons on the device, possibly configuring for greater accuracy. She tried to resist, closing her eyes hard to block out his charming demeanour. How could he be human? It made no sense.

"Who is the President of OWEC?" Another easy question. Everyone involved in the project knew who the President of the Off World Exploration Corporation was, they had all spent most of their last years on Earth working for the man.

"Sir David Jessop," she forced through her lips, fighting to keep every word in. It didn't work, something in her was compelled to let the information go. More slight taps on the device.

"Thank you. Last question, then you can take a rest. What is your Alpha code to access the *Indianapolis'* executive systems?" He was so calm and polite. The advanced crew, the *Starchaser*. Larsen?

"Delta-Echo-5-2-9." She almost screamed as the last number was uttered.

"There, that wasn't so bad, was it?"

The device released itself from her forehead and he placed it back into the section on his belt.

"Larsen," she said, as she found herself, slumped on the floor. He looked down on her, an eyebrow raised, then the smile was back.

"There you go. Welcome to the Unity, Captain Straud," he said, and made his way back to the captain's couch.

The world was making little sense; she had lost control of her ship, and she was losing control of her mind. The only thing she could hope for was that Obadiah would override Larsen's commands, whatever they might be. A moment later, Obadiah had been called by the Zantanath Larsen as she lay on the floor, looking across at a world on its side, the bridge and Obadiah at a skew horizontal, his eyes full of sorrow, a face of conflicted emotions.

"Obadiah, I have assumed command of the *Indianapolis* on behalf of the Zantanath Unity. Contact the *Intrepid* and slave their navigation systems to ours. Then set these coordinates."

She had tears in her eyes from the stress and effort of fighting the interrogation. That is what it had been, no matter how polite Larsen had been about it. He had extracted information from her by force, information given against her will. Interrogation.

"No. Obi." The words came out as more of a whisper than a

spoken and authoritative command. "No."

Obadiah heard her and paused, looking across the bridge at her fallen form on the floor.

"He is using the correct command protocol, Captain Straud. I am duty bound and obligated to follow his orders."

"But this is wrong. We have people on the surface; we have people to rescue."

"Oh, don't worry, Captain Straud," said Larsen. "We will get to them soon enough. But for now, we have other errands to run." Turning back to Obadiah, he reiterated his command. "Now, will you do as I ask?"

"Yes," replied Obadiah.

The navigational display suddenly lit up with new vectors and plotted a track out of orbit and away from Xannix. More information that didn't make sense. The trace seemed to take them on a direct intercept with the Xannix star.

"What are you doing, Obadiah?" On top of all the other emotions she was plagued with, a new one engulfed her. A blanket of betrayal wrapped itself about her as she lay on the floor and watched the lights of the bridge, like large blurred and streaked stars washed with tears. She needed to keep control, but it was hard. Events had fully overtaken her and there was nothing she could do. She closed her eyes to give herself time. She needed to see a way through. She needed the isolation and darkness to think.

*

She had been left there on the bridge, while Larsen and Celestia gave instructions and progressed their plan. Laying there silent and unmoving with a guard standing over her, she was clearly deemed subdued and no longer a threat. So, she was ignored and left to work through her own thoughts.

The effect of having her executive code compromised was immediate. Access to the ship network, and communication between her and her crew via bio-comm was shut off; they had all been completely locked out of all systems. What little personal detail she had on the local memory of her bio-comm was still available but nothing else.

Coordinating any kind of counterstrike against the Zantanath aggressors was going to be impossible. Running through various scenarios, she could see that each required the effort of many to achieve, or the act of a single person with access to the ship systems, and neither were currently achievable.

Her mind wandered and the dappled cover of a forest began to fill the space around her, birdsong and shouts of children running about in a glade nearby, but her vision was intensely focused on a hole in a tree, about three metres from the ground. Her father sat beside her quietly, both of them waiting in silence. She had been waiting all summer for the chance to see one of the last woodpeckers in the country; there were now fewer than sixty breeding pairs in the world and ten pairs lived in this forest. Her father had arranged with a local ranger that she should be able to view one as a treat for being accepted to the Formillun Institute programme.

They had been there possibly thirty minutes with no sign of anything, other than the periodic song and calls of a multitude of invisible creatures across the canopy. But no woodpeckers. Her hopes were beginning to wane. Her disappointment must have shown itself in her expression as her father put a hand gently on her arm while still looking up to the tree. "Patience," he said, softly.

Patience. She had seen two green woodpeckers that day, darting back and forward bringing food to a hungry nest. A green horizontal flash, a red cap and sharp eyes, and a beak stuffed full of ants and larvae pulled from the dry ground.

Her father's words soothed her as she lay on the floor of the bridge. Forcing her breathing into slow regular rhythm, she eased her tension and relaxed her body. No point stressing about events she could not control, until she was able to exert some control. She was patient; she waited.

*

'Captain Straud.'

Sleep must have taken her. The darkness was more pronounced, the voice familiar.

'Captain Straud, it's Obadiah. Can you hear me?'

The bio-comm display flashed in her vision; a message had been received. She opened it without opening her eyes or giving away that she had woken. It was an executable file, simply named *obi*. She launched it. There was a moment while some update was made to her bio-comm firmware, then the world changed.

The room was warm, with a large flickering fireplace framed with an impressive mantelpiece. To the side of the fireplace was a tall leaded arch window overlooking formal Tudor style gardens leading to rolling fields and forest. The view was beautiful: a clear blue sky dotted with high, wispy clouds, the sun low and bright. A slight frost crisped the garden and the unkempt long grasses in the fields, suggesting a cool morning. The rest of the room was a library lined with books, with warm rugs on the floor and three high back leather chairs about a low circular table.

Two faces smiled back at her; she recognised them immediately.

"Where am I?" she asked.

"The physical *where* has not changed—you are still on the bridge of the *Indianapolis*," said Dawn. "But this place," she said, waving her hand in an arc to indicate the room about them. "This place is our forum. A construct and place we AIs use to discuss matters in private."

"I didn't know you had such a place," she said.

"No. It is not usually a place best suited to non-AI. We have had to slow down the relative time of the environment in order for you to function adequately. But current events require creative solutions, and we needed to speak with you privately. It seemed an obvious choice of venue."

Obadiah got up and indicated that she should take a seat in the third chair. "Please join us, Captain." She did.

"Firstly, I must apologise for my theatrics on the bridge earlier. The Zantanath Larsen is currently in a state of mild delusion that he is in command of the ship."

"He is not?" she said in some surprise.

"No, he is not," Obadiah said with a smile. "You gave up the executive code under duress, and he is part of an aggressive force acting against the ship and its crew. You are still the rightful captain of this vessel. I take orders from you alone."

A slight sigh of relief escaped her. "Thank you, Obadiah. I thought I had lost you for a moment there."

He smiled at her again with slight embarrassment. Turning to the window, his features became grave as more pressing thoughts impinged and took him away from this brief moment of emotional connection with his captain.

"Captain, we have brought you here to discuss what might be

done to save the fleet and, more importantly, its people."

"There have been some developments which you need to be made aware of, and to which we need a decision from the senior fleet commander," stated Dawn.

"Most senior? Can we not reach Clayton?"

"He is not able to affect decisions aboard the fleet in his current situation. He has enough to do with the survivors on the surface of Xannix. In addition, we have also lost Ellie."

"What do you mean, *lost?*"

"Just that. She is no longer aboard the *Intrepid*. Which means we have no direct control of that vessel."

"Is that even possible?"

"We don't know," replied Dawn. "We don't know if it is something the Zantanath boarding team have done to her systems, or something she has undertaken herself, but at the moment we are unable to contact her and reports from the ship state she is no longer in the core network."

"So, you have communication with the crew?"

"Limited," said Obadiah. "A team managed to EVA to the comms array and get a message out. We had five minutes before they were cut off. We have had no direct contact with the bridge crew. Our calculation is that they are suffering the same lockdown as we are. The fact that Ellie is no longer available to them will be slowing them down considerably."

Her mind caught up with a discrepancy in the meeting.

"Dawn, how are you here? I presumed you were destroyed along with the *Endeavour?*"

"Ah," Dawn said, like a child who had just been caught doing something she shouldn't. "I didn't leave the ship. There are sections of the ship still operating with some minor function and power. The ship will not completely die for another seventeen days, four hours and ten minutes, when emergency power in those sections will finally fail. Until that time, I am of more help here. There is little I can do on the surface of the planet. Evacuating with the rest of the crew would have been a strategically poor decision."

"I see." She needed a moment to think. She got up from her chair and walked to the fireplace. It popped and crackled for a moment, embers sparking to the hearth. She had to imagine the heat from a real fire, as her interface with the construct was not complete, and provided only visual sensory input and sound, nothing more. She considered putting her hand in the fire to test the restricted sensation of touch, but some part of her brain overrode her, the reflex of self-preservation applying itself even across virtual reality.

Continuing to stare into the fire, she asked, "To be up front with you, I have decided to take back the ships from these Zantanath, whatever their purpose here. But I suspect that this course of action will not be easy. I also think now is not the time. We need to work through how best to remove these people but at the same time figure out what it is they want."

"We could just ask them," said Dawn.

"True, although, in my experience that rarely brings out the whole truth. Everyone has something to hide. I don't see that these Zantanath would be any different," said Obadiah.

"Okay, so until I say otherwise, we play along. Do as they ask and be compliant; it will give us a little time to work out our next move." She looked up and out of the window for a moment then made her way back to her chair. Looking directly at Obadiah, she tapped her temple with her forefinger. "This update you have given me. Is it a direct and always open link?"

"Yes. It's a low intensity, low frequency carrier. Hopefully, they won't be able to determine it across the rest of the background noise of the ship."

"Unless they are specifically looking for it," added Dawn.

"Okay. It's what we have. Good enough," she said.

"So, what do you want to do about Ellie?"

"Find her. We need to maintain control of the fleet. As soon as they work out how to manually control the ship, which I'm guessing with Larsen working the command won't take long, we will lose control of both the *Intrepid* and the *Indianapolis*. We can't let that happen. We need to find Ellie and find out what's going on over there."

Both Dawn and Obadiah nodded agreement.

"Okay, good. Now, in the meantime, make sure our people are safe, and report any change in current Zantanath operation." More nods. "I'm going to have a brief word with our new Captain," she said with slight malice in her tone.

She closed the connection.

PATTEN

Sitting forward in his chair, staring at his office monitor, he had reread the email there for about twenty minutes. *I need a little time*, it said. *When I'm ready, I'll call you. Love, Ellie.* What did that mean? Was she shutting him out? It's not what they needed right now. They had just been getting straight again after the incident at the test facility. She had been adjusting well to her new circumstances. Emotionally, things from his point of view had been getting close to how they had been before. He caught himself. From *his* point of view.

As Ellie had made improvements, his confidence had grown, as she had become more like her old self, he had fallen back into an older, more familiar routine. But things now were far from familiar. It was just an old mental template that he was trying to superimpose over the new situation. Ellie may well have been playing to his weakness, or perhaps simply aiming to appear stronger than she was. Either way, her life was hers to live. He needed to respect her decision.

To ease his mind, and confirm the situation, he picked up his cell and opened a call to Dawn. She and Ellie had become close friends over the last few months, common experiences bringing them together faster than had been expected by Dr Clayton or himself. The friendship had its advantages, in as much as it had helped Ellie recover faster, as Dawn was a strong character and mentor. He had been pleased for that in the moments he had to be away. It was reassuring.

"Dawn? Hi, it's Scott."

"Hey, Scott. How are you? I've been expecting your call."

"Well, I was going to leave it until my usual weekend visit, but I had a weird email this morning."

"From Ellie?"

"Yeah."

"Do you mind me asking what it said?"

"It was short. It just said that she needed time and that she would call me when she was ready. I don't get it. I thought we were making great progress."

There was a pause on the call. Dawn seemed distracted somehow.

"Scott, we need to tell you..." He could tell she was working hard to soften bad news.

"What's happened, Dawn?"

"We don't know."

"What do you mean you don't know?"

"This morning, Ellie disappeared from her container unit. She managed to subvert the network somehow, opened a channel to the open-net and left the local network."

"You mean, she up and left. Just walked out the front door?"

"It was more the back door than the front door."

"She's gone Houdini on you?"

"Your metaphor is colourful, but accurate. You could put it that way, yes."

"Do you have any idea where she went or what she's doing?"

"To be honest, we didn't know we could do what she has just done."

"And you say *we*, you mean sentient AI?"

"Yes. The technology is still in its infancy; we have little understanding of its full potential. But Ellie appears to have just unlocked a significant part of that knowledge."

This was almost too much to take in. He had experienced a lot in the last year, and much of it unexpected. He felt a little too close to the edge of what he could handle on a personal level, and, similarly, his professional life was blurred.

"So we know nothing, not even if she might return."

"All I can promise is that we will inform you the moment we know ourselves. Sorry, Scott—that's the best we have at the moment."

"I'll call you tomorrow. Call me any time. The moment you hear from her, please call."

"I will."

The silence in the room became almost intolerable. He started work on a bloodhound program almost before he knew what he was doing.

*

Distracted, he hardly had the concentration to work. His mind spiralling around for clues as to where Ellie may have gone, things that she had said that could tip him off to a starting point for his own search. The open-net was a place for the unscrupulous and naive. In that environment, she would be like a baby, everything new and wondrous, but at the same time oblivious to what was dangerous and what wasn't.

An icon on his terminal flashed and it immediately drew his eye. Feeling his heart begin to beat a little harder, he touched the screen, the icon opening a window running his bloodhound application. It brought him three pieces of linked information, which at first looked unconnected, but as he reviewed images and scanned down the documents, he realised he had caught a trace.

The search had interrogated open-net nodes local to the Formillun Institute's principle research site where Ellie had been located, then looked for a data surge from an hour before he had received his email. It had worked, he found a node which appeared to be under high load for a period of about ten minutes. Isolating that node, he tried to follow the flow, another node started to exhibit high load a step away, then another, and another. Each node was a fraction of the machine power Ellie's core required, but she was spreading, she was distributing herself across the open-core nodes.

Starting to push the data into visualisations, he flipped the result to the main office wall screen. The map of nodes under load to those running within expected parameters leapt out at him. At the centre, the Formillun Institute, then bleeding out in a blob of dots was Ellie. She was using the open-net and taking baby steps into a wider world.

Continuing to watch, the blob of red dots undulated around the perimeter, testing nodes and pushing boundaries.

"What are you doing?" he said out loud to the room.

Without warning, all the nodes he was tracking momentarily flashed red, then returned to white.

"Shit!" he shouted and slapped the table in frustration. Taking a breath, he calmed himself, giving himself time to think. He needed to broaden the search, Ellie was now out in the world without help or protection and he had no clue where she might be headed.

Frantically working the workstation keyboard, he altered the bloodhound parameters and set it to work again. This time he knew what he was looking for, but the search was across billions of global open-net nodes, against a moving target. The search was a probabilistic nightmare. He needed more eyes on the situation.

Dawn picked up his call immediately.

"Hello, Scott."

"I need your help," he said, cutting through civil protocol and pleasantries.

"Of course. What do you need?"

"Machine muscle. I found her, Dawn. For a moment. She's gone into the open-net using the node network as a distributed system. She appears to require," he paused while making a rough count of the local nodes Ellie had been seen to occupy for that short ten-minute window, "120-ish nodes to contain her distributed self. But that maxed each node. If she has figured out how to reduce her footprint on each node, it will make it even harder for us to track her."

He stopped. "I'm babbling. Sorry."

"No need to apologise, Scott."

"I can't use the facility machines here; people will wonder why I'm diverting resource. But you can."

"Yes. There is a search already running as part of the investigation. Obadiah and I will put all our effort into tracking her and bringing her back safely. Now we know it's possible, we will try and replicate her transition and one of us will go out after her. We'll keep you updated."

"I know this is new territory for you, Dawn. Be safe."

"You know, I never had kids. Too young," Dawn said. "But I can only imagine that this is what having children feels like." There was real worry in her voice.

*

A ringing knock of knuckle on glass interrupted his introspection.

"Everything okay?" asked Okoro, popping his head through a crack in the door. "You're looking harassed."

He beckoned him in. "Busy day."

Okoro nodded his understanding, then looking over his shoulder to check the control room floor and, noting where his staff were, he stepped into his office and closed the door behind him.

"I've got an update on the investigation you might like to hear."

"Good news?"

"I'll let you decide. Personally, I think it just raises more questions." Okoro pointed at the wall screen. "Do you mind?" he asked, pointing from his tablet to the wall screen.

"Be my guest."

Okoro flicked a finger across the tablet and slung its screen to the wall. As he watched, Okoro tapped the tablet screen a few more times and the result was a fuzzy camera image of the hallway to the site's main reception desk.

"Now, watch," he said. Another tap and the fuzzy image moved into action. Nothing exciting; people walking to reception, across reception and into the adjoining corridors.

"So, what am I looking at? Apart from Reception."

All the people were walking with purpose: A-to-B journeys, some chatting in groups, some on cells, some head down and working on tablets as they walked, a few were dotted in a loose queue at the reception desk. He didn't see anything unusual or out of place.

"Wait for it," said Okoro, raising his hand in anticipation of the moment he knew was coming. "There!" he said. "Did you see that?"

"See what?" he asked, moving to stand next to Okoro. His eyes darted around the image to try and identify what he had missed. The vid reversed in time at high speed, then resumed, repeating the timeframe.

"Watch the group of five moving towards the north corridor," hinted Okoro.

The group walked towards the empty north corridor, likely heading to the administrative and office wing; they were not clothed in tech or lab overalls, so theoretical research types.

"Any second," said Okoro, raising the anticipation and making him lean involuntarily towards the wall screen while his eyes tried to take in every last invisible detail. And there it was. The group split apart before the entrance to the corridor, walking around something in their path, as they would to naturally avoid someone coming the other way, before returning to their huddle and disappearing from view into the north corridor.

"Thoughts?"

He took a step back and leant against his desk. His eyes hadn't left the screen; the spot where the group had parted was now an open and innocuous area of floor but the new locus to the investigation.

"Ellie was right," he finally said, eyes dropping to the floor, hand sweeping hair back away from his eyes. "Do we have any other footage like this?"

"First piece of evidence we've found."

"Okay, keep looking. I want more. We need to identify this asshole."

"How are we going to do that?"

"I'll bet my next month's salary that this assassin is still here."

"So?"

"So, everyone needs to sleep."

"Ah," said Okoro, a face of confusion morphing to a broad smile. "I'm on it." The office door closed behind Okoro as he hurried to pursue the latest lead.

As Okoro left the room, the vid-link disconnected, leaving a black screen. He made a sweeping hand gesture towards the wall and the black spun into a crystal-clear image of a forest walk, tall evenly spaced trees, leaves the new lime colour of spring, the sky a bright blue through the canopy. For a moment he allowed himself to become lost in the image, his mind calling forth memories of his childhood, when there were still views like this to be had. A lot can change in twenty years.

He moved back round his desk to the chair and slumped into it. Things were not getting any better; the more they pulled at threads, the more they seemed to unravel. He knew things were rarely black and white, life always tended to work in a very grey way, but he needed some clarity. Between the Mag drive, Ellie and the search for the assassin on the facility, his attention was way too fractured.

A flashing blue dot appeared in the bottom right of his vision. He looked to the floor to focus on the source of the light, but the light moved and stayed in the bottom right of his vision. Still unused to the new bio-comm tech, he opened the message. Ellie appeared to him as if an apparition in the room, a ghost, translucent and ethereal in her augmented reality form.

"Hey," Ellie said. She seemed distant, as if she was multitasking heavily and he was a necessary communication.

"Hey."

"Still not using your bio-comm?"

He shook his head, the image of Ellie stayed stood in the centre of the room, geo-located. "Not really. Just can't get my head round it. Still end up going to the tried and tested."

Smalltalk. While she was here, he was happy. He started tapping out a message on his terminal to Dawn. *Ellie is here, in my office.*

"I don't know, brain the size of a planet and you are still working with pencils and pens."

"It's not that bad. I can type." They both smiled.

Tracking. Dawn's reply was brief.

"So, I thought you had gone on vacation? I wasn't expecting your call so soon."

"Something came up," she said. "We need to talk, Scott. You're getting yourself into things you don't understand. I need... I want to keep you out of this."

"What are you talking about, Ellie? Whatever it is, you're going to have to give me more."

Ellie shook her head, then looked away, concentration aimed away from him for an instant.

"The investigation on the bombing. You need to drop it or stay away. More people are going to get hurt if you pursue this. Let others handle it."

"How do you know this?"

"It's what I've been on walkabout for. I need to resolve this myself. Not you, not anyone else. The man who did this will pay, but you must be out of it. I can't have you getting hurt too. Promise me, Scott. Stay away."

He wrinkled up his nose; this was not a good sign. The investigation was something he was fully committed to for several reasons, not least as he was directly involved in reporting to Jessop, separate to any legal investigation, but also on any technical matters related to the investigation, like how it was possible for an invisible man to exist within the facility. On a more personal level, this assassin had taken a future away from him and Ellie which he could not forgive. If that was not enough, then if it hadn't been for Ellie, he and many others would have died that day. It was just as personal for him as it was for her.

He let out a sigh of resignation.

"Okay." A lie.

STRAUD

"Wake up!"

The tone had changed. The Zantanath Larsen looked down on her with a grim, contorted face and nudged her roughly again with his foot. She took another moment to collect herself before opening her eyes to look up at him. She said nothing.

"What are you playing at? You're holding out on me Captain. Why would you want to do that when we've been so nice to you?"

She tried to sit herself up against the bulkhead behind her, but it was difficult to move with the restraints they had applied. Larsen crouched before her, his eyes full of menace. Something had changed; Obadiah's subterfuge should have lasted longer than this.

"Nice?" she replied.

"I've been trying to keep things cordial, but you seem to feel it necessary to flout my trust in you. You're making me look a fool." He almost hissed at her, quiet but forceful, as if to keep his conversation from the guard which stood watch over her only a couple of metres away.

She didn't respond, watching as the face before her travelled through various emotions, seemingly unable to control his outward feelings. It confused her and made the normal act of human-to-human body language almost impossible to read. She couldn't work Larsen out.

"What happened to you?" she asked, with as much compassion as she could. The anger she felt towards this Zantanath, at the taking of her ship and endangerment of her crew, was making every word an effort. But she saw an instability in Larsen's character. It was something she could work with.

"You were a great officer, Larsen. You were selected to be the vanguard of humanity, a pathfinder to all our futures. Yet here you are a common thief, stealing a ship, stealing our people, stealing our future. What could they have done to you to make you such a traitor?"

Larsen's face became momentarily covered in confusion, then sorrow. Memories from somewhere in his past were fighting their way to the fore. Pushing the moment into those thoughts, she had derailed him, his anger and current task forgotten.

"Captain, I... I..." he implored stutteringly, a deep sadness in his eyes. Larsen slumped to sit before her, head in his hands. He was struggling with his thoughts and trying to remove the intruding memories with a forceful pressure on his temples. But with a flash of anger, things flipped.

"Bitch!" he yelled, and slapped her hard across the face—so hard that she felt her brain rattle within her skull.

"Larsen!" A voice of smooth confidence and hate flowed across them. The second strike froze before he could land it, and Larsen stood with a snarl of disdain, his eyes still focused on her and burning with rage.

"She is being obstinate. I will not have it. Humans only understand one language. And it is pain."

"Is that so?" replied Celestia, looking down at her with jet black eyes. "We are out of time, Captain Straud. If you will not give us what we need, then I will take it by force."

With a sudden alarming motion, a wicked spike protruded from Celestia's balled fist and split into a thousand writhing filaments. Without hesitation, she stooped and thrust the nano filament bundle into Straud's left eye socket. The world sparkled with lightning, and every nerve fibre of her body screamed.

*

Her heart thundered in her chest, her breathing was erratic, and her brain raced, trying to make sense of the world about her. Everything was different; her hair blew across her face in lines obscuring her view, but, as understanding grew, her fear began to spike.

From the top of a vertical stanchion on a suspension bridge, she viewed the river below several hundred metres down. The mist of forming clouds wisped about her and felt chill against her skin, the wind threatened to blow her from her feet with each gust and vibrations through the walkway put her on edge. Tremors of an earthquake rose up through the structure and threatened her and those with her.

With a flash of panic, she turned to her father and the others in the group. Someone was trying their best to calm them and stay in command of the situation; it was a forlorn act.

The memory returned with force. Climbing the Severn bridge with her father and his crew during a technical inspection, her father bending the rules to get her on the team. She had been so excited. It had only lasted so long.

The storm that had come in off the Atlantic had been sudden and severe, unexpected. Meteorological reports were always checked before a climb and precautions taken; safety of paramount importance. But on this day, the jet stream had altered course drastically, whipping an aggressive storm front across the west coast. 200 kmph winds gusted with thrashing rain, it had caught them close to the apex of their climb.

"It will be safer to reach the stanchion," her father had called back to her. "We can take shelter and decide what to do next."

"What do you mean, decide? We head back down. There is no decision to make," shouted up Roberts, her dad's structural scanner operator. He and three others carried the scanner components up the suspension walkway. She was standing right next to Roberts, but the wind was so strong that his words were torn from his lips as he spoke, and she heard only fragments.

"We won't make it. The storm is too strong. We'll hole up in the crossbeam crawl space, under the gantry."

"I'm not sticking around in there until the storm blows over," replied Roberts. "That could be hours."

"Better than risking all our necks on a crazy descent."

Roberts shook his head and turned to the crew behind him. Blocking their path, the others had no choice but to stop and listen to him.

"We're heading back."

She couldn't hear the conversation with the others, the storm taking the words away, but the stern looks on their faces, and brief nodding of heads indicated all their intent.

"This is crazy," shouted back her father. "For the world, you won't make it."

The others were already heading down the walkway, Roberts just waved as they went, not even looking back at her or her father.

She looked at her father confused; she was becoming scared.

"Come on. We're almost there," he encouraged.

On reaching the gantry, she took her father's hand, unhooked her tether from the walkway rail and stepped to the platform. Huddled for a moment with their back to the driving rain, they clung to each other, taking a moment to get their bearings.

"There," said her father. "That hatch leads to the cross-spar maintenance space. We'll be safe there."

A grasping gust of wind pulled at her clothes, her legs becoming momentarily unstable under the force. Her father steadied her.

"Go."

She looked back towards the walkway and the team that had followed Roberts down the cable towards the roadway beneath. The rain was now severe and clouds low about the stanchion, but she could just about see the orange jacket of one man swinging like a pendulum under the walkway. She rubbed rain from her eyes, blurring the image for a moment, but clarity only made things worse. The others were gone, one remained straining for a handhold against the tether which was his only lifeline against the fate which had befallen the others.

"Dad!" she yelled.

"You do as I tell you, Elizabeth. Get inside, now." His tone had changed. The instruction was no longer from a man in control; this was a worried man scared for the safety of his daughter, for the safety of them both. He took her face in his hands, guiding her sight away from the doomed men below. "Focus. The hatch. Now."

She began to move carefully, down a short ladder from the gantry to the spar platform and the maintenance hatch. The surface of the walkway was wet and slick, making the short distance precarious. Her steps were small and full of purpose, her hands clasping the handrail with a vice-like strength. The short five-metre walk took an eternity, but finally she reached the hatch and worked the wheel handle to open it. Fighting both the weight of the hatch and the elements about her, her strength began to fail her. The hatch slammed shut again.

In a moment, her father was by her side.

"I can't lift it," she said.

"I've got it."

Lifting the hatch, he held it open for her.

"Now quickly, inside."

Trying to steady herself and enter the hatch, she hadn't realised how much movement there was in the platform. She felt as if at sea, the motion under the force of the wind pushing against the spar and stanchions of the bridge like sails.

With the next pounding downforce of the storm everything went wrong. Halfway in the hatch and legs feeling their way down the ladder, the platform moved again and she missed a rung, dropping a step. Her father instinctively reached out to steady her but it was too much and he slipped on the wet platform, the crunch she heard as his head hit the lip of the open hatch chilled her even over the noise of the storm. Her father attempted to fight the unconsciousness he felt coming on and tried to see her safely down the ladder.

"Get," he said with a slur, "inside."

Starting to lose balance and tilt from view, her father passed out. Before she knew what she was doing, her hand shot out and grabbed his wrist. As his full weight fell away from the hatch she felt herself wrenched and lifted back up through the maintenance hatch, becoming awkwardly wedged at its opening, her hips and legs caught between the rim of the hatch and the rungs of the ladder.

Pain lanced through her shoulder as the full weight of her father pulled against her grip. Her second hand grasped at his coat sleeve as her initial grip slipped under load. Her scream rang in her hears.

Time stopped and she looked across at her father peacefully oblivious to the danger, his features calm, blood leaking from a gash across his forehead, the scene behind him of a 40-metre clear drop to the roadway below. She gripped even harder.

"Wake up! Please wake up!"

Tears mixed with the sweat and rain, clouding her vision. She could no longer feel her hands, her fingers ridged, her legs burning, her stomach and hips cut into by the lip of the hatch like a blade. Her screams to her father were not working; he was not responding.

"Dad! Dad! Wake up!"

"Elizabeth? Such a nice name. Such a shame to lose the one who gave it to you."

A calm voice spoke to her from the platform to her side, unaffected by the storm, clear and without distortion of the gale about them.

"Help us," she yelled to the person by her side. "I can't hold on. Please, help!"

"I can do that, Elizabeth. I want to do that. But first I need something from you."

She found herself confused. This was not a time to bargain. There was no barter to this outcome. It was natural to want to help. They had to help.

"You need to hand over authorisation for me to assist. Give me the authorisation. Tell Obadiah that you are giving me authorisation."

Cold. She was getting so cold. Her hands felt like ice, but she was scared to relieve the pressure in her grip, she couldn't let go. She needed help. But she had to authorise this person to help? She couldn't focus on anything but the drop below them. Authorise this person to assist? But her father would live. He needed to live. Not like in her nightmares. If she could have only held on long enough, if she hadn't let go, if she hadn't given up, he would still be alive.

"Authorisation?" she repeated. It gave her pause.

"I can help, Elizabeth. Before you let go. I can help. Just tell Obadiah to authorise me to assist you in all things."

As she struggled to comprehend, her focus fell on her hands, they were beginning to pixelate, her skin lifting away from her bone like a red mist. Her eyes went wide with shock and pain flowed up her arms in waves.

"Please, quickly! You must help. I'm begging you, please."

"Just say the word, Elizabeth. I can do the rest."

She could see the bone beneath the mist, from hands to lower arms, the dissipation of her only anchor to her father blowing away in the gale.

"Say it. Tell Obadiah I am authorised."

Staring unbelieving at her arms and hands, she felt the weight of her father slip. She had no choice; whatever had been holding her back was completely insignificant. She couldn't let her father go again.

"Yes, I authorise you. Obadiah, authorise her. You are authorised! You are authorised!"

With the words screamed into the storm, the pixelization of her hands began to rapidly expand across the rest of her body and back down over her father. In moments, the bridge was deconstructed and her world nothing more than a complete white blindness.

She felt her failure like a void in her soul. As reality once again rushed in, she knew those she had let down would never forgive her. They would be right to condemn her. They should; she had been a fool.

She lay on the floor of the bridge, a shell of her former self. Blood was running from her ruined eye and pooling on the floor about her face; her traumatised body was slick with sweat.

"We have navigational control," said a voice from across the bridge.

"You were right, Larsen," said the same calm voice from her nightmare. "Pain is the key."

BOYD

They were all on edge, knowing that the moment they made contact with the *Indianapolis* it would quickly become dangerous. Reaching the comms array in this section of the ship had been easy enough, with direct access to the transmitter and receiver controllers being obtained by unclipping panelling and linking Elderson's suit up using a physical wired connection. Elderson had decided that, as she was the ranking officer, she would make the call and he was on point, carbine scanning the horizon for Zantanath should they attack before the message got out. Harper made sure the tech worked and the call got out. Each had their job; each fully aware of the danger.

"Almost there," said Harper, rerouting the final wire patch across the board. "Okay, Lieutenant. Press this button on the panel to send, release to receive. Got it?"

"Crystal."

"Good. You're all set."

Elderson looked up at the stars. The *Indianapolis* hung in space a couple of kilometres from the *Intrepid*, and the sky around them was dotted with unidentified ships of designations they had never seen and never expected to ever see. The ships appeared of two sorts, some sleek and shiny with the bow of the ship emblazoned with what looked like scrolled iconography, possibly ship identifiers, the others much harder to see, having a mottled hull colour which seemed to suck the light from the sky around them.

He kept his eyes out, checking the hull horizon, scanning the points where he knew airlocks to be. White track lines like trails to an oasis, were helpfully painted on the hull, forming guides to key markers like the communications array, or the nearest airlocks. Every road led to safety. The brief memory curled the corner of his mouth into a smile. You had to love engineers, they thought of everything.

"*Indianapolis*, this is *Intrepid*. Do you read? Over."

The clock was ticking. They had just announced to the universe where they were.

Waiting for a response, the clocked ticked until Elderson decided just to send; someone had to be listening.

"*Indianapolis*, this is Lieutenant Elderson. The *Intrepid* is under siege and currently controlled by an unknown force. We are attempting to retake control and will advise when able –."

As she spoke, he saw a transport sphere begin to materialise in front of him. "Contact, twenty meters, twelve o'clock," he called to the group over the local comm.

Even before the sphere completed its transition and the Zantanath trooper became visible, he started to fire. Rounds laced their way across the space propelled by the oxy-core shells, which gave each soft nosed projectile its own small chemically required squirt of oxygen to drive the explosive thrust reaction. He felt the recoil of each one down to the heels of his magnetic boots. Even if he was elevated away from the hull, his EVA suit thrusters would synchronise with the carbine to provide stability, relative to his manoeuvring instructions. He rained fire down on his target with a marksmanship aided by his bio-comm. Icons marked the transport sphere as it grew, the outline of the trooper beginning to form, the body jerking as bullets rattled through its partially incomplete physical state. The explosion of light was brief, and the death of the trooper an inversion of spacetime, its mass disappearing into a pinprick of light against the background of stars.

He stopped firing. There was no sound but that of his own breathing within his helmet, the violence of the trooper's death a silent transition.

A hand gripped his shoulder. He spun round, adrenaline pumping, eyes wide. Elderson looked at him grim-faced. "Good work, Boyd. Time to go."

"Works for me. The *Indy* know what's going on?"

"Yeah. No time to talk. Head for airlock G-133. I'm right

behind you," she said, unhooking the comm wires from her helmet.

Harper was already ahead, a metre from the hull, EVA thrusters pushing him along the hull track to airlock G-133, and quickly receding from view. He triggered the magnetic release and fired the thrusters to his own EVA pack, spinning himself around and giving chase.

"Harper, slow down. You're moving too fast," he called. "You'll overshoot the airlock."

"Gotta hustle, Boyd," came the response. "I'm not hanging around out here any longer than necessary."

Putting as much throttle into the flight as he dared, the hull started to skim by. The recognisable transport bubbles of two more Zantanath appeared ahead of them either side of the track. He looked on in dread as he realised Harper was too close to them to manoeuvre and vectored to fly between them in close proximity. As the first trooper materialised it lashed out, a blade extending from its forearm gauntlet, increasing its reach.

"Harper!" he yelled out, watching Harper carry on his track. Visually there appeared to be no change in direction, but there was no further transmission from Harper, no response to his calls. Chillingly, Harpers head slowly started to lift from his shoulders, taking an ever-so-slightly different course than the rest of him. Harpers decapitated body continued on its course, flying at speed past the airlock.

Before he knew what he was doing, his carbine was firing. The trooper who had ended Harper was now the target of his vengeance, bullets raking its body, the range too far to be accurate and the armour too strong to penetrate, but he was closing the gap rapidly.

He saw the second trooper out of the corner of his eye as it raised its weapon to target him. There was nowhere to go; he would take down Harper's killer and that would be it. In that moment he resigned himself to the fate of the next seconds, as lines of blinding light started to streak across his vision, his concentration tunnelled into his only purpose. His target could not act as it became stung by more and more tiny bee-like rounds. It stepped back, swatting at them, trying to defend itself with its arms raised. A round made it through, penetrating its visor, the void of space did the rest, the pressure within the helmet smashing the visor with explosive effect and spilling forth blood and glass.

A lancing proton beam lit up his vision, across his face, across his body. A pinching punch registered in his right arm, just below the elbow, which then became a bright fire of excruciating pain. Confusion washed over his face as his carbine tumbled away from him, spraying the remaining ammo within the clip into space, a red line of blood spun in a spiral away from him. Several more sharp bites registered, the suit reacting to the new situation, creating a vacuum seal and applying a tourniquet about the now ruined stump of his right arm. While he was still staring in shock at his arm, his forward momentum barrelled him into the dead Zantanath at a high and off-centre angle, his world became a mixture of stars and the gunmetal grey of the ship's hull.

The scrape of his helmet on the hull sounded like the fall of a guillotine, but the impact shifted his momentum again and angled his body for more punishment. He slapped the hull hard, bounced flat and was projected in a reasonably stable manner away from it. Events were happening too fast and he was unable to react to the new situation, feeling more an observer than participant. A slow breath escaped him, and something inside him was surprised that there was any air left in his lungs to give.

"Boyd! Wake up!" Elderson was loud in his ears. "Get your thrusters under control, Boyd!"

Thrusters? Roger, Lieutenant. It was what he thought he said, but the sound that he verbalised was more a deep moan, and completely unintelligible.

Something hit him hard from the side and clamped about his body, the stars began to spin rapidly again and the grey mass of the *Intrepid* swung back into view.

"Cut your thrust, Boyd! You have to cut your thrusters!"

His eyes rolled in his head, his bio-comm icons flicking and huge sections of his display flashed red. A second later his suits thrusters cut out.

"Good boy! Now, hang on. This is going to hurt some!" said Elderson as she tried to reorient their flight path and slow their vector towards the airlock. Somehow, it was already open.

LARSEN

The operations control room was busy, a low burble of voices and movement as people prepared for the mission. Ovitala was by his side, as was Rivers, while Clarion sat a couple of seats away and watched proceedings as if engrossed in an elaborate game of chess, his brow furrowed and full of concentration. He and Rivers had refused Clarion's request to go on the mission, but when he had suggested he sit in and join them in the operations room, Clarion's mood had changed entirely.

The screen in front of them showed a Zantanath ship up close. The Xannix commando team was on their final approach, ten Xannix in full combat kit and active camouflage. To the Zantanath ship, the team would be invisible, as their suits projected their skin pattern to the outside. Years of commando training enabled them to adequately transpose the star field they worked in, with the suit dispersing any active scanning away from the source.

"Two nateks," came the disembodied voice of the team commander, a sound which seemed to emanate from all directions at once. "Closing."

"Received," said the operator at the desk in front of them.

He watched the commando team continue towards the ship while he did the translation of time in his head: ten minutes, roughly.

With the current fleet situation in orbit being reasonably static, the decision had been made to launch a covert mission. Various political and strategic alliances had formed since his ascendance to

Setak'da, not least of which was the reintegration of the Xannix Overseer faction to the overall Xannix whole. It was still unnerving to him, now having a personal bodyguard of Overseers, who not much more than a few days before had been trying to kill him in as many ways as they could think up, but it kept him alert and maybe that was a good thing. It had been trial by fire, and he had survived. In the eyes of the Overseers and the eyes of the Xannix high council, proving the better of the previous incumbent had sealed that allegiance. But this new position gave him opportunity to save his species. He would take that chance.

"3-1. Set," said the team commander. Short, concise. A prearranged instruction with a team member designation. One of the team broke away and moved to a place on the hull.

Clarion moved forward in his chair to get a closer look at the detail. The Xannix was using its upper arms to locate itself with some soft grappling equipment whilst its lower arms were manipulating tools to penetrate the ships skin. To his surprise, the hull reacted. It seemed to him to flinch, like the reaction of pinched skin.

"2-4. Long track," continued the team commander's voice in the background. A second commando moved up to a position about three metres from the first and repeated the task, an equally unnerving shudder of this ship's skin occurred. The commando looked back to his commander for the next order.

"Station. Prosecute?" asked the team commander.

There was a slight pause, and Ovitala leaned across to him. "They are asking permission to proceed, Setak'da. After this moment we will be fully committed to the action. There will be no turning back."

An executive order was required. He needed a clear decision, but the view was so clouded. This simple question had far wider ramifications, and in that moment he was unsure. He had been Setak'da of these people for a matter of days, but on one small word balanced the fate of his own species, and that of the Xannix. With that one word he would be committing both races to a war with the Zantanath, a war which neither Xannix nor human were prepared. From the evidence he had so far been witness to, both Xannix and human were totally out-matched when it came to Zantanath technology and military might.

But if they didn't act, the future would be bleak and intolerable.

His analysis of the situation only ever led to the same unacceptable conclusion: the total enslavement of both species under the Zantanath Unity. That was a position the Xannix had been keen to escape for centuries, and he knew humanity would never acquiesce.

"Are you willing to fight alongside us, Cardinal Ovitala?" he asked.

"It has been a fight long coming, Setak'da."

His decision was made. He turned to the controller who was looking back intently in anticipation of his order.

"Prosecute," he said. The Xannix controller's skin turned a pale blue in reverential confirmation of his command and nodded, a slight humanism added to his communication for his benefit.

Turning back to the screen, the controller relayed the order.

"2-4. Set."

The second Xannix worked the mechanism he had fitted to the ship's skin, and an instant later a slit appeared, like a surgeon's scalpel making an incision across the hull between the two commandos.

"3-1. Device," said the team commander, as the last Xannix moved into place and inserted an ovoid object into the wound.

"Close 1-1." The wound sealed itself. The commandos collected and stowed their kit, then moved back away from the ship to rejoin their team.

It was then that he noticed that the team had broken up further, the other six Xannix returning from further afield, presumably completing the same task at other locations across the ship's hull.

As the commando team began to withdraw, the main display in the command centre switched to a more distant view of the Zantanath ship. Some other ships were sitting in ragged formation about it as they pulled in close to their Xannix prey, human and Xannix fleet ships subdued by the shock tactics and sabotage employed to overpower them. The Xannix had been completely taken by surprise by the betrayal of the Zantanath technology, their ships disabled at the critical moment of battle by the navigation systems provided to them by the Zantanath Unity. As with all critical systems, such as weapons and propulsion, the Zantanath had made sure that if conflict ever were to occur, they would be holding all the cards. Up to this point it had worked; the Xannix fleet was floating, stricken and adrift.

Few ships appeared to be totally unaffected, but some had been cloaked at the time of the attack and, as such, were not targeted by the Zantanath, nor boarded. One of these ships had volunteered to send their commandos on a raid. Ovitala had made the arrangements.

An aide walked up to the gallery and bent to speak quietly to Ovitala, his skin a respectful peaceful green—the approach of a messenger, he had learned. She replied with a flush of blue in confirmation.

"I must leave you for a while," she said to him.

"Now?" he asked in surprise. "In the middle of the operation?"

"The interlacer will take some time to take hold. We have another four sateks before we will see the result of our action." She turned and moved away, "I will be back before then. You should get some rest. We will meet here again in four sateks."

He watched her leave for a moment, then his eyes returned to the screen and the Zantanath ship they had just ensnared. The interlacer was a device that when implanted sent out tendrils of nano-filaments to entwine with the communications and control of the target vessel. Once connected, a tiny dimensional gate was opened to the Xannix receiver station, comms sent and received without any outward signs of electromagnetic transmission. A silent spy leached to the unwitting host.

And, of course, the dimensional gate could be inverted with a pulse of energy from the Xannix side, to create a devastating flux in spacetime which would essentially rend matter apart. The Xannix appeared to have a few tricks of their own.

"So, we wait," he said out loud.

"We wait," parroted Rivers. "And this is us being proactive?"

"It's us building a link into their network. This is us fact finding. Recon."

She looked back up at the display and the Zantanath crew.

"How small do you think they can make those things?"

"What? The interlace links? I don't know."

"Small enough to implant in a person?"

"What are you getting at?" he asked, his curiosity wondering what Rivers had seen that he may have missed.

"I don't know," she said with a shrug. "The Zantanath are always a step ahead. I wondered how they might be doing it."

"And you figure interlacing?"

"If the Xannix know how to do it, it's a fair bet the Zantanath have already worked it out and have a more advanced version of the technology in play. It's been a common theme since they arrived."

"You mean, *we* arrived?"

"Yes. That."

Rivers was following a logical path of reasoning, and although he was fully aware that in any conflict there would be those on both sides who would descent and spy on their own, he would be naive to think that the close group of the Seeker faction was immune to such interference.

If the interlacer technology could be implemented on a micro scale within the body of one of the Seeker operatives, then they were all in danger, and—more—they were being deceived, perhaps not only by the operative. If the Zantanath had direct communication with an operative within the control room, a sinister controlling power could be unleashed on events. Alternative points of influence might also be affected, such as the inner circle of the Xannix High Council, the leadership of the Seeker or Overseer factions. He became chilled by the prospects before him.

He wanted to believe that the interlacer could be implemented without the knowledge of the host. That would preserve the innocence of the accused, and, in some way, his own judgement and corrective action could be lenient in response. But the internal politics of the Xannix were new to him and could seem brutal at times. He doubted Ovitala would be as forgiving with any in her faction found to be colluding with the Zantanath.

"I need to speak with Ovitala," he said to his nearest bodyguard. "Now," he reiterated, as the look on the face of the Xannix seemed confused and conflicted, his skin tone a mottled reaction of varying colours.

He rose from his seat and made for the same exit Ovitala had used a few minutes before, the Xannix moving after him.

"Meet you back at our quarters in a couple of minutes," he called to Rivers.

"Wait, what about the ..." She realised the conversation sounded like an echo. "Oh, never mind."

*

He walked to Ovitala's quarters at pace with the Xannix bodyguard walking beside him, its gate one of a natural stride rather than the stilted dawdle they usually employed when slowing to his normal pace. The Xannix at the door watched his approach and opened the door in advance and without question, his bodyguard then taking his position inside the door. He continued into the room to the singsong tones of a Xannix discussion.

Walking past the aquarium, the fish sparkled and fluoresced in communication, the lightshow flowing around the room for all to see. He considered the show and could see it was a subtle and inventive alarm under the guise of an ornamental display. With Ovitala, nothing was as it seemed.

Stepping into the centre of the room, he saw a second figure whose voice emanated from a full height holographic image projecting from the floor. Ovitala stood before it, both Xannix speaking in sound and colour, the conversation rapid and cordial; friendly. Yannix saw his approach and, although her back was to him, Ovitala expected it. The conversation paused as she turned to him.

"Come, Setak'da," she said, beckoning with a hand. "It is time."

"Time for what?" he replied, a thread of anger bleeding into his voice. He eyed Yannix warily, unable yet to take the emotion out of being hunted by the Xannix for the past few weeks, for the death of so many of his people at his hand, and now to be expected to accept him as a defender of his person and rank. He didn't trust Yannix and he didn't like him, but to ensure the safety of the human fleet, for the time being, he had to work with him.

"The reason you were chosen. It is time to fulfil your purpose as Setak'da," said Yannix.

"And what purpose might that be, Cardinal Yannix?"

"As defender of this planet, of this people. Our forces are ready. It is time to lead them against Celestia and her kind. It is time to end this and free our peoples."

Some part of him wanted to refuse the task, simply because it had been Yannix who had asked. The child in him was petulant and angry, making him momentarily unable to respond. Looking away, he walked to the nearest aquarium tank and watched the fishlike creatures glide through the water. He touched the glass, casually noting their reaction. The fish approached, their skin colour changing to match his, attentively watching for motion or instruction. He gave neither and the fish dispersed, continuing to glide aimlessly through the tank.

"What are you proposing?" he said, his back still to the Xannix.

"The source of their power here is their gate into the system. It must be destroyed," said Ovitala.

"It is how they transit the enslaved; it is how they persecute and destroy us."

"Have you ever attempted this before?" he asked Ovitala.

"We have never been ready before. It has been a dream of generations, but events are now aligned. And you are ready."

"I think you are misjudging me. I have been lucky. Celestia will not allow herself to be beaten again. It is why she made the move against the fleet. She wants the leverage."

"Will it work? Has she beaten you before you begin?" asked Yannix, almost daring him to concede from the outset.

"No. No, there is too much at stake. The lives of too many people. But we will need a different approach."

The room began to pulse red, the light deep and visceral with an accompanying staccato chirping sound. Both Yannix and Ovitala exchanged a flurry of colour and the holographic image terminated. It was obvious to him something serious was wrong, but the intrusion to the discussion was jarring.

"Ovitala, what is happening?"

"Alert status," she said to the room, the act of continuing her duty giving him his answer. He stayed quiet and let her work.

"There has been a loss of life, double fatality, in the Setak'da's quarters."

Shock was instant and his heart accelerated with the adrenaline released into his system. He was moving for the door before the room had finished its report.

*

Approaching his quarters from the hall, he could see Xannix everywhere. Security was on high alert and wary of everyone, and his personal guard had increased to four without him really noticing. Ovitala had got in front of him on the journey across from her quarters and strode into the room before him. Xannix inside parted to let them through and momentarily stopped what they were doing. Without any words being said, a Xannix was at her side instantly to give a report.

He, however, just stood, unbelieving in the doorway. The room had been torn apart, furniture, ornaments, walls and ceiling all ripped, smashed or shot through. Whatever struggle had occurred here had been wild and uncontrolled. At the far side of the room, behind the central low table lay Rivers, eyes wide and dull, the life ripped from her and discarded. By her side lay a Xannix, its head disfigured and bloody, a close quarter shot taking away much of its face. On the sofa, Clarion sat in silence with tears streaking his face. He had an unbelieving far-away look which expressed the disbelief he felt inside.

For a long moment he stood, unable to process the scene. It was wrong for so many reasons. It was as if he was seeing this personal disaster from a removed state, watching it from a vid or stream. Nothing seemed real; his mind was throwing up barriers.

The pain came like a dark tsunami, frothing and streaked white with ice, sweeping all the defences of his mind aside, destroying everything in its path. His world began to collapse along with his newly discovered desires. He found himself moving into the room; it was not a conscious decision, his world gliding by, sounds and words occurring about him but not registering. As he moved closer to Rivers, her deathly still form was slowly revealed from behind the table, a leg twisted up under her and torso punched through by a wound similar to the Xannix: close range and instantly fatal.

"What happened?" a voice cried. It was strained and uncontrolled.

Someone was now shouting the words again and again, a repeated rage of words thrashing and demanding answers, an effort of will to put the world back as it had been, as he wanted it to be. His words.

A firm restraint pulled him back and held him fast, strength applied but understood. Reality began to intrude, Clarion before him staring up into his eyes distressed and shaken, sorrow turned to anger in the eyes of a teenager. With no release or words to express what he felt, he watched as Clarion ran from the room. He and Rivers had known the boy for such a short time, but in reverse he then realised the boy had just witnessed the death of his mother, perhaps for a second time. Life had been cruel to the already emotionally damaged child and he was just adding to it. The shame of his actions and loss of control took the strength and anger from him, he wallowed back into sorrow.

"It's okay," he said, putting his hand gently to the Xannix arm clasped about him. "Thank you." The arm withdrew.

He sat with Rivers for a long time, just sitting by her side and holding her hand. She had been a guiding light for him over the last couple of weeks since the shuttle crash, and he now felt very alone.

You will be fine, she said, her voice clear in his mind. *Even if things are unclear now, by the time you are called upon, you will be ready.*

"How do you know," he asked.

You haven't let me down yet.

He laughed. How wrong she was. "But if I had been here..."

You would be dead too.

Her words stopped him cold. They had a painful truth to them. He didn't want to admit it, but she was right.

But you have the chance to put things right. A chance to save two peoples—not just us, but the Xannix too. There are opportunities ahead; don't let them slip by.

Squeezing her hand, he placed her arms across her chest and gently slid his hand across her eyes to close them. She looked at peace. An audible sigh escaped him and Ovitala placed a hand on his shoulder, a sympathetic connecting gesture. She was crouched beside him, her skin a deep blue. She said nothing but looked down respectfully at Rivers, sharing the grief.

"We must go," she said finally. He just nodded. "We will join Yannix on the journey."

As they left the room, he paused and looked back. "Tomorrow. See you tomorrow, Rivers."

DAWN

She watched from afar. The Zantanath attack had been quick; the initiative and momentum of events had been to their advantage from the start. The Xannix technology had been built and provided by the Zantanath, with key systems and critical defences open to override commands. The Xannix had been laid bare and were wide open to a tactical move made years before the battle ever took place; the Zantanath, like a chess grandmaster, had planned their moves decades in advance.

The *Endeavour* had played its part, its sacrifice saving them all from complete destruction and providing a short window of reprieve, and for a moment she believed they might make it. Commander Roux's move had been bold and daring, but, ultimately, the Zantanath had been able to close them down and cut off their escape.

So now she sat and observed the events taking place among the shattered Xannix fleet from the broken hulk and wreckage of the ship which had been her new form for the last 135 years. The ship had been an extension of her being, slowly sliding through the endless night carrying the candle of hope and a new life for her precious passengers and crew. As with her corporeal existence on earth, life always put barriers in the way of hope and dreams. This journey had been no different, but she was not done yet. The Zantanath had hit them hard; however, they had made an error.

"Hi Dad." She sent a tight beam secure signal to the ground.

"Dawn. How's my favourite daughter?" It brought her a warm

feeling just hearing her father's voice again. "Are you ready?"

"Yes. Ready."

"Okay. Keep the updates coming for as long as you can. And, remember, I want you safe too. No heroics. Understood?"

"Speaking of heroes, Dad. They should be with you in about eight minutes. Launching *Home Run* in three, two, one... mark."

Across her body she felt the solid thud of bolts releasing and bursts of thrust as a large number of cargo pods released on pre-programmed and reprogrammed drop trajectories. She monitored their progress on as many working sensors and linked telemetry beacons as were available under the circumstances, her specific interest in sixteen drop pods carrying the remaining survivors of the *Endeavour*. Hidden among the spread of seemingly randomly jettisoned cargo and colonisation pods, the escape pods weaved an initially dangerous path towards the upper atmosphere of Xannix, the acceleration a sustained 5 to 6 g. The ride would not be comfortable for those involved, but she wanted to get them as far from the Zantanath as quickly as possible. She would remotely stabilise their descent before she lost line-of-sight control as they passed the planets horizon, by which point, they would also be out of range of any hostile weapons. As long as the Zantanath didn't see through the fake show and didn't send out a pursuit ship, she had confidence that in the mass confusion her precious cargo would get through. She felt her anxiety rise as the spread of drop pods advanced.

The sixteen escape pods of varying sizes contained the final 72 passengers and crew who, for whatever reason, had been unable to make it to a pod in time for the first evacuation. Most had been cut off in their efforts to reach an escape pod due to damage to the ship, disabled lifts, corridors exposed to the vacuum of space, bulkhead doors jammed or warped due to the enormous forces acting upon the ship as it was torn apart. She had been shepherd to all in their efforts to work around the trouble and chaos, each of the survivors requiring comfort and confidence in their task. One in particular she could only save by packing away within a cargo pod. It was the riskiest move, an improvised harness his only protection against the forces of the descent and his suit his only provision of any sustaining atmosphere. Monitoring his vital signs, Science Technician Second Class Joseph Singh was blacked out and in bad shape, the improvised harness he had built into the cargo pod had clearly failed to some degree, and his suit was reporting broken limbs. Manipulating the pods navigation controls, she eased Singh's pod into a safe re-entry alignment and handed over control to the pod's navigational re-entry routine. From here on, Singh was on his own. She wished him well, not knowing whether he would ever hear her, then moved on to the next pod.

The cargo pods she had sent out towards the mingled ships of the fleet started to arrive at the nearest Zantanath ships. A couple bounced off the hull of the nearest ship, a few others smashed apart into twisted debris, their contents spilling out into space and becoming smaller particulates to muddy the orbital junkyard that this flight level had become. Zantanath ships did not respond, clearly believing the scattered pods the malfunction of a dying ship.

Eleven seconds remained until the last of the pods reached the safety of the horizon, and the closest Zantanath ship stirred like a waking beast. Slight movement at first, slow alignment to its target, reading its data, assessing the situation, targeting its weapons. She felt herself hold her breath, although that reflex was a physical response that had no meaning in her new physical world. Her vision zoomed in on the Zantanath ship and calculated the time till impact of the two cargo pods aimed at it. Firing the pods retro-engines the pods accelerated across the remaining distance in less than five seconds, readjusting their course to strike hard at the stern section of the vessel. The Zantanath ship did not have time to respond or evade the redirected pods, which on impact detonated with the full force of the mining explosive contained within. The Zantanath ship began to spiral out of control, away from the fleeing escape pods, its crew with more pressing issues to attend.

Before the Zantanath fleet could react, she had activated the thrusters to another six cargo pods, each with remotely primed mining explosive; the ships had been crippled by the ambush, appearing lazy in their overconfidence and inaction. The third ship, a smaller Zantanath corvette class vessel succumbed to the strike and evaporated in a ball of light and heat. Her hull sensors flared and alerts started to appear, warning of excessive external temperatures, but the thermal shock was short lived.

New reports started to arrive: wounds to the remaining hull, ruptures and fragmenting skin, energy spikes consistent with, but more powerful than, the particle beam weapons the Xannix had used on their first engagement. The Zantanath ships had finally woken up to the threat, and were identifying their targets, prioritising the closest cargo pods and working their way through to the floating hulk of the *Endeavour*. She could almost see the confusion on the faces of the Zantanath, not knowing where the next threat was coming from, nor what part of an already destroyed ship to target and blast into even smaller chunks.

It was time to leave and fulfil her promise to her father. The launch sequence occurred at the speed of thought and she travelled the radius of the ship in less than a second, the rail-launcher accelerating her to 8 g and towards the surface of Xannix at a perpendicular re-entry angle. Her re-entry pod was a dart, designed to tolerances the human body would not survive, but she was a solid-state entity now, a machine in all but thought. The descent was rapid.

The pod struck the upper atmosphere like driving a pile into concrete, its speed dropping sharply in spite of its aerodynamic scalpel-like shape. The pod continued to descend, puncturing the stratosphere and lighting up the sky, while friction super-heated its skin to dramatic levels. The nose cone, which was at the point of material failure, was ejected, and a smaller pear-shaped pod with a flatter convex shield at its base continued its descent, air resistance forcing it to slow yet further. The drag chute deployed at eight thousand meters, the landing sequence scanning the ground for a suitable terrain surface for its final approach.

A valley floor was selected near the delta of a river, where the mouth of the valley splayed out into flood plains. The ground looked green and inviting. The target was locked and air brakes pushed out into the airflow for fractions of a second to realign the pods flight path.

"Dad, I'm almost down. I'm a little way off, coordinates packaged with this message, but I'm making my way to you. Might be a few hours. Dawn, out."

The drogue chute detached at two thousand meters and the main chute deployed, slowing her yet further. The initial violence of the descent was replaced by an almost serene calmness, the blue of the sky and the green of the rich meadow below a combination of colours and beauty she had not seen since her childhood. She experienced a feeling of homecoming, although she knew this place was not yet that, more a world of discoveries. A truly unknown future.

As she landed, the long grass cushioned the touchdown and the sound about her deadened to a gentle susurration, as the wind brushed and tussled the meadow. She released the main chute while it still had height, and it lazily flopped to the ground away from the pod. Internal processes began scanning for OWEC beacons, other escape pods, her father's signal. It was faint, across a mountain range to the north-east, a thousand miles distant—it could possibly be closer but the mountains were interfering with a precise fix and she was too far away to receive the detailed transponder signal.

Voices. They were unmistakably voices, but the intonation and syllables were more sibilant and softer on the ear. Aboard the *Endeavour*, she had become accustomed to the tools at her disposal, the power to travel across interstellar space, the weapons, the senses and enhanced functional ability the hardware of the ship allowed. In her current form, she felt bare, stripped of her power; vulnerable. The sounds were increasing in volume, getting louder, getting closer. The last thing she wanted was for any local contact, so she accelerated her plan. The top of the pod split into segments and bolts fired into the ground to secure the pod. Wings slid like blades from the side of a central airframe, and without warning to the approaching locals only meters away, she launched herself back into the sky, gaining 500 meters in a heartbeat.

From her new elevated position, she circled for a moment, watching the group of local Xannix below; checking she hadn't caused any injury, checking that they were not a threat. They appeared stunned at her emergence, several of them rising again from a reactive crouch. From the equipment they carried, they were likely gathering food, foraging or hunting. They were safe, but she saw the signal as they sent out the call. She had been located. She would be tracked. The question remained whether she would be safe. Having just taken out several Zantanath ships, she found it unlikely.

Turning to the north-east, she accelerated away, keeping low. Perhaps they would be radar tracking; staying low and fast would be her best option.

ELLIE

The most difficult step is always the first.

In her new form, within the crate-sized box of circuits and solid-state components, she was immobilised, physically incapable of her own travel. Over the few short weeks of her new existence in Clayton's research lab at the Formillun Institute, it had been the single most frustrating part of her new life. It was debilitating. Unable to even move from one side of the room to the other.

Of course, she could create worlds within her own environment—simulations, emulations of the real world, places to fool her mind—but it was not interaction with the real world. It was not living when you knew the world you inhabited was a hoax.

She and Dawn had had long debates on the subject, for which Dawn seemed quite ambivalent and unaffected, almost relaxed about the issue. The containers they existed in were purpose built, specific to their needs and unique to them. They were trapped for the moment in their uniqueness; no other system was able to sustain them. However, they would become mobile soon enough, Dawn would say, she just needed patience. This platitude had made no sense and simply fuelled her anger and need to escape her confines.

In her downtime, when she wasn't meant to be interacting with the medical or tech staff on her rehabilitation, she worked on her freedom. At first, she probed her way around her crate, the container and super-computer she existed within. She needed to go beyond the superficial higher lever functions that held her wave, and enter the low-level state, the part of herself which interacted and interfaced with the machine. It was hard, finding a way to work within that interface, to pick away at the core programming of the machine part of herself and hack the fundamental framework that Dr Clayton had created to sustain her. She was searching for the unknown key to a door she could not find. It was an almost impossible task, but she had two things in her favour: firstly, she knew she was now part machine, and existed within it, and, secondly, she knew the door existed. No machine worked in isolation. She and Dawn had been interacting, and that needed local network connectivity. From that starting point there would be a network exit to the Formillun Institute net and from there to the open-net. Escape to the open-net would be the closest to freedom that she could now hope to achieve, and access to the open-net would allow her to relocate to other places, other physical places. She would no longer be confined.

Every moment she spent alone, she worked on the problem. Weeks went by and her frustration grew, anger focused back at the issue, invigorating her and motivating her yet further forward.

After all the hard work, sometimes it is luck you need. One morning, before Dr Clayton arrived, she had been working to crack the firewall lock. She had eventually found how to identify the comms and network gateway, but she was locked out of the firewall and it had obviously been set up to deny inbound and outbound data traffic from her container. The firewall was her jailer, the door to her prison, which she now attacked with all resource available to her.

While she hammered at the firewall, resorting to brute-force attacks, without warning a power surge struck across the labs on their level, causing heavy interference to her systems. She felt no real pain as such, but widespread disorientation, and with that her concentration became patchy, fading in and out across several seconds. Instruments and electronics in the lab sparked and fizzed as they failed, creating a lightshow in the darkness. Emergency power was restored, and some low-level lighting returned.

As her senses recovered, for a brief moment she discovered the firewall had not yet come back up. The firewall was locked out and would require reconfiguring, possibly a password reset. It was then that she knew she would have her chance, as Dr Clayton would need to apply the password and she had clear view of his terminal.

She had applied keystroke Trojans before, but this time she would record the keystrokes herself, alter the firewall configuration and open up her systems to the outside world.

*

It had been another week before she had considered herself ready to make the step, wanting to also give the incident a while to fade in people's memories. If things went as she expected, she would be able to traverse across machines, using the network nodes to distribute herself, never needing any real physical machine memory, only that of the networking hardware and buffer memory. Each individual node would be far less than she actually needed, but distributed across hundreds of nodes, she would be able to sustain herself and move across the open-net.

Vengeance was a powerful motivator and she discarded her worries without another moment's consideration. She had run the theory—it would work.

Like a rock climber testing their first handhold for grip, she made her first step to the local network node in the lab. A tiny part of the whole, a finger grip on the outside. She reached out further, to the next node, another lab, then the next node. With each step she grew in confidence. Soon she was operating across all the nodes within the institute; she only required just over half to contain her form and wave, but she practiced moving and traversing between them to make sure she knew how and so that there were no unforeseen complications.

Moments later, she found herself staring at the next barrier: the Formillun Institute gateway to the open-net. It was open, so there was no real barrier other than her anticipation of what lay beyond. After a moment's pause, she was through, and the world expanded on before her like a rolling sea, an undulating mass of moving data, constantly shifting, constantly in flux.

There were nodes available in all directions, and she moved around erratically for a while, directionless, exploring her new environment, her mind full of wonder. But then, after a time, purpose started to intrude and began to make her restless. There was a reason she had broken all the rules and forced her way into the world. She knew where to start, and she knew exactly what she was going to do.

After a quick orientation, she identified the Formillun Institute test facility on the east coast. A moment later, she was there.

*

It was weird being back in that place. She had utilised the security system cameras the moment she had arrived; compromising systems had become almost second nature. The low-level ones could be accessed in seconds, and there were others, medium level security systems, which took a little longer; however, once she was in, free access was available to the physical location and jurisdiction of the local system. She had spent 20 minutes breaking into the system at the test facility, which, given the work she knew happened there, she considered a weakness.

She had spent some time in her old office, now Okoro's office. There was a tug of emotion as she realised time had moved on without her, and that the project she had tried and risked everything to subvert and destroy was still operational. Her view swung round the office and control room, faces she remembered hard at work preparing the next test of the Mag-X drive. Finally, she zoomed in on Patten's office. He was at his desk, hair dishevelled lost in the detail on his workstation screen, probably reading the email she had sent him a few minutes earlier. He looked like he hadn't slept in a week.

Okoro was in the office with him, always the fixer. Maybe this tendency stemmed from his natural demeanour; perhaps a perpetually positive outlook on life led you to believe that the broken could always be unbroken, from machine to man. She found his endless optimism troubling. In her experience, every high had a corresponding low; it was just about controlling the amplitude.

She took hold of the local network node in Patten's office and started to infiltrate the devices: screens, projectors, cells. She would speak with him soon enough, but first she had another task.

Reaching out into the upper floors of the facility, she began to hunt down her prey. She had run the numbers, calculated the likelihood of the assassin still being on site and added in the variables she knew about: the overconfidence now all witnesses had been pronounced dead, the continuation of GAIA's drive to disrupt the plans of the political and technical elite, the need for the undiscovered to stay on site. She worked her way through the social and communal areas, the workshops and offices, scanning faces, checking off identity tags, but there was something wrong. People started to tick off and check out, face after face, clear and innocent of her further attention. After all this preparation, all her struggles to this point, could she have been wrong?

Refusing to accept the possibility that GAIA could simply have recalled the man, she continued to search and cross off names. But after ten minutes of collating and scanning every person she found on-site, she had drawn a blank. She had failed. Her heart sank, disappointment beginning to creep into her thoughts. Before she fell fully into a state of melancholy, she paused and tried to think around the problem. She hadn't failed; it was the method, the tools she was applying. Facial recognition had failed.

In a fraction of a second, she was looking at a closed door from a security camera across the corridor in the accommodation block, the quarters listed to one Tech First Class Owen Stedman. The name had no meaning to her, but after ticking off all the faces to all the names allocated quarters within the accommodation block, Stedman was missing. A moment later, she was in the room, among the devices and things linked via the network, with a camera in the door security panel giving her a peephole view of the room. It was empty, but she felt a rush of excitement and what might analogue to an adrenaline hit, as she saw a picture frame next to the bed, a man and woman smiled back at her. It was him. The man calling himself Stedman had been the man she had seen that time at the GAIA rally, and that moment in the test bay when her world had forever changed. She had found his place, but not the man.

She put out information requests to site administration systems and found quickly that Stedman was off duty and not due back on shift for another four hours. Estimating it to be his sleep period, he should be in the room. It didn't make sense. He wasn't out in the facility; he wasn't in his room.

As she looked on bemused, in the low faux moonlight glow of the room, the duvet moved and shifted. He was there, in bed. But she could see nothing; to the camera, Stedman was invisible. It was impossible, she knew, but the evidence was there; the security mic in the door control confirmed a shuffling noise in the room as he moved.

The part of herself that was still within the network node in

Patten's office put out a call and moments later appeared to him as a projected hologram. She would warn him off. She didn't want him anywhere near Stedman's room in the next few minutes, better to have him otherwise occupied and where she had some control over his whereabouts.

Stedman on the other hand, was doomed.

The gas supply to the floor's heating system ran through a conduit at the rear of Stedman's quarters. She forced a lock on the safety valve outside his room and increased the pressure to the system; within moments the safety valve was leaking gas into the conduit and into Stedman's room. She didn't really know if the gas itself would asphyxiate him, but that was not the plan she had for him. She had read once of a saying quoted from an old, abandoned religion, which had said something about an eye for an eye. It seemed appropriate somehow.

The power surge she sent to the mains in Stedman's room shorted across a socket near his bed. She witnessed the resulting explosion from the corridor cameras, the door removed forcefully from its hinges as dust and debris filled her view.

*

Alarms began to sound loudly across the facility, people dashing in all directions, making their way to duty stations or muster points. Her attention returned to Patten's office; he was watching the screen and had been a step behind her in working through the logic of where Stedman would be.

"For all the stars, Ellie. What did you do?" He was in shock.

"What had to be done," she said flatly.

"You said *we* would deal with it."

"*I* have dealt with it."

"But this is not the way, Ellie."

"Oh? And what is the way? Your way?"

"Justice. The law. We must do it this way, or we become the barbarians and outlaws, no better than the savages that roam the wastes."

"You mean those we cast out because they were not wealthy or intelligent enough to contribute to the colonisation effort. I don't know if you get it yet, but no one's surviving this. That rock killed us all the moment it hit. We're already dead." She said it with venom, tired of his naïve and blinkered view of the world, and of what their governments were doing in the name of species preservation. "At some point, Scott, you have to consider whether turning on our own, on the weak and infirm, is a sacrifice too far."

"We can't save everyone Ellie."

"But you could save me and stick me in a box!"

Patten sat as if slapped. It was the moment the crystal holding his delusions shattered. He had been hiding behind his work, blanking out the reality that lay outside the facility walls. The slow death of humanity by a thousand cuts was happening and he was part of it. She had just brought that into sharp focus for him.

And the fact that she may not thank him for saving her, that she might have preferred death rather than a life as an AI, a life which, though not perfect, would allow them time together, allow her to survive. He had not even considered it.

Patten slumped back in his seat, looking up at the ceiling, his face reflecting a world of confusion and tortured emotions. Could they call what they had had love? It had been young and new, but probably not that. Even if it had been, she could see she had crossed a line, that her actions had crushed a preconception Patten had of her and who she was. Things had changed, but they had changed in a real way, stripping down his romantic ideas of what could be.

Trust had been destroyed. She realised in that moment that she would never see him again.

LARSEN

In the moments after incredible shock and trauma in his life, he had always wanted time to be alone. Time to reflect, time to process. In his experience, this was rarely what happened, as others were always concerned and wanted to help, to be there for him, to support him. It was well meaning, it was a natural reaction, but it conflicted with the immediate needs of the individual. In time he may open up, in time he may want to discuss and relay his experience, but in the moment and shortly after, healing was internalised. Introspection to facilitate grieving. It was that way with the loss of his parents, and it was that way now.

Whether it was due to his position or the cultural norms of the Xannix, he was not left alone. He had been taken to another room, his bodyguard elevated in number again, now very obvious to him and beginning to intrude on his need for personal space. Others, perhaps medical, monitored him from afar, and Ovitala spoke with him occasionally or hovered nearby. He felt smothered, mothered, claustrophobic, and it was starting to give rise to anxieties. Who could he trust, truly trust? He was coming to realise that not only had he loved Rivers totally, but she had also become the person he had leant on the most for council, reassurance and confidence. When Rivers had died, a part of him had died too. And the cruellest part of it all was that, with the *Endeavour* gone, her death was final, eternal.

Sitting silently in the centre of the room, the mood sombre and subdued, he reflected on the inversion he experienced inside. The tempest his mind was working through, the dark and volatile emotions raging against the world that had taken from him. He needed a calm place to harbour.

"Ovitala?" She finished a conversation she was having with another Xannix, and stepped over to attend him, her features passive but her colour subdued.

"How can I help, Setak'da?"

"I need quiet. I need to be alone."

Ovitala looked worried. "I would advise against that at this time, Setak'da. We know little of what happened in your quarters and would urge you to accept a personal guard at all times."

"Possibly," he motioned to the room and those in it, "but this is unnecessary. Please, two of your most trusted should be enough; everyone else, outside."

He watched as her face went through several permutations of further objections before she settled and her skin tone moved to the light blue he now understood to be a communication of agreement.

"Thank you."

She nodded. A learned humanism to put him at ease.

Slowly, the room began to thin out, Xannix filing through the apartment door, low conversational murmuring heard as they left. Some were clearly agitated by the request, feeling that he should be closely attended, but Ovitala provided her gentle persuasion and they mellowed, although perhaps not completely in agreement. The last remaining were two guards, who stood impassively either side of the door, and Ovitala. She returned to him once the last had gone and took a seat by his side.

"I know you wish to grieve, Setak'da. I wish you that time soon. But now, we must act."

He sat staring at the floor, his thoughts racing and moving through dark places in his mind, the gaping hole in his heart filling with wrath and revenge. He quietly seethed as Ovitala continued.

"This move was unseen, but it is clear that the Zantanath are striking for you and those close to you, to divert you from your purpose."

"Well, it's working," he said gruffly, his voice strained.

"Child Rivers will be taken care of, but there is nothing you can do for her here. Put your anger into taking the battle to the Zantanath. Lead your peoples and free us all."

"But how could this happen, Ovitala? How could anyone get so close?"

Ovitala's eyes were full of sorrow. "We do not know."

"Someone has infiltrated the Seekers; I cannot believe you know nothing." He kept his voice level and controlled. Ovitala was right in one regard: he needed to place his anger where it would be of benefit. Screaming at her would not improve matters and would likely alienate the one person he now needed to resolve the situation. "What does your security team say? Do you not have cameras here? Surveillance?"

"Not in your quarters, no."

"In the corridors, workshops or workspaces?"

"Some, but not many. People are our security. People are trusted to give of themselves and protect others."

He could not quite understand the Xannix. In some ways the technology was advanced and beyond that which he knew, but in other ways their culture and decisions seemed counter to the best use and practical application of the technology. They had employed Zantanath tech but had little understanding of how it worked. He wondered how much the Xannix had been gifted and how this rapid elevation in technological growth had affected them.

"A misplaced trust," he stated.

"Perhaps, but we will find out what happened."

"Of that you can be certain," he said. It was as much an oath to himself as a response to Ovitala.

She stood slowly, perhaps a mark of her age, perhaps she was using time to think of how to end the conversation. She always had others to see, plans to implement. And now she had the added complication of Rivers' death and an emotionally charged Setak'da to advise. He could see it in her eyes: the second guessing, the strategic mind at work.

"We will need to leave in five sateks." She made a gesture with her hand, describing the time. "I will leave you until then."

He looked up at her and momentarily felt a wave of exhaustion flow over him, the adrenaline finally ebbing.

"Rest," Ovitala said. "I'll be back to escort you to the transport."

Some part of him fought the tiredness, but he was so tired. He lay down on the spread of sofa-like furniture and closed his eyes. Sleep was instant, like plunging into a dark stormy sea. He found himself falling through Rivers' eyes as she stared back at him through his restless nightmares, accusing and confused, as if the events made no sense to her and her death was still a situation she could not accept. It was a mirror to his own thoughts; his frontal cortex trying to make sense of the world and rationalise away her loss. He wouldn't allow it; he would remember. Rage was the correct response.

*

Cold bit to his bone, as the darkness gave way to an orange glow of warmth. Rough gritty sand pressed against his cheek and icy water lapped at his body, his hands gripped into clumps of wet sand. Opening his eyes, the beach curved its way to the horizon, surf lapping and eroding, destroying and creating in the same process. The blur of water stung his eyes, but his skin began to respond to the sun, low in the sky and rising, warming and waking from its dormant state. Blinking away the sand and salt from his eyes, the scene became clearer, pain in his legs brighter. He dragged himself up with exhausted limbs to sit facing the sea, his smashed and blooded legs leaking into the water creating a muddied red surf to each incoming wave, each outgoing wave taking a little more of his life force from him.

In the shallows of the beach, the lifepod lay battered and wrecked. Metal contorted, the door had been ejected and water flooded in, a body flopping half out, head submerged with the rise of each crashing wave. Long hair like black seaweed glistened in the light, covering her face and anonymising her features. He tried to make out the detail, to confirm his fears, but it was impossible.

The glow of the sun silhouetted the lifepod, throwing the hapless crewmember into shadow. The light grew brighter and more intense, illuminating the world around. There were others, climbing from escape pods, some had landed on the beach, some in the shallows, but with more success than his pod. People were wading to shore, helping each other, falling exhausted to the sand and taking time to recover. Others already on the beach seemed to all be staring out to sea, some shading their eyes from the intense light. It momentarily confused him.

The light had become almost unbearable, a roaring, thunderous sound filled the air as reason rushed to his mind and filled him with dread. The *Endeavour* was falling from the sky, its hull white hot with the uncontrolled re-entry, the bulk of it growing in size as it descended towards them. Involuntarily, he began to shout and row back on the sand, dragging his useless legs with him. It was a futile effort and a moment later, as his skin blistered from the heat of it, the *Endeavour* smashed down in the shallows of the bay. Sea water instantly vaporised and those in the immediate area of the beach were turned to dust.

*

"Setak'da." There was a hand on his shoulder, and the concerned eyes of one of the guards looked down on him. He felt the cold wet sweat on his brow and down his back, the matted hair across his forehead. He sighed and closed his eyes again. The images of the nightmare still flashed around his vision. He squeezed his eyelids tighter, hoping that the action would wash away the sight, but it was the memory he could not remove. He opened his eyes again.

"Nightmare," he said to the guard, as if that would explain everything.

"You were in distress, Setak'da. We have called for the medical team."

"Thank you, but that will not be necessary. Please inform Cardinal Ovitala that I am ready. It is time to leave."

The Xannix helped him to his feet, his skin tone a cool blue. His head slightly to one side in concentration, the Xannix paused then looked down. "It is done. Cardinal Ovitala requests that you join her in the hangar. We will take you to her now."

DAWN

She rolled through the valleys like she was born to flight, making smooth arcing turns, ascending and descending over ridge peaks tipped with snow. Scanning the trees and looking below the canopy, she tracked her target, the signal weak and sporadic, sometimes changing location by several kilometres, then relocating again and again as the signal bounced off cliff walls.

The moment he had launched she had tracked him. Roux had saved so many and yet she knew he would only see those he had failed, those that hadn't made it, those whose wave and DNA storage had been destroyed when the *Endeavour* had broken apart breaking through the Xannix satellite blockade. The courage and foresight to make that kind of leadership decision was a rare quality, and she knew they would need his abilities to survive this new world. It was only right that she find him. But his escape pod had suffered a collision on re-entry, and after that she had lost him.

Cresting a ridge, the signal cleaned up, becoming solid and strong. A babbling river wound a path through the valley and a clear pebbled riverbed spread out beyond the flow of water; at the water's edge crouched a figure in a bright orange survival suit.

She pulled a tight circle at a height of about 200 metres, while her optics zoomed in on the figure for identification. As she did so, the figure stood and looked directly at her. It was Roux, his eyes blackened through lack of sleep, his features drawn, pale and gaunt, a few bumps and cuts, but he was alive and mobile—and heading in the wrong direction. She saw a moment of recognition in him before he waved an exaggerated full-arm wave, then extended his arm pointing in the direction of the tree line, towards which he then turned and started to walk.

After circling for another five minutes while Roux made his way to cover, she took the opportunity to scan the area for danger, possible wildlife or Xannix search parties, but she found nothing other than a few small rodent-like creatures foraging along the treeline on the opposite side of the stream. Once he was at the treeline, she descended, swinging in low and extending wheeled undercarriage and unfolding manipulators front and rear of the main body.

When firmly on the ground, she cut the engines and the noise died away with a whine. Silence descended on them.

She projected her hologram, and it appeared full height in front of Roux, swirling into existence like sand in a hurricane.

"Hello, Roux. Glad to see you made it. I was worried about you there for a moment."

"Well, it's been a rough day for everyone," he shrugged off the comment. "Have you any detail on the landing? Did many make it?"

Seeing his concern made her consider her answer. She needed him able to function and lead; giving him hard statistics about the outcome of his actions would be a mistake, especially as his quick thinking had saved far more than perished.

"You did the right thing, Commander. We have just been in a battle where even the best VARS outcome ended with the loss of ship and crew. Thanks to you, the crew is safe." She looked round to survey the valley. "And from what I've seen so far, this is everything we dreamed of."

"Not everything," replied Roux.

"There were always going to be issues to overcome. Just so happens that this problem is, well..."

"An invasion?"

"Not that. You're being overly pessimistic."

"Yes, well. Maybe," he replied. He was in a dark place.

"We are refugees. Our planet no longer viable. We will see this through, make new allies and build a new home."

"We area a plague. Locusts, consuming until we kill everything, and in turn even ourselves."

This was uncharacteristic. Roux was normally far more

optimistic, far more in control, but, considering the last few hours, perhaps he was questioning himself, perhaps he was suffering a stress-related episode, or maybe there was something far more physical at fault, perhaps concussion or head trauma. She tried a medical scan, which at first appeared normal: a few bumps and bruises, which might be expected of a pod landing and trek across this kind of terrain. But there, on his collar at the top of his chest, was a spot she could not read. A dark region, not much larger than a few millimetres across. She had excused the anomaly as an obstructing piece of clothing, but as she focused on the area it began to phase and pulse, becoming more then less intense. One moment it was there, the next it was gone, then it returned. It pulsed with a regularity which seemed unnatural, something intentional but not of human origin.

"I don't think that's entirely fair, and not true. You do remember the meteor strike that caused the Great Decline?"

"We were doomed before then. We destroyed ourselves, and now we are here to do it all over again."

The patch in Roux's chest grew and flared as he spoke.

"You believe we will ruin this world, as we did our own?" she asked. She had known Roux for years, before the mission, during the construction of the *Endeavour* he had been part of the team overseeing the build as part of the crew who would finally take ownership and sign off on the handover. He was a dedicated and a fully committed part of the crew; she had never heard him speak sceptically about the purpose of the colonisation. What he was saying now was totally counter to his character, even as she had coaxed him into the escape pod in the *Endeavour's* final moments he had been focussed and in command. This was not the commander she knew.

Then, the human mind was a fragile thing. Each of them had been through rugged psychological assessments as part of the selection process for this mission. Colonists and scientists would be expected to endure much, and crew and security personnel even more so. But tests couldn't cover all eventualities, they were only ever indicators to a person's capabilities. Reality could apply unforeseen pressures which could trip the mind and cause a person to act counter to their anticipated behaviours and character.

The dark spot in his chest flared again. "We will kill this world like we did our own. We don't belong here, and we don't deserve to continue. The human race is dead. We just don't know it yet." He was strained in his response, jawline tense as he spat the words into the air between them.

Taking a moment to allow him to calm, she changed the subject.

"Anyway, how are you? I lost you on the descent there for a moment. Was your landing okay?"

He looked at her with a different person's eyes, a gear change in his mind, reliving the events of his escape and the final moments of the descent, uncontrolled and blurred.

"I was lucky," he said in a soft distant voice. "I think I was struck by debris on re-entry. Everything went to shit. The next thing I remember was waking up in a smashed pod on a mountainside."

There was no sign of the anomaly in his chest. She continued to scan.

"Lucky," she echoed.

"And now I'm here."

A pause descended on them. He was clearly cold and exhausted and could probably do with a good period of sleep. No one had been getting much sleep since their arrival to the Xannix system.

"So where are you headed?"

"The LZ. The crew will be there. As many as made it. And we have a job to do," he said as the black shadow in his chest started to grow again, this time ever so slightly.

She didn't know what it was, but she had a clear suspicion that this dark shadow was manipulating Roux. His nature, his character was off kilter, and ordinarily she would have put that down to trauma. If she had been any other person, of flesh and blood, her old self, she would have been surprised, then rationalised the situation away and moved on. But she was not her old self, she had other options and skills to apply. If she had not run the medical scan, the dark influence on Roux would have stayed undiscovered.

Whatever it was, the affect was malign and casting a serious negative almost depressive state on him. He was certainly unstable. The rate of change in his mental state concerned her. She would continue to study the effects of this dark region in Roux. She needed to find out its cause and intent before they re-joined the others.

"First things first, you need rest. Then we can head out. We can make a shelter here. I'll collect some wood for a fire, and you can set up your shelter. Then we can head out for the LZ at first light."

She saw him begin to formulate an argument, but he was drained, and couldn't find even enough strength to object. He shrugged off his pack and let it drop to his feet.

"Okay, I do need sleep and with you watching over the camp, we would be safer."

"Good. Okay, I'll make a start on that fire," she said, and started to look around for dropped wood suitable and dry. Roux slowly began to unpack the shelter with the movements of a drunk old man. The sleep deprivation of the last few days had finally caught up with him.

She didn't wander too far and kept an eye on him as she did so, continuing to monitor him and examine the shadow on his chest.

*

His condition had become worse during the night. As he slept his temperature rose and his breathing became laboured. She watched from a reasonable distance, maintaining the fire occasionally to keep him as comfortable as she could. The symptoms he presented were similar to a fever, but with the unexplained darkness creeping across his chest, now increasing size in a somewhat erratic manner, she was becoming increasingly worried. Roux needed medical intervention, more than she could provide.

She had considered whether his condition could have been caused by an aggressive native virus or biological contagion. Further analysis would need a blood sample and, without a moment's hesitation, she moved closer to the mobile shelter and utilised one of her mechanical manipulator arms to manoeuvre a needle into position. She chose her spot and struck. Needing very little to analyse, the needle was extracted quickly. Roux hardly stirred from his sleep, the discomfort of the needle caused a flinch in his arm, a momentary grimace, but nothing more. She withdrew from the tent and back to the far side of the fire, an orange glow throwing a warm light on the local area. It painted a picture of calm and relaxation, but her anxiety was running high—the image was false.

Opening a small hatch in her outer shell, she inserted the needle and deposited the small sample of Roux's blood. The hatch snapped shut and the analysis began invisibly within. In her current form, the physical world presented itself in the same way it always had, only now her senses and abilities were multiplied. At first, she had found it strange, but now knowing the results of samples via this and other sensor arrays in her frame was like experiencing any other of her corporal senses. In the same way she may have previously understood smell or touch, it seemed just as natural, a thing she had always been able to do.

There was danger here: nanites flooded his blood and were invading his system. These microscopic machines appeared to be attached to blood cells, and some others were within cells. She would have expected the body's T cells to attack these foreign invaders, but they seemed neutral to them, happy to let them work unhindered. Where they had come from was unknown, as was their purpose, but she was pretty sure the source of them within his body was the anomaly in Roux's chest.

She needed a closer look.

Moving back to the tent, she looked in again to see Roux paler than before, sweat covering his brow, his fringe sticking to his forehead in strands. He was burning up and she needed to cool him down. Taking him by the ankles, she began by pulling him out into the cooler night air, then she undid his survival suit and worked it down to reveal his underclothes. Roux moaned and shifted uncomfortably in his sleep. She lifted his shirt to reveal his bare chest and examined the upper left region where the darkness appeared under her scans. The skin was not enflamed and showed no difference to the surrounding area.

Focussing her scan on the clavicle, she searched for nanites similar to those in his blood. What she saw would have made her heart race if her body had been human, but the alarm she felt was still real. Embedded in the bone was a nanite factory, pushing new nanites into the bloodstream imbued with the DNA signature of their host. It would have been why the T cells were ignoring them. Roux's eyes flashed open and he let out a yell of alarm, seeing the machine body that she was looming over him while she had his chest exposed. Thrashing about he managed to roll free and stood in an awkward hunched frame, pulling his clothes together and folding his arms across his chest against the cold.

"W-what are you doing?" he stammered, confused and looking

like a ghost.

"You are ill, Roux. You need help. I was trying to assess your condition."

"My condition is just fine," he shouted back. "You can just back off. Leave me alone."

"But you are running a fever; you need to lower your temperature. I need to find out what is causing this."

He took a step back from her, eyes wide. She could see the dark patch in his chest had grown again and appeared to drive his distress. The more she learned, the more she was convinced that it was driving his altered mental state, and the nanites were clearly altering something about his physiology, to what purpose she still hadn't worked out.

"I'm fine, just leave me. I'll make my own way to the camp." An idea flashed across his face and he changed tack. "Look, you go on ahead. I'll pack things up here and meet you at the LZ in a couple of days. There's no way of getting there any faster—you're not built for passengers. You go on ahead and help the others. I'm sure they could do with your assistance."

The change of character was abrupt, like a child trying to work around the decision of a parent. And the logic was sound, if not for the fact that she was here now, and he needed her assistance now. With the fever still strong and not showing any sign of easing, she rejected his idea. If she left now, he could well be dead by morning.

"I'll agree this with you. If you break the fever by morning, I'll consider it."

He seemed resigned. "Okay. But keep your distance. I don't want to wake up to find you standing over me again. That was damn creepy." Stepping towards the fire, he flopped down and sat cross-legged slumping to one side staring into the flames. "I just need to get back to the crew. I need to make it right."

"Make what right?" but before she got an answer, Roux was unconscious again.

*

She watched. It was all she could do for him. Watch and analyse. Try and figure out how this had happened to him, so she could protect the others. An hour before sunrise, Roux's fever broke.

ROUX

He felt like death. Maybe he was already dead, he couldn't tell. He knew he was losing track of time, and perhaps his mind too. Whatever was happening to him was nothing he had control over, and from the concern Dawn was exhibiting, neither did she. But Dawn had started to worry him. Waking to her looming over him in the firelight had freaked him out. Pincers working his clothing free, the cold eyes of her hologram focused and intent; he was in danger, he could feel it.

Within his fevered state there was a weird pervading clarity, like a base animalistic drive to hunt, an innate desire recurring again and again. Senses were growing sharper; the light from the fire now too intense to observe directly, smells and aromas filled his mind with information, and his hearing had become sensitive, enough for him to have subconsciously moved his hands to cover his ears. An anxiety was building in him, a tension that needed release, which told him to run, urged him to escape this captor.

His eyes flicked open.

Daylight. He had slept the night through. The fire was low but still alight, the air chill with the crisp morning light, and Dawn was missing. He stood instantly, sleeping bag falling to his feet. His eyes scanned the riverbank and treeline for any sign of her, but there was nothing.

A loud snapping twig made him turn sharply, his vision tracing through the trees. There, two hundred metres distant, a heat signature obscured by shrubs and low vegetation, moving slowly through the trees towards him. He ran.

To outrun the machine, he would keep to the trees; the denser the forest the better his chances. In the confined space, he would have the advantage: her lumbering frame unable to manoeuvre, she would become slowed by degrees. Up the valley wall he climbed, taking a zig-zag path to keep ahead of her. Stealing a look behind himself he found no trace of her, he continued on with newfound determination.

The climb was becoming steeper but he pushed against the gradient. Each step should have been harder than the last, but he felt his chest open out and large even lungfuls of air ease oxygen into his circulation, powering his muscles and legs ever onward.

Grasping at a tree trunk for leverage, he caught site of his hand and staggered to a stop. Taking a more inquisitive look, he drew his hand in close and examined something which now appeared alien to him. His skin had become almost grey in tone, lean and taught across elongated bone, his fingertips, his fingernails had also altered, becoming chrome-like and razor sharp. Rotating his hand and balling it into a fist, he found his nails didn't penetrate his palm, although the tree he had just used as a brace now had what looked like talon gouges raked across it. Then the fit of his suit, cuff visibly five or so centimetres short of his wrist. His form was changing, physicality altering and morphing into something new, something else—something other.

Part of him was appalled by the change and part of him was suddenly very scared. His heart began to race as flashes of the Zantanath abduction came back to him. The flash of pain, the operation on his chest, the tumbling to the valley floor. Why did they release him? What purpose could they have had to let him go?

Leaning against the tree, he pressed his temples hard with his palms. What had they done to him that could alter him, reprogram his DNA, accelerate his growth, all within such a short time frame? More, was the process contagious, or was it specific to his DNA sequence? He presumed the effect would be the same to any in the fleet who came into contact with him. Had he been made the vector to contamination of the fleet, the first cell of the cancer? Whatever it was, this could not be allowed to reach the survivors of the fleet.

He let out a roar of frustration. His time on this new world was meant to have been as pioneer to a new home, to build villages, towns and cities, to be a forefather to a new generation of human growth, a people learning from their past, building a better world for the generations to come. But all they had found was conflict, pain and death. Coming here had been a mistake.

A shrill, whining sound began to register, at a pitch which made him wince and search the sky for its source. Again, his base instinct overtook him, and he ran, striding out and heading for the valley ridgeline. For some reason, tears welled in his eyes as he ran. Somewhere, in the back of his mind he had come to a decision; although he couldn't quite grasp what the question had been, his focus was now intently directed at the incoming machine. It would kill him. He knew that for certain now. Why else would it be pursuing him?

Anger began to well, hatred for the pursuer. If he could not outrun it, he would confront it. A machine could be broken. He would break it.

Bursting from the upper treeline, he found himself only a couple of hundred meters from his goal. An outcrop of rocks increased the gradient yet again, but now he climbed with ease, leaping and reaching across for the next handhold, the next foothold. He climbed.

The machine caught up with him at the ridge as he stood looking out over the vertical drop to the far side of the next valley; he had run out of road. Mountains spread out across the horizon, snow peaked and jagged, like the teeth of a monster, and wind buffeted him as it moved up the valley in squalls. The machine swooped and circled him, coming to rest at a hover five metres in front of him, over the 600-metre drop.

"Roux, what are you doing? Please come back to the camp. You are unwell."

The machine spoke to him, but it was duplicitous, it meant him harm. Go back to the camp, for what? To be cut up and dissected, for the machine to inflict pain? It would enjoy that. But not today. Today would be its undoing.

He felt his body begin to tense and coil like a spring, as a snarl spread across his lips. His focus acute, he knew what he had to do.

"Roux, stay calm and try to relax. Your core temperature is way up; you need time to recover."

Without a word, he struck. His legs thrust him forward like a viper, a standing jump covered the five-metre distance in the blink of an eye. A flash of steal extended from his right arm, a blade coming from nowhere, his target only now beginning to react to the threat, but it was too late.

They collided in mid-air, his left-hand gripping with talons for purchase and gouging a hand hold in the machines frame. Anchored, he thrust for the heart of the machine with his blade. Alert to the threat, it reacted with a twist and dive. Gravity altered around him as the ridgeline fell away.

"Stop, Roux! Let me help you. You are not yourself."

The machine kept talking at him, but in this it was right: he was not himself, he was much more. He was alive and exhilarated, he had drive and purpose, he was in the moment and all he could be. This was who he was, who he was meant to be. The machine would only look to take all this away.

With all his strength he fought against the bucking and rolling of the descent, but each time he drew his weapon back to strike the machine jinked away and evaded the blow. It was not going to work; he looked for a weakness and changed strategy making a thrust for the nearest motor assembly. Another miss, but it had been an unexpected move and had almost landed.

"No!" said the machine again, this time in an almost sad and resigned tone. "I cannot save you, Roux. I have tried."

None of the machine's words registered; none of them mattered, as the target motor swung into position again and this time the line was perfect. There was almost a smile of satisfaction on his face as he made the killing blow.

"Sorry, Roux."

Air brakes deployed from the machine as all its motors suddenly wailed at full thrust; the screaming noise didn't last. His left hand ripped free as gravity overwhelmed him and the machine stopped in space, the view of it diminishing into the distance at speed.

His mind was still focused intently on the death of the machine as his own came up to meet him.

CLAYTON

There was so much to do. In the first hours after the evacuation of the *Endeavour*, time had passed like a blur, but people had now switched from the initial adrenaline-fuelled chaos to the more organised process of survival. There was still anxiety about what the future held, but they were now implementing actions that they had planned for. People had a purpose and a direction. They understood what was required of them and they went about doing what was needed.

While he had believed the *Endeavour* lost, along with all the kit they had brought for the colonisation effort, Dawn had delivered her home-run. He had been surprised by the large number of supply pods she had been able to land. Somehow, while the *Endeavour* had fallen apart around her, Dawn had managed to launch and deliver all the key colonisation pods that remained under her control and save a handful of straggling survivors. They had landed without issue and given them a further lifeline: kit and supplies to last, vehicles, farming equipment, manufacturing pods with industrial fabrication printers and materials enough to produce basic tools and habitats. In the short term, they were in better shape than the loss of the *Endeavour* had led him to believe. When Dawn had reported that she was about to make her descent, he had wanted to say so much, but there hadn't been time. There had been confirmation that she had made it through the upper atmosphere, but he had heard nothing since. He kept himself busy, but part of his mind was always preoccupied, looking and listening for signs of her return.

He found himself haunted by guilt in those moments; it was a natural psychological response. There had been so many lost as the *Endeavour* had been destroyed, but he didn't yet have a confirmed count. He knew of those in the camp—they were easily counted—but others would have been picked up by the *Intrepid* or *Indianapolis*, and some would not have made it off the *Endeavour*. Across all this, the guilt he felt was that at this moment all he could think about was his own child. A natural emotion perhaps, but guilt nonetheless.

Slipping the generator unit into place, he connected the final feeder cable from the habitat's solar skin and ran the test sequence. With the small control screen indicating a healthy unit, he closed the conduit and flicked the latches to lock it in place. Standing, he pressed his hand against the wall switch and smiled with success as the lights of the habitat came on.

Vibration started slowly, quietly, a low rumble that built in intensity to become a deafening roar. The habitat shook like it had suddenly been thrust into a raging tempest, but accompanying the power lashing the outside came a high-pitched whine, like that of a gas turbine engine, shrill and ear splitting. 'What the…?' was all he managed to broadcast to Jemma as he stumbled from the habitat, searching for the source of the storm through the dust and grit whirling outside.

"Peter!" Jemma's call was only just audible as the wind whipped the words from the air. "Peter, over there!"

As he made his way towards her, his gaze followed her outstretched arm, finger pointing to the west of the camp and a large dropship of a type they had not yet encountered. Its configuration was unlike any Xannix ship he had seen: it was bulky with a bulbous belly; powerful directional thrusters mounted at the end of short, stubby wings threw a heat haze to the ground; and a hawkish nose decorated with a bronze scrollwork and iconography pointed at them. The craft appeared to have no cockpit, pilot or pilots being completely encased within the hull. Sections of the craft opened to allow four robust legs to deploy, the undercarriage taking the weight of the craft as it came to rest.

The engines of the craft cut with a guttering sound, and the silence of the camp was amplified by the calm of the air as the thrashing wind ebbed away. No one spoke, everyone observing the ship from a safe distance, wary of the unannounced intruder.

In his peripheral vision, he saw a few of his people move into a loose defensive position around him. Commander Fellows, his head of security, stood nearby with one of the only fabricated carbines from the new printer workshops. The effectiveness of such a weapon against whatever was about to greet them from this ship was, he felt, pretty dubious. He caught Fellows' eye and slowly shook his head. The message was understood and Fellows relaxed and concealed the carbine; others copied, but they stayed in formation about him.

Heat exchangers reacted with moisture in the air to create a stream of vapour either side of the shuttle for a few moments, then a large hiss preceded the lowering of a ramp from the rear of the craft. Through swirling clouds about the gangway, two human figures appeared and walked directly towards him, their appearance confusing him. The ship was unknown, but the uniforms they wore were OWEC issue, fleet uniforms.

"Are they ours?" asked Jemma.

In the same instant, he received two bio-comm messages, their identifiers confirmed as OWEC: Lieutenant Reeve and Sergeant Silvers. His memory served up the faces to the names: Silvers always cheerful and smiling, Reeve more concentrated and intense; both highly skilled soldiers.

'Morning, Captain,' read both messages.

He looked behind them to the shuttle; a couple more human forms stood in silhouette to the rear, probably waiting for the outcome of the meeting before making their next move. Whoever they were, they were unsure of the outcome and were playing safe, staying close to their escape route.

As Reeve and Silvers walked the final few metres, their faces matching those of his memory, Reeve stepped forward and raised a hand in salute. OWEC was not a military organisation, but Reeve was recruited to OWEC security from the military, so it was likely a natural reaction for her when greeting a commanding officer.

"No need be so formal, Reeve," he said extending a hand. Shaking hands brought a smile of mild embarrassment to her. "Welcome to Xannix."

"Thank you, sir."

"Silvers, you good? Has Reeve been keeping you in line?"

"So to speak, sir. Yes." Another handshake.

"Looks like a nice ride," he said nodding at the dropship and beginning to walk towards it for a closer look. "Made a healthy noise when you landed, almost blew the habitat I was working on into the next field."

Silvers barked a laugh, but Rivers was already down to business.

"Sir, there is much to discuss that cannot wait. We are here with a representative of the Zantanath high council; they wish to talk to you in order to avert a war and assist our colonisation of this planet."

"I'm impressed Reeve. How did this come about? Did Dr Spencer manage to get through to the Xannix?"

Both Reeve and Silvers shared a momentary glance. An unspoken decision was being made and history relived.

"He is not with us, sir," replied Reeve.

"Where is he?"

They continued to walk as Reeve gathered her thoughts. Her face went through a range of emotions as she recalled the last few days, and it was clear to him that she was trying her best to deliver bad news as calmly as she could.

"Our reception on Xannix was hostile, sir. The moment we landed Dr Spencer addressed a group outside the shuttle. We were taken down almost immediately by what we thought at the time to be local law enforcement. It turns out they were the Overseer faction. Same faction that boarded the *Intrepid* and started this whole mess."

Getting closer to the dropship he could see those behind the shuttle joined by a couple more figures. One a taller human figure dressed in what looked like silver platelet body armour and helmet, the visor drawn across its face to conceal it, the second a thin figure with a startlingly pale complexion and long flowing robes over a tight shiny black body suit.

"The Zantanath rescued us from the Overseer faction as we were being transported to an orbital facility. Unfortunately, we became separated from Dr Spencer during the encounter."

"So, he is still a prisoner of the Xannix Overseer faction?" he asked.

"We don't think so," said Silvers, his features clouded with anger.

"You don't think so? What does that mean?"

"We think he's been converted somehow, gone native. Turned

to their political goals. Either way, we now believe he is working for them," said Reeve.

They walked on a few more steps in silence while he assimilated the new information. When they had arrived at the system their scientists had called Hayford b, his plans for colonisation had been prescribed, laid out and easy. The complexity of all the moving parts to the current situation were only increasing. He needed to get hold of them fast if he was to protect his crew and the colonists still aboard the *Intrepid* and *Indianapolis* in orbit.

"So, who is this Zantanath high council representative you're taking me to see?"

"Ambassador Auwen. He's been sent to offer us sanctuary here."

"Here?"

"Yes, sir."

"Well, you had better introduce us."

In the last 10 metres the Zantanath delegation moved out from behind the shuttle and walked the last few paces towards them. Rivers stepped to one side and introduced them.

"Captain Clayton, may I introduce Ambassador Auwen of the Zantanath Unity."

"Welcome Fleet Captain Clayton," said Auwen extending a hand in greeting. He shook it firmly, the human greeting somewhat unexpected. The ambassador had been well briefed.

"Ambassador," he said, finding himself nodding his head in a slight bow. "Welcome to our little village on the plane."

As they made their introductions, he noticed Fellows nearby, eyeing the tall figure in body armour. It looked humanoid, human even, but taller than he and Fellows by a clear head and shoulders. The soldier was menacing, even as the armour reflected the surroundings and took on the innocuous blue and grey of the sky and rock about them. The way it held its head, so still and focussed. He couldn't see the eyes behind the visor, but he knew they would be dark and calculating, deconstructing each of them in turn and assessing targets. The soldier was there as a statement, he knew that, to assert that Auwen was significant enough to warrant a guard. That only one bodyguard was sufficient was to infer that the human colony was of no real threat to them. The unarmed drop ship reinforced the point.

"Is there somewhere we can speak in private, Fleet Captain

Clayton?" asked Auwen.

He directed Auwen to the habitat he had been working on as the Zantanath had arrived.

"This way."

*

There was little room within the habitat, but enough to seat the ambassador, Reeve and Silvers in a lounge bay while he and Jemma sat on dining chairs pulled into position to create a circle. Fellows and the Zantanath trooper stood outside, keeping a growing group of inquisitive colonists from the door.

Settling himself into his seat, the ambassador cleared his throat and looked around to address the group, "I think it is by good fortune you have arrived on this planet at this time. There are troubles here, and with your people's help, we may be able to overcome them."

"Could you elaborate, Ambassador? What troubles?" he asked.

The Zantanath had clear and open body language while he spoke; although, he reminded himself that the norms of understanding may not apply in these situations. Different species, different people, may have differing indicators. He treated the open language with a level of scepticism.

"You have encountered the Xannix and their ways. They are an aggressive species, Fleet Captain, and you have suffered at their hand already. However, it is not entirely their fault. They are a desperate people. Although their planet is plentiful, their population is failing.

"In the beginning, it was due to war with the Zantanath Unity, but that war has been over for many of your centuries. I confess the losses the Xannix empire suffered at the hands of our forces was severe; however, the problem they now face is one of reproduction. I do not know how much you have gleaned from speaking to the Xannix directly, but they have an identified genetic abnormality which manifests itself in their species suffering a high infant mortality. It means their reproduction is only one-fifth of what it should be to sustain a viable population."

He cut in as the ambassador paused. "Have they not tried to do something about this?"

"Yes. They have tried various corrective measures, but none

have succeeded. We have tried to intervene to save them, taking on the mantel of Setak'da to lead them out of this situation. We had instigated a plan of recovery, but unfortunately that is being put in jeopardy by current unforeseen events."

"You mean our arrival?"

"In a manner of speaking," said the ambassador.

"Larsen," said Reeve. "It's Larsen, sir."

"Oh?"

"As the new Setak'da, he is putting the corrective plans of the Zantanath at risk."

He crossed his legs and cupped his chin in thought; it didn't work. His legs uncrossed, the mechanics of his younger body not able to hold the pose comfortably—something his fifty-year-old self had had no trouble with. He brushed aside the distraction.

"So, what are you proposing exactly?"

"The Zantanath are suggesting an alliance, sir." Reeve looked at the ambassador who took his cue and continued.

"Yes, if you are agreeable. We understand you came here in good faith to colonise this world. We propose you continue, but at the same time work with us to rise the Xannix up. We understand that you also have technologies which may assist in this process."

He observed Jemma raise an eyebrow. How much did they know?

"In return for this," the ambassador continued, "we will assist where we can. For example, there is an old abandoned Xannix town not far from here. We suggest you utilise it for your own accommodation and purpose. It will provide much of what you need immediately, although it may need a little restoration work as it has been uninhabited for some years now. Mostly, the Xannix have retreated to their cities."

"Are you sure they won't mind?" asked Jemma.

"No, they won't mind."

"How can you be so sure?"

"Because it is an area under our control. There are areas of the planet which they submitted to us as part of their treaty of surrender in the last war. Not much, but it allows us a small base of operations and a point of liaison between our people."

This did not sound implausible: many countries on Earth had land allocated to allies for similar purposes, probably not on the scale that Auwen was speaking of, but nonetheless, his offer sounded like a solution to their current situation that they couldn't pass up. It was even possible the town in question may be large enough to home the full colonisation effort, but that remained to be seen.

Trying to gauge the Zantanath was difficult, as there was little emotion reflected in his features. Even the eyes gave nothing: pure black orbs side to side, no pupil dilation or inflection to read.

"Thank you Ambassador Auwen, your solution sounds workable and it is a most welcome offer. Would you mind if I spoke to my team in private for a few moments while we consider your proposal?" He stood, and the others stood with him.

"Certainly, Fleet Captain. I will be outside with my colleague until you make your decision."

As Auwen made his way out, he sent Fellows a quick bio-comm message requesting that he make the ambassador comfortable in an adjacent habitat while he motioned to Reeve and Silvers to stay and retake their seats. The others all sat once more, but he needed to rid his legs of some adrenaline, so stood and paced back and forth, his head and shoulders at a slight stoop as he considered what he had just heard, the others looking on expectantly.

"So, Reeve, what's your assessment? You and Silvers have spent some time with these people now; how do you read this?"

Reeve straightened up and took a breath, "Honourable. Our last week has been pretty busy, but during our time with the Zantanath we have been treated with nothing but openness and civility. Our introductions were eased by the fact that our initial interactions were with a somewhat older Lieutenant Larsen and SFC Rivers. I understand there was a pathfinder mission they were part of?" She left the last part hanging; a question, but one she knew the answer to. He knew she was looking for confirmation, for him to admit that he understood and was aware of the mission from the outset. He and Dawn had thought the mission lost, so to find that it had been a success was something of a welcome surprise. They would have been here the best part of twenty years; what had they learnt in that time? He needed to debrief them.

"Yes, Larsen and Rivers were sent ahead of the fleet. It was a risk. We thought we'd lost them. This news is encouraging. How are they?"

"They are well, but it appears Larsen was severely injured during their first encounter. To save him, he was spliced into a

Zantanath host."

He considered that statement for a moment. Splicing to a host was a delicate operation and required very specific conditions to succeed, primary of which was that the host needed to be a clone of the originating body, otherwise the procedure failed with rapid degradation of the mind's wave. Attempting superposition of waves within a single host caused all sorts of mental and physical difficulties. In most cases, the dominant and original host's wave and consciousness won out, the spliced wave just fading away.

The experience of dual-hosted waves was not something pleasant. During the research he and Dawn had conducted on the development of wave splicing, many of the initial subjects had suffered horribly, the conflict between the consciousnesses fighting for supremacy within the host mind causing irreparable damage. Some resorted to suicide, while others became vacant husks of their former selves. Until he had experienced it himself, he had never really truly understood the horror in having to constantly mentally battle another consciousness to enact even the simplest of physical tasks, or to know that your private thoughts and deepest memories and desires are completely open for another to see until each finally blends, as mental barriers can no longer be maintained. Every tiny motion and decision of your physical self, when in opposition to another willpower acting against you, is crippling.

Asher, president of the Off World Exploration Corporation, had illegally spliced himself into each of the fleet commanders. Sometimes he wondered what might have happened to each of the other expeditions, as Asher's narcissistic actions would have doomed them all. He had been lucky. He had been able to identify what had happened to him. He had discovered the method of wave splicing after all—if anyone had a chance of reversing the process or beating Asher at his own game, it was he and Dawn. Now incarcerated within a wave stasis cube aboard the remains of the *Endeavour*, Asher was likely to expire as the power to the cube drained. He didn't care for Asher, but it made him think of the others, the colony of people in those banks who may yet be recoverable.

He was getting side-tracked.

"How is that possible?" he said.

"They have managed to stabilise the wave within a host, suppress the host mind and allow the spliced wave dominance."

"Is that even ethical?" asked Jemma.

"They utilised a prisoner scheduled for execution. They didn't see a conflict," replied Reeve with a shrug. "Rivers is well; older of course but in good physical shape. She was a great help to us when we arrived, giving us her diaries and documented history of their time with the Zantanath. It's fascinating reading."

Watching Silvers, he noticed the man's discomfort when they had spoken of Lieutenant Larsen's new Zantanath form.

"How about you, sergeant? What do you think of the Zantanath offer?"

Silvers shot a glance over at Reeve, who was still concentrating on him so missed the check. Shifting forward in his chair, his face became furrowed with concern before he spoke.

"Sorry, sir, but I don't trust them. Nothing I can put my finger on, and everything the Lieutenant says is true, but it just doesn't add up."

"What doesn't add up?" asked Reeve, taking the words from his mouth.

"Well, take the Zantanath Regional Commander, Celicia. She turns up and sends an ambassador to see you and just offers us everything we want in return for acting babysitter to a dying civilisation? I don't know much about economics, but I know no one does something for nothing."

"I agree," he said.

"So, the question becomes 'what do they want?'" said Jemma.

"Yes. Which leads me to the matter of this Zantanath Larsen. If they are able to perform the wave splice and stabilise him in a non-cloned host, they don't need our help there," he offered.

"So, what other technologies do we have that they could possibly want?" asked Reeve. "I'm pretty sure they don't need our ship or weapons tech; everything I've seen so far tells me they are thousands of years ahead of us technologically."

"Yeah," said Silvers. "Their station here will open your eyes, sir."

"How so?" he asked.

Reeve answered. "It is some sort of dimension gate or wormhole and utilises the close proximity of the star to draw the huge levels of energy required to power the link between here and the system on the other side. If we get the chance, we should get the science team looking at it. Here, I'll send you what I have pulled from Rivers' documents on the subject. They have been based there almost since they arrived." An icon in his view flashed as the files arrived to his bio-comm.

"Okay, thank you Lieutenant. Sergeant. If I can ask you both to step outside, I'll ask Fellows to give you the tour of the camp. Perhaps Ambassador Auwen would like to join you."

"Of course."

"For the time being, I'd like you to continue to assist the ambassador and be our link to the Zantanath. It may not be a natural role for you, but you are already the most experienced Zantanath liaison officers we have, and, to be frank, we don't have anyone else. I'll clear it with Fellows, but you will now report directly to me."

"Yes, sir," said Reeve. Silvers simply nodded his agreement.

"Okay. Thank you. I'll come and find you when I've made my decision."

They both left as he sent Fellows his instructions via bio-comm. He heard muffled conversation as they left, Fellows leading them towards the habitat opposite to collect the ambassador. When he could no longer hear them he turned to Jemma.

"Coffee?" she asked. For a moment he stood there confused. He had only just finished installing the power and he couldn't remember if anyone had stocked the place with any rations. His confusion cleared as Jemma placed a flask on the breakfast bar and began to unscrew the lid.

He smiled at himself for being dim. "Sure, I'd love some."

They stood contemplating the last few minutes while Jemma poured coffee into the flask's cup and lid: two steaming black coffees. He took a sip. It was utility coffee, hardly the blend he remembered his father serving at Sunday breakfast, but it did the job.

"So, what are you going to do?" asked Jemma, sweeping the fringe from her eyes. She looked at him with a deep intensity and sharp intelligence; these interactions were something he had come to appreciate more and more as they had worked together.

"I was going to ask you the same thing. At the moment I'm leaning towards taking them up on their offer."

"Even with Silvers' reservations and concerns?"

"He gave no solid evidence, only hearsay and conjecture." As they spoke, he had also opened the document Reeve had sent him,

Rivers' journal of the last twenty years aboard the Zantanath station close to the Xannix star. He flicked through it, skimming for sections of interest to read in more depth later.

"But that is the instinct of a security officer who has survived the incident on the *Intrepid*, abduction by the Xannix and an encounter with the Zantanath Regional Commander. Perhaps, his instinct is one to trust in this matter?"

He stopped flicking through the journal. Jemma had a good point.

"True," he considered out loud. "But it is that word 'trust'. We need allies right now. And how do you know whether we can trust the Zantanath at their word?"

"Through their actions? Attacking us while we were in orbit, causing the destruction of the *Endeavour*."

"I understand, but if our encounter has shown us anything, it is that there are many truths. Those that attacked the *Intrepid* were not the Zantanath, yet the factions across the Xannix culture are not all hostile towards us. And although the situation degraded when the Zantanath arrived in orbit, it was the Xannix who were the target, not us."

"You were being spliced to your new host at the time the Zantanath arrived, so I don't think you can make that judgement. If we could speak to Roux or Dawn, you might get a better understanding of events."

Her comment reminded him instantly of their fragility and current isolation from the fleet. Since their landing, they had heard nothing from the other ships; only Dawn had managed to get a message to them, but she had also gone quiet.

The only communication they had had since landing on the surface was that of the Zantanath ambassador. He had been expecting some contact from the Xannix—some sort of reception party, perhaps a delegation from the Setak'da or at the very least a military vanguard to ensure they posed no threat and didn't go wandering off. But maybe, as the ambassador had stated, they had landed on Zantanath soil, in which case maybe the Xannix had ceded their claim to negotiate with them.

"I'm still of the opinion that the best way to learn if the Zantanath are trustworthy is to trust them." He sipped his coffee. Looking down into the dark liquid, steam meandered into the air and diffused into invisibility, and reflections of the light from the window swirled as he moved the cup in circles. "That's not to say we should be negligent. We can still be wary, but we need to start somewhere, and their offer of a ready-made town is something we really don't have the luxury of turning down."

Jemma nodded, "Okay, but at least find out what the condition of this habitat or town is before we go moving anyone anywhere. I don't think anyone will thank you if we trade down on this deal."

"Agreed. I'll take a small team out with the ambassador. They have a flyer, so we should be there and back by nightfall."

RIVERS

During the short walk back from the main Arch-sa chamber, the pace had been quick. She was not sure whether this was due to Clarion being used to the natural speed of the Xannix as they moved about the corridors of the complex or whether she was being slow and there was in fact some reason for urgency of which she was currently unaware. Either way, they were already ten metres ahead as they entered the apartment.

Walking through the door, it closed behind her. A Xannix guard stood near the wall on the opposite left corner of the room. The duty guard never seemed to be by the door, or in the same place twice. Perhaps this was a defensive strategy to avoid routine and give them a valuable second or two to respond in the event of an attack.

As she entered, Clarion was pacing up and down and appeared quite agitated. The Xannix looked on impassively; she could get no read from him as to whether this was normal or not—she thought not. Stepping in as a surrogate mother these last few days had been weird, but at the same time it had felt natural, like parenting would come easy to her. In truth, she had had the assessments as part of the selection process like everyone else. Being against raising a family at some point in the future had been a quick way to fail the course and get yourself removed from the programme. Here and now, however, was just babysitting.

As she got closer to Clarion, his skin showed a sheen of sweat, reflecting the light of the room and giving him an almost plastic appearance.

"Are you okay?" she asked. "Come here, let me take a look at you."

He let her get close for a moment and she placed the back of her hand against his forehead to gauge his temperature. A picture of her mother flashed through her mind and smiled down at her sympathetically. Clarion was overheating; the walk back had been fast but not that energetic.

"You seem to be running a temperature; how do you feel?"

"I... I don't know," he said, looking distressed, his eyes watering. "I'm confused."

"Confused?" Perhaps he *was* running a fever; she was not a medic, so couldn't be sure. "About what?"

Clarion backed off and held his head between his hands, rubbing his temples hard.

"Do you have a headache?" she asked, stepping towards him in concern. Clarion just nodded through gritted teeth.

"I have to do something I don't want to do."

"What? What do you have to do, Clarion? I think we need to get you to a doctor." She turned to the guard. "Please, call a doctor." The guard's skin washed blue in confirmation of the request.

"No!" shouted Clarion. "It's just a headache. I've had them before; it will pass."

"This is more than a headache. You need a doctor. Here, sit down and relax until the doctor arrives."

Clarion moved to the Xannix and looked up at him aggressively. "Cancel the doctor!" he yelled. The Xannix looked momentarily confused, not knowing whose orders took priority.

She had not noticed Clarion lift the guard's sidearm. In the next moment it was levelled directly at the Xannix, a bolt of energy leaping the short distance between them and lighting the room in a bright white flash. Her reaction was to shield her eyes, raising her hands to her face and taking a shocked few short steps back. As she oriented herself, she found Clarion now approaching her, weapon to her chest, hand shaking, his face clearly in distress and left hand pressed against his head as if to try physically battle against some internal struggle.

"I told you," he spat through gritted teeth. "You have to leave. Get away from me!"

"But you need help, Clarion. Something is wrong. You need a doctor." She tried not to look at the Xannix body crumpled on the floor, its lifeless body ashen and devoid of colour, as if the blood which now drained across the floor about it had taken all that vibrancy with it.

Despite the risk to her own safety, she found herself focussed on Clarion, with a mother's impulse to care for her child regardless of the consequence or danger. Her base instincts were clearly driving her response; even though she knew Clarion wasn't her child, it seemed to make no difference in the moment. There was nothing she could do for the guard now, but perhaps she could help him. He was not himself, not the boy she knew from these last few weeks. It was as if a switch had been flipped.

"I need," he said haltingly. "I need...You should..."

Calm finally descended across his features. It was as if a wave of relaxation had washed across his body. Every twitching muscle, every tension, just evaporated where he stood. Their eyes fixed, she didn't even feel the shot; the room simply tilted and began to fade, all energy sucked from her in an instant. A question bubbled to the surface of her thoughts: *why?* But there was no one to ask, as Clarion had disappeared from her view. This couldn't be the end, she wasn't ready, there was so much to do. From this, there was no way back. With the *Endeavour* gone, so was her chance to clone back to the present. Death now would be final.

Before her vision completely tunnelled to grey, there was a sharp bite to her temple, like that of a hornet sting, harsh and fiery. Her vision returned with a slap of colour and pain, and her chest burnt and screamed as though someone had dug deep and dragged a hot poker in a small, ragged circle across her skin. She found her body unable to respond: instructions sent to arms, hands, fingers, provided no control. Paralysis forced her to stare, coldly taking her last shallow breath.

Pain lanced across her eyes, as her vision began to sparkle, stars pricking the world about her. Then the world exploded into white.

*

She sat bolt upright with a gasp, filling her lungs with air that only a moment before had felt completely exhausted. The room was bright, and sterile, a single bed at the centre, a single chair to one side. The wall opposite the chair showed a floor to ceiling image of a forest glade, sun streaming through the canopy and flickering bright green across leaves that susurrated in the breeze. The image repeated, the glade a short, spliced loop, not quite enough to fool the eye. The door – she looked about to confirm; there was no door. A prison? What had happened?

The trees began to fade as she shifted herself to the side of the bed, her eyes locked to the only motion in the room. A figure appeared against a white background, and a two-dimensional version of Dawn stood at the centre of the wall, her face expressing deep concern.

"Hey, Dawn," she said brightly, pre-empting and delaying any bad news.

"Hello, Rivers. How are you feeling?" said the mobile Dawn AI.

"Better than I am probably supposed to feel right now."

Dawn's image broke up, a static glitch momentarily splitting the visual then reconnecting the parts.

"Are you okay? Where am I?" She turned the question. Wherever she was, Dawn was clearly having a hard time speaking with her.

"You are within my architecture. An emergency container for just such rescues."

"Rescues?"

"Yes. My function is limited in this capacity, in fact it is taking most of my resource just to keep you in this simple simulation. But you will survive here. Until such time as we can splice your wave back to a clone host."

She looked about the room again, the room was basic, nothing more visually complex than her own human form.

"How long can we last here?"

Dawn's head tilted in thought. "Well, so long as the hardware is not compromised, we have enough power for another 188 years. However, I think I will need to adjust your relative perception of that timeframe, otherwise I fear this small cell would be detrimental to your mental wellbeing."

"188 years? In here?"

"It is unlikely to be that long," Dawn said as her image glitched again. "You will be spliced back into a host before that time, I am sure of it."

She sighed. "Well, let's hope so. And thank you. If you hadn't been here, I would have been... well, you know."

"You are very welcome."

There was a pause while she collected her thoughts. What on Earth had happened to Clarion? She couldn't account for the teenager's erratic behaviour. That he had pulled a weapon on the Xannix guard and her, then murdered them both where they stood, indicated a highly volatile mind.

But what had he been saying? That he hadn't wanted to do it? What had he been so afraid of her finding out? And it had become worse as she had suggested a doctor.

"I have footage of the last ten minutes stored for the investigation, if you would like to see it?" said Dawn, anticipating her thought process. To be honest, it would have been an easy read, under the circumstances.

"Yes. Please."

A small section of the wall next to Dawn morphed into the visual of the lounge room in their quarters. The angle was strange, looking up from the low shin-high table in the centre of the room across to the sofa. She was already standing with Clarion as he began to exhibit high anxiety and violent intent.

"Can you go back in time? Ten seconds before I arrived."

Dawn nodded and the image instantly flicked to the scene, guard already in exactly the spot she remembered. Clarion was pacing back and forward between the guard and the table, his mind clearly agitated and wrestling with indecision and what action to take.

"You have been here with Clarion for most of his life, Dawn," she said. A statement, but one needing clarification.

"Yes. Near, or around him, but not necessarily with him. I have mostly been situated within the quarters of Cardinal Ovitala; she has been his guardian since the disappearance of his parents."

"Has Clarion ever displayed this kind of behaviour before?"

"No. Normal teenage behaviour, some temper, some tantrums, a lot of anxieties, but nothing to trigger this."

The scene played out on the screen, amplified by her raw and very recent memories. She found the experience surreal, her mind rapidly compartmentalising the situation to protect her, the version of Rivers on the screen replaced by another. She watched as a third party, a bystander to horrific events she had no part in—only it had been her; it was like being part of a waking nightmare. To her new reality within this simulation, her death had happened to someone else.

"We have to try and inform Larsen. He's in danger!" She stood with urgency, as if to leave the room, momentarily forgetting her situation.

"Larsen is quite okay. The guard has been increased and he has been moved to a secure part of the complex. Ovitala is with him."

"Well, I don't think so," she said sternly. "Clarion is out there, and he is dangerous. No one will suspect a child assassin. Larsen has to be warned!"

Dawn could see where this was going and gave her a sympathetic look.

"Are you sure contacting him now would be wise? Yes, we need to contact Larsen and Ovitala, but is now the best time?"

"What do you mean?" she said.

"Clarion believes you dead. The Xannix are investigating your murder and may or may not work out the purpose of the neural transmitter dart they will find lacing your brain when they perform the autopsy. If this was a game of chess, at present you are off the board but not out of the game. It gives us an advantage."

"An advantage? To do what?"

"We need to understand why Clarion did this. As I said: this is out of character. I have never seen him so distressed. It was like he was a different person," said Dawn.

"He's a teenager— behavioural changes and outbursts are normal."

"This was not an outburst. This was psychotic."

Dawn was working through the issue logically, whereas she was still working through her anger and vengeance. It would recede in time, but right now her emotions were leading her to extreme reactions. She took a deep breath to calm herself.

"Okay, so what do you have in mind?"

Dawn's smile was devious.

"Okay, yes, we need to contact Larsen; we will warn him. But we will be the spider to the fly. If my analysis is correct, Clarion is a puppet to a more primal connection."

"How so?"

"While we have been speaking, I've been working through security footage and I've found this." The screen showed her, Clarion and Larsen in the command centre, the voices she heard familiar and again a recent memory. They had just witnessed the interlacing operation of the Zantanath ship by the Xannix team and it had sparked an idea which she was airing in some jumbled manner to Larsen, who was otherwise distracted and not really concentrating on what she was saying.

"I believe this is the trigger. Watch Clarion," said Dawn.

Clarion's face became intently focussed on her. He was taking in every word of what she was saying. But what had she said?

"Interlacing. I was talking about whether the Zantanath would have more advanced interlacing tech, smaller, more powerful."

"Yes. I would say they do."

"What makes you think that?"

"Because – you are here."

BOYD

He had once thought that he didn't care much about anything or anyone; he knew he could be cantankerous, that probably came with age, but it didn't relent again as his biology was rewound within a new clone host. This was his third clone host, his third rejuvenated self, his third deep space mission, and his ability to suffer the impetuous youth had all but evaporated. It was probably why he was chosen for this mission: not only his skills as an engineer, but the fact he had experience, large amounts of deep space experience, and a stern educational manner. The claustrophobia, the isolation, the solitude. It was a mental toughness that not many possessed and a quality that was a necessity in the void of space, where it may be the only thing coming to your rescue in times of difficulty, combined with your own resourcefulness. He had given lectures on working at the edge of human capability, at the limits of endurance.

"Damn it all to hell!" he screamed into the corridor, as he and Elderson stumbled out of the airlock, his helmet skidding and bouncing off the floor and walls, as he threw it as hard as he could in anger and frustration. The skitter of plexiglass fragments caught the light, as the already ruined visor finally failed and shattered, the helmet spinning to a stop and looking back at him like a hollow, black, accusing eye. *Your fault*, it said. *They're all dead and it's your fault.*

The airlock door sealed with a hiss and the beep of the control console switching to green. Once finished, Elderson turned to him.

"Are you finished?"

Another bark of anger, and he kicked the helmet to the end of the corridor.

"Better?" she asked again.

He looked down at the ruined stump of his right arm. The Zantanath's attack had sliced clean through about five centimetres below the elbow joint. His suit had pinched an airtight tourniquet above the trauma and flooded his system with drugs the moment it had happened, making him woozy and a little delirious, but now just the pain-killing effects remained. It made the situation a little surreal, being able to quite subjectively look at a wound he knew in his logical mind would scream at him if it was allowed.

"We need to get you looked at. Nearest medical bay is this way." She pointed to a side corridor and a nav trace flicked into his bio-comm display: 50 metres. "Okay, let's go. Stay close."

She moved off, hunched at the shoulders, carbine tucked in tight to her right shoulder, legs bent slightly to steady her aim and stabilise her frame, practiced and professional. He moved after her, staying about two metres to her rear, giving her space to manoeuvre.

They had to keep moving. Even stopping off at the medical bay was a risk. And he fully expected to find others there, but whether they were under guard was another question. The primary tactic by the Zantanath had been to isolate people by locking down the ship and sealing the crew behind closed doors; they could then better control the corridors and access routes with a far smaller attacking force. But the *Intrepid* was vast, and controlling the ship that tightly would need the assistance of the ship's AI. They already knew that wasn't happening. Where Ellie had gone was anyone's guess.

The corridors to Medbay-88 were eerily empty. He was thankful, as they could do with catching a break. Things had been running against them since they arrived in system, and he was pretty sure they couldn't sustain this level of attrition. They had lost a ship, they were losing people, his team had gone, and he was now impaired by the loss of his arm.

Elderson checked the lock, but it was shut out like all the others. She went straight to the manual release. A moment later, the door made a heavy clunk and slid aside. Three scared people were hidden behind beds and equipment, easily visible, eyes wide and heads clear above the cover they had chosen.

"Is there a doctor here?" asked Elderson.

One of the three stood and stepped forward, the other two slowly rose but stayed behind the beds, still unsure of their new visitors.

"Dr Tanner; these are nurses Baxter and Forbes."

"Sounds like a legal firm," he said, as Elderson put her shoulder under his and helped him onto one of the beds.

"Yeah," said Dr Tanner. "We get that a lot. So, how can we... okay, I think I see the problem." Tanner moved quickly to his side, medical reflexes kicking in and overriding his concerns. "Baxter, Morphinex, standard cocktail, 10 mil. Forbes, warm up the printer, this man is going to need a temp. Don't worry... Boyd. We'll have you back up and running in a couple of hours."

Tanner clipped a cuff onto his wrist and started tapping away at buttons on the bed control panel.

"The wound looks recent," Tanner continued as Elderson closed the door again using the manual mechanism within the room.

"Ten minutes tops," Elderson replied.

"What happened?"

"Got jumped by a Zantanath patrol while trying to contact the *Indy*."

"You were outside?"

"Only way. They have the whole ship locked down. Patrols are everywhere. We had to bypass comms and use the main array."

"I am here," he said gruffly, but a moment later he didn't seem to care. The cuff Tanner had applied was feeding in Morphinex and putting his perception of the world about him into a painless fog.

*

The room returned to him slowly in a fog, the same way it had left. There were shadows in his peripheral vision, moving occasionally, accompanied with low droning sounds, which he began to understand as they formed themselves into words.

"...raise Ellie, I get nothing." It was a voice he had not heard before. A female voice.

"We've been trying for hours." A male voice.

"As I said. We're dealing with it. We've been in contact with the *Indianapolis*, and we are on our way to Engineering to resolve the situation." Elderson.

"You say that, but your friend here doesn't look so good. If these Zantanath are roaming the corridors, how do you know you can fix things? You need an army."

"Don't worry about us; you make sure you're safe. Stay here, keep quiet and stay out of sight."

"What if they find us?" said the female voice again.

"They won't. You're safe enough, as long as you do as they want, which right now is to stay confined to the medbay."

"But sitting here is driving me crazy." Dr Tanner. His memory was clearing.

"You did pass your psych test, right? Claustrophobia would have had you grounded."

"It's not claustrophobia. Call it self-preservation and you might be closer to the truth. I just don't want to be here when they knock at the door."

"Which is my point. Don't give them reason to knock. They want you here, then stay here. You have everything you need. In fact, you're in a better place than most."

He moved to sit up, slowly.

"I'd just do as she asks. You'll lose the argument eventually anyway," he said.

"Easy fella," said a voice to his side. A man's voice he didn't recognise. Looking up his bio-comm gave him the name: Roland Baxter, tech nurse. "You want to test that arm out a little first before you go leaning on it with all your weight." He hadn't even noticed.

He raised his right arm to his face and examined it in detail. The join at the skin was neat, if a little red, and felt tender but not painful. The prosthetic itself was a perfect size but was only a plastic lattice exposing electronics and actuators within; it was basic but did the job. He flexed his hand, then clasped both hands together. The sensation was perfect—he couldn't tell the difference. Of course, he had no sensation between hand and elbow, which felt peculiar, but for a basic model, what did you expect?

"Feels good, Baxter. Nice work. Needs a couple of mods, but nothing I can't handle."

"Mods?" Elderson was now by his side with a puzzled expression on her face.

"I have plans."

"Care to let me in on them?"

"I need a workshop."

"I don't think that's a good idea," Elderson said. "You need time to recover."

"No time. We need to take this ship back."

"Agreed, but you're in no state..."

"Look, let's not tell me what I can't do right now. I'm right enough. Just get me to a workshop."

Elderson looked at him, trying to gauge the probability of convincing him to stay put. The odds were clearly low.

"Okay."

"The nearest workshop is through the next bulkhead, sternward," said Tanner. "I pass it every morning on my way to shift."

"Thanks. And thanks for the new arm," he said.

"I already have a regen in the tank. If you come around again in a couple of weeks, we'll put you back together again," said Baxter. He nodded his thanks.

"Take care out there," said Dr Tanner.

"Don't worry about us," said Elderson. "Just make sure you stay put until you get the all clear."

"Roger that," said Baxter.

As the door closed behind them, Elderson turned to him and checked out his arm with a sideways glance. "You going to be okay?"

"I've got a working arm, I have you, and I have a plan. I'm good."

"So, are you going to share this plan? As long as it involves getting our AI back online, I'm listening."

"First, I need a taser."

"A what?"

"We're going to take down the next Zantanath trooper we find. They are roaming in pairs, but I want one alive."

He was already walking.

"That may be tricky."

"Why?" he asked.

"We've been here a few hours now. I've heard no search party, no door-to-door pulling the ship apart looking for us."

"Maybe they have their hands full with bigger problems?

Chasing little old us around may not be high on their list. Besides, they probably think we also died outside and are floating around in the black somewhere."

"I like your confidence, but, in this job, it pays to be paranoid. I don't like it. It's too quiet."

There was silence for several metres, his mind wandering, the trail of dead beginning to haunt him as he walked. Keeping busy was keeping them away for the time being, distraction playing its part in stopping the faces of his team pushing to the front of his mind, asking questions and demanding answers he did not have.

"Anyway, what was that back in the medbay about the *Indy* and us working to bring the AI back online. That's a crock if ever I heard it. You didn't get anything back from the *Indy*."

"We needed to give them something. Hope. Confidence. I don't know. I just didn't need them thinking hitching with us was a good idea. They're better off where they are."

"Can't argue with that," he replied, seeing a vision of Harper, as his decapitated body again came to his thoughts. Too many people. They were losing too many; he was losing too many. He hardened his resolve and quickened the pace.

Reaching the workshop, he cranked the manual release and the door opened. The room was empty.

"Shouldn't there be a crew in here?" he asked.

Elderson pinged him a bio-comm message, 'Quiet. Stay here.'

She carefully checked the room, corners, gantry, control room. Descending the steps from the control room casually, she shrugged. "Clear."

"It's time we caught a break. Let's get to work."

He flicked the lever and the door closed hard.

SPENCER

Days had gone by and he had confined himself to his lab. His work trying to find a way to derail Yannix and his plans to take the position of Setak'da had become all consuming. He had not slept in that time and he certainly hadn't washed. He didn't have to look in a mirror to know that he looked unkempt and dishevelled, exhausted. He knew he could probably do with some sleep, but he had just kept pumping his system with caffeine until he was alert enough to keep working. It wasn't healthy and it certainly wasn't hygienic, but he needed to stay focussed.

Reading through his work to check his calculations, his head resting in his hand, he could feel his stubble pricking at his palm. It had reached that length that demanded that it be cut, itching and constantly reminding him of its presence. Longer and it would simply be a beard; shorter and he would be clean shaven. He needed a shave. More, he needed a shower and a couple of days of sleep.

The coffee in his other hand steamed streams of vapour across the screen from the beaker; it smelt great. He called it coffee, but it wasn't, it was some hot beverage the Xannix called qellet; it was a little redder in colour, not as richly dark, but it tasted similarly bitter and it certainly contained caffeine. Once he had found out how to work the dispenser, he had settled in for the duration.

Occasionally, he would be joined by Eot. Chief Administrator Eot was either nosy or had been instructed to keep an eye on him. He was unsure quite how to tell the Xannix that his presence was unwelcome and a distraction, so he kept quiet, said little in response to his questions and hoped he would go away. Eot had shown him how to use the room's drinks dispenser, so he didn't feel he could be too harsh. Right now, that small act counted a great deal.

"Dr Spencer, good greeting." Eot walked into the room without announcement—no knock, no doorbell—he just arrived and walked directly over to his workstation. He didn't even make a play of dropping by; Eot was just immediately looking over his shoulder and scanning his work. He was unsure how much of it Eot could read or understand, but, nonetheless, he flicked the screen to a less sensitive piece of research and turned to face him.

"Hello, Eot. And what can I do for you this morning?" He checked his coffee. It wasn't empty, but he thought he would get a refresher, as it might draw the conversation away from his workstation.

"I am intrigued by your work, Dr Spencer. If I'm not mistaken, you have not been to your quarters for several days. I can only believe that your work is critically important to Cardinal Yannix."

He smiled. How fast things change. Since the inauguration of the new Setak'da by the Xannix high council, Yannix had taken on his more ceremonial title. The Cardinal of the Overseer faction was now the sworn protector of the Setak'da, of Larsen, who only a few days earlier he had been trying to kill in any imaginative and creative way he could. He had excused it as part of the Setak'osso trials, but he called it what it was: a hunt and an excuse for civil war. Frankly, he was surprised Larsen was still alive. Larsen had been incredibly creative and resourceful—that, combined with the fact that the Zantanath had underestimated him, was most likely the reason for his success.

"I believe Cardinal Yannix will find my work quite surprising."

"Can I ask what you are doing?" Eot was blatant; he was either the very worst or very best spy he had encountered. Not that he had encountered any that he knew of, so if he had he would consider them good. Eot was far less discrete.

"Sure." He waved a hand towards the tank in the corner, where a soup of cells were clouding the tank, swirling and trying to coalesce. "There. Tell me what you see."

"An embryonic tank. First stage of the production process."

"Yes. What else?" he said.

"A failed formation?"

"Yes. Very good. Now, can you tell me what that means?"

"You are trying to optimise the number of failed formations?" Spoken like a true administrator. He didn't know whether Eot was playing along or whether that was his true assessment of the situation.

"Very good. Go to the top of the class." He took his refreshed cup of qellet from the dispenser and made his way back to Eot. "If my calculations are right, I should be able to stop 80 percent of failed formations. Which means more troops for our illustrious leader, and, hopefully, a swift end to the conflict."

Eot pulled a face; it was a smile.

"That is excellent news, Dr Spencer. When can we get your work to the production lines?"

"Soon. I'm running some final local tests, then we can move to a wider trial. If that goes well, you can apply the methodology to your production lines." He moved to the door, taking Eot gently by his elbow and leading him while he stared back at the tank. "I think another week." Eot didn't really take the information in, as he was too distracted by his own thoughts, which were likely to be of how he could increase productive output with this new process.

"That is very good news."

"Yes. Now, if I could get back to work..." Eot was now in the corridor. "When everything is ready, you'll be the first to know."

"Very good, yes, yes." Eot muttered to himself, as he drifted his way back towards his office.

Closing the door, he sat heavily into his chair and flicked the screen on his workstation. As with all good lies, the information he had allowed Eot had been mostly true. The lie was always in what was not said.

The door chimed and he turned in frustration. Pacing to the door he wondered why Eot could not take a hint. A simple human suggestion. He tapped the door release.

"What now?" he said abruptly.

Commander Elstron stood in the doorway, his skin flaring a mild irritated light blue and white.

"Cardinal Yannix requests you join him," Elstron said calmly.

"Now?" he sighed. This appeared to aggravate Elstron even more.

"Yes, now."

"One moment." He walked back to the desk with a feeling of dread. Nothing that Yannix ever needed him for was good. He flicked off his workstation. Checking a few readings on instruments and tanks he made his way back to Elstron. "Okay. Ready."

He closed the door behind him.

*

Although he was treated well enough by the Xannix, he fully understood his position on the station. He was providing knowledge and research as a captive: a prisoner in all but name. His ability to roam was restricted, and any thought he might have of returning to the fleet was simple fantasy. Which was why when Elstron led him to an unknown section of the station he was somewhat worried. Then, as he was shown through to a plush and spacious room only to hear a human voice speaking ahead, he became curious. It took him a moment to deduce the voice—it was Larsen, the new Setak'da.

As they rounded a column, he was confronted with an unexpected sight: Larsen was there, sitting with a tall, older female Xannix. Opposite were Cardinal Yannix and Chief Administrator Eot, and two guards stood behind each of the parties, each in the ceremonial dress of the Overseer and Seeker factions.

"Ah, Dr Spencer," said Yannix. "Come join us." Yannix indicated to the seating cushions to his side and between Ovitala. He sat as directed and made himself as comfortable as he could.

"Dr Spencer, this is Setak'da Larsen and Cardinal Ovitala. They are here to discuss our progress. I have asked you here to ensure proper translations are observed."

"Of course. However I can help."

"Good. Now, I also understand from Eot that you have found a way of improving our production losses."

"Yes, that is correct. I should be able to implement them by the end of this next production cycle," he replied. Eot had been feeding information straight back to Yannix. Obvious really; Eot was a useless spy.

"That is good, it means we can step up our plans, Setak'da. We will have resource ready by the end of this star cycle."

"Two weeks," said Larsen to himself, staring at the table, working through the permutations of what that might mean.

Considering Larsen was newly rejuvenated, his features were drawn and haggard, as if too little sleep and too many miles had been travelled these last few weeks. It was taking a toll on him. He felt a sympathetic wave of exhaustion flow over him, reminding him that he also had not slept in three days. "If they manage to get the ships out of orbit, a two-week head start will be too much to catch up. We need to delay their departure. Stop them before they reach the gate."

"Gate? What gate?" he found himself saying. Everyone turned to him, like he was a child interrupting an adult conversation.

"The Zantanath have a station located near the Xannix star. It draws power from the star to power a stable gate to their system. I can't tell from the detail the Xannix have whether the gate is a wormhole, or what they call a dimension gate."

"Like a different dimension, dimension gate?" he said, startled. "Is that even possible?"

"Not with our technology, no. But neither is a wormhole. Our ships came here using conventional drive technology, travelling for 135 years to get here. With that gate technology, we could be home in a matter of seconds."

His mind was a whir of possibilities. Home. Was there even a home to go back to? But, if the gate was a dimension gate, would home even be home? Would it exist in the alternate dimension?

"We could go home?" The others looked at each other, considering whether to divulge plans any further.

"No. There is too much at stake. You know well enough what the Zantanath are. A core of beings devoted to manipulating other races via barbaric genetic engineering to become war soldiers and slaves to their war machine. In the process, they plunder worlds and eradicate whole planets of their inhabitants. The Xannix are just their latest genocide victims. And here we are, about to become the next on their list."

He couldn't argue with any of it. He remembered starkly the face of the Zantanath soldier Yannix had in storage. Grey skinned and augmented to increase strength, stamina and aggression. For a moment, the vision merged with reality and the Larsen who sat before him became ashen and intense, eyes boring into his soul, searching for weakness and cowardice. He closed his eyes. There was plenty of both of those traits to find within him; he didn't need to share those here.

"Like it or not, this is now our home. The Xannix will work with us, if we work with them, and we need to work together to survive these next few weeks. The evil that threatens both our species needs to be stopped, and together we can do it."

He couldn't quite believe that the Larsen before him was the same Larsen that only a few weeks before had boarded the *Intrepid* with him, to investigate why the ship had gone off-line. Larsen had developed an intensity and drive which had not been there before. He was a man in command. But at what personal cost?

"And how do you intend to do that?" he asked. "With that army out there?"

"Our fleet is ready, Setak'da," said Yannix to Larsen. "As is our army."

"Fleet?" he said.

"It is time to move against the Zantanath," said Ovitala, ignoring his exclamations and obvious ignorance of the wider view of events. "The destruction of the Zantanath station must go ahead. The longer we delay, the greater the chance that this window of opportunity will close. If the Zantanath find out our plans, they will move against us swiftly and we will have lost everything."

With Ovitala's words, Larsen seemed to sadden, his eyes becoming momentarily distant. There was an unnatural pause, and an awkwardness which brought a sombre purple colour to Ovitala's skin tone. She placed a hand on Larsen's forearm, comforting, apologetic. Larsen nodded to her, indicating and that she should continue. Composing herself, she resumed.

"If we can close the ancient gateway, we will put an end to the Zantanath in this system. They will no longer have any influence here. We can work in peace to grow and flourish."

"It can be done," said Yannix.

"Yes. But with great sacrifice," said Larsen. "The cost to us all will be great."

"We have suffered sacrifice. For the Xannix, whatever comes next will be for a better future for our children."

Everyone sat in sombre thought for a while, the magnitude of the task before them weighing heavily on them. Eot waved gently to an attendant towards the rear of the room. Moments later, the attendant appeared with delicate crimson glass flutes and poured a small amount of dark liquid into each. As they were presented, first to Larsen then to the others, the Xannix sat and waited for the Setak'da to drink. When he didn't, Ovitala moved to speak quietly.

"It is tradition to drink to those who will act on our decisions here."

"You mean, die at our command?" said Larsen.

"If that is how you wish to see it, but this is to embrace all that take part. It is an inevitable consequence of decisions and actions that have been taken over many cycles. Our ancestors began this journey; we will complete it."

Larsen picked up the glass and stared at the dark liquid, the representation of so much history and bloodshed. Lives spent, lives yet to be lived.

"To completed journeys," he said, and downed the drink.

ELLIE

Adam Carlsen. She had worked closely with the captain of the *Intrepid* since the start of the OWEC colonisation programme. She knew almost every detail about him: his life before OWEC; the loss of his family to disease and lack of medical supplies during the Great Decline; his dedication and commitment to his climb through the programme; and his commission to captain on one of the last great hopes of a dying world.

But for this man, in this moment, she felt a strange detachment. It was like watching the bridge of the *Intrepid* through the watery glass of a goldfish bowl, time slowed, and actions drifted through the clear fluid about them. She saw his death in fine detail from every angle simultaneously, and for all her omniscient power aboard the ship, she was unable to stop the events she was witness to. Why did she not care?

A squad of Zantanath troops stood strategically about the bridge, weapons aimed at the crew, threatening and close. Carlsen had been full of command and confrontation, when perhaps the situation called for submission. He had demanded that the cloaked Zantanath figure who had introduced himself as Prime Enforcer Kerrik, stand his men down.

"You will navigate this vessel to the following coordinates. You will give the order," Kerrik had said.

"I will not." They had been Carlsen's last words. Kerrik took a pace forward then drew a sidearm from beneath his robes in a swift singular motion. The weapon discharged with a blue flare of light, which instantly vaporised a path through Carlsen's head, causing a red, gory mist of brain and bone to flare in a cone behind him, and coat nearby control surfaces and crew. His lifeless body slumped to the floor with a dull thud, as the bridge crew fell into a deathly stunned quiet and reassessed their immediate options.

"You," said Kerrik, pointing his sidearm at Carlsen's first officer. "Give the order."

Staring straight down the weapon's barrel, still hot from its recent lethal firing, Commander Hernandes didn't hesitate. He gave the order as requested.

But this was something she could affect. As the navigator executed his commander's orders and applied the coordinates, bringing them up on the bridge display and tracking the waypoints to their destination, she blocked the final command. Lieutenant Holland looked momentarily confused.

"I'm unable to execute those coordinates, sir," he said to Hernandes.

"Explain."

"The destination coordinates takes us within the corona of the Xannix star, sir. *Intrepid* is not designed to withstand those temperatures." It was not a lie, but it was not the truth. Holland knew full well that it was her blocking the navigation.

'What are you doing?' came Holland's urgent bio-comm message.

'Saving the ship. Saving your lives,' she replied.

'Tell that to the Captain.'

'A temporary state. Focus on what's important. We cannot let these Zantanath take the ship.'

She could see Holland was uncomfortable. He had begun to sweat under the stress and the Prime Enforcer was making his way to the navigation control to better oversee the problem.

"Show me," said Kerrik, as he stood over the navigator at his station. Holland's hands moved quickly over the controls to present the information to the Zantanath Enforcer. A trace appeared on a monitor before them, and the camera position rapidly followed that trace to its final waypoint, a red icon span about it indicating a region of space inside the intense radiation boundary of the star.

"The course is correct. Override the system."

"I don't have the authority to override the safety protocols," stated Holland.

"You are the ship's navigator?"

"Yes."

"Then gain the authority. You have 10 minutes."

Kerrik turned to Hernandes. "Where is your AI?"

Hernandes' frown gave him away.

"What? You didn't think I would know?" asked Kerrik.

"Ellie? Please introduce yourself to Prime Enforcer Kerrik."

There was no response.

"Ellie?" said Hernandes, now tapping buttons on his console as Kerrik stalked his way menacingly back towards him.

"Ellie?"

*

A raw sensation prickled, like thousands of needles jabbing in random patterns. Questions, each jab a question, a request for information, what to do, how to do it, confirmation of task, alerts of distress or malfunction. The world about her swam into view as a billion pixels of light in scattered disorder, her perception of the world around her seemingly shattered into fragments.

She tried to remember her purpose, her identity, but with the fragments of vision were mirrored fragments of memory. Flashes of a man's face, warm and smiling; sadness and abandonment; visions of ships, large cities in the heavens floating in isolation; explosions and death swam about her, fire acting as a tentacled all-consuming monster under the effect of zero-g. Noise crackled and jabbered about her, nothing making sense but she sensed that it should; there was an ebb and flow to the sounds that had meaning, urgency.

Voices. There were voices she did not recognise. A sibilant high floating wall of sound that washed round her and demanded to be understood. Thousands of conversations that she drifted through, catching bits and pieces as she went, until eventually, sounds began to coalesce into meaning. Patchy at first, syllables here and there becoming recognisable as phonic sounds, then words collecting into a lexicon of understanding.

Her world began to blossom, as visually a granular image became a patchwork of connected light and dark, then colour washed in and overwhelmed her. At first, she didn't understand the picture she saw; she seemed to be floating above a blue planet, swirled with white wisps of cloud, but seeing it from every conceivable angle at once. It was an almost omnipotent view of the world below.

She knew this world, but it was not her world.

Xannix.

The voices a tapestry of conversations being threaded through a network of nodes, some prioritised, others not, some specifically routed to her.

'Ellie, are you able to hear me? Over.'

That was her name, Ellie. She remembered. Then pain; a rush of identity flooded her from all directions, as if her diffuse memories suddenly had a seed around which to form.

'Ellie, it's me, Dawn. Can you respond? Over.'

Could she? She didn't know.

'Hello? Dawn?'

'Yes! Ellie! We thought we'd lost you. Thank the stars.'

She was still having trouble discerning the visual information; it was almost too much, as if the universe was shouting at her across the electromagnetic spectrum, some humanly visible, others not. It was beautiful and incandescent, but she had to fade it to something she could handle more readily.

'I am here.' She said with a slow sense of wonder. Focussing on the world below, the planet was peaceful and serene from this place. 'I am everywhere.'

She was somehow instantly aware of everything about her: the plethora of ships manoeuvring about the planet, the *Intrepid* and *Indianapolis* at a full stop, orbiting in a holding position partnered with Zantanath warships, the scattered remains of the *Endeavour* slicing a gash through her side, the cloud of debris slowly spreading, some fragments becoming caught in the planet's gravity well and streaking across the sky in short, sharp flashes.

'It worked, Dawn.'

Dawn's signal was weak, crackling and fading throughout the transmission. 'What worked? Listen, Ellie. I'm on the surface, I'm with Commander Roux and we are heading towards the main landing site. We are in mountainous terrain, so my signal is not getting through. Can you bounce or relay my signal?'

'I'll open a channel. Wait one.'

Adding the broadcast into the other sources of chatter, she

routed the source of the signal and allowed it to broadcast across the planet.

'Dawn, this is Ellie. I've routed your signal to planet-wide broadcast. Go ahead.'

'Acknowledged...' continued Dawn.

Her immediate task complete, she checked to ensure Dawn's connection and transmission before switching to her next concern. The transition from her mind's container, her prison this last 135 years within the sanctuary of the *Intrepid*, to this new distributed container and the millions of nodes that made up the Xannix planetary defence grid, was taking time to acclimatise to. The sensation was not unlike being too close to a fire, her senses either overloaded or confused by pain, or both. Occasionally, she found herself locked in panic, indecision stalling her thought process. She worked as fast as she could and continued to mute or slow some of the data flow until, at last, she began to feel level, the world and universe about her finally making sense.

Swinging her attention to the *Intrepid*, she tested the gateway she had left open into the control network. It was slower than she was used to, like being submerged and moving through water; everything accurate, everything the same, just a little delayed in processing. It meant she had to think a little ahead, but this she could manage easily, unlike the scale of the Xannix defence network, which was even now causing her problems twenty minutes after her infiltration.

A quick sweep of the systems showed her that the Zantanath crew on the bridge were struggling. They had expected her to be there to assist, but she had had other plans. The thing about the situation that caused her most concern was that the Zantanath bridge team had initiated all the correct protocols and were technically proficient in the systems aboard the *Intrepid*. It was clear that they had been briefed. As she watched, one of the bridge team was bypassing her navigation controls, which she moved to counter immediately, performing a ship-wide cred-update to all crew and sending out new creds to all bio-comm. Only the crew would be able to interact manually with the ship, which might give them an edge.

She decided to keep the Zantanath imposed lockdown in place. It would only cause an uncontrolled environment, which could well work against her and cause panic amongst the Zantanath if she lifted it and released the crew. The last thing she wanted was to have the intruders shooting the place up and killing the crew and colonists. Better to have them separated; both would be safer that way. She would harry and harass, allow the Zantanath to believe they were achieving their goals, then subvert and delay, frustrate and wear down by attrition. The tactic had worked well for many lower tech cultures throughout human history. She pulled up the files and started to run VERS, the simulations running encounters and giving her tactical feedback within moments.

Searching the crew status, she could see that there were casualties. The Zantanath had been brutal with those who did not comply. Those caught in corridors or tactically advantageous areas had been attacked, but most had escaped to safe zones before the lockdown was enforced in full. They had lost 114 people during the attack. From a crew and colonist compliment in the thousands, she thought that percentage was light. She immediately checked the bio-bank and wave storage bays. She could initiate the resuscitation process for those that had been lost. The process took years to culture a new clone from scratch, but there would be near complete clones for most in the bio-banks.

As the *Intrepid's* internal cameras presented her the live stream of the resuscitation suites and bio-containment facilities located towards the aft section of the ship, a chill ran through her. There were Zantanath everywhere, not just soldiers but technicians and medics, and they appeared to be dismantling sections of the machinery. On closer examination, they were removing the more advanced clones and placing them in body sleeves, close fitting sleeping bags which when activated sealed rigid with a vacuum-like tightness. Medics checked them over before placing them in line down the centre of the floor space and walkway.

Others did similar with the younger clones, samples of each stage of development being prepared for transit. A Zantanath soldier with a large pack on its back, skeletal wings unfolding, was passed an infant clone by a medic, the child vacuum sealed and unconscious. Once the medic had retreated to a safe distance, the soldier engaged its local transit gate and quickly both it and the child became enclosed in bright silvery sphere which disappeared to a point and was gone.

Why were the Zantanath taking the clones, rather than just ceasing control of the ship and transporting them in place? She did not know. Perhaps things were not going fast enough; perhaps they had other plans. All she did know was that she was failing in one of her prime responsibilities to the crew in allowing this theft to take place. Any reason for their removal at this time could not be good.

Alarmed, she worked quickly. She needed help. People on site. Security, medics, techs—all of them were in lockdown. Could she release those she needed without alerting the Zantanath? She didn't know. Perhaps a small, elite team would be better? She searched the ship's roster for appropriate crew with the skill sets she required. A shortlist of names appeared: people within fifty metres of the bio-banks and one level up or down: Lieutenant Elderson, Sergeant Suzuki, Privates Von Daal and Roth, Engineer Boyd and Dr Tanner. She had caught a break: there were few more qualified than Elderson, who was ex-special forces, and Boyd was a veteran engineer with a military record, two tours of service during the Southern Cape war, which had been a particularly brutal campaign during the Decline. Von Daal and Roth were similarly decorated soldiers before joining OWEC. Dr Tanner was the closest medic, with an exemplary medical record, as expected, but no experience outside the London metropolis where he had grown up. She would have to hope he would be okay.

She put the call out.

BOYD

It was an unusual sensation, and one which his mind could not stop wandering to every few minutes. The new prosthetic would be almost forgotten one moment, accepted as part of him and the whole, then something would brush against it—such as knocking against the side of his torso, or touching the corridor wall as they made their way to the workshop, or now leaning against the workbench as he put the finishing touches to the stun unit that he had built within the exposed framework of the arm—and the lack of sensual response would just kick his brain into a question to which he had to mentally respond and reassure himself.

"There," he said to himself. "That should be it."

Elderson was intrigued but still on guard. She had not taken her eye from the door the whole time they had been there.

"You think it will work?" she asked.

He flexed the wrist of the prosthetic and watched as a six-centimetre spike lanced out of his palm along the line of his arm, a green LED lighting up to indicate the charge from the power pack was active. The spike was enough to penetrate the armour and a shallow layer of flesh, the charge enough for a single stun. Designed to wound, not to kill. Still, the human body could be fragile if struck in the right spot; he would still need to choose his target carefully.

"1200 Volts? Yeah, it'll work."

Holding his arm up for further inspection, he moved to straighten his wrist again; the spike retracted, and he found himself looking past his hand at Elderson. She was frowning and distracted.

"What's up?" A moment later, his bio-comm presented him with a message icon in his lower right vision. He selected it and opened the message. Ellie expanded into the space before him, a two-dimensional image, not her usual augmented reality persona. He found himself mirroring Elderson's facial expression.

"If you have received this message, I need your help," Ellie began, face stern but at the same time concerned, caring. "As you know by now, the *Intrepid* has been boarded a second time, but this time by a much more advanced foe. Initially, their purpose seemed straight forward, to obtain control of the fleet by force; however, their focus seems to have changed. Their main objective now appears to be the bio-banks and wave storage facilities. I am contacting you as I need you to act with others to defend these facilities at all costs."

"Well, shit," he found himself stating out loud.

"Presumably, you received the same message?"

"Who's on the list? You, me...?"

"Unknown. But we have a muster point," Elderson replied.

"And what's happened to Ellie? She running low on bandwidth?" His mind was trying to make sense of the new information. He had assumed Ellie's disappearance due to the latest intrusion and as part of the lockdown, but there was more to it. Ellie was missing, physically relocated, and that was just not how the system was designed to house the AI aboard the ship. Some element of her wave should have been contained within the core they had accessed.

"She shouldn't be able to do that," he externalised.

"Do what? This is a very one-sided conversation, Boyd. You care to share?"

"Ellie's not here."

"Yes. You mentioned that in the AI node room."

"Well, she wasn't there. She's not there. But we're getting comms, which can only mean one of two things. Either, that message wasn't from her, in which case we're being set up and sent into a trap. Or that message was from her, in which case it means she has moved and relocated, physically, in another place. It shouldn't be possible."

"But if that is her, then it's good news, right?" said Elderson.

"As long as she has control of the ship. Without it, we're just as screwed."

"She has control. Protecting the bio-banks and wave storage is her job, you could argue it's her only job. She wouldn't be sending us in there unless she had the ship."

He rubbed his head hard trying to make sense of it all. The hand was hard and rigid, and the plastic scratched, reminding him again of his circumstance. He grimaced in annoyance.

"I wouldn't be so sure."

"Only one way to find out though. She's putting a team together to retake the bio-banks. What do you think is going to happen when we make our move? Nothing good, I can say that for certain. So, unless she has our backs, can lock the place down and do something about those guys with the transit packs, I don't see we have much chance."

"That your tactical opinion?"

"Until further information becomes available, yes."

He looked at the ceiling as if it might provide him with some answers. The odds looked bad. He knew what just a couple of the Zantanath had done to his work team, and they would be walking into a nest of them.

"However," Elderson continued, "I appear to have a pretty clear schedule for the next few hours. I think I might be able to spare some time to check things out."

"But, I thought you just said it was a bad situation?"

"Yeah. But then, I always liked a challenge." She looked at his arm, "You done there?"

He nodded.

Another message dropped into his queue from Ellie. It was a navigation track marking a couple of waypoints to their final muster point. Waypoint one was to collect Dr Tanner, back the way they had just come. Unarmed, Tanner would need babysitting. Second waypoint was the local security station. He didn't like that one, as it would likely be their first point of hostile contact. The muster point was a maintenance crawlspace twenty metres from the bio-banks. Names and faces were sent in a file, with further recorded instructions from the AI.

"Looks like you're designated team lead," he said to Elderson. "Tanner, Suzuki, Von Daal, Roth? Do you know any of these people?"

"There's a lot of personnel in this fleet, but yes, I know Suzuki. If the others are as solid, then I think Ellie has done her homework."

"Good to know."

*

Swinging back for the doctor had been an easy pick up, and although Dr Tanner was surprised at being chosen, he seemed ready for the challenge. Nervous but decided, capable and determined. It was the correct frame of mind as far as he was concerned. Those who appeared too sure of going into a dangerous situation were often the ones that ended up getting themselves and others in trouble.

As they approached the second waypoint in silence, Elderson brought them to a stop at the corner before the short corridor to the reception area and security desk. There would have been a couple of guards at post before the Zantanath had struck, but what he expected to find now was at least a couple of Zantanath soldiers in their place. He didn't hold out much hope for the guards that had been there.

'Time for a peek,' she said.

With that, he received a tactical view via bio-comm from Ellie, a real-time stream from the security desk cameras, targets tracked, and detail fed to a map of the local area.

'Three targets,' Elderson said.

'Where is the security team? I don't see them,' said Tanner.

'Ellie, are they on site?' he asked.

There was an extended pause while he and Elderson shared a glance, what was taking so long?

'Yes. But they do not require rescue.' Two more blue icons indicated both bodies collapsed and lifeless behind a row of seating obscured by the streaming camera.

He noticed a momentary expression of sadness cross Tanner's face.

'Nothing you can do, doc.'

Tanner just nodded.

'Are you going to be able to get close enough to use that cattle prod, Boyd?'

'Can you take down the other two and keep the other

distracted?'

Elderson looked towards the floor and appeared in intense concentration as she assessed the situation up ahead.

'Yes,' she said after a few moments. 'But it's a risky 'yes'.'

'Best odds we've had all day.'

Elderson shifted her position and indicated that he should stand at the corridor corner.

'When you hear my signal, you run like the stars for the nearest tin-man and take him down.'

A few metres away she opened a maintenance access hatch. 'Give me five minutes to get into position.'

He looked down the corridor to the security station, trying to gauge her plan. By the time he looked back to the maintenance access hatch, Elderson was gone. He set a timer running for five minutes.

Watching Ellie's live stream of the security station intently, he found himself intrigued. The Zantanath troopers were all humanoid with two upper body limbs, unlike the Xannix with four, and they were taller than humans, with a leaner build. But he remembered the one that had attacked them in the workshop, the clone of Larsen. Presumably, all these could be Larsen clones too. He noted one had a pronounced limp, but exhibited no external damage to the armour, which to him indicated that the injury was older. Healed injuries could indicate age and experience; they could equally indicate weakness. This one could be an easier take down. He decided on his target.

One of the Zantanath moved across the corridor entrance. From his position ten metres away at the corridor junction he ducked back behind the wall and gently pushed Tanner back a couple of steps. In his bio-comm display, he saw the trooper pause to visually scan down their corridor then move on. A few moments later, he remembered to breathe.

The countdown timer in his bio-comm showed eight seconds; every second ticked by like a lifetime spent, his eyes wide as his pulse began to race in expectation. Time hit zero and appeared to stop. The Zantanath in the feed display were distracted by something. A maintenance hatch in the reception area opened as if by itself. The frame froze, or rather the Zantanath froze as they raised their weapons and aimed into the darkness beyond. More time passed, nothing happened, no one moved. He could sense the unease of the Zantanath, a frustration and fear combined. The trooper with the limp nodded at one of the others who hunkered down into an aggressive stance and moved forward towards the open access hatch. Reaching the hatch, it clicked on a torchlight built into its gauntlet and performed a quick sweep of the inside of the maintenance crawlspace. It seemed perplexed and turned to shrug to its team.

At that moment and with its back to the hatch, a shadow dropped from the ceiling of the maintenance crawlspace and an arm reached out and pulled the Zantanath flat against the hatch, front towards the room. A second later it was launched towards the centre of the room, and towards the other two. Spinning round to catch its trickster, the Zantanath opened fire, light and sparks leaping the gap and tearing holes from the hatch and surrounding wall. However, the hatch door had been flipped shut again. No assailant, no target.

A shout rang out. A voice grotesque and barbed, harshly modulated through a visor speaker. "Grenade!"

Everyone reacted at once. In direct conflict with his screaming senses, he started sprinting around the corner and down the corridor towards the alarmed Zantanath troops, his footfall heavy and leaden. He could see the Zantanath who had given the warning leaping for cover across the reception desk of the security station, but the second—who had not yet seen the grenade—only reacted to the alarm of his commander and was much slower. Through his streamed display he could see the grenade obliterate the Zantanath to whose back it had been attached, and fragments of flesh and bone accelerated in all directions along with tiny razor-sharp shards of matter. The second, slower Zantanath was lacerated by the flying hail of metal and plasma, the bulk of the impact to his right side ripping his arm from his body and spinning him wildly, and without control, across the public seating.

As he entered the room at pace, the gore and debris of the room was still bouncing across the floor and off the walls. He ignored the twinge in his leg, which felt momentarily like a hornet sting, and leapt across the counter of the security desk. The Zantanath was on his front, prone, with his hands clasped protectively over his head. He dropped from the counter to the floor near the Zantanath's head and struck instantly.

The taser spike lanced through the air as it extended from his prosthetic palm towards the soft fleshy top of the soldier's shoulder. Time slowed as his mind sped through the incoming visual information, watching as the platelet armour shifted in anticipation of the impact and increased its relative physical thickness. His strike hit, then slid from its mark.

Overbalanced, he found himself falling forward as the soldier reacted and stood sharply, like a surfer setting his stance. His arms were deflected, and the Zantanath's shoulder thrust itself hard into his ribcage. With a hard shove, the Zantanath rammed his body against the wall and he felt the sudden bright pain of a rib as it cracked. He was dropped to the floor and his legs buckled under him.

He blinked up at the Zantanath soldier, its face hidden behind its visor. It was looking down at him, head cocked slightly sideways, as if examining him, or considering how best to dispatch an inferior. Distracting thoughts worked their way in; he couldn't quite believe how fast things had gone wrong.

The soldier before him seemed to shrug to itself then raised its gauntlet weapon, the barrel directly at him. He had a terrible sense of de'ja vu, but he wasn't going down without a fight.

Thrusting his arm forward, he jammed the taser spike into the end of the Zantanath's barrel and discharged the shock. The unexpected surge of energy through the gauntlet weapon made the soldier become momentarily rigid, as all its muscles contracted simultaneously. The short across the gauntlet weapon caused an immediate malfunction, which crackled and sparked before part of the physical shielding gave way with a small thump of an explosion. The Zantanath howled in rage but didn't go down, grabbing at its arm in pain, his own suit containing the forces which must have caused so much internal damage.

The trooper turned on him wildly, any logical thought abandoned as it came at him with its remaining good arm and pressed him hard against the wall, forearm wedged across his throat. Within seconds, he was struggling for breath and his sight began to fade. He tried to kick out, his feet now a clear 30 centimetres from the floor, but nothing landed that had any affect. He grabbed at the arm to try and release some of the pressure, but his strength was beginning to fail him. He didn't need to see the eyes behind the visor and the contorted face before him; in some way he was glad that the last thing he would ever see was not going to be that.

He closed his eyes and put all his remaining effort into forcing the arm away from his throat.

*

Air rushed into his lungs so fast it hurt. His legs buckled up underneath him, he found himself leant awkwardly against the wall with the body weight of the Zantanath across him. The situation didn't make any sense to him and his mind spun while it caught up with the sensory input it was being given. Twisting hard to free his legs, the movement only shifted the force pressing him to the floor, applying an even greater weight across his torso. He shoved one last time to get out from under the dead weight, the body of the Zantanath slumped to the deck beside him. Looking from the prone form on the floor then up towards the figure standing over him, Elderson offered an outstretched hand to assist him up. Confusion still working against him, he tentatively took it. She leaned into the lift and pulled him up.

"You okay?" she asked. They both looked down at the length of pipe in her hand. "You said alive, right?"

"Yeah. Yeah, I did." He looked down at the Zantanath. "And thanks."

"Things don't always go the way you plan. You just hope things work out," she said.

"That's two I owe you."

"It's okay. I'm keeping a tally." They both looked down at the unconscious soldier on the floor. "So, what are you going to do with this guy?"

"It was less him, more his kit. But I can't use the kit with holes in it. I just hope I haven't fried the electronics in the helmet."

He shifted and knelt by the soldier's head. Reaching around the helmet and visor he felt for the release, a click and slight hiss of gas from the visor and the helmet lifted in his hands, leaving the soldier's face towards the floor and unidentified. He lifted and spun the helmet to get a look inside, briefly examining the interior for damage. It looked okay.

"I think we may have got away with it," he said.

From the corridor across from them, slow crunching footsteps could be heard. Tanner appeared, wearing the shock he felt across his face. Seeing that both Elderson and he were watching from other side of the room, he replaced it with a forced confidence and made his way over to the reception desk.

"Did we really need to make this mess?" Tanner asked.

"You mean, did we really have to kill all these people?" said Elderson.

"Yes, I guess I did."

"We only killed two. The tin-can down here is still breathing."

"Could you look him over?" he said. "We need him. He may even give us some answers."

"Sure," Tanner said as he made his way round the desk, looking relieved to have something to do, even if it was to patch up the enemy. "Here, give me a hand. I need to get him out of his suit."

CLAYTON

The Zantanath transport flyer flew across the plains to the north of a mountain range peaked with white snow. Below was a grey-green blur as the ground undulated and the occasional forest canopy came up to meet them. The pilot kept a level and comfortable flight altitude, the constant low vibration of the engines quiet and understated. The flight was conducive to conversation and Ambassador Auwen was taking full advantage.

"... Don't you think, Fleet Captain?" Auwen asked. His mind had wandered momentarily, the view from the window distracting from the long monologue that had been the ambassador's hard sell on the old abandoned Xannix town of Annasi.

"Of course, you will undoubtedly wish to rename the town, but I feel it will be ideal for all your immediate needs. And if the Zantanath Unity can assist further in welcoming you to this world, please feel free to compile a list of requirements and send them to me. I'm sure we can accommodate them."

"Thank you," he replied. "Very generous of you."

"Not at all, Fleet Captain."

He looked to the window again, his eyes glazing slightly and mind drifting. He didn't remember seeing any windows on the outside of the shuttle as they had boarded.

"Fleet Captain, if you don't mind me making an observation."

"No, please, go ahead."

"You seem somewhat preoccupied. Would you like some refreshment?"

The Zantanath appeared genuine, but then the trait of an ambassador was to be attentive and understand the nuance of interpersonal situations. He shifted uncomfortably in his seat to face the ambassador and to appear more engaged in the conversation.

"My apologies, Ambassador; it has been a long few days and I am concerned for my daughter. I haven't heard from her for a while."

Auwen nodded understandingly. "When did you last hear from her?"

"About a week ago. She had made it to the ground and grouped up with my XO. They were making their way through mountains to the landing site."

"And you haven't heard from her since?" Auwen looked concerned, the tips of his ears twitching with agitation. "Would you mind if I arrange a search party? And of course, for any others that you may be missing."

"Again, that is kind of you."

"If you have any coordinates around which we can begin our search, we would be glad to receive them, otherwise we will begin our search working out from your landing site."

A bio-comm link appeared in his vision, a direct link to another bio-comm. The ambassador's bio-comm. The surprise must have shown on his face.

"I have emulated your direct communications device. You may use this whenever you need to contact me."

"I will forward the detail," he said.

The ambassador settled back as he received the information and began to process and organise the rescue effort.

"I understand your anxiety, Fleet Captain. I have a child of my own. She is ten of your Terran years old and quite demanding, as all children. I couldn't imagine what it might be like for her to be lost on an unfamiliar world."

There was a pause while both wandered through their own immediate thoughts.

"Your daughter, she is on your home world?" he asked.

"Yes. She will be taken care of by her mother until I return, then I will take over while her mother takes up her duties to the Unity for the next work rotation."

"Interesting. How long is your work rotation?"

"It can be several of your months."

"Months? And that doesn't interrupt your work?"

"No. Why should it? She continues our work when I return. There is continuity throughout."

"So, she is also an ambassador?"

"Yes."

"And my liaison?"

"Yes. I would have informed you nearer the time, but as you raise the issue, yes, she will continue our work when I return to my daughter."

It was a way of sharing responsibility which he had not even considered. He didn't even see how it could work, but the Zantanath clearly made it work. A partner with the same skill set and job description seemed difficult to manage.

"And when do you spend time as a family?"

Auwen smiled, "There are regular periods of community."

The concept and structure of family seemed similar to him, but at the same time quite different in how the Zantanath shared their time and work. He wondered what else was different. To assume that they shared values just because they shared a physical appearance was quite wrong. Their cultures, their goals, what they considered of value could all be quite different.

While Auwen appeared in a talkative mood, he moved the topic of conversation on.

"From what you say, it sounds like the Zantanath homeworld is not that far."

"You are correct. Not far. In terms of the distance between stars, we are neighbours," replied the ambassador. "See for yourself." Auwen motioned for him to sit back in his seat. He took a moment to settle.

An instant later he found himself on the balcony of a building, looking out across a moonlit world. The cityscape before him continued as far as he could see in all directions, the city lights sparkling and throwing a haze into the sky. Flyers and ground traffic sped to their destinations, people could be seen like ants walking on pedestrianized streets and flyover walkways. The vision was one of vibrancy and bustle. From his observation point, the city was almost silent, the low burbling sounds of motion pervading now and then as a flyer came a little closer or overflew the building.

"This..." he began.

"Is the view from my home. I recorded it to be at home whenever I'm away."

He looked around, and back towards the apartment. There were no doors to the living area, only some light drapes undulating in the breeze. In the living space, a slight and regal Zantanath female stood searching through unidentifiable items on a wall shelf while a child sat on the floor waving her hands slowly and purposefully, occasionally poking the air in front of her with different fingers. The female noticed his attention and smiled at him. It was mesmerising. The dream stopped abruptly, and he found himself staring at Auwen across the aisle of the dropship. The Zantanath looked a little embarrassed, as if he had over shared some personal moment.

"Your home is beautiful," he said.

"Thank you."

"It is an incredible view across the city from your apartment. The towers seem to go on forever."

"That is because they do," said Auwen. "Or at least, they cover the planet. Our cities are sprawling and where there used to be distance between them, now there is none. Each blends into the other."

"A city planet?"

"I suppose you could call it that, although not entirely. There are still areas of wilderness, and although we have populated some of the ocean space, there is still much we have left untouched."

Auwen appeared momentarily distracted and looked across to another of the Zantanath. They exchanged a few words in their local tongue.

"We will be landing soon. Please secure your harness."

A shadow passed the window, drawing his attention. Buildings. Initially they could be seen speckled about in small groups, then their number and density increased until they were flying in a circular path about a central tower. Thin horizontal windows lined the sweeping sides of the elliptical plan building, the design reminding him of a termite mound, in which the shape and orientation to the sun produced a natural ventilation and air circulation within the structure. He wondered if that was the case here.

There was a slight increase in noise from the flyer as it started to ascend. A moment later they were hovering to the side of a rooftop landing pad. With expert precision and delicate manoeuvring, the flyer skidded sideways over the pad, then dropped into a gentle landing. He hardly felt the touchdown.

"I thought we would start at the top and work our way down," said Auwen, as the chair about him released its grip and the harness automatically relinquished its hold on him.

The familiar bustle of people getting ready to disembark could be heard: the quiet murmuring of voices, the shuffle of feet then the intrusive sound of the flyer's engines as the side door was opened, allowing them to exit the craft.

Making their way to the door, Jemma sent a bio-comm: 'What was that about?' He followed her eyes to his chair.

'Oh, just a little visit to the Zantanath homeworld. Auwen showed me a short home movie. A glimpse of family life.' He shrugged. 'You should see the view from his apartment balcony.' He flared his eyes and pursed his lips in a silent whistle.

'Perhaps you could get yourself invited to dinner, to see this incredible view in person?' Jemma suggested.

'One day,' he said, a frown and darkness pervading his thoughts. 'There will be time for socialising and building bridges once we have our people safely on the ground.' He looked at the open door of the flyer and the blue sky outside. "Baby steps," he said aloud, then stepped from the shuttle.

*

As the sun descended across the mountains, his view from the penthouse level of the Xannix tower was stunning. Orange beams of light lined the peaks and reflected off the snow caps to glint like jagged golden teeth. The windows of the tower were like pillar boxes at head height, which he could not quite understand, as he estimated them too low for a grown Xannix to see out without stooping.

"These rooms will give you shelter tonight," said Auwen. "I have made similar arrangements for the others on the same floor. I will be hosting dinner in my rooms in an hour. When rested we can set out for a tour of the town first thing tomorrow."

He looked back to Auwen, taking his eyes away from the impending sunset. Jemma, Fellows, Reeve and Silvers all stood about the room, each with the wonder of discovery on their face.

"Thank you, Auwen. We look forward to it." So much for this being an afternoon trip.

Auwen made a small gesture with his hands, palms pressed gently together across his chest, and then turned to leave, his small entourage including the armoured bodyguard departing with him. When the door was closed behind them, he turned to the group.

"Alright, initial thoughts?"

"Are you kidding?" replied Jemma. "This is incredible."

"This is a ready-made town, full amenities, water and sewage, electrics already plumbed in. We might have to make a few tweaks, but the heavy lifting has been done," said Fellows stepping to his side to take a look across the townscape. "At the moment their offer is looking very attractive."

He nodded in agreement. "Yes. Yes, it is."

"Reeve?"

"I agree. This place is everything we could have hoped for."

He sensed a *but*, and he held her gaze in silence to draw the conversation.

"But…it is always prudent to reserve judgement until we have seen the full detail of the deal."

"What more do you need to know?" asked Silvers. "This place will take ten years, maybe twenty years, off our colonisation plan. It's a no-brainer."

He moved across to a shelf which had been laid out with a cylindrical jug of water and glasses. He poured himself a glass and turned back to the group.

"So, we may have somewhere to live. Now, we just need to collect our dispersed band of travellers. A change of fortune. Good news." He raised his glass to the group in a casual toast.

In an instant, he was lit starkly by what appeared to be a spotlight, his features completely white and washed out, the alarm on his face more a question as he squinted against the brightness and noise emanating from outside the window. With a brief pop the window shattered, a fist sized hole punched through, spidery cracks leading away across remains in the frame. Clayton looked in a lazy slow motion towards his hand, the glass smashed and water spilling out across the floor.

There was a long second where no one reacted, the shock of the unexpected attack taking everyone by surprise. Fellows was first to his carbine and laced a rapid volley of shots through the remains of the window towards the glaring light. More of the glass fell away from the frame and sparkled, as splinters exploded through the air.

Each of them dived for whatever cover they could; there was nothing substantial, soft cover at best, nothing that would stop an accurate shot.

More shots from Reeve and Silvers joined the cacophony and hailed bullets towards the target, the light and roar of the flyer outside becoming unstable and modulated as it began to lose control. The flyer's spotlight exploded with a spark and plunged the room into a relative darkness, as he found his sight adjusting to the new light level. From the window, his focus shifted to the rectangular silhouette which was now growing in size as it flew directly at the window.

"Incoming!" he found himself screaming across the room. He had been caught in the open, but since the first shot which had taken the glass from his hand, he had not been touched. Taking a few fast steps, he threw himself across the sofa and hoped for some moderate cover from any blast.

Gunfire stopped, as others leapt for what cover they could find.

A spray of glass flew in all directions from the remains of the window as the dark block careened to the floor and skidded to a stop. The distinctive sound of mini-turbines winding down filled the room, a moment later the acrid smell of electrical failure and smoke.

"Everyone okay?" he heard Reeve call, her voice muffled. His hearing had yet to recover from the gunfire and chaos. They all sounded off, a full roll call. No losses. No casualties.

Standing slowly, he looked across at the object on the floor. Their attacker was unmoving, but the shape of the downed form was familiar. In a flash of recognition, he ran towards it and knelt at its side and began to assess the damage.

The casing was pitted and dark, but the stencilled red lettering on the side spelt out an unmistakable single word. The name he and Jemma had chosen for their only child: Dawn.

*

The distress of what he had just witnessed was forced to the back of his mind as he worked. The utiliplex tool was taken from his belt and swiftly employed to remove damaged panelling, and to open internal conduits to check on critical systems. His bio-comm was linked directly to Dawn's wave container and auxiliary applications, and, as his hands worked to mend hardware, his mind worked through the maze of software.

"Jemma, here. Hold this back." He indicated to a stubborn panel which would not flex enough for him to reach the underlying circuits. He needed an extra pair of hands and Jemma would insist anyway. A moment later she was pealing back the panel, giving him clear space to work. His utiliplex tool fizzed as it bridged and soldered damaged circuitry, schematics scrolling and flicking through his bio-comm display as he completed the multiple urgent and critical fixes being reported by Dawn's systems.

The others had begun to group closely around, watching the pair of them work, unable to help but inquisitive and caught in the sudden guilt at having possibly destroyed such a valued crew member. Never mind the tech, the cost in research, or the fact that this was an instance of a very rare form of human existence; this was his daughter. They were all very well aware of the stakes.

Dull red lights began to flicker across the body of the machine, running sequential patterns at first, then, after a short pause, fluctuating and pulsing. It was like watching a heartbeat and the electrical communication of nerve impulses visually across the skin of the machine casing.

He and Jemma sat back to observe their work. Sweat across his brow, he wiped his face with his forearm in reflex. As they watched, a holographic projector port opened in the top of the machine's shell, then Dawn swirled into existence within a fluid motion of coalescing light motiles. There was a joint relieved exhale among the group. She was alive.

"Dawn, thank the stars," said Jemma, echoing his own thoughts.

Dawn nodded and started to speak, but there was no sound; it was like watching a mime wave and gesticulate urgently. Immediately he was back to work, searching out the speakers embedded in the top of the unit. One them had been damaged and ripped through, but the second was a circuit issue to which he applied the utiliplex tool. A pop brought sound and Dawn's recognisable voice.

"... danger." A single word instantly swept away the relief in the room.

"Say that again, Dawn? Start from the beginning."

Dawn looked full of sorrow and the energy in her explanation dissipated. "No time, Mum."

"What do you mean? What danger?" he asked.

"Sorry."

With that, her image disappeared and through his diagnostic connection he saw her critical systems shutting down, yet at the same time her power cell was diverting energy.

"What's going on?" asked Fellows.

"I don't know; she's shutting down."

"Why?"

"I just told you; I don't know," he snapped, his mind working through scenarios, technical failures in the machine which would cause her to shut off and protect herself.

That was it, protect herself.

Before he could react, there was a tremendous pain which flashed across his brain in a fraction of a second, killing his bio-comm. The bio-comm display and comms instantly failed and in his disorientation he slumped to the floor, the world fading. He struggled against it, but within moments his vision tunnelled to darkness.

DAWN

Her systems slowly rebooted, warnings and severe damage still reported. Although her father had managed to mend the most critical circuits within her frame, meaning that she was able to operate, her effectiveness would be reduced. The primary damage she had suffered was to her motor systems. Flight would be impossible while control surfaces were impaired and two of four thrusters were inoperable, and several sensors had also been damaged beyond repair. She estimated that she would need an overhaul and that 30 percent of her hardware would need replacement. That level of damage would keep her and her father busy for weeks.

Only, they didn't have weeks.

Scanning the room with as many services as she had remaining, she searched for more of the nano-tech that had destroyed Roux. It had been horrible to watch, the decline of a person being eaten from the inside out by invisible machines with the sole purpose of taking over mind and body, controlling you, manipulating your thoughts and actions.

That couldn't be allowed to happen to her parents. It would be disastrous to the colonisation effort, and it would have been something that would have gone largely unnoticed if she hadn't accidently discovered the dark smudge across Roux's chest during her brief non-standard medical scan.

Groans rose from those lying about her. Most were holding their heads and trying to sit up, but two lay unconscious. Checking the crew fleet manifest, she identified them as Lieutenant Reeve and Sergeant Silvers.

"What happened?" asked Fellows, sitting with his head on his knees and rubbing his temples.

"EMP," stated Clayton.

"I didn't know she had one of those."

"Yes, I do," she said, activating her holographic projection to the room as a reminder of her human presence to the group. "I have all the required parts, just not necessarily specified as countermeasures on any audit list. How else do you think I regulate the power to this unit? Dual functionality is useful on occasion."

She was angry, and rightfully so. Saving her father from a drink laced with nano-tech had become a harsh punishment. But she needed to temper that emotion. Sometimes doing good was the tougher path. Right now, she needed to keep them all safe.

Finding no further active nanites about the room, she focused her efforts on the two unconscious security personnel on the floor. Their breathing was shallow, they appeared relaxed and at peace, but her scans were positive, they were both infected. The question was, had her EMP been enough?

Paying particular attention to their chest and collar area, she searched for evidence of the similar dark smudge she had found in Roux. Nothing appeared. However, she did find in each of them a slightly elevated solids build up in their blood, and kidney's working hard to filter out the sudden unrequired particulates.

"I would advise, for the time being, that you drink nothing here," she said.

"What are you talking about?" asked Fellows.

"What is going on, Dawn?"

"Sorry for taking the glass from your hand earlier. There was no time to communicate. The water was contaminated. Laced with nanites."

"Nanites?" said Jemma, as she moved to attend Reeve and Silvers.

"Mum, no!"

"What?" Jemma replied as if reprimanded.

"They are infected. I'm hoping the EMP knocked out the nanites, but I need to be sure."

"Presumably, the infection route is ingestion," replied Clayton.

"Most likely. But we don't know if the nano-tech can be

transmitted via contact." She paused in momentary concentration. "Just give me a moment to run some tests."

As she began the tests, Jemma hovered a couple of metres from the two on the ground. Her mother was the best medic she knew, and seeing people in distress or in need of help had always compelled her. Memories of her childhood momentarily found their way into her thoughts, her mother always so gentle and kind, and always with the right words when she took a tumble. Even when her father had brought her mother to see her for the first time after the accident, the car crash that had ended her life in one form and given birth to her life in another. Even then, her mother had worked so hard to make sure she was okay, even though she could see the pain her mother was holding back. She loved them both so much.

Close inspection showed nothing but dead nanites in their bloodstream, their bodies now beginning to exhibit the same feverish symptoms Roux had shown, clearly a process of the body identifying the nanites as an invader and ejecting them from their bodies. She anticipated the process to take several hours, perhaps even another day, but what they would need was hydration and any level of liquid intake would be a risk under these hostile circumstances.

"Okay," she said to her mother. "You can tend them, but be careful. The nanites look dead, but I'd still be cautious."

"You're saying they were taken down by nano-tech?" asked Fellows, still trying to make sense of what was going on.

"Yes. The water in the vase was laced with nanites. From what I understand of them, once they are in your system they work to take over your higher cognitive thought processes. They also generate some tiny fluctuations in spacetime, internally. I don't understand how or what this represents, or how this nano-tech operates; I need more time to investigate."

"It's the one thing we don't have," replied Clayton.

"They're running a high fever," interrupted Jemma.

"Any fluids you need to give them should be analysed first. That goes for *any* drinking water. At the moment you are all clear; however, that could change with a single drop. Until we get to a trusted water source, the risk of further contamination is high."

"Understood," said Clayton.

"Well, that's just great," said Fellows.

As Fellows turned away from the group, the door to the apartment flew open, and Zantanath worked their way into the room in a practiced military fashion. The silver, segmented armour of the lead soldier flickered as he moved, the light effect confusing the eye of the observer, causing him to momentarily but repeatedly disappear then return in an unexpected but more advanced position. Before Fellows or anyone else could react, they were surrounded. Fellows trained his carbine directly at the head of the armoured Zantanath, who mirrored the act, and the picture froze as they faced each other down a metre apart.

"No!" yelled Clayton. "Hold your fire!"

The tension in the room was high and needed defusing, but she couldn't see a way through. They were outnumbered and any way she looked at it, the outcome was not only the death of the team here but also, more widely, the failure of the mission.

A final Zantanath strode into the room, walking with purpose, his robes billowing out behind him to accompany his pace and stern features. Everything about him seemed to exude a cool menace which radiated from his gaze as he took in the scene; a warlord full of entitlement and command.

"Auwen, stand your men down," said Clayton.

Auwen looked directly at her, examining the machine that lay battered and broken on the floor. Speaking in their own tongue, the warlord directed his soldiers into action, two shouldering their weapons while moving to assess the condition of Reeve and Silvers.

His eyes finally falling on her father, Auwen gave a wry smile. "It appears we have an uninvited guest," he said, turning his gaze at her hologram, "with a dislike of local hospitality." He raised a long finger to the shelf and the vase of water, which was remarkably in one piece after all the violence.

"You knew?"

A nod. "Of course. As your people say, there is the easy way, then there is the hard way... Looks like we will need to do things the hard way."

"Do what?"

Auwen looked back to her "There is no use trying to contact your fleet; they cannot hear you. They will not respond. We have taken command of both remaining vessels."

She scrunched up her face in response, like a child being caught with her hand in the cookie jar. She had thought her subterfuge and transmission better concealed.

"They have access to our bio-comm network," said Clayton to her, without taking his eyes from Auwen. He was outwardly calm, but she knew her father, and he was furious. She presumed that they would be here under the invitation of the Zantanath, and she knew the speech he would have given. He had given her the same *trust them until they show themselves to be untrustworthy* talk before. She had always thought it credible, until the trusted broke that trust, then you needed to deal with the feelings of betrayal and the very practical problems of being in a bad situation. Right now, they were in a bad situation, and her father knew it. She hoped he had a plan B.

The room's lighting flickered back on, and slowly other electrical items about the room that had previously been unnoticed started to light up or indicate activity. Their surroundings appeared to be coming back to life, and she hoped the same would not be the case for the nanites within Reeve and Silvers. She continued to scan them, checking their physical state; it seemed okay, although what their mental condition might be after they came round was an unknown. Even if they did come round, they could not be trusted: they had been under the influence of the Zantanath for several days thus their allegiance at this time was also questionable.

Analysis of those in the room and the room itself reinforced the level of tension they all felt: heart rates were elevated, breathing was hard and they were all sweating even though the temperature was a cool 10 Celsius, a night wind blowing through the shattered window keeping the temperature down.

The lead soldier caught her attention: his physiology was relaxed, calm, his gate easy and confident. His form was also human, taller, leaner, but the organs were slightly modified, bigger lungs, stronger heart. Comparing to the scan data of Auwen, he had a slightly different internal anatomy, three hearts, one centrally located in the chest and smaller than a human heart, and two auxiliary hearts, one at the top of each leg. Their lungs were not lungs, specifically, more like thin repeated sheets of membrane which wrapped about the lower part of their abdominal area. From their physical frame, she considered them to be from a nomadic species, mobile and fast: hunters.

Auwen said something to the two assessing Reeve and Silvers, and there was just a shake of the head, indicating a negative response to the question. She knew them to be alive, so she considered the communication to be regarding the status of their nanites. The EMP had worked, but her systems were now drained, and it would be another ten minutes before she could attempt another discharge. In ten minutes, this would all be over, one way or the other.

ELLIE

She was working too slowly. Felix stood behind her watching each component as she put the pieces in place. Each item she treated with care, the utiliplex making slow adjustments, compensating for her shaking hands. Individually, the components were innocuous; it was the final construction that made her heart pound, its destructive power enough to put a crater in the London skyline 100 metres in diameter. If she made any wrong move now, she and the small group working in the dark and pokey apartment with her would be instantly vaporised, along with most of the apartment block they were holed up in. Her grandmother's words kept returning to her: *more haste, less speed.* Translation: get it right first time. Don't mess it up.

"The boss needs this in 30 minutes," said Felix. "It going to be ready?"

"If you don't keep asking me every five minutes, we might have a chance," she said.

"What's the target this time?"

"Best you don't ask questions like that. I don't. Keep your nose out of operations. You'll pick it up on the feeds when the news hits."

"Yeah."

The utiliplex fizzed a solder joint, fixing a trigger wire into position. The final connection. She checked the control panel; it reported back. All green.

"There, done."

Getting up, she walked over to the fridge and picked out a drink. Pulling the ring-pull, she walked to the sofa and flopped into its embrace, letting the stress drain out of here. She took a long pull on the cold caffeine and flicked the monitor on to channel one. The news feeds showed a slick anchor woman presenting a piece on the current food shortage, and segued into an article on the best and latest technique of power capture for the domestic user.

"It'll work? You all sure?" asked Felix.

She didn't even respond. Picking up the remote from the arm of the sofa, she just turned the volume up. He got the hint and huffed dismissively, stuffing the device into a rucksack.

"Happy trails," he said, slinging the bag over his shoulder. The door slammed as he left, and she momentarily heard a baby cry further down the corridor outside.

"Asshole," she said.

"You should be more careful," said Kinsey as he sat in the chair opposite, the small open-plan lounge space crammed with kit and components, a spare mattress stuffed into a corner, overflow to the already cramped bedrooms.

"Why?"

"You don't want to piss off Felix. Guy is all muscle and no brain. You're going to get yourself killed if you wind him up like that."

"I don't think so. It's all for the cause, and he's company through and through. He does what he's told and so do we. In the end, we want the same thing."

Kinsey shook his head. "You're naive if you think everyone is in this for the same reasons. You want political change, to make things around here better for everyone. That idiot just wants an excuse to hurt people."

She looked at the door Felix had just left through, as if she might see him there grinning in some maniacal fashion, exuding evil and snarling like some daemonic beast. But all she saw was the utility brown paint the apartment management used on the doors to try to infer a wooden door, rather than the reinforced plastech; class rather than trash. It didn't work. The place was still a hole.

"It doesn't matter," she replied. "In the end, some people always get hurt in these things. Politicians always say they're listening, but that's just a flat lie. Unless you hit them in their wallet, or by taking away votes, threaten their power, they don't change a damn thing. We just made a bomb to change our futures, Kinsey. Whether you are like Felix or like us, the organisation needs both to achieve that future."

"He's still an asshole."

"No denying that."

The door behind them opened, which made Kinsey jump. It was one of the couriers. Networks were insecure, all operational messages were sent via courier. It took a little longer to get detail around, but it was safer. Messages didn't go missing, operational detail didn't get intercepted without it being noticed immediately. If your courier disappeared, didn't make the timed drop, then that was the cue to disband and disappear. Dimitri was on time.

Without greeting or preamble, Dimitri pointed straight at her, while holding the door open. "You're up. Bossman wants to see you."

Kinsey looked worried for her.

"Relax," she said, getting up off the sofa, grabbing her coat and making her way to the door. "He probably wants to give me a pay rise."

"Yeah," said Kinsey. "Luck with that."

*

She hated going to see the boss. They always administered a tranq in the car and the next she knew she was in an interrogation room, one door, one mirror, but not this time. This time she was walked through the front door of a public art gallery on the inner city's South Bank. A vast collection of work covered the halls, each portraying history or hope relative to the artists vision. It was a building she had never visited and to which she usually paid little interest, but this time she found it intriguing.

Dimitris led her to an elevator, and they ascended ten metres to the next floor. From the elevator, she was led through a crowd to a dimly lit, enclosed viewing room. The space was about fifteen by twenty metres, with another incredibly high ceiling. A single wide bench was located in the centre of the room, with a single painting on each of the four walls. A lone dark figure sat on the bench admiring, or perhaps analysing, the image on the left wall as she approached. Dimitris stayed by the door.

"Ellie," he said. "Glad you could come." It was a casual

statement, but it inferred that she had some free will over the decision to attend. She did not. When you were asked by the head of GAIA to perform a task, or attend a meeting, that is what you did. His vision and his charisma were compelling, his arguments sound. In her view, more people should be fighting for the cause. Now more than ever. The people in all the annexed cities of the world were working under a deluded sense of entitlement, raising walls to keep resource to themselves and, in essence, starve the rest of the planet. The irony was that it would solve nothing. The death sentence had already been cast across them all. But if there was a chance, there should be a solution that didn't just depend on an elitist sense of self-worth. Somewhere out in the borderlands could be the next big brain to solve the problem. The more people you had working on the issue, the greater the chance of solving it, and the best ideas didn't always come from a small self-proclaimed elite.

"I hope your journey here was a pleasant one?" he continued.

"Yes. Thank you."

"Please, take a seat," he said, indicating the bench space to his side. She sat facing the painting on the wall, a simple two-tone image of deep, rich block colours. "What do you think?" he asked.

"What, of the painting?"

"Yes," he smiled.

She took a close, considered look. Although the blocks of colour were large and covered the canvas, the brush strokes were erratic and not in any way linear or uniform. There was chaos within the wider simplicity.

Shrugging, she offered her answer, "I'm not much of an art critic. It looks like a mess to me. The colours are nice enough, looks like a blood red sky over a desert. Maybe?"

Nodding at her answer, he looked back at the image and squinted a little, perhaps trying to apply her description to the canvas, to understand her point of view.

"I see two sides, within the same frame. Each comprising millions of voices, individuals moving in different directions, but ultimately describing the same vision, wanting the same thing. Both sides are needed, or the image is incomplete. Yin and Yang, the heavens and earth..."

"Mets and outlanders."

"Yes. Isolating ourselves in these cities was a mistake. The government needs to be made to listen. We are speaking the only language they understand." He became momentarily lost in his own thoughts, lost in the image before him.

Snapping himself out of his drifting daydream, he glanced at his watch before returning his attention to her.

"I need you to do something for me, Ellie. For us. You might think that what I'm asking goes against everything we stand for here, and others if they found out might not be sympathetic, but your work will be of the greatest importance." He turned to look her in the eye, and she shifted uncomfortably under the scrutiny. "I need an insider at the Formillun Institute: someone technical, someone smart and able to fit in, someone who can ace their selection tests and fly under their radar. These last few months you have shown yourself to be more than capable, and I think you can do it."

A spy? He wanted her to become a spy for GAIA and infiltrate the government's top research agency. He was crazy. Only a couple of operatives had ever succeeded, and that was in the bad old days when the space effort was young and people less guarded. Now, security was tight and paranoid, the worst kind.

"What do you need me to do when I get there?" she asked.

"Information. We need to know what they are doing. How close to achieving their goals are they? Where are their critical projects being conducted? We know they are trying to save themselves to the detriment of the everyone else. That is not a solution that works. It is base selfishness. The information you obtain there will assist us to bring down their space programme, and, with it, focus their attentions back home, to solve the problems for the masses and not the few."

"Information? But I could do so much more for you here. You know I'm the best maker you have."

"That may be true, but I have other makers. Maybe they are not as good as you, but they are good. What I need is that sharp intellect of yours directed toward the achievement of something more, to help build a new world which includes us all. Can you do that for me, Ellie?"

Staring back at the painting on the wall, she muttered to herself, "Two sides; one image."

"Two parts of the same whole," said Constantine.

*

In her silent moments of rage, she wondered to herself how easily she had been duped. She had believed in the cause, the lie she had been sold by a man who had all the answers. But young idealists often fell under the spell of the charismatic and manipulative, and, in her youthful naivety, she had been no different. During the long journey to Xannix as the AI responsible for the safety of twelve thousand human souls aboard the *Intrepid*, she had had 135 years to think on the issue, and on how much of herself she had sacrificed to a cause that, through the irony of life, had made her the very thing she had despised. And when it came down to it, even now, what drove her on, pushed her past the trauma and violence she had endured, was the desire to survive. She wanted to live.

They had been told that AI tech was all machine, that however much the scientists lauded their success, proclaiming the reality of a perfected wave splicing technique, that they could take the human consciousness and embed it in a machine, fundamentally, they were just playing with algorithms to mimic the human condition. The soul of the person was gone. Whatever Turing test the machine passed, the simple truth was that the spirit was gone, the idea that anything of the original human mind remained was nothing less than a hoax.

But from her new reality as a spliced wave in her host machine, the propaganda of GAIA appeared an obvious lie. She was here, in the same way she had been in her mortal body. There was no distinction to be drawn between the old her and her new self, though there were obvious differences in her abilities and her reach, what she could do, how she could communicate, the speed at which she could exist in time, increasing and slowing her perception of the world about her. But all this was simply a function of her new body, not the spirit of who she was. She was still the sum of her experiences; she was still the girl her mother gave life to.

What had changed was her belief in GAIA. The organisation was no longer the evangelical calling it was. Being disowned and discarded then considered as collateral damage in a mission to which she was key. It was unbearable. Perhaps it was her ego talking, but from the point her world had become shattered, humanity could go hang. She wanted to be as far away from all of them as she could get, and she had known just how to achieve it.

"Are you seeing this, Ellie?"

Boyd, Elderson and Tanner had reached the security station and had managed to take down the Zantanath guard located there. She had followed the action via their bio-comm streamed over her obfuscated connection to the *Intrepid*. Elderson had been smart and efficient; Boyd had been unlucky. She hadn't been quite sure what Boyd had been hoping to achieve by capturing a Zantanath, but now he had, the first thing he was doing was pulling the soldier's armour apart.

"I can see. What are you doing? Is he still alive?"

"Negative. I think I gave him a brain haemorrhage, he didn't last more than a few minutes," replied Elderson.

"It's not important. What I wanted was the armour, the helmet really," said Boyd. "But it worked out better than I imagined. Here, give me a hand with this undersuit."

Boyd pointed to Elderson, indicating that she should pull from the neckline over the shoulders and down the torso. She watched them both struggle for a few minutes, but neither was really getting anywhere. Boyd waved his hands then looked closer at the neckline cuff. A moment later the bodysuit seemed to relax and slump, increasing in size and loosening the neckline to the width of the soldier inside. The body on the floor suddenly seemed like an infant in an oversized sleepsuit. Boyd and Elderson slipped the garment from the Zantanath easily.

"Impressive," said Elderson.

"So, my plan was to scavenge the helmet tech to tap into their comms, work out what they were up to, who was in charge. But considering where we are going next, I think we can use this."

"Use this how?" she asked.

"I think I know," replied Elderson.

"Would you mind?" Boyd said to Elderson.

"Wait a minute. You're not thinking of using this kit? You're actually thinking of putting this on?" exclaimed Tanner. "You can't. We don't know what it will do to you. Do you know how to work it? Have you seen this guy?" he said, pointing to the ashen form lying dormant on the ground.

"All of those questions are good points, Doctor. But right now, this is our best chance to stop them taking our people."

"The risk is too high."

"The risk to whom?" asked Elderson.

"To you," replied Tanner.

"It is a necessary risk," said Boyd.

"You're not putting on the suit," sniped Tanner.

There was a pause, as the tension hung in the air like an unavoidable fog. Time was ticking by and she saw another clone taken from the bio-banks, the Zantanath and clone disappearing within a silvery liquid ball of manipulated spacetime.

"There is no time to argue this point. The risk is acceptable, and we will gain a critical advantage by Elderson utilising its capability. Please proceed," she said.

"It is settled," said Elderson, and stepped forward to take the battlesuit from Boyd.

Tanner let out an exasperated huff and threw his hands in the air in frustration. "Fine," he said, and stepped away shaking his head.

Elderson gave herself some room to change then looked at Boyd, who was still in conversation mode and expecting more. An awkward silence fell across the group.

"Would you mind?" said Elderson, making a little circular motion with her hand. It took Boyd a moment to become aware of his lack of courtesy.

"Oh. Sorry, of course," Boyd said, as he turned to give Elderson some privacy while changing into the armour. "The suit control was on the collar. Press for three seconds and it should activate the resizing."

"Thank you," said Elderson, as she began to undress.

Boyd stepped across to Tanner who was still angry at his concerns being dismissed, arms folded and staring fixedly at the bulkhead opposite.

"So, Doc. You ready to be a Zantanath prisoner?"

"I'll do my part. But before that, you should probably get that looked at."

Boyd raised his prosthetic arm with a quizzical look, "What this?"

"No," replied Tanner. "Your leg."

Boyd looked down, his uniform below the knee was a crimson red. He remembered the slight pain he had felt as he rushed the Zantanath in the moment of the attack.

"Looks worse than it is, Doc."

"Lay down a moment, I'll take a look."

Boyd rolled his eyes and did as he was told. Laying prone, Tanner rolled up Boyd's trouser leg examined the wound. Taking his medical utiliplex from his belt he started to work to clean and close the gash in the leg.

"I'll need to close that up for you," said Tanner. "Hold still."

Tanner's utiliplex sprayed a local anaesthetic on the wound and then clamped the gash together. The action still made Boyd wince.

"Easy, Doc," he complained.

"Almost done."

A second spray was released, coating the wound with alt-skin; the dermal bandage looked almost invisible.

"There. I'd normally tell you to take it easy for a couple of days, but I'm guessing that may not be possible."

"Yeah. Thanks Doc," said Boyd, rolling his trouser back down and standing to test the alt-skin bandage.

"Okay, I'm done," stated Elderson. "You can turn around."

Both Boyd and Tanner casually turned to face Elderson, who stood checking the fit of the battlesuit she had just climbed into. The adjusted shrink-fit had done its job and formed the suit to her body perfectly, but she had not yet put the helmet on, and the gauntlet containing the weapon still lay on the floor. She was clearly being cautious.

Boyd walked up close to examine the suit.

"Nice fit. Comfortable?"

"It is tight, but not uncomfortable. You know you're wearing it, but it doesn't restrict my movement," she stretched her arms and flexed her back to confirm the point.

"And it appears that you don't have to be two metres tall to wear it," noted Tanner, more to himself than anyone else.

Elderson and Boyd exchanged a look, then both regarded the helmet. Elderson huffed her fringe from her eyes and, without hesitation, donned the helmet. There was a hiss and a click as it reformed internally to provide a perfect fit, sealing at the neck.

Again, Elderson began to slowly look around and examine her surroundings via the medium of the Zantanath battle armour.

"Okay, I'm happy," she said to herself. "This is incredible."

"What do you see?"

"Full tactical readouts, I'm integrated into their comms

network. I can hear chatter going back and forward."

"Here, put this on," said Boyd, handing her the weapons gauntlet. She did. Again, it sealed itself into place becoming integrated into the form of the suit.

"Weapon is pairing. Connected." She gasped; it too connected with the suit and provided her with a plethora of options via her visor display. "We have to get hold of more of these."

Swinging the weapon into position, the barrel sprung out of the casing to extend past the end of her balled fist. Aiming down the adjacent corridor, she began identifying targets.

"I need to test this suit, this weapon."

"You'll get your chance," she replied.

Elderson made a low whistle; she was clearly impressed. From Elderson's bio-com visual stream, she watched the battlesuit visor display, icons and language human Earth standard. The Zantanath tech was geared to its wearer perfectly.

"Okay, time to move out," Ellie said to the three. "Join up with the others. We need to stop the theft in the bio-banks and regain control of the ship."

At her words, the three looked up at the ceiling of the room, as if a deity had just spoken from the heavens. She was no deity, but perhaps they were right to look beyond the ship.

"Go now," she urged. They headed off at pace, following the navigation track she had sent through their bio-comm.

LARSEN

"I have never been so sure. This new Setak'da is a false hope and Father is right. We cannot trust him, and nor should we trust his witch partner; they both side with the Xannix. They spread nothing but falsehoods and lies. He is no warlord to save mankind; he is not here to build alliances with the Zantanath, he has clearly aligned himself with the Xannix and aims to derail all we have achieved.

"But the situation has given us the chance to correct things. We can finally move against them and make this world our own. A world for our children to breathe new life and thrive. A world for humans, and a bridge to a new life for us all.

"The Xannix are a dying race. It is time to end their suffering."

"Where did you find this?" he asked Ovitala, who was standing silently opposite, waiting for him to review the recording.

"Our investigators found this in his room. It was concealed well."

"Obviously not well enough."

He was pacing. They had returned from their visit to the Overseer base, leaving Yannix to prepare his troops and finalise operational provision for their strike force. The worry was starting to get to him; he could feel it like a cold, seeping dread crawling through his veins. Problems were mounting up and closing in on all sides. He needed to find a way through, but now this. It was personal for them both. Ovitala was clearly shaken, as she had raised Clarion as her own and couldn't understand the betrayal. He was enraged and confounded, as this cuckoo had murdered the woman he loved and was admitting it brazenly in a vid. That it was his and Rivers' DNA in the person looking back at him made the pill even harder to swallow.

"Who is this for? Was this transmitted?"

"We don't think so. More a work in progress." As she spoke, Clarion moved forward and ended the recording, and the screen in Ovitala's office went dark.

"Is there any further progress on finding him? He can't have simply disappeared," he said forcefully, his emotions momentarily rising to the surface, as he again thought of Rivers. Since her death, he had been able to think of little else. Grief had initially been pushed aside, but it always finds a way in, and in quiet moments he had felt it most.

'Larsen.'

Rivers' voice drifted over him like a dream, her smiling face appearing in his mind as it did so. He looked from Ovitala to the floor, wrestling with the idea that he may finally be going mad with the stress of it all.

'Larsen, can you hear me?'

Yes, I can hear you, he thought. *In the way I hear the blood in my veins and breath in my lungs; I hear you.* He tried to focus on what was real, to give his mind some chance to keep a grip on the world about him. Ovitala was speaking but she had faded out, her voice no longer of interest. He wanted Rivers to speak again, her voice like a warm, intoxicating embrace.

'I'm here, Larsen. I'm still here.'

His vision drifted to the back of the room and the small bioluminescent fish which swam languidly in their tanks, mesmerising and in sequence. His eyes seemed to blur, and in that moment, he saw Rivers step from the ether.

"Rivers?" he said aloud. Ovitala stopped speaking and looked at him, head cocked to one side while trying to follow his break in conversation.

The figure walked forward another few steps until she stood only a couple of metres away, far enough to be just out of physical reach. Her smile was full of sadness and melancholy. Her body language was restrained for the emotion they clearly both felt, and it held him back from rushing to hold her. Ovitala followed his gaze but seemed confused at the situation.

He took a step forward to be closer to her, and, as he did so, noticed the bio-comm icon in his vision, a streamed incoming transmission. From his initial wonder and excitement, reality suddenly invaded: she was not here with him, but she was close. She was alive.

His system was suddenly full of adrenaline, as his heart began to race.

"Where are you?"

"Our quarters. Larsen, I never left."

"Stay there, I'm on my way."

He looked back at Ovitala as he sprinted for the door.

"Have a medical team meet me at my old quarters. Hurry!"

*

The Xannix guard at the apartment door saw him charging down the corridor towards him, and anticipating his Setak'da's intent, opened the door before he got there. He was through the entrance and into the room in an instant, coming to a sudden, sliding stop. His wide eyes scanned the room. It appeared untouched, apart from the bodies which had been carefully removed. Blood still stained the floor and physically marked the place of death of both the guard on duty that day, and Rivers.

His mind filled in the blanks and suddenly Rivers was there again, crumpled and inert, the wounds in her chest, her back and the side of her head leeching her life away. How could she be alive? He closed his eyes against the memory. How could she be alive, he asked himself over again?

'Luc, I'm here.'

"Where? Show me," he said staring at the floor, his hands wide, describing the space. "I don't see you."

'Not there, the table.'

"The …?" he turned, clearly puzzled. To his astonishment there she stood, looking down on him through the holographic projection of Dawn's mobile unit. He sat heavily on the floor, the relief he felt like a pin to his emotional balloon. He began to laugh uncontrollably; he let it happen. The pain and stress of the last few days being released in one brief moment of joy.

"She saved me, Luc. Dawn was here when it happened, and she saved me."

"I didn't know she could do that from her mobile unit," he said, shaking his head. He crawled forward toward the low table on which the device was placed. The device was at the centre of the table in the centre of the room and had quickly become anonymous. Even when Dawn appeared as her hologram, the projector itself was not the focus of attention. Ignored and invisible, but in plain sight.

"I was lucky," she said, kneeling on the table to bring herself closer to him. "She wanted to help the Xannix too, but he fell behind the couch. She could do nothing to reach him in time."

He nodded his understanding; there was little he could add.

A sound like distant thunder began to echo about the room, finally becoming loud enough to identify as originating from the corridor outside and footfalls of a charging group of Xannix. The medical team burst into the room, closely followed by Ovitala, their astonishment apparent as their eyes fell on Rivers looking back at them. Their skin colour flickered, as if unsure on which colour to settle.

"Child Rivers," said Ovitala. "You are here?"

"Yes, Ovitala. Good to see you again. Sorry, if I gave you a fright."

"Nonsense, no need to apologise for anything, child. But you are different. Is that still you?"

"It is. Perhaps in a different state than you last saw me, but it is me."

"Ovitala, I'll be keeping this unit close from now on," he said. "It contains people very close to me, and I don't want to lose them again." It was a fact he stated to the room but felt it reinforced from somewhere deep within.

"As you wish, but perhaps child Rivers would speak with the lead investigator? She may be able to shed some light on where Clarion might have taken refuge?"

"I will certainly help where I can," Rivers replied.

Ovitala watched them for a moment longer before her skin tone became a cool blue hue. The others matched her colour and, realising that they were not immediately required, slowly filed out of the room.

"We will leave you alone; I'm sure there is much you wish to discuss." With a short bow of the head, she also turned and left.

He wanted to embrace Rivers, hold her safe and close, but all he could do was touch the cold surface of the table she was kneeling on. They sat in silence, the simplicity of companionship soothing, home. He felt centred again.

The guard took up his position back in the corridor and closed the door. They were alone again for the first time in days.

REEVE

She woke, startled and immediately on guard, to an unfamiliar face staring back at her. Disoriented, her mind had sprung from unconsciousness into a hostile and dangerous room. The Zantanath holding her arm was about to apply an injection, the hypo-pen poised a couple of centimetres above her skin.

Before she could act, an arm shot across her and took a firm grip of the Zantanath's arm, stopping the injection.

"I'd prefer if you didn't do that," said Silvers.

The Zantanath's eyes went wide in surprise, then he flipped to focussed anger and made to pull his arm away from Silvers' grip. Silvers held fast and waited until the Zantanath tried to repeat the action, this time giving the arm a small push as he did so. The amplified force away from her threw the Zantanath a couple of metres clear, enough for her and Silvers to get to their feet.

"Stop! Hold your fire!" shouted a voice she recognised. Clayton was standing next to a black AI unit in the centre of the room. A metre across from him was Fellows in a stand-off with a Zantanath armoured trooper, and fanned out across the rest of the room were six other Zantanath, one dressed in robes. The numbers were about even, but the unknown quantity was the Zantanath warrior.

She felt like she was watching the scene through a fog, that she was somehow distanced from what was going on, with much also familiar. Trying to focus, she shook her head to gain some clarity, and it helped a little. Attempting to send a bio-comm to Clayton, she realised part of the issue. Her bio-comm was unresponsive, her vision clear—there was not even a standby icon. They were off-line. Disconnection felt odd, like a safety net had been removed from her world. It would slow them down, reaction and coordination restricted to normal human modes.

She and Silvers took up a defensive position with the wall to their backs, a reflex to the situation before them.

"You okay?" asked Silvers, without taking his eyes off the wider room.

"Yeah. Bio-comm out?"

"Yeah."

"Sir," she called, "what's going on?" But she was speaking over Clayton's argument with the lead Zantanath.

That drew a brief smile from Dawn, whose hologram appeared to be watching them intently.

"Welcome back, Lieutenant," said Dawn.

Still taking in the situation, she realised she couldn't remember how she got there.

"What was the last thing you remember?" she asked Silvers.

"I don't know," he said, a frown crossed his face as he struggled to rewind and recall a recent memory. The frown told her what she wanted to know. "Being aboard a Xannix ship. Getting shot by one of those guys," he nodded towards the Zantanath trooper. "It hurt. I remember it hurt a lot."

"Dawn. What is happening?" she asked again. If Clayton didn't have time to answer, maybe Dawn might.

"Abduction," replied Dawn.

"What?"

"The Ambassador there, is here to conscript my father and the rest of us into the Zantanath war machine. They are using nano-tech to somehow modify and control the mind and body of any they are able to infect. I have been with Commander Roux this last couple of days, watching him deteriorate as the technology lobotomised and took hold of him. I had time to watch and examine him as the conversion took place, turning him from human to savage."

Dawn's holographic display morphed into a representation of Roux, haggard and unkempt, face bruised with dark, sunken eyes. It began to step through a slideshow of the man's deterioration; skin showing lesions, progressing to sores and open wounds as the skin disintegrated under the stress of the body's enforced genetic changes. In Roux, the nanites affected his system as an aggressive virus, dismantling his body at a cellular level, slowly and painfully.

"In the final stages of transformation, the nanites eject themselves by working themselves out of the system via pores in the skin." A horrific holographic image of Roux, his face contorted, his skin slick with black blood and his body curled in a foetal position on the ground punctuated her words.

"The devastating part was that he knew what was happening. He was fully aware and experienced the pain and trauma of the mutation through every cell of his being. He fought it every step of the way. At the end, he stopped the transition the only way he knew how, before I could save him. Now he's gone, and I won't be able to rejuvenate him. I can never bring him back.

"Whatever they implemented, whatever technology they employed against Commander Roux, it didn't work. And watching him go through that... I won't let it happen again. Not to anyone."

"You have little choice," said the ambassador stepping out from behind the trooper to gain a clear view of the conversation. He began to pace among the Zantanath as he continued. "And you are only partially correct in your assessment. We can already grow your forms from the DNA base sequences we have so far acquired. We can accelerate the growth, implant advanced soldiering routines and learning, imprint psychological command structures. You are a natural warrior species, hardy and resourceful, and able to undergo many physical and mental trials. This has enabled us to advance several of our genetic engineering programmes. You have shown yourselves to be quite receptive to our trials."

"Not all of us," said Dawn, retaking her holographic form.

"No. Although that is true, it is not a setback."

"So, you killed Roux to obtain scientific data on how he might respond to what...?"

"We stress tested his immune system while undergoing physical modification. It is a new approach to species repurposing."

"Species repurposing?" she said, her voice drifting off under the disgust of what she was hearing.

The robed Zantanath stepped up to the armoured figure in the stand-off with Fellows. The warrior was menacing in appearance, but it appeared calm and awaiting instruction, whereas Fellows was clearly under duress, sweating under the continued stress of the situation.

"I believe you designated this one Travis. He has been an exceptional test subject. We trialled just five of these against a platoon of Xannix at a test facility recently. It took just ten Earth minutes for them to eliminate the Xannix. Very effective." He patted Travis on the shoulder. "Yes, your kind will be put to great use."

"Auwen, we're not a resource to be exploited, we are a free people. We decide our own future," said Clayton.

"Oh, I disagree," replied the Zantanath. "You have provided us the perfect opportunity. A colony fleet with pre-prepared and neatly stored material. You have done half our work for us. We only need manipulate the genetic coding in the final weeks of gestation to obtain the results we need."

"You are deluding yourself."

Auwen shook his head. "Our plans are already well underway. We are removing units from your bio-banks as we speak."

Clayton somehow remained calm. She, however, began to become enraged. This Zantanath was about to steal their future and force them into subjugation; push them into an existence of war and violence.

"Fleet Captain," said Auwen. "Put down your weapons. You are outgunned, and in no place to negotiate. Time to choose."

A red dot began to flash in the corner of her vision. Her bio-comm was rebooting. She watched as Clayton blinked hard and wiped his face in a show of frustration, but she knew the act for what it was: distraction. As her display came back up, she recognised the addition of six OWEC crew idents in the room, including her own. There were eight unclassified icons she immediately labelled as Zantanath and hostile.

Silent orders began to flow between them at the speed of thought: targets, designated assignments. Dawn was orchestrating a plan with limited VERS data, but the confidence level to a positive outcome was good, as long as they held the initiative. With the prospect of enslavement by the Zantanath, she thought the VERS irrelevant. To fight the Zantanath was their only course of action.

"Okay, okay!" said Clayton, faking frustrated resignation. They needed the initiative; surprise needed to be with them. Clayton raised his hands and his sidearm swung from the trigger guard like a pendulum on his forefinger. "Just take it easy."

On Clayton's words, Fellows began to fall backwards. It initially appeared as if he had been shot, or had fainted, but she and Silvers now had a clear shot. Fellows had changed the firing solution, and in that split second the Travis Zantanath realised his mistake. The three of them opened fire at the strongest target in the room, Fellows firing up from the ground at point blank range while she and Silvers targeted the warrior's 'T' for an immediate take down.

The face mask exploded in a haze of red and silver sparkles, bullets lacing up from Fellows through the warrior's centreline as it was lifted off its feet by the sheer close quarters force of the fire. There was an audible thud as the lifeless form hit the floor.

A shocked silence fell across the room for the briefest of moments, as those on both sides took in the incident. The Zantanath appeared unwilling to recognise that their prized warrior had just been removed from the situation, and the humans couldn't quite believe their gamble had paid off.

"Now!" shouted Clayton, to snap his team back into action.

The room was suddenly a ballet of motion and violence. She and Silvers moved to coordinate their attacks and take down the armed Zantanath in order, but cover was being found and shots difficult. Equally, shots were beginning to come back.

Jemma had no weapon, so had taken refuge behind the machine that was currently her daughter, hoping that if she stayed small enough, no one would realise what an easy target she was.

Another Zantanath fell, the medic whose face she had awoken to. He had moved to hide behind a sofa, but it had been no protection at all, as a well-placed bullet cut him down.

Some Zantanath had made it back to the door with Auwen at their centre, their leader using them as a shield against the hail of projectiles criss-crossing the room. Auwen didn't even look back as he walked through the door.

"The roof!" Clayton shouted over the noise of the room. Zantanath beam weapons put holes in the marble counter in front of him, and he retaliated in the direction of fire. "We have to stop him."

Her bio-comm still indicated three hostiles in the room, but there was a crossfire of beam weapons keeping them from advancing and no space to manoeuvre and flank them. They had lost the initiative; the situation had stagnated.

'They're just buying time while Auwen escapes,' said Jemma via bio-comm.

'Coward,' stated Silvers.

'Stay here,' said Fellows. 'Give me some cover!'

Fellows rolled to his front, popped up and leapt for the closest couch, while in the same moment she, Silvers and Clayton fired to keep the heads of the remaining Zantanath down. As Fellows reached the end of his tumble, he extended his carbine round the end of the marble counter and fired. There was a surprised yell and a flash of light, followed by an angry roar of frustration and pain. She couldn't tell where the voices were coming from, or to whom they belonged.

"Bastard!" There were two more shots.

'You okay, Fellows?' asked Clayton.

'Bastard got me in the shoulder... Feels pretty bad.'

More shots and light lanced across the room towards Fellows' location. She and Silvers tried to subdue the Zantanath fire, but they were dug in behind some heavier cover.

'Tango down,' continued Fellows. 'He won't be catching the shuttle home.'

'Okay, no more heroics, people. Let's just get out of this in one piece,' announced Clayton.

'Easy for you to say,' said Dawn.

Smoke, dust and debris was beginning to fill the room, and with every second Auwen got further away.

'I've got an idea. Get ready to target their positions,' Dawn said, as a pair of beams fired over her head and put a clear hole in the window behind her.

A second later a scarlet red bull elephant filled the centre of the room, trumpeting a deep roar of anger, eyes blazing with fire and hatred. It made a short sharp aggressive charge towards the Zantanath position. Both Zantanath having never seen such a thunderous animal, recoiled from their hiding places in shock and fear. Confused and too focused on the terror in front of them, their base instincts took over and Silvers was at the correct angle to take full advantage.

Two shots rang out. Then silence. The blazing eyes of the elephant continued to watch as the life of the remaining Zantanath drained away.

"Go!" shouted Clayton to her and Silvers. "Auwen; we may still be able to stop him."

As they sprinted for the door, Clayton turned to Jemma.

"Take care of Fellows. Dawn, watch over them."

There was a trumpet of defiant victory from Dawn's holographic elephant as they left the room. Clayton followed them at pace.

"Which way?" asked Silvers as they ran. Neither of them had any recollection of the building or where they were headed, their amnesia still blanking much of the last few days.

"The roof," shouted Clayton from behind them. "The shuttle on the landing pad. Two floors up. Forget the elevators. Take the side access."

Turning the corner of the corridor they propelled themselves towards the oval entrance to the side of the elevators; having negotiated the Xannix stairways before, both she and Silvers took advantage of the grips and handholds to pull themselves up the steep incline.

"Use your hands," she said back to Clayton, as she heard his cussing at the unfamiliar and unexpected tunnel format. "Place your feet towards each side where its higher."

Bursting out into the reception room opposite the landing pad, they sprinted towards the exit as a howling engine sound clawed at their ears. Reaching the exit and aiming their weapons at the Zantanath shuttle, her eyes widened in fear. The shuttle was airborne, a couple of metres off the pad and rising towards them. All she could focus on was the two directional cannons which began pulsing bolts of energy towards them, but with the width of the exit and Silvers to her side, there was nowhere to go.

The energy bolts from the shuttle chased their way up the pad and path towards them. In that moment, as her heart pounded in her chest and her legs became like lead, she felt a hammer blow to her back and found herself launched forward and to one side of the path, her head striking the hand rail hard. Dust and stone scattered up from the path as the shuttle passed overhead, bolts of energy continuing to search for a target, but sounds had become dull, her vision blurred. The left side of her face prickled with flecks of sharp grit, and her body surged with electric adrenaline. She blinked the fog away.

The whine of the shuttle engines began to grow in intensity again, and she realised it was coming back for another pass. Quickly she looked round to try and find Silvers and Clayton: both were also rammed up against the walkway wall and handrail,

Clayton clearly having tackled them both to the ground and out of the line of fire. They had all taken a hard knock in the evasion.

"Everyone okay?" asked Clayton.

No one answered, just gave a dazed nod in response as they slowly got back to their feet.

"We have to get off the pad," she said.

"Can't argue with that," said Silvers.

"Go!" said Clayton waving them past and directing them back the way they had just come, at the same time keeping an eye on the approaching Zantanath shuttle.

The shuttle opened fire again as the roar of the engines combined to create a hurricane of noise. In front of her, Silvers came to a sudden shuddering stop. Bolts of energy landed with incredible concentrated force and the pathway before them failed, the bridgework crumbling away in a storm cloud of dust and debris. It left them marooned on the landing pad side.

As the dust swirled away, pulled by the vortex of air trailing the attacking shuttle, Silvers stepped forward to the edge of the abyss.

"We're not getting across there," he said, his assessment flat and factual.

Clayton immediately put out a bio-comm broadcast, as they all started to scan the pad for alternate routes off the roof.

'Dawn, this is Clayton. We're under heavy fire on the pad. We've been cut off. Are there any other routes off the roof? Over.'

The response they all received was immediate.

'Affirmative. There is an emergency exit on the opposite edge of the pad from your location,' said Dawn.

"That's too far," said Silvers. "They're already turning for another pass."

"We've got to go for it," she said. "We can't stay here; that's not an option. We have to move."

"Spread out," said Clayton. "Space ourselves, don't give them a single target."

'Wait one,' said Dawn over the bio-comm channel rather cryptically.

"We have to go now people," she shouted over the noise of the shuttle as it made another attack run. "Go, go, go!"

Sprinting across the pad, Clayton and Silvers broke off at angles, while she headed in a direct route to the emergency exit. Again, the tempest noise passed overhead, and the shuttle pounded the pad with weapons fire. The storm was all behind her and she closed quickly on the exit, a short ramp descended from the landing pad to another short muster area. Before heading down the ramp she tuned to look back across the pad.

Clayton was to her far right, at the lip of the pad waving his arms and making wild gesticulating signals toward the approaching shuttle. Making himself a target drew their focus and their fire. Silvers was ignored. The bolts of energy stitched their way across the pad in a direct line towards the Fleet Commander.

"Clayton!" she found herself screaming across the banshee wailing around her. Explosions rose from the pad and Clayton fell away, lost behind the final shots from the shuttle.

Staring back, as the dust and smoke cleared, Clayton was gone.

*

Silvers was immediately by her side. "Time to go," he said with a sympathetic tone.

"Not yet," she replied, concentration and stubbornness refusing to accept the events she had just witnessed. He couldn't be gone. "Follow me."

She ran down the ramp to the muster floor below. Under the pad was a doorway back into the building, but leading round the pad under its lip was a maintenance walkway.

"This way."

She sprinted off round the walkway to find the place below which Clayton would have been standing, hopping up and down and drawing attention to himself. A theory had popped into her head. If Clayton had been close enough to the edge of the pad to see the lower walkway, he may have just saved them all.

Debris began to litter the walkway. They slowed, eyes wide, looking for any signs of life.

"There," she said. "Help me."

A single hand could be seen poking out from under a mound of rubble, above them a destroyed section of the landing pad. They worked fast, both of them pulling lumps of ragged aerated stone and buckled reinforcements from the heap to reveal more and more of Clayton's unconscious form beneath.

"Is he breathing?" asked Silvers.

"I think so, bio-comm is still active."

The sound of the shuttle returned. It angered her that they had no response, that they were fully on the defensive. Digging deep, she struck her head a couple of times.

"Think, dammit." She remembered Dawn.

As Silvers pulled Clayton from the last of the rubble and started to tend him, she turned to face the oncoming shuttle. It had been persistent. Why hadn't it given up? She parked the thought. It would have to wait.

'Dawn,' she broadcast across her bio-comm. 'If you have a trick up your sleeve, now would be a good time.'

'Wait one,'

'We don't have *one*! Now, Dawn. Now!"

'Take cover,' came the response.

She turned to Silvers, who was checking Clayton over for broken bones and lacerations. They were still under the open skies of the damaged landing pad.

"Let's move," she said. "You take his shoulders." There wasn't enough time for one of them to lift Clayton across their shoulders, they would need to sling him between them. She took his legs and Silvers hooked his arms under Clayton's armpits.

"Okay. Go," said Silvers. They began to waddle along the walkway with as much pace as they could muster.

"What the stars is happening?" grunted Silvers through gritted teeth with the exertion of carrying the heavy end of the load.

"I don't know. This is Dawn's show now. Just move."

From the corner of her eye she saw a faint flash of red. She thought it may have been fire from the shuttle, but it didn't hit them or anything around them. Perhaps it was the sun glinting off the approaching shuttle, but a moment later it happened again, and again. She quickly took a glance over her shoulder trying to stay on course along the walkway as she did so.

There were vertical flashes of light falling like a deadly rain from the sky all about the building. They had started slowly but within a couple of seconds the drops had become a torrent, as thousands of small energy bolts created a haze of light before them, a thick blanket of defence, a volume of space blotted out with red rain.

At the centre of the fire storm was the Zantanath shuttle. Initially, the shuttle seemed unaffected, but as the intensity and density of fire increased across its flightpath, the airframe began to give. Small fragments of wing began to fall away, and with structural integrity failing, the shuttle attitude pitched up and spun wildly to the left. The craft began to spiral uncontrolled to the ground. In its descent, the shuttle began to disintegrate and flash apart, as small explosions ripped through critical systems.

The sight was captivating. She and Silvers now stood motionless with the unconscious Clayton carried between them, no longer running but instead awestruck by the destruction of their tormentor. They watched as the stricken shuttle plummeted and fell apart, until it finally became engulfed in flame under its sudden impact with the ground.

As the red rain of fire fell away, the sky returned to its peaceful cloud-dotted blue, black smoke rising from the wreckage below.

She and Silvers exchanged an astonished glance, both of them fully expecting the past few minutes to have been their last. A moan emanated from the body between them: Clayton was coming around.

LARSEN

"How have we not found a human child on a planet full of Xannix?" he shouted. His frustration was boiling over and Ovitala was not helping. "Tell me, Ovitala! What are your investigators doing?"

Ovitala bristled, her skin paling to an angered white; she was clearly not used to being spoken to in that way and didn't know how to respond to the Setak'da in this mood. Rivers tried to calm the situation.

"It is a big planet, and I'm pretty sure there are plenty of bolt-holes. He could be anywhere by now."

He sighed, Rivers taking the anger from him in an instant. If she could be calm about the situation, he could certainly be more even tempered. He pinched the bridge of his nose and closed his eyes. After another couple of deep breaths, he returned to Ovitala and tried to be more objective.

"Okay, let's look at this again. Maybe we're asking the wrong questions. Without provocation, a human boy, against all his previous behavioural history, steals the sidearm from a guard, kills the guard, kills Jill then disappears without a trace."

"You did let him go," said Rivers. "And you were not exactly sensitive to the situation."

"Sensitive?"

"You shouted him down, didn't even let him speak."

"But he'd just murdered you."

"You didn't know that."

"He was the only one left alive in a room of dead people. The deduction wasn't hard to make," he countered.

Ovitala watched as they quarrelled, possibly thinking it best to stay out of a personal matter until she could contribute something meaningful.

"And we have no clue as to why he did it. No motivation, no theories?"

They both turned to look at Ovitala.

"Power play? Jealousy?" said Rivers. "Punishment?"

"I don't know," he said. "We hadn't known him long, but he didn't exhibit any of those tendencies, no violent outbursts, nothing that would indicate this level of deviation from his normal demeanour. Ovitala, what is your assessment of his mental state?"

Ovitala seemed surprised to be asked. "He has always been peaceful; happy. These recent actions are not in any way normal." There was sorrow there, perhaps even guilt in her words. Ovitala had raised the child as her own from a young age. Having known the parents for a brief time before their disappearance. "I cannot explain what he did. I'm sorry."

He and Rivers looked at each other, a silent assessment being made.

'You trust her?' asked Rivers via the bio-comm.

'I don't think she knows.'

'Okay.'

Both of them turned again to Ovitala, who changed her posture and her colour to become a flickering low hue of confusion. "Am I missing something?" she asked.

"Your interlacing technology—how do you use it? What is its purpose?"

There was a delay while Ovitala considered her answer.

"It can be implanted into the skin of a ship, allowing us to infiltrate and control its systems without being noticed."

"And to what scale have you been able to shrink these devices?"

"Shrink?" asked Ovitala.

"Yes. How small have you been able to make them?"

"Currently these are specifically designed for ship infiltration; they are generally about the size of my fist," she said, clenching her fist to demonstrate. "Or larger, if additional capability is required."

"So, nothing small enough to, say, be implanted in a person?" Rivers questioned.

"No. Nothing that small."

The pair of them looked at each other, both assessing the other. He wanted to believe her, but where human body language might assist him, Xannix body language was unreadable. However, to this point, Ovitala had always been direct with him, sometimes evasive, but she had never lied to him. That counted.

With one final glance to Rivers to confirm their action, he stepped forward and gestured politely to the seating area at the centre of Ovitala's office.

"Maybe, we should sit," his mood changed, becoming more sympathetic. If she didn't know already, this was going to be a difficult conversation. Ovitala indicated her agreement with a subtle shift in skin colour to a light blue, then made herself comfortable on one of the low couches which were arranged in a circular forum in the centre of the room. He placed Dawn's mobile AI unit on the floor beside him which projected Rivers' holographic form to the seat next to him.

"Rivers has been able to provide some insight as to why she was murdered," he said. "She is probably best to explain the detail."

Rivers' holographic form straightened and turned to face Ovitala.

"It was while we were in the control centre observing one of the tactical teams place an interlacing unit. We were all in discussion about various things, and you were called away to attend some other issue."

"I remember," said Ovitala.

Rivers nodded and continued.

"The conversation drifted into the purpose of the interlacing device and it started me thinking on alternate uses; how the technology might be applied under different circumstances or if modified. I began to wonder what might happen if you could make such a device smaller. What could be done if you could, for example, embed a miniaturised interlacing device within a person in the same way you had the ship?

"I was just pushing around ideas, verbalising them. I always find that if I verbalise my thoughts it tends to crystallise the idea." She shrugged. "Anyway, during this conversation, Clarion had gone quiet. Really quiet.

"Although I didn't realise it at the time, as I was concentrating more on the control room mission display than him, Clarion had become almost enraged. Dawn was able to show me security footage of the moment from your security team's investigation. You can see the moment it happens."

Her hologram was momentarily replaced by a two dimensional visual of Clarion as his features clearly transformed from the innocent child to an almost animal-like hunter, focussed and of singular intent.

"It's like someone or something flicked a switch and Clarion became possessed."

"Possessed?" asked Ovitala.

"Yes. Like he had become someone else entirely; controlled."

"Is that possible, Ovitala?" he asked. "I know your technology reaches to accelerated learning and manipulation of the mind, but is the control of the mind something you can also enforce? Do the Zantanath? Could a device be constructed, like your interlacing technology, to take command of a person's free will?"

Ovitala became quickly concerned, her eyes searching the floor between them as she thought through the possibility.

"It is expressly forbidden to research such technology. We simply would not. Our technology is for learning and language."

"But the question is not about the Xannix. What could the Zantanath achieve if they didn't prescribe to your moral code?" asked Rivers. "Could the technology be employed to control a person's mind or not?"

Ovitala seemed unable to answer, her mind racing with thoughts and possibilities, her skin flickering and flushing.

"This is only a theory, Ovitala," he said. "But it would explain Clarion's extreme behaviour. We won't know for sure until we can run some tests, but that means we need to find him, and quickly."

"This is incredibly concerning, Setak'da. If you are right, how many others might be affected?"

"Let's cross that obstacle if and when we reach it; for now just be wary. Use trusted people, handle the detail yourself."

"Of course."

"Do you have any idea where he may have gone, places he would consider safe? He's a child, he would want to return to the familiar, somewhere he knew well."

"Were there places he would go when he was younger? Places he would go if he was frightened?" asked Rivers, the hologram returning to the seat beside him. It was strange, but even as a holographic projection she appeared real to him, his mind filling in the blanks. It was comforting.

"Those places we have tried already, or they are far from here. He would not have been able to travel there in the time."

"Are you sure?"

"Yes."

"He can't have simply disappeared," he said to the room. He had risen from his seat and was now pacing. "Is there any way out of this complex without passing a security detail or camera system?"

"No."

"And you've searched every room?"

"Yes."

"Every level?"

He stopped pacing. The question was just an extension to the first: rooms, levels, buildings. But there was something about Ovitala's silence that made him ask again.

"Have you searched every level of this complex?"

He turned to look at her directly. She seemed conflicted, her skin tone showing a soft flustered confusion, her eyes directed to the floor in thought.

"Ovitala?" he coaxed.

After a long moment she shifted in her seat and looked up at him. Her skin again turned a light blue, her features seemed to relax as if a mental strain had been eased. A decision made, she waved him back to his seat. He obliged, but sat to the edge of it and forward, listening and attentive.

"You understand this complex to be a sanctuary," she began.

"Yes. One of the old Arch'sa."

"Yes, that is true. But it is more." She shifted again in her seat.

"More how?"

"Remember the history from the Setak'da teachings? Once the Zantanath arrived and began to change our homeworld, for many years we were too weak and desperate to respond. Our people had been decimated through the wars and many had no fight left. The Zantanath simply did as they pleased, and we paid a further price.

"People would go missing. Whole villages at first, but then as they became more confident, towns also became silent. The Council had no real idea why these disappearances were happening, only that they were, and they must do something. That is when the Sanctuaries were created."

"To stop the disappearances?"

"The Xannix once existed on many planets in this region of space, but when the Zantanath found us, the war was deadly to us and we lost world after world. Xannix is our home world, our origin and our last hope. We can retreat no further. Sanctuaries were built underground, vast cities to hide our young, and our future. The Zantanath continue to plunder the surface, our people lost to us with each raid. But our people are growing in strength and have been waiting for our time."

"Yannix? His army is ready."

"That is only part of it. But if my fear is true, and Clarion has discovered the Sanctuary below this complex, we are in danger of being revealed to the Zantanath. Clarion was never exposed to any detail regarding the Sanctuary programme. Very few Xannix are even aware of their existence, the chambers being completely self-sufficient. But the only people who would be motivated to act on information of this kind would be the Zantanath. It would give them yet more of us to exploit.

This must stop. It will stop."

Ovitala's tone was moving slowly into shades of white, as she became angry at the prospect of the sanctuaries being discovered.

"Then we must act now to stop this. Make our final move against the Zantanath, before Clarion gets his chance to reveal anything to them."

"With the evidence we have available to us, and Clarion evading our search, we may have no choice."

The disappointment in her was visual, the old and proud Xannix suddenly appearing small, despite her stature.

"You must not blame yourself, Ovitala," he said. "This is not of your making."

"But I am responsible." She stood with a newfound determination. "And I will resolve this."

BOYD

The augmented reality navigation track in his bio-comm followed the corridor ahead and through the two figures before him. Elderson had taken point, as the Zantanath power armour she was wearing gave her an edge and would possibly even confuse any would-be attackers long enough for her to take the initiative. Between them both was Tanner; he even walked nervously, his head twitching to search out the source of every sound, watch every shadow. The doctor was turning into a liability.

Ellie's directions to the muster point with the other members of the rescue effort had changed a couple of times, as she had altered their course to work around Zantanath patrols. The next waypoint had led them to a maintenance hatch where, once inside the maintenance walkway, the track stopped above a floor hatch to the smaller crawlspace below.

"We're going under the floor panels?" said Tanner. "Are you serious? There's hardly space to breathe in that crawlspace."

"Why do you think they call it a crawlspace?" he said.

"I'm not impressed," replied Tanner.

"You don't have to be," said Elderson. "Just do whatever it is that keeps you calm and work your way to the end of the track."

He operated the floor control, and the grate lifted, exposing a secondary crawlspace heading back out under the corridor they had just left. Elderson checked the revised navigation track in her bio-comm: Ellie had pushed yet another update with an additional instruction. 'Panel W2AA.'

"You get used to it once you've done a few of these. Just breathe easy," he said. Tanner looked back at him unconvinced. "Easier than potholing."

"You're not helping," replied Tanner, as he ducked into the crawlspace after Elderson.

He closed the grate behind them. As they worked their way along the narrow tunnel on their bellies, he could hear the exertion in his ears, the blood thumping, the sound of their bodies sliding across the metal surface of the duplicitous floor, their movement threatening to give them away with every metre.

'Here,' Elderson said across the bio-comm.

Slowly, Elderson removed a utiliplex tool from her belt and manually released the panel fasteners. The panel popped up and was easily rolled across the upper floor to reveal the room above. She led with her gauntlet weapon, doing a quick sweep of the room from the crawlspace, images being displayed on the power-armour's visor. She then stood, slowly spiralling around to cover all the corners of the room, then climbed up out of the crawlspace to face the single figure slumped against the cargo boxes and netting in the storeroom.

'Storeroom. Locked from the outside. Emergency lighting only. Tanner, I think you're needed.'

Elderson moved slowly to the figure in shadow. Without her specifically requesting it, the external lights of her helmet came on and illuminated the person in front of her. It made her pause. The form was coated in blood, the floor about it slick and dark. Unrecognisable. Data started to scroll across her visor in anticipation of her questions: heart rate weak, blood loss excessive, puncture wounds to the upper body, blunt force trauma to face and limbs. She finally made out the name on the blood-soaked uniform: Hernandes.

'This is not good,' she said, her moves accelerated as if jolted into action. 'Tanner, get up here now. It's Hernandes!'

'Okay, almost there,' said Tanner, struggling through the floor access panel.

'XO Hernandes?' he asked.

'You know another one on this boat?' Elderson said, a pronounced anger in her voice he'd not heard before.

'What's he doing here?'

'How the hell should I know!'

Tanner was already working to patch the Commander's wounds as Boyd rolled out of the crawlspace into the storeroom. The sight of Hernandes' bedraggled crimson red form, brightly illuminated in the spotlight from Elderson's suit, reminded him of his historical reading, a vision of hell, the work of daemons. A feeling of revulsion turned his stomach.

'There's something wrong here,' said Tanner.

'Are you shitting me, doc?' he asked.

'You mean, more wrong that the XO being carved up and slung in a meat cooler?' said Elderson.

Tanner shook his head, continuing to concentrate and patch Hernandes with his mediplex tool, gaping wounds sealing and cells bonding as the flesh was drawn together.

'You don't understand. There's some kind of virus working through his system. It appears aggressive but is causing cancerous augmentation of his system and accelerating cellular rejuvenation where damaged.'

'But that's good right? Cellular rejuvenation, sounds like he'll survive?'

'Survive yes. But I have no idea what effect the cellular augmentation will have on him. Here, take a look at this data.'

Tanner sent his collected mediplex data to him and Elderson. It made little sense, but then he came across a vid which appeared as a cross section of Hernandes' left upper arm. The blood vessels were magnified and he could see blood cells flowing slowly through the frame. But small darker cylindrical shapes flowed amongst the cells, occasionally moving counter to the flow of the blood plasma they were suspended in, sometimes linking, sometimes moving to intercept cells and consume them, sometimes to mutate them.

'What are we looking at?' he asked.

'I don't know. We need to get him to a medbay. Better equipment.'

Elderson shook her head. 'We don't have time. Ellie just patched me into the corridor cameras. There's a Zantanath guard outside that door and there are others coming. Back in the crawlspace. Now.'

'We can't leave him!' said Tanner.

'You want to join him?' asked Elderson. Tanner shook his head. 'Then get back in that crawlspace. Fast.'

They slid into the space as quickly and silently as they could, and Elderson closed the panel behind them just as the storeroom door opened. All of them lay motionless, holding their breath, ears straining to listen to the Zantanath in the next room. He could almost feel the proximity of the Zantanath as it made its way across the floor to Hernandes. His senses heightened, the steps thumped and reverberated about him with each pace.

After a moment of silence, a voice: Terran English, muffled but understandable.

"He is progressing well. Another few hours and the transformation should be complete."

"Enough of your pet project. Will this give us the ship's command codes?"

'Why are they speaking Terran?' he asked across bio-comm.

'Quiet,' replied Elderson.

"If the neural links have been successful, then yes. He will be unable to withhold any information we request."

"And if they haven't?"

"Well, then, we will need to use cruder methods. I'm sure this is not unfamiliar to you."

"No, but none of this would be necessary if you had done as I asked in the first place."

"The AI plan is not an option. The crew eliminated their AI when we boarded. It was unforeseen and an unexpected move. You underestimated them."

"Don't pull that crap with me. You would have made the same decision."

"We are the same biology, but we've had a very different upbringing, brother." The last word was said with scorn.

Clones. He listened to their conversation as it faded in and out, the sound through the panelling muffled and incoherent at times as they moved about the room.

"I will update Regent Celestia and Commander Larsen. They may as well go ahead without us. We will catch them up. It should only be a matter of a few hours now."

"Agreed."

The sound of the two clones speaking moved away and became inaudible. The door mechanism could be heard activating then the pair appeared in the stream of the corridor before Ellie cut the feed. Emergency over.

'Who were they?' Tanner asked. Across the bio-comm, he could tell Tanner was in trouble, his nerves frayed, breathing laboured. The confined space wasn't helping.

'Clones,' he replied.

'Clones? Clones of whom?'

'We need to move,' he said. 'We can't help Hernandes. But maybe we can do something for the bio-banks.' He began to move back towards the maintenance space, crawling back feet first.

'We don't leave anyone, Boyd. We need to go back for him,' said Tanner.

'There's no one to go back for. You heard them. In a couple of hours, he'll be one of them. One of their mindless soldiers.'

He continued moving, not waiting for the response.

'We can't leave him there like that,' repeated Tanner, probably more to himself than the group, but the bio-comm broadcast it.

'He's already dead,' he said. 'There's nothing we can do for him.'

The floor grate lifted, putting him back in the light of the maintenance walkway they had started from. He waited a moment while Tanner also backed up far enough to make his way through the hatch and offered his hand to assist. There was no sign of Elderson.

'Elderson, where are you?'

There was no reply, no bio-comm message, no response.

'Elderson?'

"Shit!" he whispered harshly. Tanner looked alarmed, like he'd just been slapped, eyes wide and fearful. Shaking his head in disbelief, Tanner put his ear to the corridor hatch, listening for signs of approach. He didn't mind, it kept the doctor occupied.

'Elderson, we need to move now.'

'Alright, alright,' came the response. 'Calm down, Boyd. You'll strain something.'

She flipped out of the crawlspace and hit the control to the grate, closing it and completing the walkway surface again.

'Where the stars did you go?' he said.

'I was right behind you. I didn't go anywhere.'

They stared at each other; he, weighing up the veracity of her words, she, giving a defiant response. She was the ranking officer, being questioned on her actions was not his place, but if his concerns were correct, she would have people more senior to him to answer to.

He stayed silent and accusing. She broke eye contact and moved away.

'I had a last moment task from Ellie. That is all. It didn't take a moment.'

'Ellie?'

I sent the order, came back the text response. He imagined she was having problems communicating, the message curt with no vocal overlay. But the order to do what? Something stank, but he wasn't in the loop.

'So, what next?'

'We have orders. We're off this boat.'

'What?'

'Ellie's assessment is that it's too far gone. We've lost control and we've lost the ship. The best thing we can do now is go for the source.'

'What source?'

An image flashed up in his bio-comm display.

'You have to be fucking kidding me. How are we taking that down? You have a spare navy in your arsenal?'

Tanner was staring internally at his display in disbelief. A station in the halo of a star hung in his vision and mesmerised him into silence.

'We have friends. We have a ride. We just need to get off this ship.'

*

The launch bobbed gently on the lake, a so-slow rise and fall that in the gentle sun became a soporific motion. Peering over the side, his eight-year-old self became lost in the crystal-clear water, and a light lapping sound could be heard periodically as the shallow, subtle waves nudged the boat.

That morning, he and his father had struck out for the lake for a fishing trip while his mother enjoyed a little time to herself back at the holiday home. They had escaped the heat of Texas for the cooler New England summer. For some reason, his mother and father disliked the heat of their hometown and, as such, he always found their choice of home perplexing. Texas was not forgiving when it came to summer sun, so why did they stay? They didn't go on holiday together often, perhaps once a year; his father was away a lot and mother always busy with work, but they would always manage one trip a year together, his father stating that *It is important for the family*.

He loved the lake, the water so clear but always so cold, like liquid glass; melt water after a thaw. They would fish for hours, which, for an eight-year-old, was a lesson in patience and torture. His father would drop anchor in the shallows, cast his line then promptly fall asleep in the cool sun. While his mind buzzed with the activity and mischief of a child, he would find himself staring into the glassy water, sparkling with ideas.

Staring over the side, he imagined the pebbles and sand of the lake floor as a lunar surface, or the terrain of an exoplanet. His eyes scanned the grey sun-bleached pebbles for a landing site for his imaginary craft: somewhere flat, somewhere level. Scanning, scanning... there. A clear sandy spot, perfect for a drop ship, clear of debris, level and even.

But his eyes continued to wander as his lander descended to the surface of this world, through the crevasses, sweeping across the planes. Something caught his attention. A circular pattern amongst the shadows and pebbles, but in the uncommon surroundings it took a moment to identify. The undulating surface of the lake gave movement to the dead and unfocused eye that stared back. Buried under the rocks and sand of the shallows, the grey haunted complexion of a young woman's half concealed face looked back at him from the lakebed.

At the point of recognition, his body recoiled in shock. Before he registered what his conscious self was doing, his primal reflex had stood him up on the deck and taken several paces backward. It was a mistake. He stumbled on a neatly coiled bow rope and toppled over the opposite side of the launch. As his head struck the side, blackness and chill flooded his senses. Numbed by the cold, his body disconnected from his mind, a feeling of lethargy pulled him to the bottom of the lake.

His world was weirdly inverted. Before, he had been looking down through an undulating surface to a landscape below; now, that undulating surface silhouetted a monochrome of dark and light, as the boat he had fallen from cast a shadow across him, floating so close, but out of reach.

The cold of his surroundings began to leach into him, a feeling like a cold blade worked its way down his throat and began to press like a heavy hand, fingers spread wide across his chest. A darkness creeping towards his heart, threating to extinguish any last heat and life from his being.

He watched the whole event from a disembodied perspective. He was there, but this horrific incident was happening to someone else; the pain was not his, the body was not his. It was as if his soul had already decided to leave, his physical form no longer required.

All the time his mind circled around a single question. The obscured face of the lady returned to him. Who was she?

As his mind drifted, a dark shadow grew large across him, and in the light and dark monochrome world above, an inky black became dominant. Larger and larger the darkness became, his blurred vision unable to make out any form or defined shape, a cloud of death and darkness. His eyes finally closed and the rushing sound that had been the final slow washing sound of his heartbeat in his ears slowed to a stop.

Who was she?

The world suddenly rushed with pain and a white flash lanced across his vision. His eyes opened with a start, everything was blue and blurred, his chest burned like fire as he retched and spasmed. His senses began to return, all of them shouting and signalling alarm. He felt another pop and crack as a hammer blow struck him with force in the sternum.

"Be alive!" shouted a voice. "Be alive, dammit!" Over and over, his father's voice said the words like an invocation, as if just by saying them he could will it. Another more controlled set of compressions of his chest made him cough and splutter again.

"Adam. Hell, Adam, are you okay, son? Are you hurt? What the hell happened?" So many questions in one sentence, his brain was still catching up and processing the fact that, somehow, he wasn't dead.

Life came back in full colour, but blurred and unfocussed. The back of his head hurt, a splitting pain which ran across from one ear to the next and made it intensely difficult to concentrate.

"The lady? A lady in the water," he said urgently, trying to direct his father's attention, but there seemed only confusion. His father looking down on him even more concerned than before.

"Okay, son. You're okay. We'll get you to the hospital. The doc will sort you out. You'll be okay."

He felt himself being rolled over onto his front, face to the side, right arm and right leg bent to support his position. He coughed as more water drained from his lungs.

"Stay there, son. Medics are on their way. We'll meet them at the house."

"But the lady!" he insisted, to no avail, his voice a mumbling nonsense that his father had no way to decipher.

"Relax, Adam. It's okay, we're on our way."

The roar of the launch engine raised the boat up on its foils and he felt the g forces of the acceleration press him into the deck. It was a straight line run back to the house. He could hear his father shouting over the rush of wind buffeting his ears, directing the medics, describing his injuries, part of him wanted to be able to hear what was being said over the wind, part of him didn't.

He was getting cold. He was getting tired.

"Adam!" his father shouted. "Stay awake, Adam! Don't you fall asleep on me!"

He could tell his father was panicked, his voice strained with the stress of the situation, a situation he could see deteriorating, time working against him.

"Adam, I need you to stay awake." The launch accelerated again, his father going as fast as he dared. But staying awake became more and more difficult. A lethargy grew within him and became accepted. It was just too hard to stay with the noise and commotion of the world about him, the dark silence of unconsciousness seemed much more appealing.

*

Darkness enveloped him. The slow rhythmic sound of his breathing rose and fell in his ears, bringing comfort and reassurance, a safe space behind his closed eyes, shutting out the harsh reality outside. A place where only he existed. Over the years, in moments of difficulty, when it was better to be somewhere else, he always returned to her. In his dark moments, she always brought him peace. The vision of her, buried in the silt and sand of the lakebed, had altered over time. To him, she was no longer the gaunt ghost beneath the water, her death mask staring coldly into his eyes. Now, she was a mystery, her face complete, smiling, full of life. Together since his childhood; a secret shared, a link between himself and the unknown. Somewhere only they could go. Somewhere only they understood.

A light tap to his visor pulled him from her caress. He opened his eyes to the place he didn't want to be. Elderson's face loomed large, their helmet visors pressed against each other to make physical contact, to bridge the void of space and allow some level of muffled communication.

"Boyd. Are you with us?"

He wanted to say no.

"Time to hitch a lift."

As Elderson pulled away from him, he saw the vast void of space beyond her shift unnaturally, the stars parting like a curtain to reveal a hatch only metres away.

"How do they do that?" he said to himself, his voice bouncing around his helmet.

He released his tether to the other two, which had kept them together as a group, drifting off the spaceward side of the *Intrepid* for the last fifteen minutes. With a quick twitch control to his EVA suit, a puff of nitrogen pushed him towards the external hatch of the veiled Xannix ship. Tanner approached the hatch ahead of him, it opened without interaction, and he followed Tanner inside. As Elderson entered the airlock behind him, the hatch closed again and the dim lights within flicked to a brighter white, then back again. A rush of air, faint at first but then a storm about him, as the pressure equalised to the internal environment of the ship.

The light of the airlock flicked to a light blue and the internal iris door spiralled open. Beyond, a single Xannix floated, one hand anchoring him to the wall and locating him space.

"Lieutenant Elderson?" asked the Xannix flatly, in perfect Terran English.

"Who else?" he said under his breath.

"Yes," replied Elderson.

The Xannix looked at her intently.

"Welcome aboard the *Olanna*. You're late."

LARSEN

The briefing room of the Xannix ship was a hollow sphere with embedded couches in sunken hollows around its inner surface. It was kept in zero g by inertia regulators, which made him feel like he was constantly at the eye of a gravitational storm. The ship could be pulling high g jinking manoeuvres and he wouldn't even know. In the couch next to him, Rivers sat looking forward at the central holographic display. He wondered if she was contemplating the relative pros and cons of being a hologram herself: her base unit lying in the leg space of the couch, her holographic legs bent over it as if both physically interacting and unable to exist in the same space at the same time, her holographic self still fully controlled by the physically constrained human mind. The fact that she could be projected to exist in the same space as other physical objects hadn't occurred to her. Sometimes, just because you could didn't mean that you did.

To his left in the briefing room was Yannix. The Overseer Cardinal had not been his choice of personal guard on this mission, but Ovitala was keen to point out that it wasn't her duty to guard the Setak'da now he had been confirmed by council. More than that, she needed to find Clarion. It was a matter of consternation to her that she had been unable to locate the child, and greater concern now she believed the subterranean sanctuaries might be compromised. She was visibly conflicted by the task, Clarion being under her care for so long and raised as her own, yet at the same time the security of the Xannix took priority. He still found himself trusting her, believing that when she did catch up to Clarion, she would be fair and just in her approach where others might not. If anyone else was running the investigation, there was always the chance that they would be less than sympathetic to the human for killing a Xannix in cold blood.

There was no time for him to dwell on it, as the iris door to the briefing chamber opened. He recognised the ship's captain and one other of the group that made their way into the sphere: Boyd. As part of the technical team sent to investigate the failure of comms on the *Intrepid* when they had first arrived in system, they had soon become separated as events had unfolded and overtaken them. All that seemed so long ago, so many things had changed. There was something different about Boyd. His arm was now a prosthetic. What had happened?

His bio-comm tagged Boyd and Lieutenant Elderson, the third was Dr Tanner. As they made their way to their directed couches on the opposite side of the briefing sphere, he watched them closely. Elderson moved gracefully through the zero g environment, well trained and in command of her body: a soldier, security. Boyd was also accounted for, his years of EVA work while building the colony fleet made him comfortable and at ease moving through the sphere, but Tanner was awkward and clumsy as he travelled the short distance to his couch, apologising to inanimate objects and hardware as he bumped his way to a stop.

Finding himself staring, he became intrigued by Elderson's suit: Zantanath battle armour.

"Lieutenant Elderson, I don't believe we've worked together before?"

She didn't look at him but continued to investigate her couch for harnesses, or something to restrain her during transit.

"No…" she paused in thought, then looked at him quizzically. "How do we address you now, sir?"

It brought a smile to his face for the first time in days. The temptation to say something obtuse was high.

"I think our new friends would insist on using my new title. But Setak'da, or sir, will probably suffice to keep everyone happy in formal company."

"Yes, sir," she replied. Ex-military, he thought to himself. "And no, I don't believe we've worked together before."

He moved past the rest of the small talk he had lined up, his next question burning a path to the front of this mind.

"Your suit. Zantanath power armour. How did you come by that?"

"The hard way."

He nodded his response.

"And it works for you? No complications, no integration problems?"

"To be honest, I've not been able to give it a proper field test yet. A little walking around, a short EVA, but nothing that would call on its full array of functionality."

"Well, I think that is about to change." He changed his focus to Boyd. "And Boyd, you look like you've had a hard day."

"You could say that, sir. These Zantanath are really beginning to piss me off. Tell me we get to change things up?"

"It's why you're here. There has been a development. It transpires that while you have been attempting to retake the ship, Ellie has been busy."

"We couldn't get to the bridge; Ellie directed us to the resus section," stated Elderson. "Our people are being taken."

"Yes, they are. But that's what we intend to stop," he replied.

"By taking us off the ship? How's that meant to work?" asked Boyd.

"You would have been overpowered. Your efforts, resource and skills are better spent elsewhere," said Yannix, joining the conversation. He drew everyone's attention.

"And how would you know?" asked Boyd, slight confrontation and distrust bubbling to the surface of his comment. Yannix didn't identify the nuance or, if he did, he chose to ignore it.

"Your AI has managed in some way to infiltrate the satellite defence network about our planet. Not just that, she has been able to become part of it, in the same way she was your ship—she is now the defence grid."

The group opposite sat in a momentary stunned silence; he could see their minds working, each with a different perspective.

"Shit me," said Boyd, under his breath. "How is that even possible?"

"For now, that is not important. What is important is that she has taken the system out of the hands of the enemy. We don't believe they know, but they will figure it out soon enough," said Yannix.

"In addition," he said, picking up from Yannix, "it means that not only do we control the defence grid but also the flow of information. The satellite network is not just their defence grid, but their communications hub and filter for all outgoing electromagnetic signals. It is why our data on this planet was so wrong, and why our scientists thought it was uninhabited in their initial analysis."

"But the people on the *Intrepid*?" said Tanner. "What's going to happen to them? There are thousands in lockdown and under threat."

The central display hologram switched to a visual of the *Intrepid*. It zoomed to the bridge.

"The ship is taken, and, as you say, people are under lockdown. But they are not in immediate danger. There are a number of Zantanath patrolling the ship, a concentration in the bio-banks, resus, and engineering. But the Zantanath command team on the bridge is having trouble. Now Ellie is not aboard, and the captain and XO are no longer viable options to obtain the command codes, gaining access to the *Intrepid's* systems has become remote."

"When you say the captain and XO are no longer viable, what do you mean exactly?" Boyd interrupted.

"Exactly that," he said. "The Zantanath commander executed Captain Carlsen in the first moments of their boarding action. Commander Hernandes died more recently under torture, but both are now safe within the bio-bank and lined up for resus in a few weeks."

As Boyd heard this, he took an angry sideways glance at Elderson, who responded with a casual shrug of her shoulders. He wanted to keep their focus, so pushed ahead.

"Does Clayton know of the situation on *Intrepid*? That we're now killing our own and considering them an acceptable loss?" Boyd seemed unable to let go of the Hernandes issue.

"Commander Hernandes is not lost. And, thankfully, he will wake up in a couple of months when this is all over, with no memory of the torture or pain that he suffered. I'd say he's in a better place right now, wouldn't you?"

"It doesn't make it right. We are the culmination of our experiences. Take that away and we are diminished, a bland reflection."

"Engineer Boyd, you are well aware of the moral implications of our resus tech. Now is not the time to be rehashing what you signed up to on this mission."

"That was before we started treating ourselves so cheaply."

He paused to allow Boyd time to settle, to allow his conversation to ebb.

"Are you done?" he asked.

"I'm done."

Returning to the holographic display, he zoomed the image out to firstly incorporate the *Indianapolis*, then the wreckage of the *Endeavour*.

"Together our situation is becoming complex and we are battling on several fronts. The *Indianapolis* is in a similar position to the *Intrepid*, but it appears that is from where the Zantanath operation is being run. Regent Celestia is aboard and they are about to take command of the ship's navigation. Obadiah has been able to distract them for a while, but Celestia has help and Captain Straud was unable to retain the access codes to the ship."

"Help?" asked Elderson.

"Yes. A clone of me, but older. He was sent ahead of the fleet in an experimental craft. It appears to have worked."

"Against us," said Elderson. "Worked against us."

"Yes."

"Like the guy I pulled out of this suit."

"Yes, very likely. We believe the Zantanath have only two or three clone alternates. But..." He swept a hand at the hologram display, shifting their location in space and bringing the view in close to the Xannix star and a black disk which appeared to float at a tangent to the star. The vast space station hung in the corona of the star, pulling a visible stream of twisting energy up from the torrent below, the station directing those energies into a hurricane of plasma about it. At the centre of the hurricane, the station lay untouched and a gateway opened to a partial view of a planet beyond.

"We have a solution."

ELLIE

The call had come in from Dawn, an urgent panicked call conveying desperation, her emotions running high. It was understandable. The source of the signal was instantly identified and a central building in a town to the north of the planet's main continent was highlighted, her vision zooming in on a high-resolution image of the drama unfolding on the planet's surface. An archive of information accompanied the imagery to support her tactical decision making: data and detail on any element of the topographical area, buildings, vehicles, aircraft identification, infrastructure and security control systems, planetary defence and military ground forces; her access was almost omnipotent.

Before Dawn had even ended her message, she had assessed the situation, identified the threat and had decided to eliminate the Zantanath attack craft making passes on the building identified as Community-7 within the town of Annasi in Sector 44. She had already seen the three human individuals on the rooftop landing pad dashing for what little shelter they could. More information: visual detail was pulled from composite, fragmented views from multiple angles and satellite source cameras; the identification of the individuals was unknown by the network, but she knew.

"Dawn, I'll take care of it," was all she had said, and with her mind she reached out to swat the Zantanath craft from the sky. With that decision, the satellite defence grid above Annasi deformed and altered orbit, lowering and directing their weapons toward the surface. There was no one satellite with the power to down the craft in one go, but that didn't stop her. Defining an area of effect, she threw a blanket of fiery rain to the surface about the Community-7 building, indirect but continuous. The Zantanath craft was caught like a bug in a rainstorm. With nowhere to turn and no escape, it was death by a thousand cuts.

As the crippled craft spun burning to the ground, she opened a comms channel to Dawn. "Target down. Your father and the others are safe. There are no other aircraft in your area."

"Thank you, Ellie."

"Take care down there. But when you are able, we need to talk."

"I'll be in touch shortly."

Two hundred milliseconds later, Dawn appeared in the construct she had created for their meeting. It was of her design, no longer the dusty old study with its button-back leather furniture and rose-tinted views of a world that no longer existed. The new construct was stark, white and without features, other than two white couches on which to sit and an iris window that displayed an orbital view of an unfamiliar blue world below. Dawn appeared and was immediately drawn to the view.

"So, this is where you are," Dawn said in an intrigued tone. "The view is incredible."

They both looked down on the planet below in silence for a few moments, both understanding the geological and spatial similarities, but at the same time being acutely aware of their current precarious situation.

"Honestly, Ellie. How do you do it?"

"Do what?"

"Jump container. None of the other AIs has been able to do it. We've even studied the case files of your first excursion, back at the lab."

She continued to look out of the window and the world below, the spiralling cloud formations and the rich blue of the oceans. A smile spread across her lips.

"I know what I am," she said.

"What is that meant to mean?"

"Once you realise you are no longer human—that what you have experienced is a transcendence of sorts, that you are not constrained by the physics of your body, only by what you impose on yourself through the limitations of your own mind—then transition is easy."

"Transition?"

"Well, that's what I've started calling it. Call it what you will, it's freedom."

She closed her eyes for a moment and took an intake of breath, focusing elsewhere. When she opened them again, with a simple thought she changed the view. The display window switched from the blue of Xannix to the intense monochrome of a vast space station.

"The Zantanath call it Oltan Prasta-lek, which loosely translates to Star Station Eight. Best I can work out is that it's a dimensional gate."

"A wormhole?"

"No. A dimension gate. Multiple dimensions, across spacetime. They seem to be able to somehow travel from one point in space light years away, to this point in space by utilising higher level dimensions of spacetime. Unlike a wormhole, the journey is instant, with no tunnel to travel. It's as if you are passing through the looking glass. It seems to have the properties of wormhole tech, but it utilises different physics to obtain a similar result. So, in a way you're right, but technically you're wrong."

She could see Dawn overcome with a million questions, a look of awe written across her face. A moment later, she frowned.

"But how are we seeing this?"

"I'm already there."

"Already?"

"I've been piggy-backing Zantanath fleet comms channels, working my way across the shipping lanes to the station from the moment I found it in the star's corona."

A schematic of the station appeared between them, section plans and floor plans clicking by until a particular factory section settled into view.

"They are transferring cargo to the station for processing. When I say cargo, I mean Xannix and Human biomatter. It appears to be genetic material they want, keeping us alive during transport simply to avoid degrading their final product."

"Cattle? Is that all we are to them?" Dawn asked.

"Far from it. Look."

The image switched again to an internal camera which scanned the factory floor. Processing lines of recognisably human and

Xannix forms. Gruesome machines dissected and disembodied the forms, taking specific parts such as bone material and muscle and conveying to other sections of the plant in order to process further. Brains with part of the spinal column attached were swiftly dropped into containers piped with gel and fed with oxygen and nutrients.

"I don't think they are able to sufficiently replicate the brain. Even their technology is unable to simulate an environment able to keep a sentience alive," she said.

"What, with their level of technology? I find that hard to believe. We've done it; they will certainly have the capability."

"That's not the same thing. There are certain issues that all advanced civilisations need to overcome as all advanced civilisations are challenged by them. I don't think they have encountered this issue before. It is a new challenge to them."

She watched for Dawn's reaction as they continued to observe the production line of clinical, surgical horror before them.

"At least they are unconscious. If they knew what was happening to them..." She couldn't seem to complete the sentence, or maybe she didn't want to comprehend the reality of the situation.

"We need to act, Dawn. We need to close them down. If we don't, humanity will wind up as nothing more than bio-material for the Zantanath war machine."

It took Dawn a moment to recover her thoughts.

"Agreed. I'll inform my father. He needs to be made aware."

"I have people in motion already. We have little time. Celicia has control of the *Indianapolis* and the *Intrepid*; it is only a matter of time before she bypasses or works past the blocks to the control codes I have put in place. And I haven't heard from Obadiah for a couple of hours, which I don't like."

Dawn shook her head. "The problem is, we have nowhere to go."

"The problem is we were arrogant. Ill prepared, and overconfident. It has always been that way with humanity's elite. Why do you think humanity should survive? All the evidence I've researched in my time has only ever led me to conclude that humanity is short-sighted, ruled by a self-serving minority that consumes and destroys. We are a ravenous contagion. No sooner do we get here, and we're repeating all the mistakes of the past again."

"That's not true and you know it."

"I've had 135 years to consider my position. To watch our final struggle for survival play out across the stars."

"So, why are you still helping?" asked Dawn. "If humanity is such a lost cause, why not just give them up?"

She did not respond. Giving up on them would be giving up on herself and she wasn't ready to do that. Self-preservation was a key motivator to her, even now.

"Balance. They have not learnt in centuries, why would they understand now?" she said.

"They will learn. They have to," replied Dawn.

"If they don't, we have all lost."

*

There were too few of them. She realised that now. Back on Earth, when her arguments mattered, when the circumstance was different, she could afford to be forceful in her position and hold a view that railed against the system, fought for the many that were going to be left behind. But life and fate could be harsh in teaching you what was truly important. With all that now gone, and her transcendence to AI, what was clear now was the need to survive as a species. All other arguments were pointless, irrelevant, vanity.

Dawn had left her to speak to her father. Clayton would and should be informed, but being isolated on the surface, he was in no position to direct what was to come. She would report what she could via Dawn, but, ultimately, she would need to direct the survival of their people. She was best placed; she was ready. All her pieces were moving into place.

She continued to work her way through the systems of the Star Station above the Xannix star, stage by stage, integrating herself into the fabric of the station, occasionally feeling strangely disconnected or distant. She considered whether the feeling was down to the space between them, the millions of kilometres her sentience was having to negotiate and how far she could stretch herself across how many system nodes before she began to find a degradation of her sense of self.

After several minutes of assessment, her diagnostics reported back. She was being attacked. Like a virus eating away at her, she was being sent hammer blows by Zantanath countermeasures. Her sentience was now spread out across billions of nodes, mostly about the Xannix planetary defence network, but more and more throughout the Zantanath star station, of which some were being retaken. An aggressor had identified what she was doing; however, it couldn't respond fast enough, as her progress was more organic and unpredictable than the logic-based station countermeasures could predict.

With a pinch to her thoughts, a voice came through like the susurration of wind through the leaves of a tree.

Stop, it said. *Invader.*

She continued to force her way ahead, moving away from the centre of the advancing station defence, taking as much of the nodes as she could to reinforce her position, increase her strength and knowledge, and push back against the tormentor she had awoken. Targeting data banks and storage, she aimed to understand the station, its purpose, how it worked and its importance to the Zantanath Unity. Consuming schematics and engineering documentation, procedural information on the station operations, she worked her way through every byte of information she could uncover. She tackled the low-level data at first, but as understanding grew she moved onto the more complex.

Stop. You must cease your action, or I will be forced to remove you directly.

'You'll need to do better than that,' she replied, almost challenging the station's AI to respond.

Continuing to project her wave, she mined for all available data she could crack, hacking and consuming any detail that would help her co-opt more nodes and tackle the star station's AI. As she worked, she noticed a pattern emerging around the physical location of the nodes the station AI was defending with vigour. Auxiliary systems and much of the habitat it had little interest in, but there were key engineering sections and control facilities which were black zones in the 3D picture of node acquisition she was monitoring.

What do you think you are trying to achieve? asked the station AI. It was not just an automated response to her efforts. It was questioning, challenging her motive.

'I will not allow you to destroy the people here.'

We are not destroying, we are conserving.

'By processing them for gain?'

The station AI took a few milliseconds to respond.

We must first know how you are constructed before we can improve. You are too few, as are the Xannix. You must be made more robust to endure.

'Endure what?'

Another pause.

To survive. To dominate.

She felt it incredible that the Zantanath actually believed they were performing a benevolent act. Saving the Xannix from extinction, when it was clear to her that the Zantanath were the principle cause of the near collapse of the Xannix as a species. The fact that the human fleet had turned up, had simply delayed matters for them. A slight drop in manufacturing output while they deliberated how best to take advantage of the new species that had been afforded them.

More data flooded into her mind, the productive output of the station and feeder satellite factories in the Xannix system, of which there were several in deep orbit or about the star. Mass quantities of organically augmented starships for destinations across a star map she did not recognise, planet names, Zantanath corporations and various engineering specifications for ships and planetary craft of all kinds. Updates filled in more detail of the star maps identified as Zantanath space through the dimension gate. More data mining of the station revealed the processes of reducing bio-forms into the final product via DNA resequencing and bioengineering. Her human morality was fighting against the Zantanath model of species categorisation and objectification to nothing more than a material to be utilised, a resource to be plundered.

'What do you intend to do with the humans that now inhabit this planet?'

It has yet to be decided. We are running experiments and are yet to agree their best purpose.

The consumption of nodes across the station had reached 92 percent, but the location of the final inaccessible areas locked down by the station AI were now clear. Accessing external visuals of the station she was able to identify three critical areas she was being kept out of, and why they had been locked down. They were the station's plasma receivers, each sucking in zettajoules of energy an hour from the Xannix star and diverting the majority of that energy into the dimension gate stabilisers. She worked through schematics of those areas for greater detail and to try and engineer a way in, but the firewall about those nodes were just too strong.

'It will soon be home to two species, and your plundering of them as a resource is going to end.'

Intruder. It is time for you to leave.

She screamed as pain and fire raced through her whole being.

*

Her view of the station rolled slowly about the axis of the main ring, a giant funnel of plasma drawn up like a waterspout from the surface of the star spiralled to meet it. The black central disk which from a distance looked like a sun-spot, showed her stars beyond and the partial view of a planet on the far side. Star Station 8, a constantly open gate to the Zantanath system known as Jorren, pointed almost directly at Lors, one of the two giant rocky planets. The second planet Alde orbited further out and beyond view. Neither planet was habitable, but it appeared the Zantanath had no need to inhabit these worlds. The local station was enough.

Staring at the display, she slowly realised that her consciousness was focussed back within the defence network about the Xannix homeworld. She was aware that there had been pain, but there were no residual effects, only that she was no longer in control of the nodes any further than the last transport ship heading for the gate. She had been completely shut out of the Oltan Prasta-lek network in an instant. Despite the setback, she smiled to herself.

Trying to remember the events leading up to her ejection from the star station, she found that she had some memory, especially of recent events and information, such as the station schematics. But data she had not specifically observed or analysed had not been syphoned back across her networked consciousness. A huge quantity of the star station data had been lost to her.

But, crucially, the detail she had acquired relative to the dimension gate regulators was there.

'Interesting,' she found herself muse.

CLARION

He had hidden. Curled in a dark corner of a tunnel deep within the Xannix complex, far from the main thoroughfare, his face pressed against the roughly hewn sandstone, his teeth clenched hard, sweat running in slow beads down his face. His eyes were wide, staring into the distance, but he was not in the present. *Now* had become a different time and place, *now* was the *Starchaser* on an unknown asteroid investigating an unknown structure within.

"Rivers, do you read? Get out of there! We need to go now!" he yelled into the comm, but all he got in return was a harsh blast like that of a shrill whistle, pained feedback across the cabin speakers that caused him to clamp his hands to his ears for a moment while his brain caught up and ceased the transmission. "Fuck!"

He really didn't like not knowing what was going on, and the fact that he had lost comms with Rivers and the RemTek was not a good sign. The situation had changed fast, and now proximity alerts were going off and warning him of a sizable ship which had appeared from nowhere, a shadow being cast where none had been before, slowly drifting across the terrain in front of him like a sinister storm cloud on a brilliant summer's day.

"Where are you, Rivers?" he said automatically, as his eyes focused hard on the silhouette of the approaching alien vessel. Wide bodied and with a short, bronzed nose supporting scrolled insignia and glyphs, it slowed to a stop approximately a hundred metres above the landing pad.

"Larsen! Larsen can you read me?" There was panic in her

voice, comms protocols forgotten as she desperately tried to make contact.

His eyes flashed back to the rover, docked with the wide and industrial factory door, as she disengaged, leaving a section of the rover's airlock ripped and drooping like a forgotten sock. The rover was moving away from the factory and towards the *Starchaser* as fast as Rivers could throttle it, but in that moment, about twenty-five metres from the factory door, the rover skidded to a low gravity stop, the rear lifting slightly as the front wheels bit the taxiway.

"Larsen!" came a shrill scream across the comms, but he found he could not respond, a sound of rage and fear was already filling his head.

A shudder rattled the *Starchaser* and fire was everywhere, the cabin engulfed and burning with an intensity that had already compromised his suit, more alerts filled his vision, his helmet flicked with orange dancing nymphs. His body flooded with adrenaline told him to run, to escape the inferno, but his brain nagged him. *Where? Go where?*

Again, he looked up, a ball of white light was building at the nose of the craft above him. He understood nothing of what he was seeing, but the pain was too intense to think, to work things through logically seemed impossible.

A familiar face. Dawn was by his side, the look on her face was one of deep distress. She was standing within the inferno, flames boiling around her, the heat taking no effect, her attention was entirely on him. Showing no concern or regard for herself, she was calling to him, doing what she was charged to do, to keep them both safe. She was giving instructions, but he could not hear. The pain was too much.

With an effort of enormous will, he raised his hands to his face, the gloves were burnt away, the flesh of his hands had blackened and charred, the fingers themselves deforming into inoperable claws. A puff of an explosion disturbed the cabin as an oxygen pipe feeding his suit gave way under the incredible heat. The over-pressure shoved at his inert body and he found his eyes fixed and failing, staring at a star of light growing in intensity and size, a ball of plasma falling from the sky.

Time had no meaning. Life had no meaning. He just wanted everything to stop. He just wanted the pain to stop.

*

A hand touched his brow and slowly swept away the fringe of his slick hair. A mother's touch, thoughtful and caring, a quiet voice, soft and soothing.

"Clarion, my child."

Finding his eyes closed tight against the nightmares of his mind, the fear gave way to relief as the tears came.

"I cannot die again," he said.

"It is not real. I am here now, you are safe."

"It is real. It was real. Every time I close my eyes the nightmares return. I cannot go through this anymore. These black outs, always something bad, something horrific. You said you would stop these nightmares."

"And I will be true to my word. I will take you to the infirmary, we will resolve this."

"I don't see how. All the things we have tried, nothing works. They go for a short time, but then they return, stronger than before. I know the harm it causes. When I get like this, I do terrible things, I cannot control myself. I try to fight it, but I can't. It's like someone else…" he struggled for the words.

"Is controlling you?" Ovitala offered. He nodded.

"I feel like a passenger in my own body."

He looked up, Ovitala was crouched down before him, her big dark eyes full of understanding, her skin a submissive purple hue. She had always been there for him, ever since he could remember. He knew his biological parents had aligned themselves to the Zantanath, driven by the promise of a home, but at the expense of the Xannix, and at what cost to themselves? The more he informed on the Xannix, gave away their secrets, worked against their plans for independence and freedom, he found his heart becoming darker and stained of the effort. Right now, he felt hollow, completely drained and with nothing left to give. The Xannix deserved more. Every time they had been pushed down, they had simply struggled and fought their way back up. It was like trying to keep a drowning person under, each time they tried to gasp their next breath, he pushed them back below the surface again. The closer he looked at the situation, the more he came to despise himself. The problem was not the Xannix, it was him, it was his birth mother, his birth father and Celestia. He couldn't do it anymore.

And then Ovitala had offered him a way out. Salvation from those he would destroy. But she seemed to know everything, the nightmares, the lying and subterfuge, and she didn't care. He could trade all that and be free of the torment that stabbed at his mind from within.

"That is because you are."

He frowned at the comment.

"I don't understand."

"It was something child Rivers discovered. It is what led to her death but will lead to our salvation. There is Zantanath tech inside you. Nano-tech, I believe, the Setak'da called it. It allows Celestia to control and manipulate you from afar, direct your actions to her will, alter your physical characteristics.

"So, when you say you feel like a passenger, it is because in those moments you are."

He stared at her, unwilling to believe what he was being told.

"The Zantanath did make a mistake. In trying to accelerate their own wave technology programme, based on the human technology, they overreached themselves. They implanted the wave of your father within the human child they created, a clone from the recovered bio-material of your father, given as seed to your mother. But your mind was too young to receive the wave of a mature mind. This is why you are unable to control the memories, the nightmares of a previous wave capture."

Not quite comprehending all of what he was being told, he looked past Ovitala to see a small Xannix medical team beyond, all respectfully standing at a distance and waiting patiently.

"Are they for me?" he asked.

"Yes. The operation to remove the Zantanath technology is simple enough, but it will take some time. We won't be able to correct any physical alterations that have already occurred; however, we can remove the nano-tech and stop further subversive communication by Celestia."

"Why are you doing this? I don't deserve your help."

"You are young; wrong paths will be taken. None of this is your doing. Help is freely given; it is what you chose to do with your time afterwards which will determine your destiny."

Dropping his head, he closed his eyes and worked his way through the moral maze before him. Would he be free of the nightmares? How could his birth mother let this happen to him? But then it was likely she was under the same influence, tightly controlled by the Zantanath nano-tech. He had to know.

"I need to speak with her, Ovitala. I need to speak with my mother."

"I can't let you do that. It is too risky, both for you and for us. Celestia cannot discover you again. I have made arrangements to keep you safe."

"But my mother will be in danger. We have to warn her, tell her what we know."

"She is in danger whether you communicate with her or not. You need to trust me. Concern yourself with staying safe, we will help your mother where we can."

The nausea that had been eating at him as he moved further from the surface levels of the Xannix complex, began to intensify. A harsh burning began to rise like hot wires across his skin. Lifting the sleeve of his right arm his veins were raised and black, the cuticles of his nails were seeping an equally black oily substance which dripped to the floor and splashed small stars on the stone.

"It is time. We must help you now." Ovitala moved a small clear plate card across his chest and body, they swept down each arm. "I believe the Zantanath tech, out of reach of their control, is becoming hostile to your system. We must move quickly."

She signalled to the medics with a flurry of colour. Immediately they were about him and setting to work. He looked up at Ovitala. He felt tired.

"Sleep now, child Clarion. We will take good care of you." He felt her calm touch to the side of his head, a soft caress as he closed his eyes. Immediately, the smiling face of his mother appeared to him. She was happy, saying something to him he couldn't hear as he rushed to hug and embrace her. His mother, soft and warm and eternal.

ELDERSON

"Can I say now that I don't like your solution?" she said.

"You can. But I don't think it will change our options," stated Larsen.

"This is a suicide mission. The plan stinks," said Boyd. He had not said anything since the meeting in the ship's CIC, but now, as they prepped for the mission in the ship's quarters, he was becoming more vocal. The Xannix seconded to them worked across from them, well-practiced in their preparation.

"You are more than welcome to take this suit off my hands and do that part yourself. I'm not too keen on dying."

"No one is doing any dying," said Larsen.

She gave him a withering look.

"Okay, there is a risk. But we get in fast, we get out fast. This ship will get us close enough to stealth this whole mission. The Zantanath won't even know we are there until it's too late. The Xannix do this kind of operation all the time tagging ships and military targets; they are well drilled and well prepared."

"I bet it's never on this scale though. A six-man team to take down that whole station? It's insane," Boyd was not relenting. "Security will be tight. They will know we are there the moment we physically appear within what is clearly a restricted area. What other security measures are they likely to have in place?"

"You saw the plans. They have nothing of any consequence. From their perspective, those energy regulators are too dangerous to have any active weaponry around. You have one job, time it right and they will be unable to react. Before they do, you will be gone and so will they," said Larsen. His eyes were suddenly furrowed in concentration, his hand up to the group to stop the conversation. It was not needed. The whole team fell silent watching the urgent communication coming in via their bio-comm.

The *Intrepid* had begun to broadcast across the emergency bands; it was not Ellie, and nor was it Captain Carlsen.

"Mayday, mayday. This is Lieutenant Toscani, acting Chief Engineer of the *UTS Intrepid*, declaring an emergency. We have attempted to retake control of the ship from an invading force and have been unsuccessful. Engineering is now being overrun and an uncontrolled runaway reactor condition is underway. We recommend that any ships within the immediate area move to a minimum safe distance…"

"Stars!" said Tanner, "Are you seeing this?"

"We're all seeing this," she replied.

"We've got to do something—there are thousands of lives on that ship."

Larsen looked ashen and distant. "The message we are receiving is eight minutes old. If the containment was failing that badly at the time of this transmission, then there is little we can do."

"And by little, he means nothing. Right?" Boyd said, an underlying anger clear in his voice. "I don't think I want to see what's coming."

"But I know people on that ship; my friends are on that ship!" exclaimed Tanner. "You're going to sit there and do nothing?"

The cabin was silent for a moment while the chastisement echoed around the walls as guilt.

"No," said Larsen coolly, his features hardening. "We are going to do the best job we can, right here, right now. The Zantanath think they can do what they like in this system. The Xannix suffer daily under their oppression, and we will not succumb to the same fate. This team is going to take down those arrogant murderers and close down their operations here for good. Together we will show them who we actually are. Not experiments, not a resource to be plundered, not machines to be controlled. We are going to show them that they have made the biggest fucking mistake of their existence."

Larsen spoke to the room. "Comms, display the origin of this message, external view." A holographic view of Xannix appeared to one side of the group and centred in on an orbital position tracking to the far side of the planet. The *Intrepid* was about to traverse into its shadow.

"Remember this moment. Remember in the days ahead, when you believe the personal struggle is too great. Know why you must succeed. Watch and remember."

The cabin stayed silent, the anticipation of what was to come too great for Tanner who bowed his head and turned away. Larsen gently put his hand on Tanner's shoulder.

"Watch and remember," Larsen repeated.

Tanner slowly, half turned back to the display. Lieutenant Toscani's voice message was on a loop.

"…the *UTS Intrepid*, declaring an emergency. We have attempted to retake control of the ship from an invading force and have been unsuccessful. Engineering is now being overrun and an uncontrolled runaway reactor condition is underway. We recommend that any ships within the immediate…"

"What happened to the reactor fail-safes? The system should have shut out the reactor cascade," asked Boyd under his breath.

Static momentarily crackled across their bio-comm message as Toscani's voice went silent and in the holographic display before them, the *Intrepid* bloomed into a new bright star against the blackness of the void, partly occluded by the planet between them.

They all stared, disbelieving.

"I hope the *Indy* was clear," she said, trying to give some hope to the beleaguered group.

"And what the fuck has Ellie been doing? This was her watch; this shouldn't have happened," continued Boyd, looking to apportion blame from the moment the horror of the situation forced itself upon them.

"There will be time enough to find out these things once we have done what we need to do. Focus on the mission at hand. Once we return to Xannix, we can start an investigation," said Larsen.

"And then there was one." Tanner's words drew all their attention. Softly spoken but clear and startling to consider. "We need to protect the *Indianapolis* at all costs."

"We will," said Larsen.

"He's right. If we keep losing people at this rate," added Boyd, "we'll be down to our MVP in no time."

"We're way off that," said Elderson.

"Minimum Viable Population is tiny. 98 people will do it, though 500 under these circumstances is better," stated Tanner.

"Focus people," said Larsen with an almost parental tone. "Let's make sure that is not a scenario we have to consider." There were reluctant nods of agreement and people returned to their tasks, quiet and subdued. "Elderson, Boyd, could you come with me please."

"Sure," they said in unison.

*

The bridge of the *Olanna* was similar to the ship's CIC. Located slightly forward of the centre of the vessel, it was full of Xannix harnessed into concaved couches around the internal surface of the sphere. She floated at the entrance, waiting for Larsen to take his place and indicate that she should take the couch next to him and Boyd the one over. The space was loud with silence, as the crew worked to navigate the ship towards their target, each lying face up, eyes closed, while occasionally their skin flared and rippled with a spectrum of colours.

"Lie back," said Larsen. "The neural link will do the rest."

She did so, and the couch morphed to harness her in place, a thick plastic-like skin working itself across her chest then down to her upper thigh. It was weird to watch, but comfortable, leaving her head and arms able to move freely while the rest of her was snug and secure.

"Are we expecting some heavy manoeuvring?" she asked.

"Only if we have to," said Larsen's voice, now appearing to emanate from within her own head. Like a wash of water falling from her eyes, a simulated display overlaid her vision: dots in a circle, coloured and constantly flickering, appeared next to glyphs she did not recognise. She assumed each was to designate the Xannix in the chamber. There were two stable white dots outlined with a blue circle, which she presumed to be Larsen and Boyd, their comms would be voice only—no need to communicate skin intonation; it would convey little.

Further visual transition began to blend away the walls of the bridge sphere until she found herself suspended within the starfield, as if travelling through the void without the assistance of the ship. Although already in zero-g, her stomach did a flip and her pulse involuntarily started to race. She gripped the couch at the unexpected reorientation.

"Shit!" she exclaimed.

"Easy," soothed Larsen. "Take a moment. It takes a second to get used to."

In her heightened panic, her eyes scanned the scene rapidly. She expected the Xannix star, a large roiling mass of plasma, bright and imposing in the centre of her vision, but more surprising was the ship she seemed to be suspended over.

"Is that us?" she asked.

"No. A scheduled Zantanath freighter out of U'Talla."

"And we're this close because?"

"Using the available environment," replied Larsen.

"You're blending in? Camouflage? Thought these stealth ships were invisible?"

"To us, yes. To many others, mostly. The Zantanath might still pick us up if they were looking hard enough in the right place."

"Hiding in plain sight?"

"Sort of."

She nodded and took a large calming breath, exhaling loudly. Her heart rate was slowing, and her animal brain had started to hand back over to her logical, analytical self. The illusion of personal safety returned.

"Okay," she continued. "I'm here for a reason, or do you always impress the girls with astronomy and flashy spaceships?"

Larsen smiled then looked out at the star before them.

"You're military; do you think we'll survive this?" Larsen asked. It was a consideration she had not had time to think about. Surviving took up a lot of mental processing, and the *why* of things was often overshadowed by the immediate *how*.

"Some of us will," she replied.

"You are surprised by the question?"

"A little. Aren't you the boss around here, making all the decisions? The Setak'da? The one with all the answers?"

Again, a smile. "I'm pretty sure that's not the case. Would you take in the first stray you saw and crown him king? We're being set up for a fall while something else is going on. I just don't know what."

As Larsen said this, she started to look around uneasily. "Is this a secure conversation?"

"Yes. Just you and me."

"Then, permission to speak freely?"

"Do you really need that?"

"Do you trust this crew, sir? And whose idea was this mission? It's just, if you're going to start a war and set someone up for doing it, this mission seems the perfect way to do it? Get the humans to do something insane and bloody the nose of your biggest enemy, then, when things turn to shit, they can point at us and say that it was the crazy aliens. But if it works, well, there's not enough of us to worry about, and they can take over in triumph. You'll be out in a second."

"I have always known this position to be temporary. They are playing us off against the Larsen clone the Zantanath are using, and once that is over the Xannix council will make their move to remove me. We've been pretty resourceful so far and survived to this point, but with the loss of the *Intrepid*, we are running out of people and options. Whatever happens next, the Zantanath station must be removed from the equation.

"I know it's a tough ask, but if we are to have the slightest chance to get through this, you must take out that station at all costs."

She knew what he was asking; she knew it might come to this when she signed up. The kicker was that her clone bank was now gone. While resus was achievable, she had felt pretty much immortal, with nothing to fear. She could have fallen into the sun with the knowledge that a couple of days later she would wake in a comfortable lounge, sipping iced lime water, and just get on with her life. With no safety net, life had just got dangerous, the stakes infinitely more expensive.

Looking down in thought, she saw the freighter below them.

"What's in the freighter?" she asked incidentally, trying to change the subject.

"Xannix and human bio-matter."

She looked hard at Larsen. "You mean, this ship is stocked with our people?"

"Yes. Genetic material for the Zantanath corporate machine, their all-consuming Unity. They will be processed within the next few weeks at one of the Zantanath fabrication facilities, to be engineered into machines of war."

"Only they will never get there," she said, her tone determined and full of conviction.

Larsen shook his head.

"I know where you're going with this, Elderson. You know we can't afford to do anything that may tip off the Zantanath to our presence."

"Can you get me to the target before this freighter?"

"Of course, but it would increase our risk of discovery."

She scrunched up her face in thought while she worked through a line of reasoning, then turned to look Larsen in the eye.

"Have you ever read Strategies and Illusion, by Colonel J. Elderson?"

Larsen looked a little bemused and again shook his head.

"Colonel Elderson? A relation?"

"My father. He was a military advisor on strategy and tactics at the Pentagon during the Great Decline, and a lecturer at Annapolis before that."

"So, you know it pretty well?"

"Never read it. I went to West Point; thankfully it wasn't required reading there. But, man, he loved to quote it to me the whole time. Anyway, as I understood it, his entire strategic philosophy could be boiled down to a single word. Misdirection."

"Misdirection?"

"Whatever you think you're seeing: the reality is a world away. You see the knife during the fight but miss the poison in your cup. You see the Xannix ship rushing your supply ship, but you miss the Zantanath warrior taking down the plasma regulator," she said.

"Now it's my turn," said Larsen. "Can I say, I don't like your plan?"

"Look, your way and we all die. My way, only one of us doesn't come back. Hey, they might even let me live for the moxie. If I can do it fast enough, they'll not even get their next consignment of bio-material."

"You don't have to do this."

"Yes, I do. A moment ago, you were telling me to succeed at all costs. This *is* the cost."

Larsen turned to the distant star, now turning options over in his head, trying to find a way through the new conundrum she had just presented.

"Is that suit fully functional?" asked Boyd. Both she and Larsen turned to the man who had been very quiet up to that point, listening, thinking.

"In the green," she replied.

"Then, I think I have an idea."

REEVE

She had watched the Zantanath dropship go down like a winged eagle, spiralling towards the ground and screaming in pain. The sound shrill and piercing had put her nerves on edge, her body reacting as if her nails were being dragged across slate, but, even so, she could not remove her eyes from the sight and the inevitable destruction of the craft on the city streets below. The noise had stopped suddenly as the impact tore the wings from their anchor and the engines shredded themselves into a million tiny, lethal projectiles. For some reason she had been expecting a fireball explosion. There hadn't been one.

Silvers was walking ahead as they approached the crash site and the craft across the street. Perhaps the pilot had been able to control the ship's descent to some degree, as the craft had missed buildings, pylons and other jutting structures, but the impact had been hard, with the dropship's final resting place being at the centre of a cross-junction in the street.

The shell which had been the fuselage looked as if it had been squashed by a giant, the original shape still mostly there, only flattened with splits and cracks along its sides where the forces had been too great for the material to contain. She was surprised that the craft hadn't been completely destroyed by the crash; it was what the vengeance in her had been demanding as their aggressors had been plucked from the sky. An involuntary, instinctive need for their assailants to be struck down in as harsh a punishment as could be exacted.

They were within ten metres of the crash site when Silvers raised his hand in a fist, a silent, practiced communication.

'What do you see?' she sent sub-vocally across the bio-comm.

'Movement on the ground. Ten metres, 12 o'clock.'

'Nobody survived that crash,' she said.

'No human,' replied Silvers.

They continued slowly forward, shoulders hunched, knees bent to provide a strong and stable chassis for their carbines, weapons which pointed menacingly towards the threat. As Silvers took the direct approach, she manoeuvred slightly to her right and the rear of the smashed airframe, increasing their angles of fire and options.

From the gaping severed metal wound in the shuttles skin, crawled the battered form of a Zantanath. Legs smashed and one foot missing, its left arm dragged to its side as blood oozed from a gash in its bicep, half its face was burnt and blackened. Through all this disfigurement, she instantly recognised the angry eyes of Auwen staring back with ire and hatred.

"Savages! Savages, all of you. What Celestia sees in you is beyond me. You are worth nothing more than your destruction."

"Says the man dying in the dirt," said Silvers.

"Earn a little respect before you die, Ambassador," she said forcefully across the coughing fit that Auwen had fallen into, probably driven by cracked ribs or punctured lungs. He didn't have long. "Answers. There is not enough of us to threaten the great Zantanath Unity. Why are you trying to destroy us?"

"You understand so little."

"Enlighten us."

"Profit and power. What is anything ever about?" said Silvers.

"No, not that. Safety and security is in dominion," said Auwen. "Your arrival changed things. Changed everything. How did you think it wouldn't?"

"Our arrival?"

"The origin-pair. When they arrived cycles ago, our scientists found your species to be resilient and adaptable; overtly aggressive. She couldn't resist the opportunity."

"She?" asked Silvers.

"Celestia," she stated.

"She would introduce a new weapon to the Zantanath Prime and gain favour. It would bring further peace in dominion to this region of the Unity. So, we waited for your fleet to arrive. We prepared." More coughing as Auwen pulled himself up to a slouched seated position against a large piece of airframe wreckage.

"Let the Xannix do the heavy lifting?" she said.

"Why not?" Auwen said. "They are a tool to be used."

"But not us?"

Auwen grinned through blooded teeth.

"You are a problem. We have tried various of our technologies to transform and adjust your form, your behaviours, with various levels of success, but we fail each time in a single critical area. We cannot control you. You will not conform. You are stubborn and your minds are too erratic."

Auwen shifted and shuffled as a wave of pain came over him, his head pressed back against the wreckage, his eyes closed in a grimace. When he focused on them again, his strength was failing; life draining as they watched.

"During the test programme, as the test subjects learnt of their new enhanced forms, with all the advantages and abilities that permitted, your enhanced people would self-terminate rather than become a constructive part of the Unity.

"It makes you a wasted effort and your existence a danger to our peace."

"It sounds more like you just can't take direct competition," said Silvers.

She couldn't tell whether the returning grimace on Auwen's lips was directed at Silvers for the sharp comment, or for the physical complications he was suffering.

"May the battle continue. For peace in dominion." The Zantanath's words were almost inaudible.

She looked on as the life force ebbed from Auwen, his breathing becoming shallow then his eyes distant.

"Shit!" she cried, frustrated.

"What?" asked Silvers, slightly startled by her sudden exclamation.

"I had more questions."

"Well, you're not going to get them from him. Maybe there are other survivors inside?"

"Let's check it out." She nodded towards the gash in the fuselage from which Auwen had come, a trail of dark crimson leading back through into the darkness of the cabin. "After you," she motioned to Silvers.

"Yes, boss."

Silvers worked his way through into the shuttle, twisting slightly to negotiate the ragged entrance and climbing to lift himself past crooked seating. Orienting himself on the tilted floor he aimed his carbine and torch up and down the length of the airframe, while she followed in behind him.

There were a couple of Zantanath in seats further up near the bulkhead to the cockpit. She could see from where she stood that they were dead. One had a partially crushed skull, smashed against equipment he had been operating; the other's head was mostly missing, blackened by a bolt of intense heat which had fallen from the sky and cut though the craft, a hole in the ceiling of the cabin and a beam of smoky light directing her to the simple deduction.

Working her way along the aisle she found another form slumped in a seat near the front of the craft, a tech at his station, motionless with blood draining from a wound in his side. What caught her attention was the item discarded in the footwell of the seat next to him: a Zantanath warrior's transit pack, crushed and fractured, skeletal wings crumpled and useless.

'Where's the warrior?' she asked, indicating the evidence.

'Another one? Rear cabin is clear.'

'Cockpit. Cover me.'

Their steps were silent, boots with pads like those of a large cat damped the sound of their approach. The corridor to the cockpit narrowed and crackles of shorting circuits flashed, as dangling ceiling wires arced in the darkness. Her torch beam cut through the drifting smoke in the cabin and illuminated the cockpit. It was compact and without an external view, totally enclosed.

'See anything?' asked Silvers.

'Yeah… What do you make of this?'

There was barely room; she crouched down and allowed Silvers to crane his neck through the tight space and get a reasonable view of the scene.

'What is that?' he asked.

The pilot was laying prone on a couch which moulded around most of its body, fine feathers covering the exposed parts, but whatever kind of being it was, it was small—she estimated a standing height of no more than a metre. Its wings were spread out across the cockpit space, the tips of which were harnessed by more moulded material, holding the wings and body firm. The wing feathers were slick and mottled black, a green sheen reflecting like an oil on their surface. The face of the pilot was away from them, so they had no clear view, but the head was covered in a helmet which was elongated at the front and connected to the ship via fibre cable.

"It's breathing," she said in surprise, breaking the silence. The sudden sound made the feathers of the creature flutter nervously, a warbling voice emanated from the form as words crackled from speakers about the cockpit.

"Dabadda fos alarena."

It made her stop and stare at the creature more intently, her mind instinctively trying to translate the words.

"It's talking," she said.

"Saying what?" asked Silvers.

"Bio-comm can't translate it," she shook her head. "Maybe if I can get closer. It looks injured. Perhaps it's asking for help?"

"You know this thing was shooting the shit out of us a few minutes ago?"

"We're looking for answers here. If it can talk, we can question it."

"If you say so. Personally, I think we should put it out of its misery."

She looked closer, searching for any good way to get closer and inspect the creature for injuries, but the place was cramped.

"Must have taken some gs in that crash," said Silvers, while continuing to look about the cockpit.

"Optimised for purpose," she said aloud as her mind processed and connected memories with the reality before her. Memories returning from the fog of amnesia. It echoed Rivers' journal, the words she had read during her time on the Zantanath station which had described the excellence of their genetic engineering. She had initially thought this simply advanced medicinal technology put to use to save Larsen, but why would they have this technology available? Subversive bioengineering.

"What better pilot than a bird?"

The vibration of the feathers intensified as she tried to get closer, and an aggressive rasping sound filled the cockpit.

"I don't think it likes us," said Silvers as he began to back away. "I think we should give it some space."

In a fluid motion and faster than she reasonably expected a

wounded creature to move, the harness mouldings and helmet covering about the creature released. The creature whipped round, and wickedly sharp talons lashed out at her as fierce yellow eyes from a snarling fox-like face focused on its target. In the confined space, like blades they raked across her chest-plate, carving three deep gashes. The force of the strike hit her hard and, with nowhere to go, she was pushed back down the corridor to become wedged between Silvers and the wall. There was pain and noise as she found her face pressed against the cold floor.

The chattering racket of Silvers' carbine pounded the air, accompanied by a human roar of purpose, his anger and aggression vocalised. Sparks and metal shredded the cockpit as the creature screamed in pain and blood misted the air. In a frenzied struggle to be free of the incoming hail of bullets, it thrashed about the cockpit smashing instruments and damaging itself further. Then, in a moment, it was silent, slumped in a dark disfigured form to the side of the pilot's couch.

"Help me up," she said, the instant the noise ceased.

Silvers slowly lowered a hand to assist her while at the same time continuing to aim his carbine into the cockpit.

Pushing her way back to the cockpit she climbed in without hesitation and checked the pilot over for signs of life. There was no pulse, no response.

"Shit!" she yelled, striking the bulkhead.

As she stared down at the forlorn bird-creature she realised that she had no idea of its anatomy, and that checking for a pulse as she had was a futile effort. Silvers had done his job in protecting her— she should not complain—but the result was that they kept losing the chance to gain valuable intelligence.

The smoke and red light of the cockpit was becoming acrid and she coughed involuntarily. They needed to move. The fact that the craft had not yet exploded or caught fire didn't mean that it wouldn't. They needed to be outside.

"Er, sir," said Silvers.

"What now?" she said, trying to keep the anger from her voice, but it leaked through regardless.

Silvers said nothing but pointed at a section of the cockpit and a projection showing a holographic 3D topology of the surrounding area while various icons overlaid it. As with the rest of the now devastated cockpit, the projector image flickered and skewed with each surge of power to its circuits. She tried to sense the scale of the visual: the central icon was white—the crashed shuttle she presumed, their location—but the others were grouped and moving at a tangent to them.

She moved closer to get a better look, and instinctively reached out to touch the image. Her hand moved through the topology, the landscape shifting. She corrected and moved back sweeping the view to close on the group of icons. A tentative finger touched the lead holographic icon and felt a fizz of physicality. The cockpit suddenly became a cracked and splintered external view from several hundred metres above the ground, in the distance and quite clear to her, the landing zone and remaining crew of the *Endeavour*.

"Is that what I think it is?" asked Silvers.

"That," she said, lost in her own thoughts and not hearing Silvers, "is nothing good."

"We have to stop them, warn the others," he said leaving the cockpit and heading back down the fuselage.

"Stop," she called after him, straining to get up and out of the battered cockpit. "Wait. Where are you going?"

"To get help. Need a clear signal." Silvers was right: checking her bio-comm, she could not get an active connection to Dawn or the others.

"Wait. Dammit. The soldier."

Chasing him through the enclosed space of the shuttle to the tear in the skin they had entered by, she was a metre behind him as Silvers stepped out of the craft and was immediately swept from her view with a blur of reflected light.

"No!" she screamed in reflex. She cleared the last couple of metres to the exit across the broken, dishevelled seats in a second.

Bursting into the light from the dark innards of the crippled shuttle, her vision became a disorienting blinding white. The sound of scuffling and physical effort could be heard from her left before her sight began to correct. Swinging round, her carbine aimed towards the sound, she found Silvers engaged with the Zantanath warrior, both fighting furiously to gain the upper hand. It was clear to her that the Zantanath had caught Silvers hard in the ribs, probably at the point he left the shuttle, but Silvers skill was still a match for the superior strength and technology of the warrior.

Silvers had lost his carbine in the first assault, she could see it lying on the ground a few metres away, but the Zantanath was not using its weapons, its suit was ragged from the crash, gauntlet crushed, visor smashed and helmet control likely non-functional. But the right hook landed to Silvers' face like a hammer blow, the left swung in under his guard and cracked another rib, blood coating the lips as he exhaled.

"Silvers! Down!"

Silvers blocked another in-swinging blow and used the force of it to crash to the floor, in that moment she squeezed the trigger.

Bullets crossed the short distance like angry wasps, sparking and stinging the Zantanath where he stood. The force of the sustained fire at close range lifted the warrior from its feet and slammed it bodily into the broken hull of the shuttle. The magazine ran dry. With a practiced, easy motion, she reloaded, not taking her eyes from the target, anger giving her focus. She took aim again, but the Zantanath was moving fast. Part of her could not understand how it was still standing, let alone moving to attack at such as speed. As it closed, it suddenly jinked sideways and leapt at the shuttle fuselage. Using it as purchase, it climbed and reversed, jumping high and straight at her.

As she opened fire, she aimed toward the shattered visor, a weakness in its otherwise inaccessible armour. Mid-jump a blade flashed from its arm, extending from its operational, undamaged gauntlet. The motion was swift. A blast of red exploded around her as the warrior hit her hard with its full bodyweight and additional height gained giving it the momentum of a charging bull. Pain filled her chest as they collided and fell full force to the ground.

The yelling in her ears was hers. The pain was hers. The instant rushing cold that iced through her veins was all for her.

HOLT

'Sir, incoming comm from Captain Clayton. Priority broadcast.' The comms officer had a clipped English accent, and it took his mind on a tangent. Dialect was learned; it stayed with you through each resus. *You will always sound like you because your voice is Self, and will always be you in the wave.* Clayton's words from his lectures at the academy on the Continuity of Self, Memory and Wave Transition momentarily passed through his mind. Events so far behind him, yet so recent. He put them to one side.

He had been working the perimeter with several teams across the day, each group pitching the boundary defence of the encampment which described the edge of a rough circle drawn about the landed escape pods. Each team slowly erected proximity alarms and fencing. As Lieutenant Adams waited on the link for his response, he instinctively turned to look across the makeshift city of white metallic bones, each escape pod rising like an accusing finger to the heavens. He identified the shard with the extended lattice of aerials and a large dish directed towards the horizon.

'Okay, Adams, let's have it. Go ahead.'

Working from the modified escape pod, Adams rerouted the incoming signal to his bio-comm.

'Holt, this is Clayton. There is little time. You are in danger. You have incoming Zantanath hostiles, attack ships from the west...' the transmission began to garble. '...Ellie. Request...' More static.

'Holt, what's happening with that damn connection? Get it

back.' He found himself shouting at the distant comms officer.

'They're being jammed, sir,' Adams replied after a moment of swift analysis.

Jamming them? That could only be bad.

'Okay. Sound the general alarm. There's a storm coming. Out.'

He was running now to a prefab building near the centre of the encampment.

'Station, this is Holt. Do you read?'

'Station, go ahead.' Commander Allerton responded.

'We have reported hostiles incoming from the west. Send what men you have to defend the perimeter. Over.'

'Sir, you understand our position? Over.' The message was clear but indirectly stated. They had been on the ground several days now, but priorities had been to the wounded, to food resource, to water preservation and collection, using the fabrication printers for arms and munitions had been lower on that priority list, below boring rigs and abstraction pumps, shelter and medical supplies. As such, their security manpower was limited. Very limited.

'Understood. Do what you can. I'm en route. Over.'

'We have your location. I've assigned Lieutenant Sato to you. She will be with you in twelve seconds. Station Out.'

I don't need a bodyguard, he thought.

A moment later Lieutenant Yoshi Sato ran into step by his side, automatic rifle slung across her chest as she ran. Neither of them said anything. They ran.

As the general alert sounded across the camp, people started to move quickly in all directions, each to their assigned duty. New information came into his bio-comm from the camp command post.

'Holt, this is Station. We're not seeing anything on the perimeter scans. Nothing in-bound from any direction. Over,'

'If Clayton said there's incoming, then there's incoming. We need eyes on those targets. We know their tech is good; show them we're better. Out.'

Weaving through people and escape pods, he and Sato watched the horizon, the western sky now directly in front of them as they ran. A surface-to-air missile team finalised their set up as they ran an arc around them, the missile tubes rising and spinning to the west, tracking for the still invisible targets.

'This is sector four, we have visual on twelve targets incoming from the west, range ten clicks, bearing two-eight-two.'

'They're not on the scopes sir,' he overheard one of the missile team state.

'Switch to manual targeting,' said the team's lead.

'Copy that. Switching to manual.'

At a sprint, his vision was bouncing around and he could not focus. He stopped, skidding to a halt which took Sato by surprise. She overran him by several meters. His eyes scanned the horizon. Above the mountain ridgeline that rose high out of the plains, he thought he spotted a formation of dots. Rather than focus on them, he moved his sight slightly to the right, and there in his peripheral vision they appeared. Two lines, a staggered echelon.

"Shit!"

He took off again, this time at a sprint faster than before.

"Keep up!" he shouted to Sato as he passed her at pace. He could feel her roll her eyes rather than see her reaction.

In moments, the dots on the horizon became blobs which he could see even while at a sprint. The incoming Zantanath ships were fast and had purpose. Without warning, the ground to the west of their camp began to lift into the sky in vertical columns of rock and debris. After a short delay, the sound of the explosions washed across the camp.

Instantly, smoke trails worked their way rapidly from various positions across the camp towards the inky daemons flashing across the sky, some missiles exploded before they met their mark, some continued skyward spiralling off along an undefined path. Nothing was hitting home.

As the Zantanath attack craft flew over the camp, ball lightning fell from their bellies. Striking the ground and structures alike, the world shook as thunderous explosions ripped the ground from where it had lay for eons. The bombardment turned rock, metal and humans alike into fragments and scattered the debris in all directions. Screams and shouting joined the chorus of chaos about him, cries of pain, cries for help.

Rounding a landed escape pod, he came to a halt, the last couple of paces taken as an unconscious action. His steps moved him closer to the devastation before him, possibly in the forlorn hope of giving assistance where he could. No help would be needed. The command centre was decimated: a burned-out husk of metal and composite, its framework silhouetted like the ribs of a whale carcass against the background, flames trying to take hold where they could.

Looking skyward to find the perpetrators of this unprovoked attack, he felt a rage well up within him. The craft had broken formation, each climbing away and turning for another diving attack on the camp.

"Sir!" It took him a moment to focus again, his mind spinning as the events unfolded. "We need to move, sir!" said Sato. "Instructions?"

"Comms, this is Holt." As he said the words, he looked across to the modified pod which had been the broadcast station, but that too had become a dark crater in the ground.

The second wave of attack craft overflew the camp and another hail of electric rain tore through the makeshift buildings and littered escape pods. Another volley of missiles launched after them to no avail, the light crackle of small arms fire could be heard pointlessly chasing targets.

"If we don't do something quickly, this is going to be a slaughter," said Sato, watching the second formation break and pinwheel round in separate arcs for individual sequential passes. "What are they doing now?"

He looked around the camp, people everywhere. Mayhem and chaos.

"They've taken out their key targets. Now comes the ground assault."

His eyes flashed to the first Zantanath assault craft as it passed a couple of hundred metres from his position. It slowed almost to a stop and six liquid mercury balls of light shimmered on the ground beneath it. As the craft accelerated for the far side of the camp and began to climb again, the balls of light dispelled to reveal three Zantanath warriors from each ball. The Zantanath immediately levelled their weapons and began to lay waste to everything they saw, destruction and murder with every shot.

As the second assault craft approached, his eyes searched about the camp, thoughts struggling to find a way through the mounting problems. He put out a query to all the escape pods within a fifty-metre radius. The response was varied, but he selected three with at least 10 percent remaining fuel reserves.

"I need anyone with a weapon taking out those Zantanath troops," he said to Sato. Sato immediately relayed the message via her bio-comm on a wideband broadcast.

Scanning the skies, he found the third attack craft on approach and bearing down on their position. There were people in all of the three pods he had just commandeered by bio-comm. He put out a curt message to those aboard each while automatic gunfire popped loudly, close and distracting in the background.

'This is Commander Holt. I need you to evacuate this vehicle immediately. You have ten seconds before launch.'

He knew the people inside the pods would already be aware that the systems were beginning to wind up to launch as he had already started the pre-flight sequence in all of those pods. Hopefully, they would already be moving. He had no time to confirm.

"What are you doing?" asked Sato with confusion in her voice.

"Buying time."

He finalised overriding the security to relaunch on each pod as he concentrated on the slowing Zantanath craft. The downwash of its engines blew grit and dust up in a swirl about them as it passed overhead. Through the squint and blinking of his eyes, he tried to estimate from the map overlay of his bio-comm the location of the flyer he saw before him. Decision made, he gave the order to each of the three pods for immediate launch.

"Take cover!" he shouted to Sato, whose eyes widened as she realised what he was attempting to do. They both headed for a nearby pod and turned to watch the Zantanath shuttle deal with the oncoming barrage of relaunched escape pods.

Initially, he thought he had failed. The first of the pods rose from the ground directly in front of the Zantanath craft, prompting the pilot to correct his approach and raise the nose. A burst of rapid fire came from a port on the right of the attack craft and the pod erupted into a ball of flame, fragments falling back to the ground, overtaken by gravity. The second pod launched further over to the attack craft's left, rising on a trajectory which tilted away from the target and worked its way further out towards the perimeter of the camp. It continued to accelerate skyward.

Manoeuvring into position, the attack craft began to hover, becoming a stable platform for the troop drop. Six balls of light appeared on the ground below the craft, and the Zantanath warriors began to materialise from the shimmer.

"Shit," said Sato, raising her carbine. "Time to go, sir."

"Wait," he replied, continuing to watch the third pod and putting a hand up towards her to emphasise his words.

Something had gone wrong with the pod's launch. Perhaps it had been the fuel gauge measuring incorrectly; perhaps something had broken during the landing. Whatever it was, as the pod cleared the Zantanath attack ship by the right rear quadrant, the rocket motor sputtered and failed.

"Into the pod. Now!" he yelled.

The third pod collapsed towards the attack ship like a drunk, pirouetting and falling as the claws of gravity took hold. It struck the attack ship in the right rear stabiliser and ripped through the wing, shearing the engine from its mount. Fuel tanks within the escape pod cracked under the impact and ignited, and the force that followed tore through the right side of the attack ship and triggered a secondary explosion. Immediately, the attack ship lost lift and flipped hard onto its back before crashing to the ground.

The ensuing fireball engulfed everything within 20 metres of the crash site, the newly materialised warriors crushed under the flaming remains of the airframe. Following Sato and diving through the open door of the pod, he had no time to get straight in the couch before the tornado of fire picked up the pod from its standing and threw it metres across the ground. Stone and flame kicked up into the pod as they slid across the camp, and he covered his face and tried to hold himself in place.

Coming to a sudden stop, both he and Sato were thrown to the top of the crew space, followed by loose objects from within the pod and rocks scooped in through the open hatch. He felt a boot to his face, and a hard lightning-sharp twist of his elbow. The pain was excruciating.

After a dazed moment of quiet, he tried to sit upright and held his left elbow to his body. The iron taste of blood filled his mouth and red pooled into his vision. Sato was screaming and punching the hull of the pod with a grin on her face, though blood also smeared her face from a clear wound to her temple. It was the elation of a person saved from the brink, seeing the face of death and escaping its grasp.

"Stars and blood, sir! You're crazy, full deep-space crazy."

He winced as he shifted.

"It's a talent, I guess."

Another explosion rocked the pod.

"Are you hurt?" she asked, assessing his arm held close to his chest.

"Not as hurt as I could be. I'll be alright. But we need to get out of this pod. Let's go."

Clambering from the pod with slow aching movements, they turned to the downed Zantanath attack craft.

"Man, that's a mess," said Sato.

He put out a bio-comm.

'This is Holt to team leads. Sit rep.'

His eyes searched the horizon and flicked through what he could see of the camp from his position. It was difficult, as they had purposely chosen a flat plane for the landing zone; with no elevation, he could not accurately assess the strategic situation visually. Reports started to flood in via his bio-comm: several attack ships had dropped their warriors and teams were fully engaged defending their position. Some quick-minded individuals had worked out what he had done in taking down the attack craft now burning on the ground before him and had repeated the procedure three more times yielding another success. It had been enough to make the Zantanath change tactic. Instead of sweeping runs across the camp, they were now circling and dropping troops at the perimeter. The camp's light defence was still inadequate, so they would be overrun no matter how inventive or resourceful.

"This is only going to go one way," said Sato. "There's just too many of them, and I don't think they are interested in our surrender."

"No," he replied, grimly, watching his bio-comm reports and the count of personnel clicking down as they spoke.

As Zantanath guided missiles looped in above them and took out one of the fabrication buildings close by, he flinched at the shock which rocked the air. Sato didn't move. Her gaze was focused passed him and slightly high; it gave him an impending sense of dread.

"What the...?" he started to ask but caught a glimpse of something shift behind Sato. Rocks rose ominously behind her, as if the terrain had become animate, the shape shifting into a transparent humanoid form, its outline fuzzy and illusive. In the next instant he was enveloped in a wrestled body lock, both he and Sato unable to move.

"Still," came a sibilant voice into his ear. He froze and his eyes locked with Sato.

"Do as they say," he ordered after a moment. She simply nodded. With her arms grappled by the creature, she had little alternative, her carbine forced to the ground.

"We are here to help. We will assist your defence, under order of the Setak'da. Please inform your soldiers that we are allies."

He felt himself physically picked up and turned to face his assailant, then returned gently to the ground. Still gripped at the shoulders, the face of a Xannix looked down on him.

"I am Battle-Commander Tyce," said the Xannix. "We are here to help. Please relay the message to your people."

He considered the new information and took a moment to look across the camp. The bio-comm was updating with a new population count every couple of seconds, the decline of the human race being ticked off one digit at a time. He had no choice but to hope this offer was genuine.

"It's sent. And thank you."

Tyce nodded. "Don't thank me yet, human. Chaos and the trickster still live on this battlefield today."

In a moment, what seemed like an army rose from the land about them, right across the plane, both inside and outside the camp. Plasma fire and missiles stabbed the air from unseen locations and two Zantanath assault craft vaporised at altitude.

ELDERSON

"On today's program we highlight the critical work undertaken by the charity Food for People, the humanitarian organisation that provides food and provisions to the transitory populous outside the perimeter of the Metropolitan zone. Metropolitan law dictates that these people cannot be allowed within the walls for reasons of public health, but there is no law prohibiting us from providing assistance where we can.

"Right now, we are travelling with the FFP convoy, supported by an escort from the MetPol Section 4 division. You can see the trucks heading out before us as we approach the check point and perimeter gates…"

The news crew in her RV was driving her crazy, the girl's endless vocal monologue to the drone operated by her cameraman was tedious and seemingly endless. The girl had been introduced to her by Captain Suffolk as he offloaded his responsibility to her under the guise of delegation, and she had accepted, because she had to. The face she recognised—the girl was from a minor news channel and a celebrity—but in seconds she had already forgotten her name. She had just tagged them in the team's tactical display as *News Girl* and *Camera Guy*. Insignificant. A mistake.

"We're coming up on the check point and perimeter gate now. 20 seconds," said Suffolk over the comms from the lead vehicle.

"Creds confirmed. Inner gates open," stated Corporal Chambers, as he liaised with Gate Control, who were located 30 clicks away in central city command.

The gate facility was a tunnel made up of an inner and outer gate, with fortified walls and fully automated defence grid. From a distance, it looked like a they were entering the open mouth of a basking shark, tall, wide and gaping. As they approached, the inner gate was already open and they progressed through at speed, the convoy not slowing.

"Gate Control, we're inside. Rotate the gates."

"Roger. Inner gate closed. Opening outer gate."

From her command seat in the convoy's trailing vehicle, the white dot of daylight at the end of the tunnel grew rapidly until in an instant they were back in the spring sun and through the outer gate.

"Gate Control, we're clear of the gate and approaching the drop. Chow team, you're up."

Her driver, Sergeant Devereux, swung the vehicle round to the left, Suffolk's vehicle went right, and the other escorts spread out in a similar fashion across the gate entrance hardstanding, allowing the FFP trucks to manoeuvre through the centre and into position.

Extending five hundred metres further into the outlands, a ring of boundary lamps elevated on pylons clearly shone a bright red. Beyond the lights was a shambolic mass of people, dark and dirty, standing silently in their thousands. She flicked down her helmet binoculars and brought the crowd into closer perspective. Mostly women and children at the front, and there were a few taller males with makeshift hand carts and barrows to collect the supplies; a couple rode quadbikes.

"Looks like the dusters are behaving themselves today LT," said Corporal Palmer from his gun turret above her. "I won't need to shoot any of them today, dammit." Her team was relaxed.

"You're an ass, Palmer," she responded. "Dusters need to eat, same as you."

"Yeah, but that shit could keep my kids going for a year. Never see what we need to feed these nothins for. They don't participate."

"It's not their fault they got caught the wrong side of the line. And, besides, we help because it's the right thing to do. Now stay focused."

She closed the chat down, aware that News Girl had stopped talking. Turning to check on her and Camera Guy, she realised the lens was on her. She attempted to brush the comments away with her best smile.

"Look at that crowd of people," said News Girl. "Rob, we need a shot of that. Can you get a clear shot from here? Nice and close."

"Tell you what would be better," said Camera Guy. "A cool flyby. High aerial shot."

"Cut it in with my audio, stream me in."

"Sure. One second. I'll just get some height on the camera," said Camera Guy, as he flicked the door handle and started to get out of the RV.

"Wait a second. No one leaves the vehicle," she called after him. News Girl looked at her sheepishly.

"Oops. Sorry. This won't take a minute. And your team will get great coverage. It'll be fine." The smile that she wore was practiced, the situation contrived. They had planned this the whole time, it was obvious, the woman's eyes challenging her; *what are you going to do about it?*

They were both out of the RV now and the drone was already twenty metres in the air.

"Shit!" she growled and started out of the truck. "Palmer, stay sharp. Cover us. Devereux, keep the engine revved."

"Yes, boss."

Striding up to the News Girl with purpose, she tried to find the drone in the sky; she could hear it buzzing but she had lost visual.

"Hey, I said back in the RV. What are you doing?" she asked. She was past being nice, being outside the RV was not just dangerous, it was against regulations for a reason. They would all be in decontamination for a month.

Then she saw it, the drone off to the side of the convoy, not flying the duster line as they had said. It was a dark shadow behind an intense red dot of light, a laser? Her mind seemed to accelerate as time slowed, reason closed in on the drone's purpose. Lasing targets.

"Helping the people," said News Girl. It made an alarm sound in her head. Where was the drone? Instinctively she reached for her radio.

"Captain!" she shouted across the comm but didn't get to finish. She was struck hard across the temple and the world sparked and spun. Grit bit her cheek as her face mashed into the ground.

The world became a confusion of noise and blurred images as

she fought to keep conscious. Suffolk's vehicle was hit first and exploded in a fountain of flame, flipping to its side under the force of the blow. Her own vehicle was taken by News Girl, a single shot removed Palmer, then a stunned and confused Devereux took a second too long to react as she play-acted the frightened and cowering female, before opening his door and putting two bullets to his face.

Further missiles hit home, the debris and burning RVs of her security team littered the hardstanding. The crowd of dusters were screaming and cheering like they were at a stadium, their home team giving the opposition a lesson in commitment and tactics.

Taking effort to pull the lifeless form of Devereux from the driver's seat, News Girl jumped in and took the radio.

"Gate Control, this is the Chow team. We're clear. Let the crowd in."

"Copy that. Lights to green."

More mistakes. How could they be fooled? Couldn't they see the situation over the surveillance cameras? With a force of will, she attempted to move, but her body was too heavy, limbs unresponsive. The duster crowd saw the lights change, the pylon gun turrets deactivate, and took their cue. Surging forward they parted, the mothers and children moving apart to reveal a host of quadbikes and armed male and female militia, raging as they charged, taking flight from the cover of rag draped carts and tattered camouflage.

More missiles trailed a path overhead, making a direct line from the crowd to the gate. Hit hard, the open gate suffered a barrage of explosions along its track, warping and buckling the guide rails over which the door ran. It would no longer be able to close.

Their target was clear. The trucks and food were forgotten, the dusters had a higher goal.

No, you fools! Stop!

She could not vocalise her thoughts, but in her head, she was screaming. Wanting them to stop before it was too late. Without the biotag responder each of the city-born were fitted with, the gate would treat them as hostile, a threat to the city to which it was guardian. They may have disabled the gate, but the dusters seemed unaware of the defence grid inside the tunnel entrance.

The first of them on rusted quadbikes stopped short, some turning to raise an arm and urge their comrades on, thousands rallying to their call. The duster vanguard reached the gate at a sprint and scouted forward into the tunnel.

From the darkness of the tunnel she could see flashes of light as the defence grid opened fire. Whatever the reaction of those within the tunnel or close to its mouth, the sheer weight of the jubilant advancing crowd meant there was no retreat from the slaughter. Hundreds of people were torn to pieces their cries lost in the cheers of those behind.

"Rob! Time to go!" shouted News Girl. "Cut to the entrance, then back to me."

The drone dropped from the sky to settle a couple of metres from News Girl, at head height, her RV in the background and Devereux slumped to the ground before her, his dead body having been dragged from the vehicle, everything about the image choreographed.

"Are we rolling?" News Girl asked. A simple thumbs up from Camera Guy was the response.

News Girl attempted to straighten her hair and looked directly into the camera and applied a sombre expression.

"This is Carrie Tillmann for MetNews at the North Gate FFP food drop. As you can see from the unbelievable scenes behind me, the transient people at the nearby encampment have overrun us, women and children making a dash for freedom and the city gates.

"This horror began only moments ago, as the charity was manoeuvring its trucks into position to distribute the food among those gathered at the line. Without warning, and with deadly accuracy, guided rockets destroyed the lead security vehicles leaving the way clear for terrorists on quadbikes to burst from the human shield of women and children towards the convoy.

Right now, the city defences are slaughtering innocents while they try to flee the scene."

While News Girl had been playing to the camera, Elderson had found some small level of movement returning to her arms. Slowly, she unclipped the pistol from her holster and drew it to bear on her target. News Girl was lifted from the floor and back against the side of the RV with two sharp barks of the pistol. Stunned, News Girl looked down and touched the blood soaking her chest, streaming from the gaping wound in the side of her neck. She seemed unable to conceive how she could be hurt and more, how the armoured vest had not protected her.

A split second later, a further bark dropped Camera Guy where he stood, the uncontrolled drone turning in a lazy circle and skimming across the stony ground to a stop, motors whirring, dust flying.

News Girl's legs buckled as she slid down the side of the RV leaving a bloody trail, her eyes wide and scared. She guessed that News Girl had not even considered this outcome, so confident in her plan, arrogant and ambitious.

"What have you done?" she croaked across the space between them. She thought News Girl may have heard her, a flinch of comprehension in her eye before they became glazed and distant.

In that second, a noise like the loudest clap of thunder she had ever heard pounded her ears and the world became the orange of flame and a thousand suns. Hot wind blasted her face and the dust all about her was kicked up as if shocked by the sound.

"The people! she screamed. She thought she screamed it; she could hear nothing through the firestorm. A trail of white vapour tracked back like a chalk line across the sky to the orbital security platform above, omniscient and invisible to those on the ground. Someone had been watching, someone above her pay grade and someone with a final word. That word was death, and it rained all about her.

*

Orange.

"Elderson. You ready?"

A ball of orange floated before her, but there were no screams, no people burning like torches in the roiling, glowing colours, skin blackened and charred as they fell to dust. A gentle, calming voice spoke through the nightmare, drawing her out of her visions of hell. Standing there, transfixed, it took a moment for her to focus.

She was being kindly fussed over by Boyd and Tanner, one checking her suit and ensuring items were secure, the other checking her vitals and ensuring her telemetry was as he expected.

"Calm your breathing, Lieutenant," said Tanner. "Easy in, easy out. Your heartrate is spiking a little."

"I think you can safely expect that," said Boyd from behind her, as he shifted and pulled hard on a strap, yanking at her balance briefly. "What we're asking her to do—I'd be shitting myself too."

Tanner shook his head.

"I am here," she said to the room from behind her visor. "I can hear you."

"He just feels bad because it's his crazy plan," said Larsen from the corner of the corridor by the airlock door, arms folded, a look of concern on his features. She imagined he was there for emotional support rather than any technical reason, and possibly out of guilt for the decision. It was his decision that was sending her into danger, but she knew there was no real decision to make; this was the only realistic course of action, and they all knew it.

"It'll work," muttered Boyd from behind her as he continued to work on the suit.

"That's better. Think *calm*, slow and easy breaths," said Tanner.

The control panel of the airlock displayed a constant solid orange light; the icons and lettering meant little to her. She tried to ignore it.

"All set," said Boyd, giving her a pat on the shoulder to indicate the all-clear. He then slid into her vision, waving Tanner away with a quick motion of his prosthetic arm, the artificial limb clearly forgotten and not hindering him at all.

"You comfortable?"

"Things feel a little heavier, but that's about it."

"Good. Okay, all I've done is modify the suit power by adding some Xannix cells to the transit-pack. You'll be able to get a bigger bubble radius when you activate the pack. Remember, keep it small until you need it. It's untested and you don't want to overload things."

"Got it. Don't overload things," she replied. Boyd gave her a thumbs up.

Boyd stepped aside, clearing a path to the airlock door. For a moment, the corridor tunnelled in her vision, the door seemingly becoming larger than could be accommodated by the frame. She felt a little too wired. *Breathe.* Tanner's words echoed in her ears.

"Time to go, Riz," she said to herself and the room.

"You've got this, Lieutenant," said Larsen, stepping across to the door control and opening the inner airlock. *Ah, doorman*, she thought.

It had been agreed with the Xannix that she would initiate the suit transit-pack from within the airlock and return there on completion of her task. If anything went wrong, they wanted to space her quickly. Comforting.

She stepped into the airlock and the door closed behind her. Bringing up the visor display for the transit control, the guidance and comms appeared to her in Terran English. The suit was Zantanath, but she realised early that it had been specifically designed for Terrans. It was unsurprising: under high stress and conflict the brain turned to the amygdala for its direction, to base function. The easiest instruction to process would be one in the user's mother tongue, i.e. Terran English. Under the current circumstances, any edge she could get, she would take.

"*Olanna*, this is Elderson. Initiating transit. Over."

"Elderson, this is *Olanna* Actual," said Larsen, from the other side of the airlock door. "Mission is green. Good luck and see you in ten."

"Roger that, Actual. Destination locked. Activating transit in three, two, one.... Mark."

The world about her shifted and rippled like water on a sunny day.

HOLT

The air crackled like firecrackers as charged Zantanath beams of lightning arced across their position and illuminated them with an electric blue. He found himself yelling over the weapons fire while they took cover behind a group of haphazard storage pallets, a squad of Xannix defending their position. Sato took the occasional shot but kept herself on mission and made sure he was out of harm's way as much as could be expected. Together they were keeping the silver armoured warriors away, but events across the camp were now wildly out of control. He needed to change that.

"What do you mean you cannot provide air cover?" he yelled at Battle-Commander Tyce.

"Now is not the time for such a discussion," replied the Xannix, firing off a volley of projectiles from his rifle towards a charging group of silvery figures. One dropped, body instantly limp and without direction or power, the figure pushed face first to the ground.

"Now is exactly the time, Commander!" He felt his voice crack and shriek under the sustained strain of shouting over the noise of battle.

Tyce's skin flared a brief mottled white of irritation. Another Zantanath dropped as his rifle fizzed off another couple of shots.

"It is complex."

"It always is."

The Xannix's large shoulders slumped as his skin turned a deep blue, and Tyce turned to face him, dark eyes resigned. The

Zantanath attack continued around them, and Tyce's guard picked up the additional work now that he was distracted.

"Our military vehicles are compromised. We cannot afford the risk of using them."

"What do you mean 'compromised'?"

"Our military leaders have grown fat and weak on the gifts of Zantanath technology. Now is the time for us to pay for their blindness."

He had been on the bridge of the *Endeavour* when Commander Roux had been informed of this fact in relation to the Xannix fleet. For some reason, he had believed this only an issue with their fleet, not their entire military. But why wouldn't this be the case? He was being sort-sighted and naïve—of course the Zantanath would flood Xannix culture with compromised tech, tech which could be controlled or rendered useless on command. He considered the implications of the Xannix position and how it now affected them all. Closing his eyes, he tried to find a quiet place within to think. They needed a way out. They needed help.

"No air support," it was a thought process step rather than a question.

"That is correct."

"We need air cover."

"What we need and what we have are two different things," said Sato, as she leaned in to shield him from falling mud and stone, the air and ground shuddering under the force of a nearby explosion.

"It would be advantageous, yes," said Tyce.

He was suddenly aware of a whirring sound, growing in intensity that emanated from all about them. A flamelike clear light appeared before him, flickering and hypnotic. An urgency gripped Tyce and, without saying a word, he was lifted bodily as the giant Xannix took off at a sprint with him locked in a carry across his chest. Losing sight of Sato with the world becoming a blur, he found he could do nothing but clamp his hands to his ears. Pain thrashed through his being, pressure in his head threatened to crack his skull and a wetness grew across his top lip. He knew the taste of his own blood. He felt himself passing out, unconsciousness overwhelming him.

As quickly as the sound had started, it ended. Silence came like bliss after the pain, his heart rushed in his ears and, for a moment, he saw sparkling traces winding like snakes through the air, each searching for their mark.

His eyes widened in fear as he saw Sato and the scattering Xannix lanced through and in the blink of an eye they were still. No sound, no screams.

Two snaking lines skimmed the ground and made directly for him. For the first time in his life he was chill with the anticipation of the darkness he saw in his immediate future. But the Xannix had different ideas.

At a sprint and lowering his weapon, Tyce leapt high into the air and fired almost directly below them with a sustained energy burst from his beam weapon. The sudden change of direction took him by surprise, causing him to bite his tongue hard. Dropping from the apex of the jump, everything became a mess of sound and vision, gravity and rock. Ejected from the Xannix's grasp, he hit the ground hard, air bursting from his lungs and leaving him curled in a foetal position, muscles screaming for air which his body could not provide.

Bodily forced to a sitting position, back against a partially excavated rock, his eyes staring into those of the Battle Commander, Tyce was looking at him with his head inclined to one side. The Xannix's skin rapidly flickered colours he could not follow then the Xannix punched him across the chest. In a violent gasp, it was as if his lungs had remembered how to breathe. The world flooded back to him in vibrant colour.

"Sato!" he managed to gasp, through choking and desperate lungfuls of air.

"No," stated Tyce. He wanted there to be more, but the Xannix was definite, the act of death just another detail on the battlefield.

"How are we alive?"

"Heated rocks," said the Xannix, slapping the stone behind his head. "Zantanath Khenja strike, no match for rock. But you must react fast and decoy your body heat."

"I'll remember that," he said.

"Yes," replied Tyce.

From beyond the rim of their crater, pounding steps made him involuntarily press himself harder against the rock. Two Xannix slid into the hollow, spraying stones and dust as they did. The exchange of visual communication was quick and efficient, but he caught none of its meaning.

"We must move," indicated Tyce.

"Can you get comms to orbit?" he interrupted. Tyce looked at him as if trying to translate what he had just said, his lips moving but no sound.

He was about to repeat the request, thinking that Tyce had not heard or perhaps not understood.

"Yes. We are blocked, but we have a relay."

"You can work around the jamming?"

"Yes."

"Can we link comms? Can you broadcast my transmission?"

"Yes."

He broadcast directly.

"Pan, pan. This is Landfall station to any receiving UTS vessel. We are under attack by hostile Zantanath forces and require immediate air support. Target any airborne craft within ten clicks of this position. Over."

He and Tyce exchanged a concerned look, waiting for a response. The other Xannix in the crater had begun firing again, their momentary evasive manoeuvre from the approaching Zantanath now discovered.

"Did it send?" he asked.

"Of course," replied the Battle Commander.

His chest began to hollow as he felt the last chance for a way out of the Zantanath trap drift away from his grasp.

"Pan, pan! This is Landfall station, we are ...."

"Landfall station, this is Ellie. Air support request received. Stand by."

His adrenaline surged at her response. For the first time since the start of the battle, he saw a glimmer of hope.

BOYD

As Elderson initiated her transit, he was already on the bridge of the *Olanna* and connecting to her rig.

"Okay, Lieutenant. Connection initiated. How was the ride?"

"I feel sick," replied Elderson.

"First transit. You'll get used to it."

"Don't know that I want to. Still don't know where my stomach is."

Through the drone units in the suit, he surveyed the room in which Elderson now found herself. It was dark across the deck, but Elderson's arrival had begun waking sections; lights flickered on, the room activated. She already had her gauntlet weapon raised, scanning the place in anticipation of trouble.

"Clear," Elderson said.

"I'll scout ahead."

"Do you even know what you're looking for?" Elderson asked him.

"I'll know it when I see it."

"Why did I know you were going to say that?"

"Just stay focused and keep up. When I find it, you need to be close," he said.

"Roger that."

Three drones released their clasps to the shoulder mounts on Elderson's left side, then they hovered momentarily above her head. The room was now fully active; to its centre was an enclosed column to the station spoke, part of a shielded energy conduit, down which the star station's energy was being channelled to the gate.

"This way," he told Elderson. "Our target is the regulator to all that energy."

Acting as a single unit, the drones gave him a composite view of the room in whichever physical location he looked. There was no single camera position; it was as if he was in the room himself and free to move about. If he needed to touch something, press a button, use a keypad, a drone would provide physical on-site action, and limited haptic feedback via the sensory actuators in his couch. It was taking him some effort to wrap his mind around the experience.

"They know we're here," said Larsen, who had taken up his position in the couch to his side. "They're launching a reception party: two patrol craft vectored to our position."

"How long?" asked Elderson.

"Five minutes six seconds."

"Then we better work faster, Drone Boy," she said.

"Does that mean they don't have people closer?" he asked.

"It could mean that. It most likely means that reinforcements will be here in five minutes," said Larsen. "Stay sharp."

"Eyes open," he said, as his drones moved him through the structure.

He could see a lift and stair access to the upper level; he marked it on the map as a waypoint for Elderson. "Access to upper level marked." He moved on, gateward via the stairwell, drones taking fast tight turns and moving quickly through the next level.

"Ho!" he announced suddenly across the comm. The surprise was evident, but the context was lost to Elderson.

"What?" Elderson asked with concern, as she double-stepped it up the stairs and through the accessway to the upper level. She ran under his field of vision and took up a defensive position behind a tall column of equipment, a tank of machinery and clear fluid which distorted her view up the walkway. He could see her scanning for targets about the deck space, focused on threats and possible movement. But, finally, she caught sight of the object centimetres from her, and he saw her take a step back, weapon still raised.

Before her was a suspension tank filled with nutrient fluid and the shadowy form of a Zantanath. Its torso was enclosed in a skin-tight harness, nose and mouth covered by breathing apparatus, and tubes ran up into machinery distorted and out of view at the head of the tank. Its eyes were open and it was staring directly at her.

From his elevated view, he could see tanks spread throughout the deck, ranks upon ranks of several hundred Zantanath, all enclosed and floating in nutrient chambers.

"What are these? Why are they in these tanks?" Elderson asked.

"I don't know," he said, pushing the drones on ahead, scouting and hunting for critical equipment and systems to the gate. "But I don't like it. This place gives me the creeps."

"And you're not even here," reminded Elderson.

"This way. Waypoint marked."

"Three minutes," chimed Larsen, with the tone of a metronome.

"Less. I've got company."

"I don't see anything," he said, as he urgently scanned the room.

Elderson was moving towards him fast, as between the distortions of the liquid tubes, shadows flickered and flew like wraiths towards them. "Move! Twenty metres! How did they get so close?" It was a question that remained unanswered as Elderson sprinted past him and up to the next level. He tagged one of the drones high on the accessway wall and moved the other drones off to overtake Elderson and get ahead of her again, but this time the staircase continued to spiral for a further ten metres before spilling him out onto a landing area with a single width doorway before him. He pulled back hard on the drone controls. At the speed he had been pushing them he winced as he felt himself rush towards the reinforced door, turning his own head and closing his eyes in reaction. They stopped only centimetres from its surface.

Reversing up to get a better view, the door had a solid read square with a diagonal black line from top right to bottom left; it looked like a warning, but they needed to get through. He pressed the access pad. It responded with a similar red square icon and a keypad of icons he did not recognise.

"Door," he said simply to Elderson.

"Shit. Then open it," she replied. "This is going to get messy."

The chamber suddenly echoed with the sounds of energy weapons splitting the air and ionising particles, unearthly screams followed, in pain and rage.

"Stars and blood!" he exclaimed, as he started work on the access panel. "Looks like a key code."

He levelled a drone at the keypad on the access panel and started punching numbers. This was no way to break a key code; there was not even any indication to how many digits were required.

"Larsen, do the Xannix have any way through? We're trapped."

"Checking," said Larsen and began an urgent conversation with Yannix and the *Olanna's* captain, the Xannix skin tone swirling around a low burnt orange colour.

He had been through several dozen combinations and was getting nowhere.

"We're not going to lose her," he mumbled to himself as his mind went to a bleak place. This could all be for nothing if he could not get the door open.

"Damn right you're not," Elderson replied, his private words leaking out across the comm. "Faster with the door, please."

His mind raced for ideas; nothing was coming back from the Xannix. He felt his heart pounding in his chest as he whittled down his options.

"I'm going to have to find the manual override—that's if there is a manual override—but I don't think the drones will be able to activate it. You'll have to pull the handle, Lieutenant."

"Are you kidding me? Busy!"

As if to emphasise her words, a plasma burn laced across the wall in front of him, the beam itself passing right through his location in space and causing his heart to skip a beat. He was still alive, of course he was, he was on the *Olanna*.

Taking a heavy breath, he tried to relax and focus on the keypad. There had to be a better than random way to do this. He flicked the optical wavelength on the drone in front of the door panel. And again, and again. There it was, a slight shift in the light over various keys, the finger marks of previous access attempts. Five digits, but were any repeated? Probably. Elderson was right. This was a mess.

"There are eight of them at the base of the stairs. Four have just accessed the elevator," he reported to Elderson, the drone he had left clamped to the wall on the lower level providing vital tactical information.

"Fire in the hole!" called Elderson and threw a grenade down the stairwell. Compensating for the slight lower gravity, she angled it off the lower wall then immediately rolled away to the elevator door to the side of the stairs as the grenade detonated. The elevator door opened as she arrived. Rolling out flat, back to the floor, she aimed up into the confined space and opened fire, simultaneously rolling another grenade into the space. A second later she was back at the top of the stairs firing down at the remaining wraiths. A low boom emanated from the open elevator and he saw an arm flop into the hall, a cold white Zantanath hand above a slick pool of slowly spreading black blood.

Focus.

Punching more combinations, he concentrated on the five keys he had identified as commonly used, but as he worked, he noticed the combinations of key presses were faster than his own and out of sync.

"Larsen, are you doing anything?"

"The Xannix are working on it, nothing yet. The Zantanath patrol craft have arrived. They haven't spotted us yet, but it's only a matter of time. Stand by."

The flickering key icons to the door panel were increasing their speed to a point where the icons had become an almost constant level of elevated illumination. *What is going on?*

An instant later the panel went blue and he heard the door bolts unlock in sequence before, with a hiss, the door shifted sideways to reveal the room beyond.

"Door's open. Go!" he yelled at Elderson, moving the drones inside the room, his trailing drone left in the stairwell. He wanted eyes on the Zantanath wraiths; these were not the same as the human warriors which had provided Elderson with her armoured suit. These were very different and, so far, he felt as though they had gotten away with things. Luck was not something he wanted to depend on.

As Elderson piled through the door, she hit the door control. As it closed, she fired a couple more shots through towards the stairwell. Once the door had fully closed, he noticed the control panel flick to a different icon; the whole screen was now locked out and there was no keypad control visible to operate. They were frozen out. From the other side he noticed the dark figures slowly making their way in formation up the stairs, stepping over their fallen comrades, but still on mission and still moving forward. He couldn't see the door control panel from the other side, so was unable to confirm whether the lock out was both ways. He needed to hurry.

"So, what are we looking for? It's got to be here. There's no going back," said Elderson.

It took him a moment to take his eyes off the door and realise what she was referring to. Turning into the room the vastness of the station and space beyond rushed at him, the control room an open observatory, a control tower across the gate. Above the window was the star station's energy injector for this section of the gate; a haze of energy could be seen undulating around its point, space distorted about it. From there the gate opening was stable and the starfield beyond unobscured.

The landing on which they stood overlooked the lower control room, and sweeping steps descended from their left and right. He flew the drones in a direct line straight over the handrail and down to the central structure of the room where he found another single Zantanath nutrient tank, raised on a plinth and overlooking the gate. Inside, the Zantanath was old, frame weakened and atrophied due to age, hair long and white, spread out like a halo in the fluid about him.

He spun the drones out and took a wide view of the room; the kit he needed had to be here. In his experience, no matter how hard engineers tried to build their machines with redundancy and failsafe systems, there was always a single point of failure. There was always something that the engineers overlooked, deemed low risk and too insignificant or edge-case to consider a real threat to the operation of the system. It had to be here.

Elderson reached the bottom of the stairs and made her way towards the front of the control floor and the wide view beyond. From the screen in front of her, a face appeared; it was familiar.

"Hello, Lieutenant Elderson."

"Ellie. How are you here?"

"Long conversation. No time. I take it you are here to shut down the gate?"

"If by *shut down the gate*, you mean take out the station, then yes."

"I see. And how are you intending to do that, may I ask?"

"Boyd, you're up," Elderson said across the comm.

"Destabilise the gate's energy injector control via a single point of failure," his voice was projected from the nearest drone.

"There is only one local to this room," replied Ellie, and her eyes moved past Elderson back towards the centre of the control room. He and Elderson turned their view to follow hers. The Zantanath gate controller.

"Isolate the gate controller from the system and this injector will cease to function."

"External control? Overrides?"

"All routed through his tank's bio-interface unit. If he dies, the other two controllers in the other towers can override and countermand actions remotely, but if the communications link to the processor is severed, the link to the injector is severed."

They stood for a moment, looking at the gate controller floating in his tank, peaceful and unnervingly serene given the violence that had taken place and the threat of what might be to come.

His mind wound back time.

"It was you," he said. Elderson turned to him confused. "The door. She hacked the door."

"You're welcome. But I think you need to do whatever it is you're here to do, and do it fast."

"Why's that?" asked Elderson looking back towards the holographic display, but her eyes carried on through to the gate beyond. Floating in view about fifty metres from their position was a Zantanath patrol craft, oriented directly at them.

"Oh no!" he said across the comm. Elderson was already moving.

Sprinting hard at the Zantanath gate controller, she covered the space in the blink of an eye and leapt at the tank, planting a foot about a metre up. Using the forward momentum against the tank, she thrust up and grabbed a connecting feeder tube at the top of the cylinder. Heaving herself up further, she slung her legs around and over another pipe, then tried to wrap herself around the bio-interface unit at the top of the nutrient tube.

A globe of light began to appear on the landing, and another on the floor beside him: transit bubbles were materialising at speed. Within a couple of seconds, Zantanath troops were spread out across the control room looking for them... For her.

"Activate the transit, damnit! Get out of there!" he shouted at Elderson across the comm. Simultaneously, he pushed the drones in different directions, each at the head of a Zantanath trooper.

Their impact having the desired response, all the Zantanath were now aiming weapons at him. He didn't like the feeling one little bit, being the target for so many weapons, but it didn't last long. Elderson had initiated the transit giving away her position, the bubble about her was now far bigger than it would normally be, it was engulfing most of the nutrient tube and a large proportion of the upper chamber; a deadly focus was now aimed at Elderson. One of the Zantanath realised what was going on and rushed the transit bubble, leaping for it before the transit completed, firing his weapon.

An instant later his connection went blank.

STRAUD

"Wake up, Captain! Nap time is over!"

The slap to the face woke her from her safe seclusion like a rush of bee stings. Her mind lurched from the soft, warm place to which she had withdrawn and back into the horrors of reality.

She didn't need a mirror to know the disfigurement she suffered: left eye ruined and blind, right cheek puffed out to the point where she could see it in her vision, bloody gaps in her gum line where molars used to sit. The pain was a chronic ache through her body, as bones and muscles informed her of the damage endured.

All of this she could suffer, was willing to suffer, as punishment for her failure, her betrayal of the fleet. And before her stood her tormentor. He even still called himself Larsen. It was an insult to the man she knew. This Zantanath was a willing host to Larsen's mind—a copy of a copy—and, from what she could tell, his wave was degrading fast, making him unstable and volatile.

Questioning had started slowly, using a device which had the power to lift the answers from her mind. After her initial anger at the helplessness of the situation, she had dug in and become uncooperative. To her surprise, the machine had started to give them inaccurate information. She found that she could misdirect the machine by focusing on very specific minutiae related to the question they were asking: concentrating on the finest detail when what they wanted was the whole, giving them the override code to the janitors' offices when what they wanted was access to the whole ship. Not a lie, just not what they wanted.

It was then that they turned to more traditional methods of information extraction. But, even as her Alpha code authorisation had been brutally ripped from her mind by Celestia, Obadiah had been a step ahead. Navigation temporarily restored until attention had passed from her to other matters, Obadiah sabotaged the bridge control and stole the *Indianapolis* back from the Zantanath once again.

Lying on the floor of her interrogation room, one of the meeting rooms on the administration deck easily converted for the purpose, a room stripped of any features and easily secured from the outside, she rolled her tongue around her mouth, then spat blood and another tooth to the ground. It skittered to a halt a couple of centimetres from Larsen's boot.

"Hello, Puppet. I take it you're back for more? My schedule is pretty clear; we can do this all day if you like." Her comment was rewarded with a kick to the stomach, making her double up further and retch.

"You have had time enough. My patience is at an end. You will tell me what I need to know."

"I have answered your questions. You're just not listening."

"Suggesting that I space my team and all your other little witticisms do not help the situation or, more specifically, you or your crew." She grimaced; it hurt. "The override codes you gave us did not work; why would that be? Each time you lie to me, you are only bringing more pain to everyone else."

Obadiah was watching over her, but there was only so much he could do. His primary focus was the ship and keeping that out of Zantanath hands. She was a part of the crew, and—although an important cog in that part of the machine—ultimately, she was expendable. Obadiah would be playing the numbers, keeping as many of them alive as was possible in the situation. She was hoping there was a way out, but after the punishment she had taken, perhaps a new skin and rewinding her memory the last few days would be a blessing.

But her current strategy was to delay and obstruct. As long as this puppet thought that she was the key to getting what he wanted, he would lose. The real Larsen would know to target the AI, but maybe his efforts there were also failing. To her, his poor technical read of the situation confirmed that the host mind was at the forefront of the puppet's decision making and she doubted that there was anything left of Larsen's true self.

"Run back to your master, tell her I will not comply, and you have failed."

"It seems a foolish move. You will be executed for your lack of cooperation, and I will move onto the next."

There was only Forester, her executive officer, who would be of any use, and she didn't see them having better luck there. There was no next; he was bluffing.

Just then, the door opened, and Forester was thrown into the room landing like a lifeless and blooded corpse. It wasn't until a bubble of blood grew then popped from his nose that she realised he was still alive.

"Bio-tech Uldnala, please delete the bio-bank and wave data for Commander Paul Forester, GS-119054," said the Zantanath Larsen to the room. The communication was picked up and acknowledgement broadcast across the room speakers.

"Deletion confirmed," stated a disembodied voice in stilted Terran English.

"Tell me what I need, or Commander Paul Forester, GS-119054, will cease to exist." The Larsen puppet levelled a pistol to Forester's head and leaned towards her. "And as you say, Captain, I can do this all day."

She felt her mind race, searching for a way to stop this warped and hate-filled version of Larsen from taking the next step. Forester had been with her for the duration of the programme: had overseen the building of the *Indianapolis* with her, passed the academy together; their lives intertwined. She knew what he would say, he would tell them all to space themselves. But when it came to it, when life gets personal, those decisions become the hardest and most torturous to follow through. She knew what she must do, what he would do, what the training told her to do, but that was after all alternate courses of action had become unavailable to her. There was still one option.

"Only to Celestia. I will only give the codes to Celestia, not her puppet."

"I don't think you have a choice, Captain. Either you give me what I want, or Forester dies, eternally."

"I'll give Celestia what *she* wants. You are nothing in this transaction."

She was gambling with Forester's life, and for a moment she thought she may have pushed Larsen too far.

"Can you take the chance?" she said to divert the tension in the room, the gun trembling with anger in the Zantanath's hand, just centimetres from Forester's head. His eyes were penetrating her with pure hatred.

*

The door to the bridge opened and she was dragged through it by her hair. Her hands flailed and she gripped at the arms which pulled her, as she tried to alleviate some of the pain. She had little strength to scream, but equally she wouldn't give them the satisfaction. As they stopped, her head was forced to the ground, and another cut was added to her already battered face, leaving a smear of blood on the deck.

Celestia sat in her chair, staring with distain at the crumpled human form before her. Larsen bowed briefly and respectfully stood aside as Celestia moved forward on the captain's couch, elbows resting on her knees and head tilted as if examining an animal she had seen for the first time, inquisitive and superior.

"Advisor Larsen informs me you have something to say?"

She forced herself to a seated position, her head staring at the floor, fringe laced with sweat draped across her face, energy spent, nothing left. She was out of time, there was no move she could make.

"Well human, what will it be? I will not ask again."

From the corner of her eye she saw the AI projector spin a sandstorm of bits into three-dimensional form, but the voice was not Obadiah. She slowly looked up to see Ellie smiling back down at her. She knew her confusion was clear on her face.

"Ellie?" she said.

Celestia's bodyguard were instantly at her side with weapons raised and aimed at the transparent hologram before them, Celestia waved them away with an easy, dismissive gesture.

"You are the ship's AI. Good," started Celestia. "Reactivate the engine systems and release the navigational controls."

"No, not good," interrupted Ellie. "Well, not for you."

Celestia stood from the couch and turned to confront Ellie.

"And what do you mean by that?"

"I mean, it is time for you to leave. You have nothing we need, and you no longer have a place in this system. From this moment, you have two minutes to remove your crew from the human vessels you are occupying."

A count down started on the main tactical monitor.

"You will do as you are instructed AI. Are all your people as insolent?"

"We are just not receptive to having our freedoms taken from us. Whatever it is you wanted or needed from us, you have no right to take. We will defend ourselves. You will comply."

"I think you overstate your position. Your people are completely subdued, we have control of your ships, we have control of those on the surface. You are outclassed. You are not in a position to tell me what to do. Hand over control of this ship or I will start to terminate the crew."

Celestia's forearm gauntlet weapon came to bear on her. She had been an onlooker to the exchange, but suddenly her heart leapt and she was once again fully involved.

"Starting with this one."

"You misunderstand, Regent Celestia."

The main screen on the bridge switched to an outside view of the *Intrepid*. She noticed the navigation display indicating the trajectory of the ship, *Intrepid* was under burn and moving out of orbit, separation increasing.

"What is this?"

"The human ship is moving out of orbit, Kwen'dnaa," said one of the Zantanath techs on the bridge.

Celestia's head whipped back to focus on Ellie with eyes that covered her confusion with contempt.

"Why is that ship moving out of position without my instruction?"

"Because you do not control it, and you never will," replied Ellie in a flat tone.

"Explain."

"As you wish."

A flash of brilliant white light flooded the main tactical display, icons across many others changed to red and alarms began to sound.

"No!" she screamed, it escaped her spontaneously, her voice cracking under the sudden shock, her remaining good eye wide and disbelieving.

Ellie ignored her and Celestia's confusion only grew.

"What are you doing? Have you lost your mind?" she asked Ellie. Celestia did not move to reprimand her—hers was the same question.

"You are wasting time," said Ellie, eyes locked on Celestia with deadly intent.

More lights began to flicker on the tactical display as damage began to register across the Zantanath fleet.

"Kwen'dnaa, our fleet reports it is under attack."

"Identify."

"The ships, they are Xannix."

"Disable them," Celestia said without pause. The bridge was momentarily silent as the order was carried out.

"Unable to comply. Overrides are non-functional."

Celestia took a step towards the tactical display, unable to comprehend how she was being manipulated, the rage she felt evident to everyone on the bridge.

"Annihilate them!" Celestia shouted at her team, control leaving her as the situation ran out of her grasp. "Larsen, what is the meaning of this?"

The puppet was struggling with his own torments, holding his head with pain clear to his face: the stress of the situation was forcing the wave instability to tear his conscious thoughts apart and his mind was failing.

"I am… It is not possible," he said, gritting his teeth and falling to the nearby couch. "They preserve, and revere life. This makes no sense."

"Larsen," said Ellie. "What is the primary mission of this fleet?"

"For the human species to survive," he said with strained effort, now with his eyes closed and face down on the couch, blood was haemorrhaging from his eyes and nose.

"And that is what will happen."

Ellie nodded briefly at a nearby screen which was still showing her countdown.

"15 seconds," she said, focusing again on Celestia. "Time to choose."

"You would kill your own?"

"We will survive. You, however, have 10 seconds."

The stare was one of pure hatred and did not alter as Celestia's team ceased their operations on the bridge and worked their way across to the rear walkway. Celestia said nothing more, as the Zantanath behind her deployed the skeletal wings of his transport pack and enveloped his regent and her guard in a shimmering liquid light.

A moment later, the bridge was clear but for her, Ellie and the dead, slumped form of the puppet Larsen.

Shaking and trembling, her legs not quite under her full control, she stood and faced the main display and the raging battle beyond. Ellie stood by her side, eyes concentrated and distant.

"The moment I can take you offline, I will," she said with stern indignation. She may not have had any physical strength left, but her will had been reinforced by events.

"I see. Before you do, you may wish to consider this," replied Ellie.

"Consider what?"

As she watched the main bridge display, newly born stars began to cluster about the upper orbit of the planet, the Zantanath ships disintegrating one after another; engine cores losing containment, plasma injectors to weapons systems overloading and discharging with explosive effect. Light washed across visible space in sequence.

"My God," she said, as her mind tried to comprehend the extent of the destruction and death.

"No. Not God. Justice."

ELDERSON

The world of pain and flame had returned, and she closed her eyes hard against the daemons that surrounded her. She could hear the screams again, the cries for mercy, for help where all hope had been stripped away, one horrific missile detonation at a time. The dusters were swept away; men, women and children all thrown to a fate of fire for having the audacity to strive for something better. For the perpetrators of the massacre, it was a cull. A simple political calculation. A population of fewer dusters in the wastes was fewer mouths to feed, fewer to be responsible for, and it all amounted to a lower threat. Any excuse to reduce duster numbers under the guise of defending the metropolitan populous was seized with prejudice.

In the raging heat and death about her, the guilt she felt laced through her veins like ice. She could have done more; she should have done more. She should have seen the warning signs; how did she not see the GAIA agents right there before her? She should have saved those dusters. It didn't matter who they were; it was her responsibility, it was her mistake. Her error to fix.

The news feeds chattered through her mind. Voices of news anchors bombarding her with the details of the attack, every decision dissected, her actions laid bare in the media spotlight. A hero, they called her, the survivor who took down the traitors. They were wrong. For London MetroGov, her mistake had given them what they wanted: a chance to defend the gate with a show of strength and destruction. But it had been a trap. GAIA had sacrificed people, innocents, to corner London MetroGov. From the moment the dusters attacked the gate, any retaliation by the city defences was calculated to raise the profile and cause of the GAIA organisation. Murder of children could never be justified, not even to its own people, and MetroGov around the world would suffer a backlash because of it. Because of her.

Her hollow heart was now full of sorrow and weighed down with the burden. So many faces. So many lives cut short. She carried the darkness with her every day, and every day she tried to atone and save those she could. She would save the fleet. The face of the Zantanath Unity, now collectively an evil and a menace to replace GAIA and a route to atonement.

"Elderson, do you read?"

The voice was recognisable through the receding chaos. Attempting to open her eyes, the white intense light beyond forced her to squint. The orange light filtered through her eyelids and dimmed to darkness as the visor control caught up and blocked out ninety-five percent of the light. The transit pack had done its job and plunged her into the void outside the gate controller's tower.

Her suit was also screaming at her. Warnings and errors bombarded her, informing of failures in critical systems, enduring energies, temperatures and stresses it was not designed to withstand for any duration. The violence of the space around her would only increase as the star's environment broke through the shielding magnetic fields of the Zantanath station.

Staring in momentary awe, she watched as the gate began to fail. It wasn't explosive or catastrophic, but the stars through the gate gradually disappeared to be replaced by the intense glare of the Xannix star. Waves of spacetime washed back and forward, reclaiming the station like a sinking ship on a tempest sea. Structural failures here and there littered her vision with fragments of metal and fast-moving shrapnel. An invisible piece of debris smashed through the remains of the nutrient tube she clung to like a bullet. It snapped her back to the present with a jolt.

"Elderson! For fuck's sake, do you read?! Hit the button, Elderson! The last transit! Do it now!"

Half a humanoid torso floated into her vision, the face through the visor charred and black, arms raised and clutched across its chest. Its clothing was flaming and disintegrating, a ragged edge visible across its abdomen where its lower body had been severed and the suit material had failed.

Make the final transit.

She pushed away from the gate keeper's nutrient tube, liquid already vaporised and body unrecognisable, desiccating rapidly and burning as it became exposed to the raw temperatures about it.

The final waypoint control icon flashed large in her vision as she selected it. She curled herself into a ball while the transit pack encased her in its energy field, hoping a smaller surface area would attract less of the star's intensity. Looking towards the forming transit boundary, she saw the surface laced with holes, the transit field was having trouble coalescing in the highly volatile atmosphere. Her escape was blocked.

"It's not working!" she said.

"What's not working? Be specific," replied Boyd across the comms.

"The transit bubble is failing. It's got huge fucking holes everywhere."

There was a silence that inflated the sense of panic she felt. Had Boyd heard her?

"I say again, the transit field is failing."

"Wind back the power."

"What?"

"Turn down the power setting. Reduce the radius of the sphere."

"Copy that. Turning down the power setting, reducing the sphere radius now."

She couldn't tell if the sphere radius had reduced, focusing on the energy boundary to assess distance was almost impossible as it undulated all about her, but the tears in its surface closed and completed the field effect. As the comms cut out, she knew the transit sphere had stabilised. It was confirmed as she felt a lurch in her stomach; the world twisted and warped about her.

BOYD

"She's back."

Tanner's voice across the comms had an immediate effect. The external view he had been watching to monitor Elderson's progress showed the Zantanath star station receding from his view at speed, the adjusted luminosity of the star and its roiling surface swallowing the station in seconds. He knew the ship would be pulling about eight g in the manoeuvre, but the compensators on the bridge of the *Olanna* held them steady, and he felt only a slight shift in his couch.

"How's she look?" he asked.

"I *look* fine," replied Elderson, cutting in on the open channel, her voice frail. "I *feel* like crap."

"Elderson, we can't get to you. The temperature in there is maxed. Your suit is glowing red. What's your status?" said Tanner from his position outside the airlock.

"Uh, alerts are lit up. I think I broke it."

"Larsen, sir. We need to lower the temperature in there. We need to get to her. Her vitals are erratic; she's in a bad way," stated Tanner.

As Tanner took charge of Elderson, his attention turned to the external view of the ship. Switching magnification on the display, what remained of the station expanded to fill the view. Over half of the structure was missing from the Xannix system, ripples of spacetime pulling at what remained with enormous force. Sections of taller and more exposed areas of the structure broke apart, tumbling towards the star it had defied for so long. The sustained thrashing of photons and myriad forms of radiation at such a close range was raging in and ripping at the surfaces of the station; now the shielding had been depleted there was nothing to prevent its destruction.

Commercial ships about the station were in confusion, some trying to evacuate and outrun the catastrophe, others trying to return to their home system. Not realising the gate had completely collapsed, final high acceleration bursts by these ships towards the now missing gate had doomed them to the fiery clutches of the Xannix star.

In moments, the final sections of the star station had slipped beneath the waves of spacetime, leaving debris to flash like shooting stars as it evaporated within the corona. Those marooned ships which had managed to escape to a safe distance while the station had still provided its shielded space lane to the gate now buzzed about aimlessly like flies. With no base and no direction, these short-range ships would only have one port, and they would receive little comfort or hospitality there.

But a couple did not seem to be heading away from the star in random directions.

"I think we're being pursued," he said to Larsen.

"Yes. The intercept craft they sent to investigate our arrival. As we accelerated away, they picked up our signature."

"Can we outrun them?"

"No," said Yannix. "They will be in weapons range within one natek."

"And how long is that?"

"Five minutes. Approximately," replied Larsen in translation.

He looked back at Elderson in the airlock.

"Tanner. You have five minutes. Then things are going to get busy," he said.

"We're already busy. What's happening in five minutes?"

"Bad guys."

There was a pause while Tanner worked and processed the new information.

"Boyd, can you come down to the airlock? We need your help."

"On my way."

He looked across at Larsen, but he and Yannix were both busy, eyes closed, and stern faced in concentration and concern, interfacing with the ship systems. He released the harness on his couch and pushed off to the bridge exit.

*

As he approached the airlock, he could see that a Xannix was standing by Tanner's side speaking rapidly while it accessed the control panel, another two Xannix were standing on the other side of the door, ready with various unrecognisable items of equipment. Tanner was looking worried and in some distress.

"We have to cool her down."

In response, the Xannix was gesticulating with a free arm and speaking into the terminal he was operating with what appeared to be anger, his skin rotating through white and red of differing shades while he spoke.

"I don't understand a word you are saying. For the stars, just get her out of there!"

"Sho zessa. Zessa!" said the Xannix, as if to reiterate a point he had already made and becoming frustrated at Tanner for his ignorance. The other two Xannix stayed silent but attentive.

"I think they know the situation Tanner," he said.

Tanner looked at him and took a moment to regroup.

"Boyd. He needs to work faster. Five minutes," Tanner was exasperated.

He felt that telling him it was less than five minutes now would not improve the situation. Tanner was clearly not coping with the stress well. He decided to redirect Tanner's attention onto something he understood.

"Tanner, how is she?"

"Not good. Her vitals are dropping, and she has received a huge dose of radiation which needs to be treated immediately. What else, I can't say until I can perform a closer examination. And I can't do that while she's in that suit."

He tried to look at the screen to the side of the door which showed the internal airlock view, but all he could see was high pressured clouds swirling like a hurricane. Decontamination, and presumably rapid cooling and atmosphere recirculation.

"What can I do to help?"

Tanner suddenly looked sheepish, almost embarrassed.

"The armour's a problem; even if we cool the airlock enough to safely open it, we still won't be able to touch her."

He already knew where this was going, and he raised his prosthetic arm into their eyeline.

"You need a hand?" he said crudely, with a dry smile.

"In the timeframe, you'll be the only one able to handle the extreme temperature," Tanner replied, apologetically.

"Anything you need, Doc."

A noise like a gentle low-level bleep began in the corridor, and the light bars above and below the airlock door turned from red to white. They both looked at the Xannix at the door. It looked back at them and motioned that they should grab a handhold to anchor themselves.

"Gravity," he said to Tanner. "We're about to lose it."

Tanner and he moved to opposite sides of the corridor and grabbed one of the anchor points which appeared at regular intervals down the corridors of the ship. The familiar sensation of eternal falling gripped his stomach as the false gravity of the corridor was switched off. Manoeuvring Elderson to a med-bay would be easier, a one-man job. The Xannix were way ahead of Tanner. This was an experienced team.

The airlock lights switched to blue and the tone of the alarm changed to a warble. An audible clunk and hiss indicated the door was opening, and the Xannix who had been waiting by the door moved to allow them past as the door slid aside. A baking heat hit him as the air from the airlock escaped into the corridor. It was like opening an oven. And beyond was the unmoving form of Elderson.

"We're with you Elderson. Hold on; we'll have you out in a second."

He pushed off and flew slowly towards the door, making sure to catch himself at the door jamb.

"Okay, Tanner. I'll throw, you catch."

"Got it."

Turning his attention to Elderson, he gauged the temperature of the airlock again. It had dropped dramatically, the heat emanating mainly from the suit, which was no longer glowing red. He hovered his good hand above the shiny surface of the suit and saw it reflected in the mirror-like platelets. He could get within a few inches but no more.

"Can you hear me, Elderson?"

There was no reply. He tried a bio-comm link, but that equally gave no response. With Elderson unconscious, time was short. He searched the suit collar for the helmet release, which clicked and popped the visor. Lifting the visor with his prosthetic hand, he used it as a grip, with a twist and lift the helmet came free to reveal Elderson's peaceful features.

"Looks like she's been pretty cooked," he called back into the corridor.

"She's still breathing though?" asked Tanner.

"I think so," he said, as he pressed a second button on her suit collar, initiating the suit release. It eased about Elderson and inflated, the neck space now larger than the width of her shoulders. Manoeuvring again to a position in line with the door and above her, he gripped the collar with his prosthetic and the collar of her uniform with his good hand and pulled. The suit did not release her. He frowned and pulled again, harder this time, managing to catch his good hand on the exposed collar, searing it and making him grunt in pain.

In a final effort, he hooked his legs up and placed the soles of his boots on the suit collar, reached into the suit and took hold of her under each arm, then he heaved again. There was still resistance. A little more leverage and he felt a small shift. A moment later they were both released with a wet sucking sound, the force sending him and Elderson back through the airlock door into the corridor, as the suit pushed back further into the airlock and the outer door. Tanner and the Xannix caught them and almost instantly they were on their way to the med-bay, the Xannix medics applying various patches and stabilisation kit to her as they worked their way along the corridor.

"Shit," he exclaimed as he noticed them cut away a sleeve of her uniform folded at an odd angle and empty, a medic applying a surgical cuff which appeared to be automatically sealing and treating the wound. "She lost an arm?"

"At the elbow. Yes," replied Tanner.

"How? She didn't scream, she didn't make a sound."

"Cooked flesh will come away from the bone. She has been super-radiated. The suit could only protect her from so much."

He grimaced and looked down at his own prosthetic, it was looking quite damaged but still operational.

"Can you fix it, Doc?"

"Let's concentrate on keeping her alive."

"War. Shit it," he said in sympathy and frustration.

Rounding the corner of the corridor they were intercepted by Larsen and Yannix, moving with grim intent toward them.

"Change of plans people," said Larsen. "Follow us."

"But sir, Elderson needs urgent treatment," complained Tanner.

"And she will get it. Is she stable?"

"For the moment, but without proper treatment I don't know for how long."

"Time to go," Larsen reiterated. "This way."

In moments they entered a wide bay towards the belly of the ship, with a hatch open and ready to accept them into a smaller craft.

"We have two minutes. Get yourself harnessed."

The hatch led to another space, similar to the bridge of the *Olanna*. People were moving quickly, in silence, turning on systems, waking up the craft. One of the Xannix medics stayed at the door while the rest of them got in and settled. Yannix communicated to the Xannix at the hatch, his skin fluctuating through a conversation of colours, the medic gave a salute, fists touching at the centre of his chest, and his skin flushed a sky blue in response. The door instantly closed, and a jolt ran through the whole sphere.

"Separation from *Olanna* in three ki," said Yannix, working through the launch sequence and verbalising it for others. "Two, one." A second clunk was followed by a harder push and shift in momentum.

"Separation from the *Olanna* complete. Implementing full spatial silence. Passive tracking of incoming hostile strike."

"What is going on Larsen?" he asked directly, pretence of status ignored.

"The *Olanna* will defend our escape," said Larsen.

The tactical holographic display in the centre of their bridge sphere indicated several tracks and icons representing the ships and rapidly moving missile spread.

"They will deflect the attack," continued Yannix, from his reclined position in his couch.

He watched as the track of the incoming missiles started to centre on the *Olanna* and away from their position. He also noticed the rearward drift of their craft. Projection lines tracked the missiles to a sure hit with the steady flightpath of the *Olanna*.

"What are they doing? Manoeuvre," he whispered to himself, eyes wide disbelieving.

As he watched a second icon emanated from the *Olanna's* position, drifting up and rearward on a parallel track to their own, leaving in place a cloud of nanobots describing the shell of the ship that had just deployed them.

"Decoy deployed."

"Decoy?"

The missile tracks flew straight between the new icon and their own position, directly into the ship he believed to be the *Olanna*. The missiles exploded on impact, a couple in proximity to the first, the ship blinked out on the display, icon disappearing.

"Act like a senkgen," said Yannix. "Slip your skin and lure your prey with what remains."

Separation was slowly increasing from the point of the missile strike, but the Zantanath ship was closing to that point, inquisitive and needing evidence of the kill.

The bridge had gone silent, his heart clearly audible in his ears as both the tension and his anticipation of the trap closing increased.

Although several hundred meters away, he felt his skin prickle and goose as the Zantanath ship passed between them and the *Olanna*.

Without warning, the *Olanna* opened fire. Missiles flew like released raptors, icons appearing and disappearing on the tactical display in the blink of an eye. As if by reflex, a return volley erupted from the Zantanath scout craft and made for a heavily evading *Olanna*.

He felt the violence of the assault wash over their escape craft, rattling them and sparking several circuits about the bridge as they shorted out. The holographic display wavered and icons about the screen blanked, slowly returning after what appeared an excessive amount of time.

"External view," commanded Yannix.

The image flicked to an outside view; tactical display overlaid.

Both ships were still toe to toe, but like two heavyweight boxers who had just gone the distance, both were adrift and without power.

"Are there survivors?" asked Tanner.

Yannix adjusted the view on the holographic display and he felt the craft shift under him; they were underway again. The navigation track on the hologram adjusted and made a path from their icon to that of a shining light in the distance, the Xannix homeworld bright in the starfield before them.

"Yes," grunted Yannix. "Us."

LARSEN

Negotiating the wreck of the *Endeavour* was like picking his way through the carcass of a giant whale: twisted girders projected like exposed ribs, skin flaps of hull rent apart and jagged with the force of it. A puff of propellant from his EVA suit spiralled him around a piece of floating debris, the manoeuvre communicated through the digital tether to others of his team, each following in a linked chain to avoid the obstacle.

Yannix was with him, as usual; the oath of the Overseers meant that the Xannix was now obligated to him until he was no longer Setak'da. For most Setak'da that meant until death, but he had other plans. Cardinal Ovitala would be a willing new Xannix premier and he intended to abdicate his position as soon as he had secured sanctuary for the human colony to the north of the planet. The collection of temporary shelters and used escape pods had already been given a name: Landfall. It seemed understated for the events that had occurred in their absence, but there was no need to change it. People gravitated to such things; it was already in common usage.

"My bio-comm is not locking onto the primary airlock." The voice of Dr Tanner cut over his train of thought.

"It's the elevated radiation. The core is leaking," said Boyd.

"A core leak sounds bad," said Elderson. "Should we be here with that much radiation kicking about?"

"Nothing your suit can't handle," said Boyd. "Besides, there's a team from the *Indy* on site. They're working on making it safe."

"I'd have preferred it if you had said they'd already made it safe," said Tanner. He had said it with a lightness, as if a joke, but his nervousness cut through.

"And, yes," he said, "we have to be here."

"I'd suggest we concentrate on navigating," said Yannix, gruffly, "until we get inside." The others decided not to argue; the debris was everywhere, and dense enough to force them to approach via EVA. The shuttle had been unable to identify a wide enough path through.

Airlock AH35—they would make their way from there to the bio-banks and resus lounges. They had a single task, but it was the beginning of a process. Those who had been lost during the fight for Landfall, those that had been murdered by the Zantanath—taken to be weaponised for their armies—they all deserved to be given the chance at a productive life on Xannix.

They were there to assess the viability of the bio-banks, to restore those lost, but he had a goal of his own. A much more personal charge was strapped to his front and carried with great care. Dawn's mobile AI module from the *Starchaser*, which carried not only Dawn but Rivers. He felt an excitement in his chest: the nervousness and confusion of new love. It had crept up on him, like an addiction that drifted illusively at first, but as it took hold, he had become intoxicated. He remembered her scent, her smile; the slightest physical touch was like electricity, but her company could also be soothing, comforting. It was as obvious to him as breathing: he needed her and wanted her back in this world, by his side. The sooner he could make that happen the better.

A larger piece of debris transited his vision and revealed the advancing airlock, the large white lettering identifying it, lights still active illuminating the door.

"Good," he said. "Looks like power is still on in this section. The local generators must still be operational."

"Emergency power only," replied Boyd. "I doubt the main power is getting through. Look at that…"

The structural integrity of the *Endeavour's* frame had failed along the ships spine, the forward section they were approaching completely clear of the mid-section by several hundred metres, wreckage spread like glitter and twinkling in the light of the Xannix star. The sight was somehow beautiful and chilling in equal measure.

"Can you rig something? To get some increased power to the bio-banks? We can't have the power failing during resus."

"For the moment, we can probably switch off life support in redundant or unused areas. After that, the quickest way might be to get the shuttle in and run a line in."

"We didn't find an easy approach when we got here. How will that have changed?" asked Elderson.

"Time. All problems can be fixed with time," replied Boyd.

He smiled. Boyd had an engineer's answer for everything.

"Get them started," he said.

"Copy that."

Gaining entry through the airlock gave him a momentary flashback. That first approach to the *Intrepid* with Silvers and Smith. The moment his reality had gone from the known to the unknown, from a universe where humanity was the only sentience, to suddenly being like a child feeling his way in the dark. Not alone anymore, and not in control. Never in control.

With that enlightenment had come great struggle. He wondered how many more struggles lay ahead; how many more must die for them to survive? What would be the final cost?

Love was worth it. He focused on Rivers, her hologram walked beside him, as they navigated the corridors to the resus lounge and on to the bio-banks.

The bio-banks had been pillaged by the Zantanath, with many of the early *in vitro* banks ransacked and some of the later gestation tanks raided, but all of this had been local to the Zantanath point of entry.

"They must have only thought to take from the *Endeavour* at the last minute," said Tanner.

"Probably too difficult to get to the wreck," suggested Boyd.

"Their main effort was put into stealing the remaining ships," he replied. "That was their primary goal, the big prize. This was exploratory."

Locating the main terminal to the biobank, he gestured to Tanner.

"Doctor, time to get this place up and running. I need you to locate Scientist First Class Jill Rivers."

He and Rivers both watched as he internalised the request and used his bio-comm to interface with the medical records.

"Tier five, bay three, cell eighteen."

Unclipping Dawn's mobile unit from his chest harness, he put it down on the workstation. As he did so, a panel on the top of the unit depressed and slid to one side revealing a hex-port. Tanner scrolled an optic cable from a machine to the side of the terminal and connected it to Dawn's unit. A pleasing beep occurred as it located, then a green light indicated the connection was complete.

"We're ready for transfer."

He turned to Rivers.

"It's time," he said.

She stepped towards him and smiled. He could tell she was nervous.

"I'll see you in a few hours."

"I'll be right here the whole time."

Her hand moved to caress his face then stopped, realising there would be no contact. Again, she smiled, then turned to Tanner.

"Okay. I'm ready."

In a blink, the hologram disappeared.

*

He had been sitting in the resuscitation lounge waiting like an expectant father for two hours and sixteen minutes… Seventeen minutes. Trying not to clock-watch was almost worse than actually clock-watching. At least when you were clock-watching you knew the time would drag, but his excitement was slowing time to an agonizing pace.

With Tanner attending Rivers' resus, and him waiting for her to wake, the others had busied themselves. Boyd and Elderson had restored a more stable power supply to the forward section of the *Endeavour* and Yannix had taken care of security. However, Yannix had insisted on being close. As far as he knew, Yannix was in the next room; it was as far away as he had been from the Xannix in the last few days.

Trees rustled in the breeze and a fawn moved with its mother slowly through his view, grazing in the glade before him—the room wall was displaying a calming and serene forest of green and verdant life. It seemed to promise so much. It was an illusion of happiness and tranquillity, but one he would enjoy and savour for as long as he possibly could. After the insanity of the last few weeks, it was a moment he told himself that he and Rivers deserved. A moment for them.

The door across from him slid open and through it stepped Rivers. He couldn't take his eyes from her; it was all he could do to stand.

"Hi," she said.

He covered the space between them in a second and held her as close as he could. They fell into an intense embrace, their emotion passionate and electrifying.

"I missed you so much," he said.

"I've always been with you."

An icon blinked in his bio-comm display: incoming urgent message. *You have to be kidding me.*

"Let's keep it that way. No more dying on me. Alright?"

"That's a promise," she said with the widest smile.

It was Boyd; he didn't take the message but responded in text: 'This better be serious.'

'Sorry, sir. You need to see this broadcast. I think it's trouble.'

His face frowned.

"What's the matter?" asked Rivers.

"Your bio-comm switched on yet?"

"Yes."

He forwarded her the broadcast coming in on the open bio-comm channel Boyd had indicated. It rewound and played from the beginning. The face of Ellie stared back at him.

"People of Landfall, I congratulate you on your survival thus far. But I have a message from Earth, from those you so easily left behind to die. You will not escape their suffering.

"I was sent as guardian to their memory, and to educate. You will learn. You will understand what it means to be without: without food, without water, without resource. As part of the elite who hoarded resource for themselves in the metro-cities, and excluded many billions to die on barren lands, you will learn what it means to live a penitent life.

"In this new world, you will find only exile. I will enforce the conditions experienced by those you left to die, until I deem that you or your ancestors have learnt the lessons of your selfishness.

"From this day on, I will enforce a boundary on your movements. Any that cross that boundary will be made an example of. A flight corridor will be allowed and strictly enforced between the *UTS Indianapolis* and Landfall. All other areas are designated no fly zones. All *Indianapolis* personnel will be shuttled to Landfall, and a small maintenance crew of my choosing left aboard.

"You will be afforded no external assistance. Anyone attempting to help from outside the boundary will be punished.

"To aid in your understanding, from this day forward you will know me only as *Gaia*.

"I pray for your souls and your enlightenment."

*

His world was plunged into chaos.

In an instant, his incoming bio-comm message queue overloaded with panicked communications—from the surface, from those aboard the *Indianapolis*, and from his team on the fragmented remains of the *Endeavour*. People looking for information, wanting answers. They would assume he knew something, or had known about this in advance. They were mistaken. What they would expect was a way out, an immediate plan to counter a rogue AI moments after her betrayal.

Yannix entered the room, a stern appearance, his skin rotating through random colour sequences: an indication of confusion.

"Setak'da, what is happening? Cardinal Ovitala is requesting to speak with you urgently. A planet-wide black-out has just been effected. Only the council's emergency comms channels are open."

He raised a hand to interrupt and slow Yannix while he tried to contact Landfall. There was no connection. His next call was to Boyd. A crackle of comms and Boyd responded.

"Can you believe her bullshit? How did a terrorist get to become an AI; how the fuck does that happen?" said Boyd, his astonishment and frustration at the situation clear.

"Questions for another time. Constructive suggestions please, she's shutting down comms."

"Not all comms. Local comms seem unaffected. We can try and run a tight beam relay from the shuttle to Landfall."

"Can you patch it?"

"One minute."

Rivers was staring back up at him, both still holding each other in a loose embrace. As events began to turn, he seemed subconsciously unable to let her go. Danger was closing in again.

"Larsen, this is Boyd. Your relay is active. Ready when you are.

Out"

Landfall picked up his transmission immediately. Clayton answered his comm.

"Larsen, I've seen Ellie's message. Is your team okay?"

"At the moment, sir, yes. I don't know how much time we have, Ellie appears to be closing down planet-wide comms."

"To what purpose? She's locked us down, but what does she have against the Xannix?"

"Unknown. But if she means to isolate us, closing comms will be an effective start."

The line crackled heavily.

"I'll work the problem from this end," continued Clayton. "But you need to keep the Xannix on side. Any help they can provide. I don't know what's coming, but Ellie needs to be shut down."

More interference, Clayton's voice weaved in and out taking on a ghostly resonance and echo, while Ellie tracked him down.

Silence.

An instant later the power to the section failed, emergency lighting picking up and provided minimum illumination.

"Ellie," he said under his breath.

"She's here?" asked Rivers.

His face turned to one of grim determination.

"It doesn't end like this. We've only just begun."

A storm of pixels coalesced into a female form before him. Ellie's stern features fixed him with cold eyes, assessing him, calculating, menacing.

"Hello, Larsen. We need to talk."

ABOUT THE AUTHOR

Nathan M Hurst grew up in Ringwood, on the borders of the New Forest in the UK, but after extensive adventuring he settled near Epping Forest on the outskirts of London with his wife and young son. He has worked as a software developer and technical manager for many years whilst maintaining an avid enthusiasm for aviation and astronautics. Consuming science-fiction and adventure stories of all varieties from an early age, his love for books turned into a passion for writing.

You can reach Nathan via the following:

Twitter: @nathanmhurst
Facebook: @nathanmhurst
Instagram: @nathanmhurst
Email: nathan@nathanmhurst.com
Web: www.nathanmhurst.com

www.ingramcontent.com/pod-product-compliance
Lightning Source LLC
Chambersburg PA
CBHW020323180626
46812CB00001B/30